FRISCO

TIJAN

Edited by: Jessica Royer Ocken
Diversity/Inclusion Editors: Renita & Curtis
A Book A Day, www.abookaday.net
Beta-read by: Crystal R Solis
Proofread by: Virginia Tesi Carey, Kara Hildebrand, Paige Maroney Smith,
Serena McDonald, Kimberley Holm, and Amy English.

For my readers, especially those in my reader group.
Your support is amazing!

1

KALI

When two bikers started trading punches in the middle of the soup aisle, and my first thought was *Why couldn't they have picked the bakery section?*, the universe was telling me something.

What was it telling me? That my life was sad. But newsflash, universe: I already knew that. I've known that since I came out of my mom's vagina in the alley behind Grumps and Hoes. That was their witty name for a hardware store.

"Kal." Otis was huffing as he ran up behind me, and even though I didn't look, I knew he was pulling up his pants. They liked to sag down, a lot.

Otis was the manager of Friendly's Grocery Mart. He always meant well, but Otis didn't much like to manage. He came in, said hello to whoever was in his path, did a walk through the store, and then checked in with me. I didn't have the official title, but *I* was the actual manager. I handled the scheduling, the inventory, and making sure everything ran smoothly. This wasn't a position I'd volunteered for, but my second day back, the assistant manager took a smoke break and never returned. Maybe it was my age (I'm thirty-six), or maybe it was because Otis was flustered and came to *me*, asking *me* what was needed for the second shift.

My second day back.

Otis and I had history, but not that kind of history.

We'd both worked here in high school. I moved away, got married, never had kids, and I was back since my divorce was seriously fresh. Otis was the opposite. He never did anything. He stayed, and he just kept getting promoted. He'd made it about four positions to the general manager now. Friendly's Grocery Mart was locally owned, but the owner spent most of his time hunting or drinking beer and talking about hunting. I could attest to this because he was at Bert's Pub every night, drinking beer and—you guessed it—talking about the mystical buck all the local hunters liked to discuss.

But since the day I'd returned, everyone took note of my ability to have some idea of what was going on. And like an idiot, I couldn't handle seeing a store falling into chaos. I'd run the store when I was in high school and college. So it was like pulling on an old pair of tennis shoes. There might've been mold, and holes where toes were supposed to go, but they still fit. Unfortunately.

"What are you going to do?" Otis panted as he asked.

"Kali, you want me to call the police?" asked Ben, our bagger who was only supposed to work part-time.

He ended up being here most of the time because Otis was an asshole and called him nearly every day, asking if he could pick up some extra hours. The schedule was handled. I did it, and the point of me not scheduling Ben every day was so that the actual bagger scheduled to work today would have to, you know, do his job. But unlike Ben, who was a hard-working high schooler who probably should've been given more breaks in life than he was going to get, the actual bagger wasn't so great at his job... I didn't know why he kept it.

I gave him a look, finding him on the edge of the gathering crowd. Noah Berrman, high school jock. The girls liked to come in and whisper, giggle, flirt when he was scheduled (which is probably why Otis hadn't fired him), but Noah didn't work. When a cute girl was in line, suddenly he was great at pretending to bag groceries, but he excelled more at standing, talking, winking, flirting, being the cool guy. Right now, though, he wasn't looking too cool. He was as captivated as everyone else.

Seeing Mrs. Johnson gaping and Viola Prinnesly looking faint, I sighed. It was time to wade in.

"No," I said to Ben. "Go back to work. Noah."

He looked at me.

I motioned toward the registers. "Get back to work. Everyone, go back to shopping."

"Don't you stop this. This is better than *Jeopardy*." Viola shook her wrinkled finger at me, but she wasn't looking my way. She was busy drinking in all the biker goodness.

I had to admit, I understood. Muscles. There were muscles everywhere.

"Kal, you sure?" Otis breathed behind me.

I suppressed a shiver and a roll of nausea. "Yes, Otis. If Mike comes in, send him back out. These guys are Red Demons. You do not want to call the cops on them. Trust me."

I heard the hitch in his breath and decided I didn't want to know if it was from fear or excitement.

Most of the patrons had gone back to shopping, though Viola and Mrs. Johnson were doubling down. Mrs. Johnson had sat down on her walker. Viola leaned against the side of it, her cane resting beside *her*.

The two guys were trading punches, using cans of soup as weapons.

I liked soup. The soup didn't deserve this treatment.

I didn't know these particular two, but I knew the Red

Demons. They were relatively new, but they'd been expanding fast, and normal folk like myself wouldn't usually know this about them. I did because my brother had been friends with the Red Demons' current VP, or at least the *rumor* was that Shane King was their VP.

They didn't have a charter here, but they'd rolled into town a week ago. They'd been spending most of their time at Ruby's Dexterity, a bar where the rougher folks around here could be found. Bert's was where the tourists and not-rough crowd hung out. But if you wanted to hire a hitman, go to Ruby's. I mean, that was the joke around Friendly, Indiana, but people said it for a reason. Because it was true.

Anyway, I still had two bikers and about five hundred dollars in damage to handle, so I waded in.

"Guys!" I shouted, my hands up.

One growled, holding the other up against the shelves.

Sidenote: I was impressed those shelves stayed. I needed to check who the manufacturer was. Good shelving was key.

"You little fuck," the guy growled. "You don't think I know, but I know." He punched the other one.

The other one looked remorseful, and for a moment, I thought maybe the fight was done. He was just going to take his beating.

But then his face twisted. Fury lit him up.

Nope. The fight would continue.

"It wasn't like that, Corvette!" he snarled, twisting and somehow slipping from the guy's hold.

He whirled and came at him with a leap and a punch. Corvette was winded, and he fell to his knees from that one. Then with a snarl, he was up, and they were back to shoving each other around.

Not good.

They hit the one section of cans that had been left alone.

Thirty cans fell to the floor.

Lovely.

I was watching three roll past me when I heard a yelp.

A curse.

A shout.

I turned—both bikers were on the ground, and from the scattered cans, it looked like soup had won the fight. *Good!*

Corvette put a hand to his chest and the other to his face. Seemed he was clueing in to the fact that his face was basically all blood. The other one didn't look any better.

He cursed and locked in on the second guy. He was winding up another hit or at the very least, a tackle.

I stepped in. "No, you don't!"

I was too late.

He grabbed a can and prepared to hit the other guy smack in the face.

I stepped in again. "I said, no!" I kicked the can out of his hand. (I could do that. Eight years of soccer—high school and college. Thank you very much.) It was my turn to be a bit dramatic.

I knelt down on both of them. Literally. Knelt down. My knees and hands on their chests, I was thankful I'd worn pants instead of shorts to work today. I glared at them. "I don't give a fuck how big your motorcycle is. You hit each other one more time, you're going to regret it."

Corvette grunted, but he didn't smart back.

The other one grumbled, "Yeah? You gonna call the cops?"

"Worse. I'll get you banned from Ruby's. I'm aware how much you guys like that bar."

Corvette hissed, touching his face. "How you going to do that?"

"She's my mama."

That got their attention, and I knew it was coming.

"You're Gloves' little sister?" Corvette asked.

"I'm Gloves' *older* sister, by a year."

I had to add that last part because I was already feeling down. Didn't need to bring my age into this.

That changed everything, which I'd known it would.

The Red Demons had history with my brother.

"This your store?" Corvette asked, starting to sit up.

I stood so he could finish.

The other sat up, leaned against the shelves, and cursed, probably starting to register the pain that the adrenaline had been keeping at bay. Corvette tried to move, but his hand slipped on some blood and he winced.

I caught his arm, steadying him and helping him sit back.

I realized the blood had a milky texture to it. Some of the soup had opened.

So awesome.

I cleared my throat. "I work here, yeah."

Both were squinting at me. Or they were trying. Each had one eye completely swollen shut.

I sighed, figuring I should get this over with. "You got two choices. Give me your phone and let me call your club to come get you, or I gotta call the ambulance. If I do that... This is a small town. I'm positive the cops already know, but I had our manager head 'em off from coming in here. It'll be a different story if the paramedics make a call."

The second one grumbled, tipping his head back and pinching his nose.

Corvette just handed me his phone. "Press three."

I did, after wiping it clean of blood, and heard, "Ghost here."

Ghost. The biker name for Shane King, the one that I actually did know.

"I'm calling from the Friendly Grocery Mart. You've got two members here who need assistance—medical assistance."

"What?"

Gah. His voice was a low baritone, and raspy in a way that hit my vagina, in the right way.

I handed that phone off asap because I did not need to be reacting that way to just a 'what' from him. Nope. No how. I had enough drama to handle right now as is.

Corvette took the phone, and as he continued the conversation, I stepped over toward the remaining crowd. Viola and Mrs. Johnson leaned to the right so they could see around me. Noah was also still there, which had me ready to grab a can of soup myself.

"Are you serious?"

He jolted, his eyes wide. "What?"

"Work. Do something!"

Yep. My control had snapped. I was blaming Otis and not Ghost's *very fine* voice.

"You come in here every day and do nothing. Ben does everything. If you don't get your ass working, you're fired."

His eyes narrowed. "Right. Like you could do that."

I stepped closer and lowered my voice. "I'm thirty-six and just divorced from a truly authentic piece of shit. I can walk, and my life will be better. This is my low, so when I go to Otis and tell him it's you or me, who do you think he's going to keep?"

His eyes went back to being big. He hadn't thought of that.

"Get this aisle cleaned, and you've got ten minutes to do it."

With that, I went to update Otis.

He was more than open to staying in his office and hiding for another thirty minutes, and Red Demons who? No Red Demons had been in his store.

I HIT call on my phone.

He answered right away. "Daughter! How's it going? Tell me something funny that happened to you today."

I told him about the soup cans. And about Viola and Mrs.
Johnson.

My dad laughed so hard he had to hang up. "Excuse me, my
daughter and love of my life, but I went and almost had an accident. You got me laughing so hard."

2

KALI

The bikers left the store within minutes, but they didn't leave the parking lot right away. I steered clear of the front, content to finish up the inventory list we needed done by the end of the weekend, but I knew the Red Demons were outside because of their bikes. Trust me. You can't *not* hear a Harley, let alone twenty of them.

This group sounded like fifty. Once they left, everything settled down in the store. It was almost boring.

Wait. No. It wasn't almost boring. It *was* boring, but I was not complaining.

Noah begged off an hour early.

I sent Ben right after.

It was Sunday night. We usually had the church rush, but after that people were home for the evening, hoping to catch up on their sleep before work or school in the morning. That's why I loved working on Sundays. A slow shift was peaceful to me. I said *boring* before because that's the deflated feeling I got from those still in the store. Two Red Demons fighting had given everyone a rush, and now we were on the other side of that high.

"Kali." Macy Rodding, the last checkout worker, came up

from the back, her purse and keys in hand. In a way, she wasn't so unlike me. In her forties, going through a divorce herself, but she had two little ones at home to feed, and I knew it was all on her shoulders. Her husband was the town's lawyer. It wasn't going to be a fair settlement. Everyone knew what Phil Rodding was like. If he'd been in the soup aisle earlier, I would've figured some way to *accidentally* deck him with a can. I had a feeling Viola and Mrs. Johnson would've backed me up.

She came the rest of the way down the aisle to where I was working the only register still open.

She frowned. "I bet you could close early. No one's going to be coming in. Or I could stay, if you want? I don't mind. Gets lonely in here when you're the only one working."

I was shaking my head before she finished. "I know Natalie and Oliver are waiting for you, and you know it too. No way they went to bed at their bedtime."

She grinned, softening. "I know. They're so damn cute. Little buggers, but cute."

"Go home. I won't be long behind you."

She perked up. "You're going to close early?"

I gave a nod. "I'm thinking Otis won't get mad—not after today."

She gave a hearty laugh, and her cheeks flushed. "You can say that again. I knew those bikers were in town, but they'd not come in before. You handled them well." She cocked her head. "Any other time and Otis would've been having a fit at the loss of product. What'd you say to him? You know those bikers?"

I shrugged, deciding then and there to close up, as she'd suggested. "I gave him a little lesson about the Red Demons, and told him if he didn't say a word about the damage, they wouldn't burn down the store."

She gasped, her eyes getting big. "They'd do that?"

I gave another shrug. "Who knows? Maybe. Probably not. We'll never know now."

She chuckled and nodded toward my register drawer. "I can stay a few minutes. Walk out with you?"

"Nah." I locked my door. "Go. Seriously. I got this."

"Okay. See you tomorrow?"

"See you tomorrow," I called, heading to put my drawer away.

The door pinged. That would be Macy leaving.

I was coming back with my drawer locked up tight when I heard the door ping again.

I frowned, my feet faltering. "Mace?" I rounded the last aisle, turning to see the front. "You forget..."

It wasn't Macy.

It was a biker, and I had to stop because *holy hell*. It was the biker of all bikers.

Tall. Well over six feet. Maybe six three?

Lean.

Muscled.

Seriously tan. *Holy.*

And he wasn't wearing a shirt under his Red Demons cut. The guy had tattoos all over his body.

My gut flared. My body grew hot because even though it'd been twenty years since I last saw him, I knew who was waiting for me.

I wondered why they hadn't singled me out yet.

When the Red Demons came to town, they found my mom. They found my sister. But not me. I hadn't heard if they'd found Gloves' (my brother's real name was Connor) and Claudia's father, Patrick Hinton. He was a good man, and he'd tried to father me as he could, but I had a dad. I spent time between my dad and my mom, but was with my mom during the school year.

But back to Shane King, because that was who was standing and staring right at me.

Good Lord, his eyes.

He had an almost heart-shaped face, with pretty, long eyelashes over dark eyes, but it was the square jawline with some serious, dark five o'clock shadow that I'm sure caused ovaries to explode. He looked pretty, almost *too* pretty to be a Red Demon, but then his eyes flashed. *There* was the hardness.

He'd had that in high school too.

We'd been in the same grade, but he'd befriended Connor, who wasn't called Gloves back then. They'd been table partners in shop class, and since Connor had already been on the path toward criminology, I guess now, thinking back, it made sense. Shane never had a tolerance for any bullshit from teachers, principals, or classmates. He'd been fostered by our neighbor, another connection that cemented his friendship with Connor, but Shane hadn't lasted long in Friendly.

He got into too many fights, was arrested too many times, and was sent to juvie. That was the last I heard about him, except I knew he kept in contact with Connor, and I'd gotten a call from my brother seven months ago saying he'd done a favor for some Red Demons in prison, and one day, they'd come to pay him back.

I'd had no idea what he was talking about then, and since the Red Demons showed up, I'd been hoping I still wouldn't find out.

But that seemed to be over.

I stopped at the candy section. "You know me?"

"I know now."

Right. Shane had known me back in high school, but as he gave me a once-over, and I struggled not to let it affect me, I knew twenty years was a long time.

"You don't look like Connor's sister."

I frowned, looking down at my dark hair and golden brown skin. "My dad's Black. He was Black back then too, you know."

My mom had red hair and dark eyes, and because of her pale skin, she kept inside as much as possible. She was white, and there was a history of skin cancer on her side of the family. But my two younger siblings, from a white father, didn't care about the cancer—or at least Claudia didn't. She had straight-from-a-bottle blond hair, dark eyes, and was hella tan. Connor had dark hair and dark eyes.

My eyes were hazel, and I had no idea where they came from. No one in my dad's family or my mom's had hazel eyes.

"I know." He gave me another once-over, lingering on my legs. "But you didn't look like this back then."

"Like what?" I raised my chin.

"All fucking woman."

Damn.

Damn!

Heat traveled through me. "What do you want?"

His eyes flickered, cooling off. "My club owes Gloves. We came to pay that debt. Part of it is helping his family the way they need to be helped. I didn't know you were in town. He said you were in New York, married with a husband. A good life." He took in my sneakers and my employee ID. "Your mom wanted more customers, so we're setting it up so other charters stop in, and spread the word. We take care of our own, and that'll spread too. Your sister mentioned opening her own salon. We'll help set that up, but we'll have a percentage of the ownership. I know you helped my guys today, kept the cops away and the manager from being a pain in the ass. We'll pay the damages. In my eyes, that makes us owe you twice. So, I gotta ask, what do you want?"

Jesus. "What kind of favor did my brother do for you guys?"

"He saved a bunch of our brothers' lives. Them, our club, and their families are grateful. We reached out to Gloves' dad, but he didn't want anything. Said just take care of the mama and the girls and he was good with that. I also gotta ask, would Gloves want this offer extended to your father? We don't want to leave any stone unturned."

I shook my head. "No. He's an attorney in Chicago. He's doing just fine."

This was a surreal conversation. Out of the blue, Shane King —a guy I'd crushed on for a full year and then every time after when Connor would mention he'd heard from him—was standing in front of me wearing a 1% motorcycle club patch on his cut and offering to "help me out" in some way.

"I know what your club does, what they're about. Why are you really here?"

His eyes flashed. "I told you. We're paying off a debt."

I shook my head, my stomach churning. "This doesn't feel right to me. Feels like you're trying to buy off Gloves. What did my brother actually do?"

A wall came down over his features. I could feel him growing distant.

It felt cold between us, and wowza—I didn't like this feeling.

I gritted my teeth, because *fuck this guy*. Fuck any guy who had the power to affect me in any way. Not anymore. I didn't know if ever. One asshole in my life had been enough.

"We're here for a few more days," he finally said. "You think of something you want, let us know. As you told my guys, you're aware of where we hang."

Right. My mom's bar. Which I hadn't stepped into since coming back to town.

I might've told those guys I could get them banned, but that wasn't true. It was so far from the truth that it was sad. I loved Gloves, but a relationship with Ruby or Claudia? Nope. That hadn't been a thing for the last twelve years, not since my wedding day.

He was still watching me.

"Leave my brother alone."

Now those eyes narrowed, then chilled even more. "You know enough about us not to issue an order to a Red Demon."

A shiver sped up my spine, inflaming my neck. I knew, which was why I'd said it anyway.

"I love my brother. He's one of the only three good men I know. I cannot lose him. Your club messes with him, and I know what'll happen." My brother had truly awful luck. A strong argument could be made that he was cursed—had been all his life. Connor had no gut hunches. It was the opposite. If someone yelled that a house was on fire, Connor would run inside, but not to rescue anyone. He would just go in and stand there, confused about why it was on fire.

Shane's nostrils flared, and he spoke softly. "Watch yourself."

"You want to do something for me? That's what it is. Leave Gloves alone."

His chin rose, and I felt a whole new level of chill in the air. Goosebumps broke out over my skin, and dread took root in my gut. *Dammit.* This guy, his whole club—they were bad news.

Then, as if coming to a decision, he shifted, and some of the chill in the air faded. "I'll consider it."

He turned to leave, and I tried to pretend I didn't feel a sort of disappointment when his gaze moved away from mine. Right.

My God.

I was a mess.

The door pinged. Shane King walked out.

I hoped to never see him again.

My vagina was calling me a liar.

———

I HIT call on my phone.

"Daughter!"

I smiled. "Hey, Dad."

"Daughter, daughter, daughter. What are you doing? You getting off work? Heading home? How are the soup cans? Viola and Mrs. Johnson still doing good? They didn't break a hip craning their necks for more bikers, did they?"

"All's good. I'm just leaving the grocery store."

"Can you tell me again the reason you ain't moved in with your pops? I got a real nice brownstone, you know."

"I know." But I didn't go into detail because this was a normal conversation between James Michaels and me.

"Okay, okay. I know. You're with your friends. I get it, but you got family here too. Just reminding you."

"I know, Dad."

"How was your day before the soup cans and after our last call? Tell your pops all about it."

So, I did.

3

KALI

There was a disco ball in our living room. I glimpsed it as soon as I came in through the garage door.

What.

The.

Awesomest?

I stared at it in confusion, sparkly and rotating, sending pink, purple, blue, and all sorts of colors around the room. Once the door shut behind me, the music started.

Aqua's "Barbie Girl" filled the room, and on the beat, my roommate, Harper, slid across the floor from the hallway and past the kitchen doorway. His arms were up, his head back, sunglasses on. He wore a white dress shirt, underwear, and socks. That's it.

He turned to face me and struck a pose. He brought a bottle of bourbon to his lips, as if it were a microphone. Then, with his entire body bobbing to the music, he lip-synced the entire first section of the greetings.

Black hair. Dark eyes. Gangly form. Seriously pale skin. This was roommate number one. Like my mom, he enjoyed hiding from the sun.

When the second verse started, our other roommate moved

past the doorway and reappeared holding a wine bottle for her microphone. Aly was doing the robot, and also wearing sunglasses, but she hadn't gone with the full Tom Cruise look from *Risky Business*. She'd gone '80s glam, with hair and bangs high up in the air. She had multicolored slap-on bracelets, pink leggings, and a black top that was off one shoulder with a neon-green bra underneath.

They did a full rendition.

Their moves were choreographed.

Harper went left, Aly went right.

Harper bent low, Aly jumped high.

The chorus had two moves—a hair primp and a hair flip.

At the end, both jumped in the air, and it was impressive. They finished as if they were *Saturday Night Live* cheerleaders.

"Hey!" Harper chirped, his smile wide.

"Hey." My greeting was a lot less chipper, and his smile dimmed.

Instant regret.

I flashed a grin, trying to ease some of the shittiness I felt. "That was amazing, you guys."

In perfect sync, they turned to each other. They pulled their shades down an inch and shared a look. Then, they moved.

Harper took my purse and keys and maneuvered me into a chair. "Sit."

Aly's eyes narrowed behind her sunglasses. She gave a firm nod. "You need alcohol."

I loved my roommates, *a lot*. The three of us had been friends since high school.

Harper had gone to design school and came back to start his own business. His schooling had been for clothing design, but he had a niche now where he designed specialty costumes and that was for anyone. People ordered for high school plays, community productions, or even a really amazing Halloween party. Aly did dispatch for our local fire station—and live cooking segments on her social media, which Harper co-hosted at times.

I was the sampler of everything—food, liquor, whatever they needed. We all had our sacrifices to make.

When Foley (my ex) cheated on me, Harper and Aly had both showed up on my doorstep that night. And when I say *cheat*, he was *really* cheating. He had three women in the bed when I walked in.

And if that's what I found, I shuddered to think how long it had been happening. Surely he hadn't just gone right into a foursome? Was he the cheating overachiever? Had there been a single cheat partner to start with? Just one lady?

But back to the scene I'd walked in on.

Two were going down on each other, and he was in the other, his hands gripping the backs of her thighs, watching as she did something else, which I didn't see because my mind had snapped at that point. I was looking for a weapon. There was a lot of yelling and threats, but I didn't leave. That was important to me. I'd held my ground and sent them all packing—Foley literally. I'd been giving my house the sage of all saging when my doorbell rang. I'd assumed it was Foley, but nope.

I broke down when I saw how much they'd packed. Harper had three rolling suitcases.

Aly said she had plenty of vacation time from the fire station, and could do her segments anywhere. Once I made the decision to move back—at least until I got my feet back under me—they hadn't given me a choice. They moved me into their basement room. Harper had the top floor. Aly had the main floor. It was a big enough house that all of us had our own space.

We'd had a fourth roommate for a while, Harper's boyfriend, but they'd ended things a week ago, so now it was back to the three of us.

"What happened?" Harper asked, eyeing me in my spot on the chair.

Just one question from him in that knowing voice of his, and I told them everything.

The fight.

Me snapping at Noah.

Me commiserating about the soup that was damaged.

Me talking with Macy.

I did some venting about Otis, because who wouldn't?

Then the finale, Shane's visit, and when I was done, both of them sat in total silence.

I'd told them almost everything.

"There were..." Harper began.

"Bikers?" Aly asked. "Like motorcycle bikers? Like—"

"Sons of Anarchy and Mayans?" Harper said.

"His name is Ghost?" Aly started fanning herself.

"Was he hot?" Harper raised an eyebrow.

Ping pong to Aly. "Of course he was hot, look at her," she said. "She's still worked up. Or maybe that was our routine. We *were* amazing."

He nodded. "You're right. But also, Kali never gets heated like this. A foursome had her like this one time in a different way, though those were extenuating circumstances. This dude just talked to her."

"You're right." They nodded at each other.

"Cool and calm Kali," Aly added. "That's what we call her."

"Guys!" I held a hand up. My head was starting to hurt. "I still need a drink."

Aly needed to be the bartender, always. She could be ferocious if we got inventive with our own mixology. It wasn't allowed.

Her eyes got big, and she stood. "Right! I'm on it. We've been drinking since four today."

I frowned. "Four?"

Harper's eyes got hard.

Harper's eyes barely ever got hard.

Now I was alarmed. I leaned forward. "What happened at four today?"

"It was more like three when it happened." Aly went to the bar.

Yes, we had a whole bar. It was a counter set up on the far side of the kitchen. Wine glasses, shot glasses, and glass mugs lined the bottom and the top was shelved with all the hard liquor a regular bar would have. Wine had its own shelf. Next to the counter was a smaller fridge that housed the chilled wine and beer. Harper enjoyed beer. He liked his Coronas, but recently he'd been on a dark beer kick. We did a brewery tour last weekend. He'd been enthralled the whole time.

Anyway...

"What happened at three?" I looked between the two.

They were looking at each other.

Harper pursed his lips and looked at his lap.

Aly pressed her lips firmly together and turned to the bar, giving us her back.

I zeroed in on Harper. "Harp. What happened?" I didn't have a good feeling.

Please let it be a good thing that happened. Please, please, please.

"My manufacturer called me. They're shutting down, like forever."

"What?!" *No! No way.*

He dipped his head down in a quick nod. "Yeah. I know. I can try to find another one, but this one was perfect. They did all my products. I never had an issue with them. Now..."

"We've already come up with a plan." Aly came over, setting a drink in front of me before taking her seat. "My views always double when he's with me, and today we did one in costume. It tripled, and the shares have been amazing. It's not much, but we're going to try to be smarter about branding. Though without a manufacturer..."

She swallowed, and I reached for my drink. My arms felt like lead.

I didn't know what was in the drink, but it burned, and that's all I needed at that moment.

"Wait." Harper held up a hand, blinking a few times. "You didn't actually tell us why that biker came to see you."

"Yeah." It was my turn to swallow, and I took another drink. "This is good stuff, Aly. Real good."

She pulled her sunglasses all the way off and leaned forward, crossing her arms over her chest. "Spill it, woman. Also, I'm blaming the fact that we've been drinking since four that we didn't think to ask why he came to find her. I mean, that's Basic Interrogation 101."

"I know." Harper bobbed his head. "We're slacking in our skills."

"*Totally* slacking."

Two more large gulps, and then I gave them the CliffsNotes.

There was a beat of silence.

Then, *explosion.*

"You knew him before?!"

"Wait! That guy that Connor was friends with?"

"What guy? Why am I not remembering? I need to remember too. Help me remember!"

"The guy that beat up Hank and Miller and that whole group. You know. Connor's friend. Sophomore year. He wasn't back the next year, but *that* guy." Aly slammed her hand on the table. "I had no idea you had the hots for him! You totally iced me out. We were best friends. Best friends tell each other everything!"

"*That* guy?!" It seemed Harper had just remembered.

Both their voices went shrill.

I told them about Gloves, about the prison favor. I kept out the help they were going to give to Ruby and Claudia, but I loved my friends. They were still stuck on who Shane King was from high school.

Aly fanned herself. "Too bad he's not a farmer. I'd totally do him then."

That was another thing Aly liked. Farmers. She'd been burned by a guy out of high school, and after that, she started a quest for a millionaire farmer. She kept hoping to meet one, but so far, she'd not been successful. She met a lot of guys. A few of them had met Harper afterwards, but that was pre-Harper's boyfriend.

I wasn't sure if we were saying his name yet. I took my cues from Harper on that. Sometimes he needed to vent for days. Sometimes it was a while until he started talking. In high school, there'd been an incident he didn't talk about for six months. That was the hardest for me to handle, because it'd been a really bad situation.

Also, once I found out all the details, I'd told Connor. On the down-low, he'd beaten the shit out of the guy who did the bad thing to Harper. I had no clue if Harper ever found out.

"Wait. So he's helping you with something? Why you?"

Aly answered that with a knowing snort. "Because she's Connor's favorite. Duh."

I gave Harper a small smile.

His eyes narrowed, and he dropped his shades on the table. "They're helping out the Demon and Spawn?" His names for Claudia and Ruby. He wasn't real original with his naming.

"Yeah."

Aly frowned. "How are they helping them?"

I told them, and immediately Harper rolled his eyes. "Why is Connor so nice? I know your sister never visits him, and he's always emailing you and asking you to handle something for your mom, so that's her interaction—she asks him to do shit, knowing he can't because he's in prison, but he'll still want to help and so he turns to you. And you do it, because you love your brother, not for that Demon."

Have I mentioned how much Harper enjoys my mama and sister?

He shoved back in his seat. "Ridiculous, if you ask me."

"So you're going to think of something?" Aly asked.

I shrugged. "I don't know. They're one percenters. Like, the real kind of one percenters. That's terrifying, you know?"

"But you know Shane." Aly was being all gentle with me, speaking in a soft tone.

"Does that matter? I mean, look what happened to Gloves."

I should also clarify here that I interchanged calling my brother both Connor and Gloves, but Aly and Harper did not. They didn't know the reason he had that nickname, and both had known him as Connor before he went to prison, so it was out of respect that they continued to call him Connor. I asked my brother once if that was okay with him, and he said he liked it.

"*It makes me feel like a person,*" he'd said. "*In here, it's not always like that. I'm still Connor to someone, you know? It's like someone remembers me for me.*" That sealed the deal. He'd always be Connor to them.

After my reminder about Gloves' fate, they both made the same *hmm* sound, nodding in unison.

They got my point.

My brother had seriously bad luck. And once Connor went inside, his same luck kept striking—a fight here, a fight there. His time kept being extended, not that it mattered because he was in for life, but now he had a motorcycle club doing favors for him. I wanted to scream when I thought about what he must've done for that to happen.

I did know one thing.

No way was any of this going to end well.

Not going to happen.

It wasn't in our DNA.

I had a feeling we were well and truly fucked, and no matter how I tried to shrug it off, I couldn't.

What did I do instead?

I finished my drink, and Aly made me another.

Then another and another until I stopped counting.

And then I was doing a dance routine with them. It was going to go on one of Aly's lives.

I HIT call on my phone.

"Daughter!"

It was late, super late, but he still answered and he made me smile. "Hi, Dad. I'm drunk."

"Oh, no."

"And we did dance routines tonight."

"Ooh. Tell me more. With Harper and Aly?"

"Yep. It was fun."

"You know," his voice dropped, getting serious. "I could do dance routines with you, too. Might not be moving as fast as those two, but your pops has some *skill*."

4

SHANE

My phone started buzzing and I headed out to Ruby's parking lot.

Since we'd come to town, the bar's regular crowd had thinned. Gloves' mom had expressed concern about that a few times, but I told her the word would spread, and we'd be taking off. The regulars would return, but she also needed to remember we were sharing about her place to the other charters, other bikers we knew. They'd produce a decent amount of revenue for her bar, so this would be something she'd need to get used to.

Stepping out to the back, I could see only a few people at the tables. I answered the phone, stepping down and starting through the bikes. "Yeah."

Maxwell Raith, the Red Demons' national president, was on the other end. "How's it going out there?"

"Good. We're squared with Gloves' family, except for the older sister."

"The older one? I wasn't aware she was there."

"Neither were we. I'm not sure if Gloves knows or if he was keeping her away from us, but she's here. She's not married either. Working in a grocery store."

"Really?"

"Of all of them, she's the one I'd worry about. The dad gave us a pass. The mom'll be under our thumb, and the other sister, she's been cozying up to Roadie."

"Cozying up?"

"Yeah. He's having fun, but she wants more. I've seen the look before."

"He's not interested in an old lady?"

"No."

He grunted. "Right."

Sometimes that happens—girls who want more than a fun-time, want the old lady status, and don't take to a guy's no. An old lady was the equivalent to a wife in our world.

But she was local, and we'd be heading out, so she shouldn't be a problem.

"This older sister. What's she like?"

My gut tightened.

The Kali from high school wasn't the Kali in that grocery store. That girl was long gone.

I needed to not give a fuck.

"She's smart."

He cursed. "You laid the terms out to her?"

"I did. Her favor is for us to leave her brother alone."

Another low curse from him. "Yeah. She's smart." He cleared his throat. "What's her situation? Why's she back in Indiana if she had a good life in New York?"

"I asked Roadie to hit up the sister about her, and there doesn't seem to be a relationship between them. The mom too. Ruby got cagey when I brought her up earlier."

"That's really not good."

I sighed. "I'll make some calls. I don't want to approach Gloves about her. That could backfire. I do know she's down on her luck and not biting at getting a handout. That should tell us something."

"You knew her back in the day?"

My gut tightened again.

I ignored it, again.

"She was pretty back then. Ran with a small group, loyal to each other. I'll look them up, see if she's kept in contact with them. Already told you she was smart. Gloves worshiped her back then, and the feeling was mutual. She's got a different dad; he's an attorney."

"What kind of attorney?"

"Had our computer guys do a search. Attorney in Chicago."

"You think we should move on the dad? Could take his firm on retainer."

"I don't think so. We approach her dad, she hears about it, and that could backfire too."

"You have them look into her?" he asked.

When I didn't respond, he added, "You set our computer guys on the dad, but not her?"

I stilled.

I needed to tread cautiously here. "I knew her in school. Respected her. She was chased by a bunch of the jocks, but she knew what they were like. Saw through them, but handled them smart. She never had a problem."

"You have a thing for her?"

My hand tightened on the phone. "Back then? Yes."

"You got a thing for her now?"

"I don't know her now."

"You want to stick your dick in her?"

I didn't answer that one.

He laughed wryly. "If you need to move in on her, you willing to do that?"

"I'll do anything for the club."

Another dry chuckle came from him. "Let's pretend that's what I was asking for."

"What Gloves is going to do is for the club, so it would be for the club."

A long sigh came over the line, followed by a yawn. "Okay. It's been a long day. I have another situation for you to handle, but let's wait for now. Do what you need to do to move things in place on the sister. You know what I'm talking about. If she's a problem down the road, I want you to pull on whatever strings you have to take care of her. Can you do that?"

My gut was so fucking tight now, I felt like he had a grip on my balls. And I didn't like it. Not one fucking bit.

"Yeah," I bit out. "What's the other situation?"

"Got a call from the Frisco charter. The president is in prison, but he reached out. He's worried about some of his members, got a bad feeling and feels like he got set up."

I frowned. "You want us there to help sort it out?"

Sometimes that was a good idea. Usually it wasn't. Charters got along for the greater good, but on local territory, they liked to rule it the way they ruled it. If there was a difference in opinion, or the wrong personality took root, that could be a problem. A big one. And that could spread to other charters. The whole club was always affected when that poison took hold and was allowed to grow.

"Yeah, but it's twofold for me," he explained. "We're leaving the Goose, and I'm thinking about backup. There's a family from Canada looking to move south. Might be an issue for us, or could be a solution. I'm not sure yet."

There was only one family in Canada I knew that had that sort of reach. "Bennett."

"You go, handle the situation there and we'll figure the rest out later."

"I'd want ten to go with me," I said.

"That's what I was thinking. With ten, you're beneath their numbers. But you're the national VP. I want to send Stripes to help you. He knows the area."

Stripes had been an inmate at Potomahmen. He'd helped us out of a spot, and he'd been with our guys on the inside ever since. He was smart, but he was the sneaky/crafty kind of smart. He got out of prison a year ago, had been riding with our charter ever since, and he was officially patched in a month ago.

"What are my orders for now?"

"Stay put. Do what I said on the sister, and start compiling ten guys to go with you."

I amended my question. "I'll make eleven. Stripes will be twelve."

"That'll keep you guys one below the local charter. You okay doing what you need to do on Gloves' sister? Considering I know how tight you and he are, and if you liked her in school... Those feelings might still be there."

I loved my club.

I'd joined after coming home from three tours overseas. I grew up in foster homes and had no family. Gloves had given me my first semblance of family. My unit gave me my second brothers. The club was my last family.

Prez was right about Kali. He was fucking smart, which made sense since he was nearing his sixties and ran the Red Demons the way he had. He was ruthless, but a mastermind. He was also the sniper in our group. He'd set up a mark and wait months, if he needed to, before he hit it.

Me? My job was to wade in like a ghost—get in the thick of it, get things done, but leave no trace. Both our roles were vital to the club, but right now, I was cursing the role he played, and I wasn't much happier about mine. Still. *For the club.* That was our motto for a reason.

"I'll handle her, but not in a way that'll hurt her. I can't do that, Prez. Not to Gloves. He doesn't deserve that."

I knew how he wanted things handled, and usually I was on board with it. Not this time. I was pushing back, and I rarely pushed back.

He sighed softly.

He was giving in. I could already hear it.

"You're right," he said. "Find a way to handle her, but do it right. I'm giving you free rein on this one. It's your call." After a pause he added, "It's the least we can do for Gloves."

The very least.

5

KALI

The first one approached me in the store as I was going over a list. I was by the ham.

Mr. Baldeaver gripped his basket with both hands. That first got my attention—that and the fact that his green cardigan sweater was the same kind my dad liked to wear in the evening. Mr. Baldeaver was in his eighties, and my dad was fifty-eight.

I was *so* going to use this to tease Dad. The cardigans were showing his age. We still couldn't acknowledge the salt-and-pepper hair, but cardigans, oh yeah. I was going there.

"Kali." Mr. Baldeaver adjusted his grip on the basket and looked down at the floor. To the ham. The other meat products. He checked out the freezer behind us.

"What's wrong?"

"There's a man asking about you. He knows I taught you piano when you were young, and he found me at Martha's Café this morning. You know me and the husbands all meet for coffee. It's a gossip hour, but gives us a break. Most of the time we want to see who's still alive. But anyway, he came up to me at the table. Randy and Freddie were there too, but they don't know you as well as I do. I heard you moved back. I've not said anything. You like your privacy. But since I'm approaching you now, I figure it's the right time to let you know your ex was a fool. He'll realize it too, and be coming back. Don't let him back in. You got a better one coming. I know it. Anyway, I thought you should know because I don't know what this man's intentions are toward you."

My heart melted and twisted all at the same time.

I'd hated taking piano lessons, but now that I was older, I could look back on those days fondly.

Also, Mr. Baldeaver always kept candy in a bowl, and I really loved the little gummy bears he kept stocked. I knew he did it for me because none of his other students liked them.

"What did he ask?"

"Just about you. What you were like when you were younger. There wasn't much to the questions. Felt like he was scoping out how folk around here feel about you. I set him straight on that. Said you were the second-best student I ever had, and anything else was none of his business."

My heart melted and squished all over again.

"What'd he look like?"

"Tall, tattoos. He came in from a motorcycle."

My stomach sank all the way to my toes with a hard thud. Shane King. If it wasn't him, it was someone acting on behalf of him.

Seriously?

Why was he asking around about me?

Mr. Baldeaver seemed like he might keel over. He kept read-justing his hold on that basket, but his chin was up, almost defiant.

I nodded. "Thank you for letting me know. I know who it was. I'll take care of it."

"I need to ask and I'm not meaning this in an intrusive way, but in a way where if you need something, you know I'd give you anything you needed. If I didn't, the Missus would come out of her grave to lecture me so with that said," he took a big breath.

"Are you in trouble? I'm sorry. It's not my place, but I know the crowd your mom's bar serves, and your sister, well... And your ex-husband. I just—my Melanie adored you."

My heart yanked up to my throat. It pulsed there as my throat closed up around it.

Damn. I didn't want to cry. No way. Not here. All my bad-ass cred would be gone. Noah was working today, and he'd taken one look at me and started *actually working*. If he saw me crying, he'd likely *stop*. I couldn't have that.

"She always said you reminded her of our daughter, Sarah," Mr. Baldeaver continued. "She passed when she was young. Don't know if you knew we had a daughter, but when you started taking piano from me, Melanie was always around. She liked when you had a cookie with her, though *I* knew you preferred the gummy bears."

"I didn't know she felt that way. I appreciated the cookies *and* candy."

He smiled, his head bobbing a little, his neck jiggling with the motion. "No, no. I taught a lot of children, but you had a special place with us both. Also, I need to warn you that this mister asked others about you. You might be getting more warnings."

It didn't take long to realize Mr. Baldeaver was right.

After he departed, AnnaBeth Marcella was next. The 'motor-cycle fella' had hit her up at the bakery.

My Spanish and biology teachers from high school also shared their experiences. Both let me know, though they weren't as concerned as Mr. Baldeaver had been, but they still gave me a heads up.

Shane was getting around or the man on his behalf was getting around.

After lunch I was half expecting other childhood friends—or hell, even my college friends—to start texting or calling. The thing with the townspeople is that Shane had opened the door for them to approach me after my divorce. I'd been back three months and hadn't had many conversations. Mr. Baldeaver was right. I was private, but not really.

Mostly I was embarrassed.

Thirty-six. No kids. I'd caught my husband having a foursome on me.

Yeah. I was humiliated and embarrassed, if that was possible. If there was a distinction between the two, I needed them both. This should have been the time of my life when I was with family, when I might've been struggling in my career, but around now was when everything was supposed to start coming together.

I was so far off that bullseye, I wasn't even in the gun range. I was trying to hit it from the parking lot. Or worse, I was still on the road, not even in the parking lot.

This whole day had me in my emotions. Wanting to cry. Crying, at times (in the bathroom), and thinking I should maybe take up smoking. I also wanted to cry because I had no idea how many people didn't just like me—they *cared* about me.

This process was also giving me the 411 about Claudia and how many guys she'd dated over the years. People seemed to be hoping to make me feel better (after they realized I was feeling a certain way), so they told me about Claudia's exploits in a whole scrambling sort of way.

Still. They cared.

I was taking that to the bank.

But also, I was livid by the end of my shift. I mean, I was livid before that, but that was when I let myself actually *feel* it. Now I could do something about the Friendly Questioning Inquisition from Shane Fucking King.

Honestly.

Shane Fucking King.

Is that what he thought?

That he was some motorcycle king?

Ghost? That was his road name.

He wasn't living up to it with this, because everyone saw him, everyone knew about his whole Kali Michaels whatever-he-was-doing. There was nothing stealthy about him, though I guess it was pretty haunting.

Or stalking. *Can I go there?* Because one more day of this, and that'd be what I was feeling.

My shift ended at six. I clocked out at 6:01 pm.

Otis was in a tizzy, since I wasn't staying late, but I knew he wasn't going to protest too much. He'd seemed uber grateful to see me this morning, and I wondered if he'd done some internet searching on the Red Demons last night.

I didn't want to know what he might've found.

By 6:05, I was in my car and heading to a place I hadn't visited in twelve years.

I was going to my mom's bar.

I HIT call on my phone.

Right as he answered, I cut off his usual greeting, "—I can't talk tonight, Dad. I'm about to murder someone."

"Oh, no, no, no. You can't be telling your pops that stuff. I need deniability, Daughter. Thought I taught you better."

He still made me smile.

"Thanks, Dad."

He knew what for. "You know it. Love you, My Little Girl No Matter How Old You Are."

"Dad!"

He just laughed and laughed. Then he told me he started trying his own dance routines. "Me and Cousin Nick. We're thinking of putting together an old guys' dance crew. What do you think?"

"I think you're going to break a hip, and you need three more members."

"You're right. I can get Stevie, Phil, and Pappy."

6

KALI

The gravel parking lot was filled with Harley Davidsons and ten to twenty trucks. I recognized a few that belonged to the regulars. Yeah, some things never changed. It comforted me in a way, and then that made me sad.

A few guys sat outside at the tables, and a few others stood on the porch.

The music blaring was Kansas, but as soon as I walked inside, there was dead silence.

The music stopped.

In an uncomfortable, high-school kind of scene, all eyes would've turned my way. They didn't. Instead, all heads turned toward the jukebox.

The song had stopped in the middle of the chorus, and holy —no one messed with Kansas. Especially "Carry on Wayward Son."

"Hey! Where'd the music go?" That was the first grumble.

"What the hell?" came the second.

"Put it back!" That was a female grumble.

Then a new song started, and damn. *Damn!*

I recognized the first beats and looked at my mom, standing

behind the counter. No one knew she could control the jukebox from her phone. She'd put on "Nasty Letter" by Otis Taylor. The whole song was about leaving a nasty letter for someone.

My mom started laughing, but I glared. "Not. Funny."

She kept laughing, but reached for something under the counter. The music stopped, again. She yelled, "Everyone! A nice welcoming hello for my daughter. She hasn't graced Ruby's with her presence in twelve years."

There was a smattering of cheers. More grumbling. I caught some chilly looks.

Someone yelled, "Put 'Wayward Son' back on!"

My mom waved a hand. "Yeah, yeah. Don't forget who runs this place."

The same voice returned, "I mean, bring on more 'Nasty Letters'! We love those nasty letters."

She chuckled, the same hearty and almost baritone voice she'd always had, and Kansas came back on. A cheer rose up.

I walked to the end of the bar and my mom came to meet me, her arms out.

"Oh goodness, girl." She enveloped me, though I was four inches taller than her five feet, five inches. Didn't matter to Ruby Hinton. She was petite, but a bionic kind of petite—her hug was like cement. She rocked me, and I realized my mom didn't have any fat on her. She was all muscle.

She patted my back, her voice in my ear. "I have missed you something fierce!" She gave me another tight squeeze before she stepped back, her hands still resting on my arms. "How are you? You look good. Holy shit, Kalista. Claude's going to get so mad, because you could still model. I think you look better the older you get."

I tensed and stepped back, out of her reach.

Her hands fell, and so did her smile.

"Hey, Mom," I said.

"I used to be Mama to you," she responded.

We weren't talking about those days.

Noting my silence, sadness flared in her eyes before the corners of her lips moved up. The smile didn't reach her eyes. She gently tapped me with her knuckles under my chin. "You got my looks and your dad's smarts."

"I got Dad's height."

"Yeah," she said fondly. "You did." Then her eyes flashed. She got serious and moved back behind the counter. Picking up a towel, she motioned to an empty stool. It was the only one considering the place was packed. "Whaddya want to drink?"

"I'm not here to drink." I turned, scanning the bar. I'd been focused on my mother first. But now that I was looking, I remembered that Shane King was a Red Demon. All day I'd just remembered him as Shane, Connor's Shane.

But also Ghost.

A whole bunch of scary bikers were watching me, and oh boy...

What had I just walked into?

I tensed, because how could I not?

There was a good group of biker ladies in here too. They were spread out. Some hanging on guys' arms. Some on laps. There was a high-top in the back corner by the pool table, and a whole bunch had congregated there. They were playing pool against some of the bikers.

"Are these all Red Demons?"

I felt my mom moving closer behind me.

"Look." She touched my arm. Her tone was serious.

I turned back, remembering that Shane had said they were helping my mom out. Did that include other MCs? I hadn't known they were inclusive.

"I'm not saying this because of our past, and I'm due for you to be starting trouble for me, considering, you know..."

My wedding day. My chest tightened.

"But these guys can be dangerous," she finished. "You should go."

"No! Fucking! Way!"

We both sucked in our breaths at that high-pitched, female voice.

Well, now I knew where my sister was spending her time.

"No way! My sister! That's my sister."

Ruby grimaced. "She must've been out on a smoke break." I caught the curse under her breath.

My sister's body hit mine before I finished turning all the way around.

She hugged me, her arms wrapped tight and her cheek pushing into my shoulder. "Oh my word. I have missed you. You have no idea!"

You'd think family members who showed up drunk on your wedding day, crashed into three vehicles in the parking lot, stumbled into your wedding dance, and proceeded to claim the DJ's microphone and inform your new husband that they had it on good authority (she claimed to be her own source) that he had a three-inch penis and would never fulfill their little Kalista would have better personal boundaries. We'd had no relationship for twelve years.

But nope. My sister was trying to pick me up and shake me like she was reenacting a Minion meme.

She was also three inches shorter than me. She got Mom's height.

"You look so damned good!"

Whiskey breath was still a thing. My sister hadn't changed her favorite drink.

"Damn." Claudia released me and stepped back, panting slightly with sweat beads on her forehead. She tucked her hair behind her ears. Her eyes were bright, shining. There was some moisture there.

They were both so happy to see me, and here I was, locked down behind a cement gate.

"Hi." I couldn't help myself, looking her over. I softened, just a little. She couldn't hurt me with a mere conversation. Or, I didn't think so... "You look good."

"Yeah." She smiled, scanning me up and down. "You too. Foley was fucking *stew*-pid."

Claudia and Ruby both looked good. Healthy. There was a glow to them.

"That's what I said too," my mom chimed in.

"No, you didn't," I countered.

"Oh." She lifted a shoulder, a grin stretching her lips. "Well, I was thinking it. Fucking stupid."

"Hey." Claudia stepped close, grinning up at me. "Did you really walk in on him doing a foursome? I mean..." She shared a look with Ruby. "How ironic is that, right? I told him he had a three-inch dick, and that's when he was hard."

It wasn't true. I was loath to defend him, but he had a normal dick size. The three inches was a fabrication.

She'd tried to defend herself later by saying she'd heard it from someone else. She never shared who the someone else was, but she assured me the woman had said three inches.

"And hey." She bumped her hip to mine, tucking the same strand of hair behind her ear. "Were we right or were we right? Piece of cheating fucking asshole shit. Right? Right?!" The glazed look in her eyes, the almost sloppy smile—my sister had been drinking for a while. That said a lot because my sister could hold her own.

A pang sliced through my chest. She was right. She had been right, but...

"Jesus, Claudia!" Ruby smacked her arm with the towel. "They *just* got divorced. Some fucking tact, woman."

"Wha—Oh!" Her eyes got big, and she took a full step away from me. "Yes. You're right. I'm sorry. I, uh, want a shot? On me?"

Ruby snorted. "When's the last time you paid for your booze?"

Claudia started laughing, the awkwardness forgotten that quickly. "It's not like you pay for me either." She focused on me again, and her eyes filled up. She grabbed hold of my arm. "Whoa! I should introduce you to Roadie. He's my new man. He's great. He's a Red Demon too. They're *all* hot—even the big ones are hot. It's something about their cut, you know? And the mustaches. And the beards. There's a guy whose beard goes past his stomach. I don't even want to think about giving him a blow job. Can you imagine? Sucking and the hair's right there? Weird. I think... " She cocked her head to the side. "Maybe not. Maybe I'd like that."

"Jesus Christ. My daughters. One's talking about blowing a beard and the other's barely speaking." Ruby shook her head, glancing down the bar. "I gotta go. I gotta work. Only got so many employees, you know?"

Claudia snorted. "That's Mom's not-so-subtle hint for both of us to pitch in." She hopped up on the empty stool I'd never taken and propped her elbow on the bar. "So. How's it going? I heard you're living with your two buddies from school. You went to school to be a nurse. Why aren't you working at the hospital and not at the lame grocery store? You're enabling Otis. You know that, right? Such a lazy piece of shit."

I...had nothing. I shouldn't have been surprised by any of this.

After a moment the stool next to her emptied, and I took it because as much as I tried to pretend, I'd missed my sister. I'd missed my mom too. Damn family, you know? You love 'em until you want to kill 'em.

Claudia wheeled to face me directly, her shoes resting on my stool's footrest. "So." She tapped her toes. "I want all the details. I know that cheating asshole didn't want you to work, so I figure you didn't keep up with your license? Did I get it right? Is that something you can study and get back?"

She was ripping off *all* the Band-Aids.

"Why aren't you married?" Even as I asked, intending to turn the interrogation her way, she perked up. I'd forgotten how much my sister loved talking about herself, and everything that was going on in her life. I shot a hand up. "No. Never mind. I changed my mind."

"Oh." She deflated, her shoulders slumping forward. But her grin was back in a flash. "I know you're all reserved and cautious, the type that wades into the lake. Not me. I run down the dock and do a belly-flop in, no matter if there's water or ice or whatever. That's me, but I need to respect you. You're big on boundaries and shit. So yeah." She eased back, straightening on her stool with a nod. "I'm here. Respecting that."

Oh Lord.

This was painful to watch.

She was going to puff out her cheeks, move her tongue around. She was five years old sometimes.

Fine.

She was here. I was here.

Also, drunk funny Claudia could be fun sometimes. It was when she got sober, that was the other story. Or a mean drunk.

Caution be damned, let's do this.

"I had two boyfriends in high school," I told her. "You blew both of them."

"I like giving blow jobs," she shot right back. "And you're welcome. It was a test. They failed."

"You lied and said you slept with my husband."

"I lied about the part that it was me. So again, *you're* welcome."

"I worked three jobs in high school to buy my first car. You crashed it the day I brought it home."

She opened her mouth.

"If you goddamn say 'you're welcome', I will find your vehicle and drive it into the river. Tonight."

She closed her mouth and blew out a breath, laughing a little.

"Same Kal, that's for sure. And I was going to say your car wasn't safe. *That's* why it crashed."

Right. I'd take a bat to Claudia's car first. Might as well get some therapy done.

I started to slide off the barstool.

Claudia, knowing me just as well as I knew her, stopped laughing and grabbed my arm. "I'm kidding! I'm totally kidding. And I don't have a car you can crash. I already crashed it. Seems there's a pattern there with me. Roadie's letting me borrow the cage while they're here."

I frowned. "Cage?"

She grinned, a laugh snorting from deep in her throat. "What they call a car—or a truck in his case. He said they needed to bring it on this trip. I don't know why. He doesn't say shit to me about anything with the club. He just likes to get drunk and fuck, and he's really good." She giggled and leaned close. "And he likes blow jobs too. We're perfect for each other." Her eyes trailed past me, lingered on someone, and then softened. "Goddamn, sis. I'm in love with him." She blinked, sniffing, and sat back. "I wasn't expecting that. *You* do that. You make me see things clearly. Everything gets all muddied up, and then my sister comes back in my life and it's like—" She whistled, her hands touching each other and moving in opposite directions. "—the parting of the Red Ocean."

"It's the Red Sea."

"—the Red Sea. Just like that." She beamed at me. She patted my arm. "I *really* missed you. I'm glad you're back, but for fuck's sake, get a job at the hospital. You're too smart to be doing Otis' job." She jerked, sitting straight up. "I just had an idea. Let's get Otis fired! Tonight."

My sister had been uptight, jealous, and insecure when we were younger. A sinking realization came to me: I could've been friends with her if she'd been like this back then. I mean, I couldn't have trusted her, but we could've been friends.

No.

We *had* been friends.

That's why it hurt every time she did a "Claudia."

She stole from me.

She took credit cards out in my name.

She hit on Harper, thinking he and I were hooking up. That was before she learned he was gay.

She spread rumors about me. She spread a few about Aly.

There were so many other things, too many.

I wasn't here for her. I needed to remember that.

She watched me, waiting. In her way, she was asking for forgiveness, or maybe she was just asking to be let back in, but... I wasn't here for her.

I took a breath, pushed back from the counter, and slid off the stool.

I looked around the bar.

That's when I saw him, at the back.

My eyes caught his immediately, and everything went blank for a full beat.

Shane King.

Connor's friend. Connor's "brother."

He stood in the doorway of the back section, holding a beer. He looked like he'd been waiting for me to notice him. Once I saw him, he took a step back and walked outside.

The door shut behind him.

Well, alrighty then. Seemed he *was* waiting for me.

I didn't look at my sister as I said, "I gotta go."

I heard her suck in a breath.

And as I walked past the bar, making my way to the back, I didn't look at my mother either.

I tried to ignore that I felt her watching me the whole time too.

As I stepped outside I heard, "Took you long enough."

SHANE

GLOVES' sister. I still couldn't believe it.

I remembered her, remembered her crushing on me from afar. *Fuck.* Connor knew. He'd teased me at times, but only because he knew I'd never touch her. But damn, I wanted to.

She was all grown. All woman. Long fucking legs.

Her body was strong. She wasn't slender. She had some meat, and I loved that. I didn't like fucking someone I could break, but her? She looked like she could handle rough. She looked like she'd give it right back.

But, fuck. Fuck, man.

With what we were going to ask Connor to do, I couldn't do what I wanted with her. Not really. She'd kill me, and she'd have every right.

We were going to ask Connor to do it anyway. Hated it. But there was no one else.

The way she showed up to her mom's bar—all defiant and pissed off—she wasn't thinking of me as a biker. I was that guy she remembered from school, and she was pissed at me.

I loved that shit. Fucking moved me.

I liked this look on her—challenging me, wanting to rip my ribs out and probably spear me with them.

I'd never cared about attitude from my women before, but it was different with Kali. *Kalista.*

She'd been the one taking care of Connor back then. Claudia too, but Claudia had always been a hellion. I wasn't surprised by how she'd turned out, and my investigator had warned me, said there was some bad blood between the girls and the mom.

Looking at her now, my gut reacted. I wished, for a second, that she had stayed in New York, that her fuck husband hadn't been cheating on her since day one. I wished she was happy, and not here, not in front of me, because I knew I wouldn't be able to leave her alone.

I was going to ruin her.

She still hadn't said a word. The door closed behind her, but still nothing.

Her eyes flared as she looked me over.

She'd checked me out in the grocery store, and she was doing it again.

My gut churned. No way in hell I could leave her be, though if I was any sort of man, I would.

But I wasn't. I hadn't been that kind of guy since the service. I wasn't before, and I hadn't been after. No way I'd be going back. No more fucking sacrifice, unless it was for the club. Only the club mattered.

"Why the fuck are you interrogating half the town about me?"

I grinned. I hadn't been, but I liked that she thought it was me. "Got your attention."

She wanted to snap her teeth at me. I knew she did. If she was her sister, she might've.

"What are you guys doing here?"

"Told you. Taking care of some things for your brother."

Her eyes narrowed. "Why?"

"He did us a solid in prison, helped take care of some of our guys. This is what we do."

"He's not in your club."

"He's my brother all the same." And there was my gut moving again, because everything I said was true. Connor *was* my brother.

Fuck.

Fuck!

"I want you guys to leave this town."

"We'll leave when we choose to leave."

She kept on as if I hadn't said anything. "I want you to leave my mom's bar."

"Same answer, woman."

And again, as if I hadn't spoken, she added, "And I want your Roadie to stop fucking my sister."

I grunted. I was right there with her on that one. "We fuck who we want to fuck."

"And I want you to stop having any correspondence with my brother."

I started for her. She'd said enough, but when she jumped back, I frowned. I didn't like that happening. "You know bikers?"

"I know you."

"We do what the fuck we want to do. You keep issuing orders, we'll start responding. But trust me, it won't be the way you want."

"You guys are bad news."

She wasn't wrong.

I stepped closer, almost within arm's reach, and her eyes flashed.

She knew. She knew, all right.

Fine. It was time to scare her a bit. "Your husband slept with two hundred and six women, and three men."

Pain flared in her gaze before she shuddered. A wall slammed down.

She was a numb zombie now, but I added, "That was in the course of your marriage. Got a couple of investigators on you, and that's the number they got in a day. They're good at their job. Also found out the scene you walked in on that made you leave, but you knew he was fucking around before that. Why'd you stay?"

Her eyes flared again before that wall took out all her shine. "None of your business."

"You love that hard? Accept that shit from him? Or what? Don't know your worth—"

"Shut up!" She flew at me, but restrained herself a foot away.

I wished she'd kept coming.

"Why'd you stop?"

"Stop talking about my marriage."

"Just now, why'd you stop yourself?" Fuck, I wanted to rile her up. I wanted her eyes to come alive. I wanted her skin to heat. I wanted to feel every inch of her against me.

She sighed. "This was pointless, wasn't it?"

I gave her a once-over. Her tits strained against her shirt. She was bothered by me. I liked that—meant one touch and she'd burst alive.

"Not from my point of view."

She groaned. "You used to be a nice guy..."

Now my grin was slow, because that was funny. "I was never a nice guy."

She flicked her eyes upwards before looking away. "You weren't a bad guy, not to Connor."

Yeah... "Listen, we'll leave, but you gotta give us something." I dropped the flirting. It was riling her up, but she was a slow burner. "I'm not lying about your brother. Give us something to do for you, and we'll leave."

"*Leaving* is what I need you to do. Leaving my brother alone."

I stared at her, long and hard.

Fuck. She meant it.

That asshole did some major damage, but why would she stay with him?

I nodded, giving in because there wasn't anything I could do to help her except what she wanted. "We'll go in the morning."

Her eyes got big. "Really?"

I nodded, then moved close and touched her face. I smoothed a finger along her jaw, then cupped the side of her cheek. I raised her head up and moved in even closer. She felt amazing. Smooth. And there was no makeup. She was fresh-faced and gorgeous.

She wasn't anything like any other woman I'd known.

She was rare.

And she was Connor's sister.

Still.

I looked down at her, feeling her chest lift up and pause. Her lips parted. A dazed look came over her, and I moved my thumb over her mouth. The best mouth I'd ever seen. I could dip in and taste her for weeks.

"Why the fuck did you stay with that piece of shit?" I almost groaned the question, because he should be put down for sheer stupidity.

Her glazed look deepened, and I ceased thinking.

VP of the Red Demons, my ass.

Right now, I was a man wanting to touch his woman, though she didn't know she was his woman. So I dipped my head, touched my lips to hers, and I tasted.

7

KALI

I t'd been three weeks, and I was still thinking of that kiss.

God. That kiss.

That was the downside, that I hadn't been able to get ~~Sha~~—that kiss out of my head.

That *kiss*.

God.

The way he held my face with such gentleness...

How his lips touched—nope. I needed to stop. There was no reason to keep thinking about it, except that I needed to get laid.

But the upside? They left!

Things felt more calm and settled around town after they left, but there was also a restlessness. I could say that because I saw it. The grocery store had been slow, but then while the Red Demons were here, people had started coming in with an extra urgency in their step. The way they talked. The way they looked around. It was like the motorcycle club had woken something in the community, something new and exciting and edgy. Now it was gone, and people were like, "When are they coming back?"

That lasted until the new bikers arrived.

Who these new guys were, I didn't know, but they wore cuts

and they rode Harleys. Shane said they'd be spreading the word about my mom's bar, so bikers would become the new norm for her establishment. They stopped through town, filling up or getting food, but mostly her bar was their pit stop. I'd heard that they'd also been spotted hanging out at Gorman's Auto Repair, which wasn't too surprising. I knew Allen Gorman from school, knew his dad had been in a riding club. He wasn't in a motorcycle club—or I didn't think he was. Maybe he had been, but it wasn't a 1% one. Still, they'd recently renovated some of the buildings on his lot with bunk beds, so there you go, I guess.

I heard all that from the same people who wanted to know if I knew the Red Demons personally, since they'd been hanging out at my mom's bar. That was everyone. Everyone wanted to know.

The only two who didn't ask were my roommates, and that was mostly because they were worried about their jobs. Harper still needed a new company for his costumes, and Aly said things had been more stressful at the fire station. She didn't elaborate on that. Because of those situations, neither of them brought up anything. To their credit, I wouldn't have been surprised if they'd forgotten about the Red Demons. Either way, I was appreciative of the silence.

But everyone else wanted the details on when or if the Red Demons were coming back.

Were they doing a charter here?

What would that mean for the community?

Probably bad, right?

How would they mix with the new bikers? Would they get along?

Even Otis came out of his office more than normal, hitching his pants up and pretending to ask about the weather, which was the worst segue into the motorcycle club. He tried, though. Ben's eyes got bigger and bigger the more he heard. Noah seemed put off, and I didn't know what that was all about.

I was at work stocking cereal when the next person came over.

I was used to it by now, so I waited, feeling whoever it was at my side.

People either finally asked what they wanted to know, or they left.

I waited, grabbing the next box and putting it on the shelf. The person still stood there, so I looked—could be a customer needing something... Nope.

"Ruby."

It was my mom, and she'd been quiet as long as she had been because she was biting her lip. Her hair was pulled up in a frizzy bun, and I winced because I knew I had a mirrored look on my head, except darker hair. I'd been going the natural way lately, but I needed to get my usual products.

Her hands went to her hips. Her face was tight as she watched me stock the boxes.

"You're doing this?" Her voice went high. "This?!"

I sighed. "Mom."

"Mom." She snorted. "*Mama.* I was Mama until you were thirteen. Then you hit the teens and fuck the mama shit. I'm all about Mom, and now you're an adult and calling me Ruby. I know you don't want me to make a scene in the Un-Friendly Grocery Store." She raised her voice even higher, tilting her head up. "You hearing me, Otis? You hearing how pissed off you're making me because you got my girl shelving goddamn cereal when she's got a four-year nursing degree?"

I sighed and picked up the chocolate cereal box to shelf it. "Everyone's hearing you, Mama."

That got her.

She stopped, but let out a small growl with her mouth closed. Her fingers started tapping on her hip. "I'm pissed off, that's what I am, and not just at you, but the other one too."

I frowned. "Claudia?"

My mom went still, freezing in mid-glare at the Cheerios.

"Mom."

It took effort, but she jerked her gaze away and blinked, refocusing on me. "I need you to go and get your sister. Bring her back."

"What? Where'd she go? And no."

She was *so* not looking at me.

Something had happened here that I didn't understand. Ruby Hinton was not being Ruby Hinton. She was a stranger right now. "Where'd Claudia go?"

Her frown was seriously fierce. "I don't want to—they've helped me. The bar, but... Screw it." Her eyes snapped to mine, and they were so clear, so piercing. "You know your sister was with that Demon?"

Roadie. I nodded, not letting my mind follow my body to the other Red Demon... Nope. Not going to happen. "Yeah."

"She followed him."

I tilted my head. I needed that to digest a bit.

I had to repeat this. I needed to get it right. "She followed him?" There was no MC that would be okay with that—no MC *ever.*

"She called today, said she's not coming back. But..." Her voice wobbled, and she stopped, her throat jerking before she could talk again. "She won't come back for me. Won't listen to me. I don't want to involve Gloves. We all know he's gotten involved enough with that club, but..." She faltered, her eyes flicking to mine.

I could read between the lines. Claudia might listen to me.

And fuck, because just fuck.

Nope.

If people couldn't understand my mixed feelings about my mother and my sister, this was a classic example. Claudia went off, following a motorcycle club, and I was the one who would have to go and get her out? I didn't even want to think about the damage that could entail.

"Mom." I shook my head.

"She called, said she's staying put and there's nothing I can do to persuade her otherwise." She gulped again. "Gloves is gone. I mean, he ain't *gone* gone, but he ain't here. I don't see him for lunch or when he used to drop in for a beer, if he would've done that sort of thing. And you... You moved back and I thought, *finally*, I got both my girls here. I can make things right, can make her love me again, let me be her mama. But now..." She looked away.

Ruby Hinton was not like this.

She wasn't uncertain, fearful. She didn't stand with her bottom lip moving and her throat choking her up. I'd never seen my mother like this, not even the day Gloves was convicted and sentenced. I'd heard her in her bedroom those nights, but not in public, not where others could see her.

And goddamn, seriously, fuckitity fuck fuck fuck.

I sighed. "Where is she?"

She fixed her eyes on me again. They were clearing. I could almost see the hope coming back.

"Some place called Frisco, California. And I don't mean San Fran," she clarified.

Otis came down the aisle, hitching up his pants. "Now, Ruby, I could hear you all the way in my office—"

My mom whirled on him. "That was a good ten minutes ago. Took you that long to grow a pair and face me? After how you're putting my daughter to work? My daughter who is more educated and just got a whole fuckton more common sense than you—"

I decided to cut through any more bullshit. "Otis."

He looked. She looked.

"I quit."

Now where is Frisco, California? And not San Francisco.

IT WAS that night when it happened.

Harper and Aly came to my room, saw me packing, and wanted to know what was going on. I filled them in.

"We're going where?" was Harper's first question.

I frowned. "Huh?"

He was no longer paying attention to me. He was looking around, his skinny arm bent back as his hand gripped the back of his neck.

"Oh, dear." He held his hands out in front of him, palms toward me and Aly. "This is going to take some coordination. I need to pack. I need new suitcases. I can't use the normal stuff, not for this trip. This is a life-changing trip. I can feel it in my bones." He breezed past us, hollering over his shoulder, "I have to prepare for this. Big things will happen. My grandmama was a psychic. I can feel her telling me to prepare. I gotta prepare! Aly, go and prepare too. Don't forget Billy."

Aly growled. "Why did he have to name my vibrator? You'd think if someone's going to name a vibrator, it would be the person who uses it." She raised her voice. "HIS NAME IS GABRIEL! Because he makes me feel heaven every time." She gave me a lopsided grin. "Right? Get it?"

I groaned and held a hand up. "Don't elaborate any more. Please."

She snorted. "Yolo. Fomo. All the omos."

"That makes no sense."

She was out the door.

I called after her, "Where are you going?"

She turned back. "Gonna need to pack Gabriel and maybe a few others—Michael, Uriel."

I grunted. "Why do you have to name them after archangels?"

Her eyes went wide. "You know your archangels. I'm impressed."

I went back to packing. "Don't test me about Jesus."

She laughed. "I'm not testing Harper either. His grandmother is saying to prepare. No way am I missing out. I've got six months of vacation. It's time I call some of it in."

It took me a second to digest what had just happened.

I was packing, preparing to go on this trip alone. My roommates came home, and just hearing the story, they were going. No questions. No discussion. No trying to talk me out of it. Nothing. Just instant, "We're going with you. I gotta go and pack my vibrators because a dead grandmother told me to." Those were my friends.

Damn.

I reached up and flicked a tear away.

Damn.

Moving back after what Foley did, I hadn't—no. That wasn't true. I was going to say I hadn't taken the time to appreciate my friends, but that wasn't the truth. I had. I was so seriously appreciative of them that sometimes, I worried I was too appreciative. I depended on them too much. Was that fair to them? For them to deal with me, to come "bring me home," as Harper had put it, and now this?

Oh yeah.

My throat swelled with emotion.

Life was not easy. It wasn't easy at all, but with the right friends, it got a little less hard.

I HIT call on my phone.

"Daughter! How are you? How've you been? The Old Gents started a YouTube channel. We're uploading our first dance routine this weekend."

"I—what?"

"Oh yeah. I told you about that, didn't I? We got a name. Old

Gents. It's catchy, right? Stevie thinks it'll bring in a bunch of the young crowd. You know. All those gals who go crazy over rich millionaires. He's thinking 'gents' will come up as 'gentlemen' and boom. There you go. Our dance video will show up."

Harper and Aly started laughing, and I had to clear my throat because I'd dissolve as well. "Dad."

"Yeah? Who's that? Who are you with?"

"Uh. I'm with Aly and Harper."

"Oh, hey everyone! Kali, tell them hi from me. Did you do it? Say hi. I want to hear you say hi for me."

"Dad."

"What?"

"We're going to California. We're going on a road trip."

Silence for a moment.

He cleared his throat, and got all serious. "You know, Kali. You know you don't have to go all the way to California for your road trip. You can come here! Harper and Aly can join in on the next dance routine."

"I'm so down for that, Mr. Michaels," Harper yelled from the front seat.

"Who was that? Kali, which one was that? They're down to come here and dance with your Pops?"

8

KALI

We didn't fly, and to this day, I couldn't tell you why that didn't happen. We just didn't. Aly offered her SUV, so after she and Harper made their plans (I didn't know what those were), we piled our suitcases into the vehicle. Then Harper brought out a cloth grocery bag of food, and Aly started bringing out the coolers.

Not one, or two. Three coolers.

Those were just the food.

The beverages filled up another two. I didn't want to look at what she'd put in there, but I knew Aly liked her alcohol. I just hoped none of it was open.

But the next morning at ten, we were ready to go.

Aly wanted to drive. Harper wanted to ride shotgun—"the navigator," he said. He looked the part with actual navigator sunglasses on and a huge map spread over his lap. I sat in the back, and when Aly started off, she handed her phone to me.

"Okay." Harper smoothed his map, finding Friendly on it. "What route are we taking?"

Aly didn't answer, she just looked at me.

I programmed Frisco, California, into her GPS app, hit the fastest route, and handed it back up.

The lady said, "Turn south onto US-50 W."

Harper put the map down and gave us a look. "Fine. I was going for fun and adventurous, but if you two want to be bored out of your minds so early on, who am I to object?" If he'd sniffed, he would've sealed the whole thing.

He didn't. Instead he slumped down in his seat and pulled out snack bag #1. As it crinkled, he popped two gummies into his mouth and lounged back. "So, Aly. You're up."

She tensed, her hands tightening on the wheel. "Why are we starting with me? Who needs coffee?"

She didn't ask what the whole "up" thing was about. Those two knew.

I was missing out. "What's going on?"

Harper ignored me, staring at Aly. "Your tank is full. We have beverages to last us for days. We both know Kali isn't going to open up about her decision to go after her sister, when she just quit on Otis and she's still digesting Foley's cheating-capade, so the way I'm thinking, you're up."

"Keep on US-50 W for nine miles, where you'll use the right lane to merge onto I-65 S using the ramp toward Louisville."

Harper started laughing.

Aly groaned. "We talked about this last night."

I leaned forward. No one had talked to me. "What talk? What'd you two talk about?" My hand curled over the back of Harper's seat.

He continued to ignore me, his eyes on Aly. "We got her in the car for thirty-two hours, at least. We got time to grill Kali. You're up. You might as well just start telling us about Mr. Hot and Sweaty Fireman."

Aly's eyes threatened to bulge out. She shifted in her seat, squirming.

I frowned. "I thought you wanted to date a millionaire farmer?"

"I do!" she burst out. "That's my plan."

"It's not happening," Harper said. "You're almost forty—"

"I'm thirty-six."

Harper shook his head, grabbing more gummies. The bag crinkled. "Let's talk about who's warming your sheets, and I heard you the other night. The floors aren't that thick, not to mention the whole..." He hit the palm of his hand against the dashboard in a soft, tapping rhythm.

I fought off my laughter.

Aly looked ready to burst. Her face was all red.

Harper laughed and gestured to her hands on the steering wheel with his bag. "Hope you didn't grip his dick that hard."

"Agh!" she yelled, throwing herself back in her seat and releasing her hold on the wheel for a moment. One hand slid to the bottom as she took a more relaxed driving stance. "No one's talked about Justin since he left—"

Harper sucked in his breath.

"If we're blasting everyone, and saving Kali for last..." she continued.

"Hey," I protested half-heartedly.

At least I now knew why they'd both come on this trip with me. To an extent, I owed them some conversation. I'd really not talked about Foley, and I knew I needed to start or that dick would be inside me forever.

I shuddered at the literal meaning of that last thought.

"My age has nothing to do with me spending time with Scott," Aly added.

Scott! We had a name—oh holy shit!

I jerked forward. "Scott *Campinah*?"

"Exactly," Harper confirmed.

"The Campinah fireman from the Campinah family who basically own Vernon?" I asked.

That was our neighbor town, and it was well-off. Unlike Friendly, which didn't have a ton of businesses and was truly a dying small town, Vernon was not. It was a tourist town that was thriving, with six production warehouses there. They had a brand new hospital, a new high school, and their biggest debate was what color to paint the water tower. The fights on social media were nasty.

Vernon was privileged.

And North Campinah, along with his three sons and one daughter, owned or ran almost the entire town. The main drive had been renamed Scott Campinah Drive.

That Campinah, the one who volunteered at the county's fire station because... No one really knew. He was also twenty-six. No wonder Aly was shitting bricks right now.

I grinned. "I bet he has staminaaaaa."

Harper barked out a muffled laugh.

Aly flushed, her shoulders loosening up. "God, you guys. He's ten years younger than me."

I shrugged. "Love is love."

"I know, but ten years? Everyone we know has kids. I feel like I'm fucking a kid. And his dad..." She sighed. "He's a member of the Good Ole Boys Network, if you get my drift."

That soured me. Right. *Asshole.* But still... "Fuck him being a kid. He's twenty-six, and I bet you he had to volunteer against his dad's wishes. You know his dad just wants him to work for him. That takes character. Say it straight. I bet he's mature, isn't he?"

"I just don't know what I'm doing."

"Hello?" Harper burst out. "Why are we not talking about the good part? How's the sex? You two were thumping all night that night."

Aly turned red all over again.

I shook my head. So far the road trip was quite entertaining.

Aly shot Harper a glare. "You just wait. We've given you time after Justin left, but it's your turn to talk too, buddy."

He eyed her. She eyed him right back, for as long as she could before needing to look back at the road. Then Harper rotated around, finding me. I sat back, finding Aly watching me in the rearview mirror.

Right.

This was a coming clean sort of road trip. I'd not signed on for that.

I remembered another reason why the three of us became friends. We'd bonded over the not-talking part of hard life situations. Aly getting it from a rich twenty-six year old, Harper's breakup, and all the shitshow in my life—dammit.

Why weren't we flying?

IT WASN'T until we were driving through Sullivan, Missouri, that Harper broke.

"Justin wanted to marry me. That's why we broke up!"

"What?!" Aly said. "That's amazing."

"For you maybe, Miss I Want To Marry a Millionaire Farmer and Instead I'm Boinking a Super Hot and Young Fireman Stud. Marriage isn't for everyone, sweetie."

I grunted, on his side.

No one should get married.

Ever.

WE'D BEEN SWITCHING OFF DRIVING, and I took over in Oklahoma City. I could go another four hours before needing to stop.

Harper had sprawled in the back, needing nap time. He'd been the last to drive. Aly could handle four hours. Harper could do two. Not me. I enjoyed a good eight hours. I forgot how much I loved road trips.

Good thing we hadn't flown.

I WAS OVERRULED.

We stopped in Amarillo, Texas, for the night. Sixteen hours on the road, and everyone was tired... Or they should've been.

I wasn't.

I was wired, and I didn't know why.

The closer we got to California, the more tight I felt.

It was as if I was a wire, and both ends were being tightened, tightened, tightened. I wasn't quite to the point of snapping, but I was close.

Aly found me in the hotel's bar. I was ready for bed, head wrap and all except my pajamas were a normal legging and an oversized sweater. My sleep tank was underneath.

She slid into the chair across from me and eyed my drink.

"You know all about my bed-capades with Scott, and now we know we don't need to hate Justin. Him wanting to marry Harper is a good thing. But hon?"

I bristled, hating and loving that *hon* part. I knew I wouldn't want to hear what she was going to say. But I also knew she loved me, and that's why she was going to say what she was going to say.

"It's been three months, almost four. You don't get on with your sister, but here we are—on a road trip going to get her. You gotta talk." She dropped her voice to a whisper. "You know you gotta talk."

I didn't want to talk.

That meant thinking about what he'd done to me, remembering it, being back there, and God, I didn't want to go back there. Also, Shane's question haunted me.

Why had I stayed? I didn't know myself.

I shook my head. "I can't. Not yet."

She tapped my drink. "You are not a drinker, and you're here after riding for sixteen hours, having a drink. Kali, that says everything."

That wire tightened another notch, but I still didn't snap. Not yet.

It was coming.

9

SHANE

"How's it going in Frisco?"

I was surprised Max held off as long as he had. We'd arrived two weeks ago, and since then it'd been a shitshow.

Which is what I told him, adding, "What did you expect?"

I'd taken his call outside The Bonfire, a local hangout we'd adopted with the other Red Demons already in the local Frisco charter. It was a bar just for us, and instead of being on the outskirts of town, which is what we usually chose so we could be rowdy and not get complaints, The Bonfire was smack dab on the main street that ran through Frisco.

It was a small town, barely a town at all—population of three hundred and seventy two residents. The school was gone. The local post office had one worker. Two diners. One gas station. Two bars. A small nursing home. Some volunteers made up the local fire station, and there were no cops. The neighboring towns had those, but they were a decent distance away. That's where the nearest hospital was too.

We were twenty miles off of a major interstate that connected California to Oregon, to Washington, and all the way to the border. On the other side, we were another ten miles from a

second major highway that ran east, all the way through
Colorado and on to the east coast. It went right through middle
America, and Max had been right. This was a prime location.

Tonight the party was in the back, gated off by two giant walls
of chain, steel, and wood—pallets, to be more specific. Open that
gate up, and on the other side you'd find thirty motorcycles, two
RV campers, an auto repair warehouse, and the backside of The
Bonfire, which lived up to its name. A big fire ring had been set
up in the middle of the whole shebang, and the guys were having
a good ol' cookout, complete with beer, women, and blow.

All that was a bit noisy for my call, so I moved through The
Bonfire's interior, giving a nod to those who greeted me, and
stepped outside to the front along Frisco's main road. A line of
bikes was parked out here, along with two prospects watching
them. Both said hello, but saw I was on the phone and moved
away to give me privacy.

It didn't matter. I wasn't planning to stay there. I was restless,
and I didn't know why.

No. That wasn't true. I *did* know why, but there was nothing I
could do about it. Not yet.

Moving past The Bonfire, I went over and sat on a bench
outside Mama's Diner. It was closed, and no one was around. It was
an older building with giant windows and white paint that was
half stripped off, but it had the small town charm to it. It'd become
a popular eating place with the guys, and I could understand why
—good-sized helpings and cheap prices, especially for California.
And since there were barely any locals, it was almost like our own
diner. Mama herself didn't have any objections. She was doing real
well these last couple weeks. The guys enjoyed the high school-
aged servers too. There was a lot of flirting and giggling going on.

"I want to send Wraith out there," Max told me.

"Prez..." I stopped myself, though. Respect was everything in
our club. But he was wrong here. Dead fucking wrong. I took a

beat. "You sent me to help with this charter. I'm here. I'm doing it. They haven't balked too much. They enjoy the partying mostly, but I cannot help this charter get where you want us to go with your nephew coming. He's good. He's smart, but I can't risk it. That could lead to unnecessary death, and then we got police involved, outside police."

"What about Stripes?"

"He's smart, wily. It's an asset to have him here."

I liked Stripes. He got the road name Stripes from inside Potomahmen and it stuck. He'd come clean about what he had to do in order to get a reduced sentence for the reason he was in. That hadn't sat well with some of the guys, but he struck a deal after. He gave us some vital intel and since then swore his loyalty to us. We'd kept a good eye on him, but there was always a little hesitancy about him, though what he helped us with *really* helped the club. It was the kind of favor that saved our hides from going and being in a cell next to him. He was also young and he had a daughter. He talked about her a lot, which wasn't a problem, but his daughter was in Florida. He'd gone to see her a few times, though it wasn't enough. A lot of the guys understood, having kids of their own.

"That's good. We got a charter in Florida, but I'm hoping he stays with us. I've been thinking about the Bennett situation. When you think you could do a meet?"

Jesus. One, it was news to me that he did want us to do a meet. And two, he wanted us to get right to it. That shit didn't happen, not just like that. Maxwell Raith was the most intelligent and ruthless man I'd ever met, but he also tried to be fair. I respected him, but this wasn't how things worked.

The local charter had thirteen members, and I'd showed up with twelve of us. If I moved forward too fast, they could protest. *They* were the charter nearest to where the Bennetts had their headquarters. We didn't have a charter in Oregon or Washington.

If I made the approach and it went bad, their charter would be the one first impacted.

"If we don't want to have the guys digging graves out back, I'm going to need three months," I told him. "At the least. I also need that time to do the initial job."

"The window for our move is gonna be tight," he countered.

I grunted because selfishly, I was okay with that.

"Gloves made his choice," he said in a low voice. "We've upheld his wishes, helped the mother and one sister. We're moving forward."

I ground my teeth. It wasn't right.

"What about the other sister?" Max asked.

"She wanted us gone, so we split."

"You still think she'll be a problem?"

The way he said that... I didn't get a good feeling. Killing wasn't something I second-guessed—not now, not after so long in the service and after doing this life. There was no way up if you didn't take a life. But I didn't want it to come to that with Kali.

"We did what she wanted so why would she be a problem?" I asked. It was the most non-answer I've ever given him.

"What the fuck does that mean?"

I gripped the phone tighter, hearing laughter burst out as The Bonfire's doors opened. Some of the guys spilled onto the sidewalk, their arms around some sweet butts.

"I gotta go, Prez. There's not a lot of privacy where I'm at."

"You set on those three months?" he asked.

I'd stood up from my bench, but paused. "No ditches need to be dug in that timeframe."

"Make it happen because I'm not being bitch for the fucking Estrada cartel anymore."

With that, he hung up. He'd said his piece. I'd said mine. I got the extension I wanted, and he'd ended with a reminder of what all this was for.

Max made a call years ago and got us in business with a cartel.

That cartel had been weakened over the last year. No one knew why or how it happened, but it did. We'd voted, and all of the Red Demons wanted out from under the cartel's thumb.

"Ghost." Stripes came toward me, a beer in one hand. He glanced up and down the street, which was empty except for a few Frisco residents driving through. "We gotta problem with Roadie's lay or sweetie, or whatever the fuck she is."

I grinned. I meant what I'd said to Maxwell. Stripes was smart, and he could be an asset, but also, he was maybe *too* smart. He was the kind who could mastermind shit without blinking an eye. That made me think he could work something against us, and we'd never see it coming. I wasn't sure if he had the balls, but we'd see. He was young and had caught the eye of more than a handful of women on our trip, but to my knowledge, he hadn't taken any of them to bed.

Another weird thing about him.

"Gloves' sister?"

He gave me a tight nod, which told me he agreed with my sentiment. Claudia Hinton was a problem. She'd followed us on our trip, driving separately with a couple of her friends, but when we set up shop here, she'd stayed put.

"What's going on?"

"She's throwing a fit—found Roadie balls deep in her friend. The two are catfighting."

Well, shit. I sighed. "Get Roadie out here," I barked, knowing Stripes would repeat it exactly that way.

He disappeared with a nod, and a few moments later, Roadie hurried his ass out here, zipping up his pants at the same time.

I gave him a look. "Your two bitches are fighting and you didn't find the time to put your dick away?"

He gave me a lopsided grin, raking his hand through his hair. "Hey, man."

"Hey, man, my ass. What the fuck you think you're doing?"

His eyes widened, and he dropped a bit of that grin. Straightening up, he swallowed. "You mean the girls?"

"I mean *Gloves'* sister. She's Gloves' *sister*. You forget what we're asking him to do? And you're what? She gonna be your old lady? A sweetie? If she's a lay, it's a long fucking lay. You think Gloves will be happy if she turns into a sweet butt?"

That grin was gone, and panic crept in. He blanched. "I didn't really think it through, to be honest."

"No shit."

He grimaced again, rubbing a hand over his face. "Fuck. What do I do, Ghost?"

"You don't want her to be a sweetie?" I knew he wasn't mature enough to take on an old lady.

He considered it, regret written all over his face. He went so white he looked like Casper. This fucking idiot.

"She's followed us the whole route," I pointed out. "No one's said anything because of who her brother is. Now you've created this situation, and you better be real fucking thoughtful in the way you're going to fix it."

"I don't want a sweetie, but..."

He was considering it.

Goddamn. He'd tell her the words, she'd be over the moon, and he'd be back inside her friend by the end of the same night.

"She like anyone else?"

He gave me a weird look. "How you mean?"

"She look contemplative about spreading her legs for anyone else here?"

"You." He paused. "Don't suppose you'd—"

"No." *Wrong sister.* "Give me another name."

"Uh, she was looking at Stripes earlier today."

Fucking hell. "Another name."

"I caught her eyeing Machete the first day we hooked up." He hitched his pants with a jerk and adjusted his junk. "Didn't think of it till now. He was eyeing her back."

Machete was quiet, and he wasn't known for making the first move on a sweet butt. He liked to stay in the corner and see who came to him. But he didn't seem too picky about who he sunk his dick into. Roadie was the opposite in almost every way, except the picky part.

I gave a grunt and nodded. "Go get him. Grab your two girls. Put Gloves' sister in a room, and get that other one out of here. I don't want her around the club for a month."

"But—"

"Fucking now, Roadie!"

He shut up real quick and gave me a nod before making a hasty exit. The prospects gave me uneasy looks.

I didn't usually bark commands or roar like I just had.

I gave orders, and I killed. Those were my two main functions. This was unusual, so them being uneasy made sense. I was uneasy myself, hoping not to do something that'd put the club in a bad spot. But goddammit, my patience was wearing really thin.

Machete came out a moment later, looking for me, and his eyes flickered before he headed my way. Like me, Machete was quiet when he walked anywhere. I didn't know why, but I could tell there were a lot of haunts inside him. I knew to respect him, and if he shared, we'd be here if he needed us. Till then, we let him be quiet.

"VP." He was one of the few who addressed me that way in our smaller group.

"We got a problem."

"Gloves' sister."

I gave a nod, short and tight. "You guessing where I'm going?"

"You'd have to be deaf, blind, and in a whole other building not to know what's going down in there. Roadie fucked up."

"Right."

He gave me a knowing look, but there was something else

there I couldn't quite decipher. Anticipation? I wasn't sure. Wasn't sure I wanted to know either.

"She'd be open to me," he said after a moment.

"You'd do that?"

"For you."

"The club?"

"For *you*." He glanced back at The Bonfire. "In my forties. Not a bad time to take a woman."

I cursed under my breath. "You think you can handle her?"

He flashed me a smile, and I was struck dumb for a beat. Machete didn't like to smile, but when he did, everyone smiled with him. He gave a nod. "I can handle her just fine."

The front door shoved open and someone screeched. The other girl, I assumed, huffed her way out, jerking her shirt to cover her stomach as she did. One of the prospects walked her to his bike.

He waved to us. "Giving her a ride home."

The girl did not look over. She avoided everyone's eyes, brushing her hair back.

Couldn't say I blamed her.

Machete sighed. "The girl likes Roadie a whole lot, but she's intrigued by me. Don't know if it's 'cause I'm quiet or 'cause I'm Black."

"You sure about her? We can figure something else—"

He held a hand up, stopping me. "Ain't no problem. I know what we're asking Gloves to do. That means something. We ain't all stupid like Roadie."

"She might want to go back to him."

"It's not about that, though, is it?" He turned to go, but paused and looked at me. "It's about holding her off until Gloves does what he's gotta do."

Right. We were assholes.

"Thanks, Machete."

He gave another nod, then turned and went back into The

Bonfire. He'd do what he needed to do, and Roadie would probably have her back in his bed within a week. *No. I made a decision.* Roadie and I would have a talk. Leadership didn't weigh into who our members took to bed unless it affected the club. This would affect the club, and one of our own. That shit wouldn't go over with anyone.

I would make sure Roadie was aware of that fact.

"Prospect."

Another one had come out to replace the one giving the girl a ride home. Both looked over when I called, but I only needed one to do my bidding.

"Call Stripes out here."

One of them disappeared, and Stripes came back out thirty seconds later.

"What's up, VP?" He gave me a wary look. He was the other member who referred to me by that title.

"Take Roadie out to the T. I'll meet you there. We need to have a talk away from the others."

Understanding flashed in his gaze, along with satisfaction.

That gave me more pause about this guy.

He nodded. "Sounds good. Should I tell him I saw some fine tits out there to get him away or tell him you'll be waiting for him?"

"Tell him about the tits."

A hint of a grin showed before he schooled his features. "Tits it is."

He went inside, and I finished my beer before I went to my bike.

10

KALI

I was starting to daydream about how to murder my friends.
Just kidding.

Thirty-six hours in the car, and that wasn't counting the hotel stay.

So... maybe I wasn't totally kidding.

No, really. I was kidding.

Or—*ugh*.

Besides the fact that we'd all picked up a certain smell around hour twenty-eight—one that refused to budge, no matter how much we showered and could only be described as "travel smell" —we were peachy, and fully hyped up on caffeine and sugar. Harper was the sugar, Aly and me the caffeine.

We were having a discussion over who was the best mean girl from *Glee*, and Aly got so upset, she lit up a cigarette.

I didn't even know she smoked.

She started to light a second one, but Harper started coughing, pounding his chest. "I'm allergic to smoke. No more smoking. Please, Ally McBeal."

That got her laughing. The dancing naked baby always got her in a good mood—or a better mood. At least she set the cigarettes aside. Based on the strain lines stretched tight around her mouth, she hadn't enjoyed the fact that Harper didn't want to talk about Justin today, so he'd gone right back to Aly's love life. I was pretty sure he was on a mission to end her fantasy of finding a millionaire farmer.

Indiana had lots of farmers, but not too many millionaires in our county, and I knew Aly. She stayed in Friendly to take care of her grandmother. She wasn't moving, even to a different county. But *geez*, Harper. Why take away her dream?

Some of us might wish we still *had* a dream.

I kept that to myself. Otherwise Harper would jump on it the next time he wanted to avoid talking about Justin.

Thinking about Justin, I pulled him up on Insta and sent him a message.

Kali: Harper told us why you two broke up. Anything you want me to share with him when we finally get him to open up and talk about it?

I felt like Harper was scared of marriage because of, well, fear. He was just scared.

I needed to get both of them to talk.

My phone beeped.

JustinBanana: Hi. Nothing. He knows. Good luck. If you crack him, send him my way. I'll love him back together.

Oh, man.

I hadn't let myself form a firm opinion about Justin, mostly because I didn't know what happened and because I was loyal to Harper. Now that I knew, and based on this response, I kinda wished Justin wasn't gay. The guy was hot. And loving. And kind. And intelligent. And patient. And wise. And Harper needed to get his head out of his own ass. That's just how it was.

I was going to share that with him too.

Except, maybe not until they'd nailed me down and tortured my own shit out of me.

After *that*, I'd say something. All bets were off.

I gave Harper a look. His eyes seemed a little glazed. Too much sugar. He felt me looking, gave me a silly grin, and popped in another Mike & Ike.

I sighed internally because I knew I wasn't about to bring anything up with him, because he'd turn the tables on me. Me. Foley. Why I'd stayed—it all haunted me.

"Why'd you stay?"

"You love that hard? Accept that shit from him? Or what? Don't know your worth—"

What a dick.

Well.

Maybe not.

That kiss, though.

I was sighing all over again.

"Holy shit!" Aly shrieked.

She was at the wheel, and we'd been driving down back roads. Or trying to. The last few roads had been a bit desolate, so I'd tuned out.

Harper blinked a few times, looking around as if returning to reality.

We were back on the highway now, and I saw nothing unusual. Well, maybe a tumbleweed, which was kinda cool because I'd never seen a tumbleweed before.

Then I saw what she meant.

Aly was right. It was a *holy shit* moment.

I saw the Harley first, parked on the shoulder. There were two others.

No, there were three.

One of the guys punched another guy, and he went back down. He'd already been on the ground. The last guy wasn't doing anything. He just stood there, almost like a guard.

The holy shit part wasn't seeing bikers punching each other. We could see that at my mom's bar. The holy shit part was that all three were wearing Red Demon cuts, and my extra holy shit moment was when the guy who'd delivered that last punch stopped and looked up.

In an instant I could feel his touch again, the way he'd held the back of my head, how his lips at first had just grazed over mine.

They'd been a tease. A caress.

I'd wanted more instantly, and I'd reached for him, not thinking, just needing. I'd surged up on my toes, fusing our mouths, and then he'd taken over.

I was breathless again, remembering it all because that biker stared right at us, as if he could see into the backseat and right through me. Shane King. AKA Ghost. AKA the guy I did not want to see during this trip.

The guy now struggling back to his feet was the opposite. He was the reason we were on this journey in the first place.

"Whoa. Tell me you know them, Kali." Harper fanned himself with his Mike & Ike bag. "The blond is hot. Holy shit indeed. You said it, Aly."

"Do you?" Aly sounded breathless too.

They hadn't recognized Shane.

I couldn't blame them, but I didn't answer—not right away.

We kept driving.

The bikers watched us as we passed.

It wasn't until we saw the sign telling us we were entering Frisco, population 372, that I spoke.

"That was Shane."

AS WE DROVE THROUGH FRISCO, it felt like something out of a movie—where outsiders rolled into a town of serial killers. Except our windows were up, because it was hot. We had the air conditioner on, so no wind made our hair move through air in slow motion. And no one stepped out of their homes or buildings because they sensed the new prey. Though I did see two prospects outside the biker bar, eyeing us as we went past.

A shiver moved down my back, and I tried to ignore a tickling at the back of my throat. It didn't matter what I was feeling. Claudia was here, and I'd told Ruby I'd bring her back.

I needed to try, or move to California.

"There's nowhere I feel safe stopping," Aly commented.

No one argued.

I wasn't just willing to bet money that my sister was at the biker bar. She *was* there. That tickling feeling turned into dread. That's how sure I was, but Aly kept driving. And I didn't stop her.

There was a diner when I looked up again. I'd missed the other buildings, but it seemed you just blinked, and you were through Frisco.

Aly kept driving.

"Oh, look at that. They have their own nursing home." Harper sounded like he was cooing at a puppy.

"Pull up the map," Aly said. "There's no place to stay, and I'm not asking the nursing home if they have an extra room for us. We need to set up somewhere and have a meeting before going back."

"Right." Harper pulled out his phone, sounding businesslike now, but he twisted back to me first. "You think there's any gay members in there? Did Shane say anything about that when you saw him?"

"I have no idea, but no matter his orientation, he's a Red Demon. Are you insane?"

Harper frowned at my tone. "What?" He shrugged. "It's not like I'm going to shack up with the guy and be his cute butt."

Aly snorted and started giggling.

She'd been driving for the last five hours. We'd made one gas-and-pee stop, but I was pretty sure she was delirious. Maybe not, but she'd definitely been through the emotional wringer. Harper had laid into her about fucking her fireman again. He wanted all the details.

"It's sweet butt, and don't say that again because you don't know what that term means."

He shot me a grin. "I can google it."

Aly started giggling even louder. "Let's learn all the biker language."

"I'm on it!"

I needed to pick my battles with these guys. I noted a sign that said Fallen Crest was thirty-two miles away. "Harper, look up Fallen Crest. See if that town has a hotel or motel."

Turns out, it did.

Turns out, Fallen Crest was the complete opposite of Frisco.

I HIT call on my phone.

"Kalista Calliope Michaels. I did not receive a call last night."

I groaned. "I know. I'm sorry, Dad."

I told him about the rest of the trip. I didn't leave any of it out.

"That's not right, Kali. You shouldn't have messaged Justin-Banana behind Harper's back."

My mouth dropped. "Dad! He wants to marry him."

"That don't matter. Your mother wanted to marry me, and see how that turned out. And don't start because we would've had you no matter if we were married or not. You were destined to be in our lives and we're all the more blessed because of it. Still do not think it was cool you messaged JustinBanana behind Harper's back."

"His name is Justin, not JustinBanana."

"You told me it was JustinBanana. Why would you tell me it was JustinBanana if his name is not JustinBanana? A man has a name for a reason. I'm of a mind to refer to him as the name he was given."

"His last name is not Banana."

"Then why would you say his name was JustinBanana if Banana is not a last name? Some folk have unique last names. It's not my place to judge. I still get a kick of everyone who's got a last name of Johnson. That shit is funny. Johnson because it makes me think of a johnson. Can you imagine the name of *Dick* Johnson? Wait. Do we know any?"

"Tell me about your new dance routine, Dad."

"Oh. The Old Gents broke up."

"What?"

"Yeah. That's what happens when you don't call your old man for a whole day. The world can turn upside down."

11

SHANE

"Was that...?" Roadie's eye was half swollen shut, but evidently he'd gotten a good look.

"Shit," I replied.

Stripes looked between us. "What am I missing?"

Roadie spat out a mouthful of blood and wiped his face with the back of his hand. "That was Gloves' other sister."

Stripes' eyebrows shot up as he turned to look at me.

Oh yeah. He knew the implications of this new arrival. Roadie was too stupid to get the other part, but not Stripes.

"Why do you think she's here?" he asked.

Fucking hell. "My guess is to take the other one back."

And I doubted it had been Kali's idea to come. That meant either Gloves had asked her, which I doubted, or her mom had. Connor had said there wasn't a lot of connection between Kali and her sister or mother, but that wasn't what I'd seen at Ruby's. I saw a mom and a sister who'd missed Kali.

Roadie moaned, touching the side of his mouth tenderly. "Shit, Ghost. You didn't have to hit me twice. I mouthed off and earned the first. Didn't do shit to earn the second one."

I gave him a look.

Stripes snorted before quickly turning away.

"You were always going to get the one hit," I explained. "You got the *second* because you mouthed off."

Roadie shrugged, ducking his head and moving out of my reach. "I wasn't going to bug her again, anyway. I wouldn't do that to Machete."

Stripes snorted again, this time hurrying away. He moved ahead of us, and I was out of patience for Roadie.

"This was serious with one of his sisters around. Now we got two, and you know it all could blow up in our faces. You get that?"

His head bobbed up and down. "I do. Yeah."

"You're not just fucking with your own life stringing Claudia along. This one is smart—or smarter than your girl. She figures it out, some of our guys could die. You fuck this up..." I let the threat hang. I needed to. Roadie was a lot, but he wasn't careless when it came to other brothers' lives. His, yes—especially if pussy was involved. But the whole scenario had just been flipped upside down.

Why the hell is Kali here?

"She's not mine anymore," Roadie muttered. He risked a look my way. "You talked to Machete. I saw him heading for her room before we left. You know she'll go for him."

That was the problem now.

I assumed there'd be no way Gloves' sister would leave. She'd sunk her claws in on Roadie. She wanted *him*. Me sending a different guy her way just stalled the inevitable: her realizing Roadie wasn't going to make her his old lady.

"You think Claudia will go back with Kali? That's why she's here. Right?"

"*You* think Claudia will go with her?"

He clamped his mouth shut, finally making a smart move.

Stripes was on his phone when we got back to the bikes, sitting with his feet stretched out. "Got it." He hung up, standing, and lifted his chin toward me. "That was one of the prospects. That car rolled right past the bar and kept heading out."

That was smart.

Roadie started laughing. "No hotel in Frisco for them."

Stripes didn't laugh. He was watching me.

"What are you going to do?" he asked.

There was only one town in the direction they'd been heading where they might stop, and knowing Kali, she'd stop. She was traveling with her best buds from high school. She cared about them, so they'd set up somewhere. She'd make sure her friends were distracted, or happy enough not to put up a fight, and she'd come back for her sister then.

That meant I had some time.

"I don't want her at The Bonfire."

Both guys knew I meant I didn't want her around the other Red Demons. They weren't in our group. I didn't trust them.

I headed for my bike. "Make some calls," I told Stripes as I got on. "I either want Claudia's cell phone collected or a cell phone jammer on her. Let's find a place to stash her for a bit too." I focused on Roadie as Stripes nodded. "Claudia's been around you and Corvette most the time. I don't want to let her talk to her sister until I know there's nothing she could've overheard."

In an ideal situation, Kali would talk Claudia into going back, but I knew that probably wouldn't happen. Instead, if Claudia knew anything at all, she would try to talk Kali into staying. Kali was already suspicious about us and Gloves. Claudia only needed to give her a hint that something more was going on, and Kali would dig in.

Stripes got off the phone, putting it in his pocket. "Claudia's phone has been collected, and Machete is apprised of the situation. He said not to worry. He'll take her on a trip, hole up somewhere for the weekend or until we call to have him bring her back."

"They're probably in Fallen Crest. Tell Machete to go north."

"Roussou?"

I shook my head. "No. We steer clear of there."

"Callyspo's a ghost town, so the next town up is Crete Lake."

I nodded. That sounded fine. "Have him book a cabin—no hotel Kali could find her sister at."

"You think she would do that?"

Roadie had fallen silent, listening to Stripes and me.

I noted that, and gave Stripes a nod. "Yeah. I do."

I reached for my keys.

"What are you doing now?" Stripes asked.

"I'm going to try to head Kali off, get in her head and send her home." Those were lofty goals, and from the grin on Stripes' face, he knew it too. I gave him a slight nod before starting my bike and heading off.

A part of me hated that Kali was here, but another part didn't. The part where my dick got hard the second I saw her—that part was *thrilled* she was here.

I was going to let both parts out to play once I found her.

12

KALI

I was coming out of the room when a hand on my stomach pushed me back inside.

"Wha—" Alarm and fear spiked in my chest, and my blood seemed to freeze, until I looked up and recognized the face staring back down at me. He had a hood pulled up over his head, over his cut, but I could see up close and personal the fury he kept a tight handle on.

Shane King. Though he felt more like Ghost right now.

He shut the door behind him, locked it, and threw the deadbolt—all before I managed to think maybe I shouldn't be letting this happen.

I made a move to get past him, but he growled, "I think not." His arm wrapped around me. It was like hitting a cement wall, and he walked me farther into the room. When I felt the bed behind my knees, he shoved me down. My legs folded. I was dumbfounded by how quickly it had happened.

Then he began moving around the room. He checked the window, the patio door, and the door that connected to the adjoining room. He waited, listening, but there were no sounds.

It hit me then. He thought Aly and Harper were in there.

I almost started laughing.

"What?" he asked. His voice was soft, and I couldn't suppress a shiver as I felt it wrap around me in the room.

"This is a motel. A two-star motel. You think I'd bring my friends here?"

"Where are they?"

"At some fancy hotel. New. Built on a golf course." This motel was the outlier in this town, like how I felt. Fallen Crest was rich. I couldn't figure how big it was, but when I spotted a Lamborghini and a Ferrari at the same intersection, I knew this town wasn't anything like Frisco. Millionaires lived here. "This place is nuts."

"What do you mean?" He went back to the front door, checking the locks before looking in the bathroom. There was no window there. No way out.

He came back, and I shrugged.

"There's a dying town thirty minutes away from here, and then there's this one. Doesn't seem right that they let that town get the way it is. I saw the bones of it. It wasn't big, I bet, but there was a school. Kids used to be bused there. Where do the kids go now?"

"Here?" He frowned. "Who gives a fuck?"

"I do."

"We want Frisco the way it is."

I almost snorted. *Figures.* Good route for drug transportation. But I didn't say anything, just nodded. "Why are you here?"

"Why are *you* here?"

"You know why I'm here." I paused, and then asked again, because it wasn't making sense. "Why are you here? I know you. I know my sister. I'd think you'd want me to find her and take her back."

A hint of a smile showed, but it was gone within a second. "You're overestimating your ability to talk sense into Claudia. She's exactly the way I remember her from school."

Right.

The air in the room chilled. I didn't like the reasons that came to mind about why he might be in this room with me. My gut clenched. This was about Connor. Had to be.

They'd showed up because of him. Shane was all about him. Any other reason, and he'd handle this differently—whatever *this* was. He wanted Claudia gone so... Did Claudia know something about why they were involved with Connor in the first place?

"Not like you."

My mouth went dry. "What do you mean?"

"High school. How you looked out for Connor, endured your sister. How you took care of those friends of yours too. Took one look at you, knew I wanted you."

"What?"

"Yeah." He was looking *right at me*. "Stayed away because of your brother, but gotta admit, you're the reason I first approached him in class."

"What?!"

He grinned, it was so faint. "He took one look at me looking at you and told me to keep my pants zipped or he'd take a pencil to my dick." He snorted. "Gloves has a crazy side. Think that's why he and I clicked so well, and kept clicking even after he went to prison."

I drew in a breath. "What are you guys really doing with my brother?" My voice came out as a whisper. I was scared of the answer.

Shane's eyes stayed steady. "Told you. He helped us out. That's all."

"If he helped you out, then why won't you let me see my sister? I'm assuming that's why you're here? You knew I'd be coming back for her."

He nodded, looking around. "You were going to have your talk here."

I nodded, but that didn't really need to be answered. He knew it as he'd said it.

I felt a flutter in my stomach, one I liked but also didn't like. It was uncomfortable.

If the issue was something in the past, it was a done deal. There'd be no need for any of this unless Claudia had overheard or seen something else? Maybe it was something else? That was the only thing that made sense.

My head was messed up. Too many hours driving. Too much effort waiting, prepared, for when Aly and Harper would start the questioning about Foley.

Now Shane was here, and his presence was overwhelming. All he was telling me. Just standing there, staring at me, I felt him all the way to my toes. My blood was on fire, and it took effort to tamp it all down.

"Look, whatever she saw or overheard, I don't want to hear it," I told him. "I don't want to know it. She won't say anything. I promise. I won't let her. My mom won't let her. We know what you guys can do."

He tilted his head. "Your sister tends to do her own thing."

That was an understatement. "Let me talk to her. I can reason with her."

"Can you? Actually?"

I winced, because he was right.

Then, as if he'd decided to take control of the conversation, he started for me. "I know you."

Fuck.

"I know her."

Jesus.

My throat tightened with each statement, each step he took.

He was dangerous. I'd always felt that from him, even back in high school. But it had been honed to perfection in the years since. I'd known that immediately when I saw him in the grocery store. My feelings were muddled up a bit at my mom's bar, from that kiss. But this tiny room seemed to get smaller the longer we stayed in here. It was once again front and center in my mind that he was a killer.

Knew it in my gut.

No one could've told me differently.

Yet I still didn't quite know why I was scared of him, except the obvious. He was a Red Demon.

Oh, right. My brother.

I took a breath, closed my eyes, and let it out. "Why do I feel like I'm going to lose someone I love because of you?"

He made no sound.

I waited, tensing for his response, but after ten seconds, nothing had come out.

I opened my eyes and half expected him to be gone.

He stared at me.

He looked haunted before he caught himself. Then he growled and lunged for me.

Maybe *lunge* was an exaggeration.

He stepped toward me, but I was so attuned to his movements that I jumped up.

He kept coming, and his hand went to my stomach. He walked me to a wall.

I couldn't breathe.

My whole body heated. The hold wasn't painful. It was possessive. When I hit the wall, he stepped close to me, his chest brushing against my breasts, and he stared.

I stared back.

My whole body was an inferno. "What are you doing?" I asked hoarsely.

His fingers flexed before he let out a hiss and removed his hand. His eyes darkened, falling to my mouth, lingering there. Then slowly he leaned even closer. His hand moved to rest against the wall by my head.

"You are a problem."

A problem?

He was the problem.

His club was the problem.

The problem wasn't me, and *fuck him.*

Anger flashed through me, and I jerked forward, but there was no place to go. I hit his chest. He didn't move. It was that cement wall again, except his hand moved from the wall and went to my back. I tried to step back, but he caught me. His hand slid down my back, molding me to him, and my head tipped back.

I felt every inch of him.

His chest.

His heart.

His stomach.

My legs shifted. One of his moved between mine, and he pushed me back against the wall. His body moved against mine. He grinded against me, and goddammit, I wanted him.

I wanted more of that.

Lust surged inside of me.

The feel of him moving against me was so good, *soo* good.

I gasped, and his hand went to my throat. It was a gentle hold, cupping the side of my head and his thumb grazing my jaw. His fingers moved over my cheek.

He slowly dipped, his whole body moving against mine, and his other leg moved between mine. He lifted me with him as he straightened, leaving me pinned in place.

I was at his mercy.

"Do you want this?" he rasped.

This?

Already pleasure coated my insides. Everything was hazy, except for the feeling of him.

My mouth opened to answer, and he began grinding against me, slow and purposeful. *Fuuuck.* Pleasure ripped through me.

I couldn't answer. I just held on.

"Kali." He murmured my name against my throat. His breath misted my skin.

I didn't want him to stop. The throbbing grew.

"I need to know. Do you want this?"

I didn't know what he meant, and I couldn't answer him. I couldn't speak, but I moved with him. My hips pushed against his, and I wrapped a hand around his back and neck. I began to ride him, and that was enough.

Another growl ripped from him, and he took over.

There was no other way to describe it.

His mouth found my throat, and he tasted. He pushed up and into me so hard that I could almost feel him inside of me.

My God.

I wanted that.

My hand moved between us, catching his jeans and finding the top button.

But something held me back. I had mostly ceased thinking by now, but somewhere in the back of my head, I knew. I just knew. If I undid this button, it was over. We'd go all the way. So I held off, but as he continued grinding up and into me, I was fast losing interest in that instinct telling me to wait.

His mouth moved up my throat, and he pulled us away from the wall.

One hand held my leg and the other was around my back. He turned and took two steps. His hand slid down my spine into the back of my pants. He palmed my ass before laying me on the bed. Then he rose above me, watching.

The separation felt like a bucket of cold water.

I protested against it, wanting him back. My chest rose and fell, and I couldn't catch enough air.

Then I heard what had stopped him.

A phone was ringing.

I looked, still in a daze, my body aching from wanting him, but it was my phone.

He knelt, putting his hands back on me. He searched, and his hand went to one of my pockets. He pulled out the phone, and his whole face went hard. He showed me the screen before hitting accept.

I gasped, jerking upright. It said Foley was calling.

"Why the *fuck* are you calling her?" he growled into the phone.

13

KALI

I was in another universe. That's the only thing that made sense as I lay back down on the bed, struggling to think clearly again and listening to Shane King rip apart my husband. *No. Ex-husband.*

Shane King.

I couldn't wrap my head around that, around him. That he was here. That he was in my life again.

That he sounded like he wanted to murder Foley.

That was making me feel a certain way, a good certain way.

"Yeah, dipshit. You don't know me. You don't want to know me. Why are you calling her? Divorce was final, wasn't it? She walked with nothing, you piece of shit. She wanted to get away from you so fast that she walked with nothing. Far as I'm thinking, the only reason you should be calling her is because you woke up and realized how unfair that shit was, after all the women you went through behind her back, and you want to right some of your wrongs. Is that why you're calling?"

Whoa. I think Shane really did want to kill Foley.

He was listening now. I could hear the murmur of Foley's

voice and recognized what he was feeling. He was scared, but angry and panicky at the same time.

I sat up on my elbows and raised my head. It felt so heavy. I should've gotten up, taken the phone away from Shane, but there wasn't an ounce of caring in my body. I was all cared out, and I couldn't deny that it felt nice hearing someone take up the fight for me.

I was tired, and there was a heaviness inside of me. I'd always felt it, but it had been more the last year. It felt like an anchor trailing behind me, always pulling me back. I had to strain against it. To keep going. To keep fighting. To keep persevering.

I was just fucking tired.

Shane glanced my way, and his eyes were so fierce I felt seared by them. I was starting to like that burning feeling I got from him, from being around him, from touching him, from him just looking at me.

"You want to know what right I have to be saying any of this?" he demanded, turning his attention back to the phone. "I know the names of all the women you cheated on Kali with. How about that? I know the men you dipped into too. And yeah, she's here. She's hearing this. She's letting me talk to you this way. Think on that." After a pause he added, "She wants nothing to do with you. Do not call her unless it's to apologize with an offer of compensation, what you owe her from the divorce. Any other reason, you'll get me every time."

He hung up and tossed the phone next to me on the bed. It landed with a soft thump. His eyes never left mine, and I couldn't look away from him.

I didn't understand any of this, but I could tell it was affecting him too.

I sucked in some air. I needed a moment. I needed my brain to work once more.

Why was I—*my sister*. Connor. His club. The reminders landed on me with a hard thud.

"He call you a lot?" Shane sounded disgusted by that thought.

"No." Which was the funny thing about it. I hated Foley, legit hated him, but he called me after three months of total silence and that was his reception? I almost felt sorry for him. Almost. Not really. I had to laugh a little. "I wish I'd been in the room with him when you told him about the guys. He doesn't know I know about them. He just thinks I know about his foursome."

Shane's grin was faint. "You want the names?"

I started to say no, but remembered what Shane had said on the phone. All those names. All those women. He was right. I'd walked with nothing because I wanted nothing to do with Foley. I nodded. "Yeah. I think I do."

"Good." There was a glint of approval in his eyes, but then the atmosphere shifted again.

The ex was out. Now it was just him and me.

"Why are you here, Shane?"

He didn't answer right away. "It's weird hearing that name. I'm VP or Ghost."

I shook my head. "Not to me."

"Yeah." He didn't look happy about that.

"Shane, why—"

"You can't see your sister. Not yet."

A surge of irritation sliced through me. "Why not?"

"Because I don't know what she's overheard while she's been following us around."

So I was right. "Is it about Connor?"

"We're a 1% club. Could be anything."

That made sense. "So when can I see her?"

"After I know she doesn't have anything to tell you."

Okay. I was going to try one more time. "What about Con—"

"Stop asking me about your brother. I can't talk about him." His voice was gruff, rough. A note of authority rang out. "Who sent you out here?"

I gave him a smirk. "What? You don't think my own sister might've called me?"

He shook his head. "Like I said, I know your sister. Who sent you? Your mom?"

I narrowed my eyes. "If she did? She told me you guys are spreading the word about her bar. You going to rescind that?"

He seemed to consider it. "Maybe I should, if she's sending her daughter after the other daughter. Your mom's observant as hell. If you think she sent you after Claudia for Claudia, you're fooling yourself. She sent you out here because she saw how I reacted to you that night."

I opened my mouth and clamped it shut. "Why would my mother do that?" I finally asked.

"Who knows with Ruby." He raised an eyebrow. "You wanna ask her? Share the information with me?"

I repeated what she'd said to me. "Gloves is in prison. She and I are not close. Claudia was it for her. She misses her daughter."

His phone started going off. He pulled it out and cursed. "I have to take this." He started for the door. "Don't come to Frisco. Your sister's gone. I'll be in touch when you can talk to her."

And he was gone.

I was left with an ache inside of me and a ball of fury threatening to fill in the space.

SHANE

I'D THOUGHT it might be Maxwell, having heard about Kali's arrival. It wasn't.

As soon as I was out of hearing distance, I hit accept. "Stripes." He wouldn't call unless there was a reason. He wasn't like that.

I could hear shouting before his voice came over the phone. "We need you back."

"What is it?"

"Marco Estrada is here."

14

SHANE

Even with his cartel's recently diminished power, Marco Estrada was one of the most powerful men south of the border.

And the entirety of the Red Demon MC helped transport his products throughout the States.

He went through Maxwell for everything, and I wanted to think Stripes had misspoken on the phone a little while ago, but he hadn't. This could only mean a handful of things, and none of them were good.

I rolled up to the meeting spot, a place outside of Callyspo, near an abandoned store. Weeds grew up through the pavement, but on one end of the lot was a line of Red Demons on their Harleys. I counted all of them except Machete's. Across the lot were three black SUVs, and as I rolled in, the back door of the middle one opened.

Marco Estrada got out, dressed in a business suit. Tall. Wiry. Dark features.

I parked next to Stripes and turned my back only once. "Prez called?"

I'd tried calling Maxwell on my way over here, but got no

answer. Judging from the small shake of Stripes' head, it was the same response.

Well, shit. I didn't know what this meant.

I turned and took stock.

Every charter had voted to remove ourselves from a working relationship with the Estrada cartel. We just hadn't made the move yet. So Marco being here... I was hoping that didn't mean he'd found out and was making *his* move instead.

A phone started ringing, and one of our members called out, "It's Heckler."

He came over, holding out the phone.

I took it. "You heard who's here?"

Heckler was with Maxwell. He was also the national sergeant at arms, which meant he ranked right below me. "Maxwell's in the hospital. Somebody put a hit out on him. He's in surgery, and we're hoping he'll pull through."

Fuck.

Fuck!

Damn!

I'd process later. Had to.

"Estrada order that hit?" I turned, looking right at him. "Because he's here."

"Right now, we don't know. It's possible."

"Why would he be waiting for me to finish this call, then? He would've made a move by now."

"He might be there to ask you to take over the Red Demons."

I didn't like that idea.

"You want me to send some of my guys?" he asked. "We'll keep a group here for the prez."

Estrada had three SUVs, but that didn't mean he didn't have more men here. We had twenty-four men, with Machete off playing babysitter for Claudia.

I made my decision. "Wait for my call."

"Will do," he said before hanging up.

I handed the phone back and started forward.

"You want us with you?" Stripes asked.

I paused, but shook my head without looking back at him.

Marco met me halfway, which was a good sign. He was alone —*also* a good sign—but all of his men did step out from the SUVs, assault rifles in their hands.

He nodded. "Buenos días, Ghost."

I nodded back. "Señor Estrada. What's the reason for this visit?"

A smirk started to show before he smoothed his features. "To the point. I always liked that about you."

"I was just told someone shot our national president, and now you're here. I'm wondering how you're going to convince me that's a coincidence."

A hard look flashed in his eyes. "You were in the Army, special forces."

"You telling me about myself doesn't convince me of anything."

"I'm letting you know that I'm aware you could kill me right here, but still, I'm here. I'm standing, talking to you." He held his arms out, opening his suit jacket. "You see, I have no guns with me."

"The assault rifles behind you say otherwise."

"But I'm standing here with you. I was notified about the attempted hit myself not long ago. We were in the area. I was told the Red Demons' national VP was a two-hour ride away. I came because I wanted to reassure you that I was not behind the hit."

"You were in the area?"

A shadow of a smile crossed his face. "I enjoy my business relationship with your MC, but you are not the only connection I have in the States. Yes. I was in the area visiting."

"Why would you think I would assume you were behind the hit?"

He moved his head back, assessing me. "Am I the only one

who doubts my own business alliances at times? If so, I must work on this paranoia. I assumed. Was I wrong?"

I didn't know what to think, but he hadn't pulled his guns on my men. So far, we were peaceful. Making a move right now, with him in front of me, would be a stupid decision. I had to go with caution, and caution meant being polite.

"Señor Estrada, I thank you for your reassurance and for taking the time to travel, rather than making a phone call. It's appreciated by myself and the rest of the club."

He gave a small nod. "Muchas gracias, Señor Ghost."

Señor Ghost. That was a trip, but fuck. I couldn't do anything here except play my part.

I stepped back and motioned for the local VP of the Frisco charter to come over. He'd been waiting outside the line of Red Demons. He came forward at my signal.

He was an older member, a little grizzly and rough around the edges, but he was smart.

"This is Crow. Crow, this is Señor Marco Estrada. He's up for a short visit. Do you think we could get some of the old ladies to help with a cookout?"

I had to give him props. He didn't miss a beat, holding his hand out immediately for Marco to shake. "We sure can. My missus will send out the call. We'll have a big roast tomorrow night. You like pork, Mr. Estrada?"

Marco smiled. "I love a good roast."

I ignored the double meaning and clipped a nod. "It's settled. You'll stay the night then, Marco?"

"I have men in the area. I can stay with them."

"Will your men be joining us tomorrow night?"

"Just myself and perhaps plan for ten of my men, for the food. The rest will have eaten."

Jesus. A fucking roast with the head of a Mexican cartel. This had happened before. A surprise visit from someone as powerful as Marco also had happened before, and I remembered. It was always a reminder of the ramifications and implications of this life, this world I was in. I knew when I'd signed up to ride next to Maxwell that he was going to take the Red Demons far, and he had.

Crow turned back toward his bike, but Marco called out, "Ghost. A word."

"Yeah?"

"I've told you why I'm here, but I'm wondering why the national vice president of the Red Demons is in the area as well. Since *your* president is in Texas."

Crow froze.

I heard it, though I didn't see it. His feet sliding over the gravel came to an abrupt halt. I looked back, and he was watching me. I nodded for him to keep going.

Once he'd gone a few more feet, I answered.

"With all due respect, Señor Estrada, that's internal Red Demon business, and I'd like it to remain that way." I hadn't a clue if he bought what I said. At this point, I was starting not to care. But my spine was itching, and when that happened, I paid attention. I just needed to suss out what was making my spine itch.

As soon as we went our separate ways, with a plan worked out for Marco's arrival and where to go for the cookout, I called Heckler back.

I'd need any and all Red Demons he could muster up. There was nothing coincidental about Marco Estrada being here. He knew our plans, and because Crow froze the way he did, it made me wonder if he did too.

Heckler picked up after the first ring. "What's he there for?"

"He knows." I ignored Heckler's sigh. "What's the plan with Prez?"

"He's here. We've got security around him, but until the doc says he can move or he's in the clear, he's here. We don't know anything else. They won't tell us."

"I want you here."

"You sure? Max was just shot."

Damn. I still needed time to process that.

I shook my head. "Wait until he's in the clear. I'm moving forward on the belief that he will be, because Maxwell is a stubborn asshole. If he's going down, it won't be that way. Once you get the clear, and he's hidden and safe, come. Send half your men now. The head of the cartel is here."

"I know. The guys will be on the road in an hour." He sighed. "They'll ride all night."

"I'll bring everyone up to date here." *Goddamn,* that was going to be a bitch to explain.

And fuck, Kali was here too.

I made another call.

Machete picked up, sounding out of breath. "Yeah?"

I *did not* want to know why he'd be out of breath answering the phone after one ring. "I need you to come back."

"The sister's gone already?"

"No. Marco Estrada is in town."

15

KALI

I'd found Harper and Aly at a local bar that looked like a trendy eatery. The gravel parking lot was filled and there were tables in front, to the side, and behind. The gravel road kept going past to a cute older house behind.

That was nice. If the owners lived there, they could just run over to open up.

Getting in had been a different story.

There was a line out the front door.

I knew they were already inside the bar, so I'd tried a side door. No go. This place had bouncers, so I stepped back, made a call, and Harper came for me.

"We love this town," he gushed as he guided me to a corner table. "Oh my God. It has *everything*. Famous people. I recognized two NFL players, and that was just driving around town. Luxury cars. The *mansions*. OMG! The mansions! They have gates. Have you seen the country club here? A real motherfucking country club, like from the OC."

Harper rattled off everything they'd seen in the two hours since I'd dropped them at the hotel. Apparently, a power nap did wonders, along with the amount of caffeine and sugar both had inhaled. Also, they still thought I was staying with them. They didn't know about the motel, but I was going to explain later, *after* I got Claudia to come back home with me. With us.

We sat down, and Aly joined us a second later, smoothing down her shirt and throwing some hair over her shoulder. She'd been in the bathroom.

She leaned forward, her palms flat on the table and fingers spread. "I'm in love. *Love.* I'm moving here. I wanted a millionaire farmer? Forget that. I want a millionaire! I've gotta meet one here, don't you think?" A worker walked past, carrying a bin of dirty glasses. She stopped him. "Hey. Are you a millionaire? You single?"

He was tall, with dark hair, attractive. He blinked at her a few times before he grinned. "I'm Brandon, and holy shit do I wish I were a millionaire. Maybe for you, we can pretend I am." He gave her a once-over with a slight leer that seemed more like a compliment than actually dirty.

Aly blushed. "Oh, wow. Did I make a fool of myself here?" She looked at us. "Did I just do a thing I shouldn't have done?"

I glanced over her shoulder to Brandon, who was still waiting beside our table. When we made eye contact, he gave me a wink and a grin and disappeared into the kitchen.

Harper started laughing, pounding the table. "You just hit on the busboy, asking if he was a millionaire. He could be eighteen."

Aly folded her arms and dropped her head to the table. "I'm an idiot. I'm the friend you can't bring out in public. That's who I am."

I frowned. "I don't think he was eighteen. He didn't look eighteen."

"None of them look eighteen here." Harper grabbed his drink. "This is California. Eighteen is really code for forty-one. They look eighteen, but are forty-one inside. Which is golden for us." He turned, raising his hand for a high five.

Aly slapped it with hers. "Hell yeah! Forty inside and eighteen outside!"

A few people around us turned to look, but neither of my friends noticed. That's when I knew. They were well and truly blitzed. Good Lord. They'd driven over thirty hours on the road with me. They did it hoping to talk to me about my ex. We hadn't actually talked about my ex, and now they were here, in some super cool bar/eatery, hitting on busboys that I wasn't sure were even busboys, and they did it because they loved me.

Truly blessed. That was me.

I wanted to cry, just sitting here, when a beer landed in front of me. I hadn't ordered it, but it was perfect. Corona.

When I looked up, Harper was smiling at me. One guess at who ordered it.

I took my beer and mouthed "Thank you" to Harper, who just smiled and waved.

I took a sip. Best beer ever.

WE STAYED UNTIL CLOSING.

Aly still wanted to hit on the busboy, who turned out to be a bartender. So we moved to the bar. And by the end of the night, we'd figured out he was the main bartender. There were a few regulars sitting near us, and they were fun to talk to. One of them told Harper all about a period in his life where he'd had a male lover. He asked if that made him gay or bisexual or fluid. He wanted to know the differences.

I looked over and shot the busboy/bartender a look. An Uber showed up ten minutes later, and Brandon told the guy that Roy was outside, waiting for him. Reluctantly, he disappeared.

Brandon set my fourth beer in front of me. "We've got a few regulars here, but don't worry. Roy can handle them."

I didn't know who Roy was, but I was pro Roy. Go, Roy.

I leaned forward on my elbows. "So I'm guessing you're not the busboy?"

He flashed me a grin, pouring a drink for a big guy at the end of the bar. "What gave you the first clue?"

I glanced over. Harper was half listening to us, and half paying attention to Aly, who was talking to the big guy waiting for a beer. He smiled and lifted his chin.

I focused back on the bartender. "Just tell me you don't own the place. That'll mortify my friend."

He was pouring, but had to stop because he started laughing so hard. After a bit, he shook his head and went back to work, finishing the drink. "No, but my sister does. I'm a one-third owner. I run the bar section. She runs everything else."

"Oh."

Oh. My. Lord.

Aly would be so embarrassed. *I* was so embarrassed.

He just laughed, and since he didn't have another drink to pour, he picked up a rag and started wiping out an empty glass. He leaned back against the counter. "Why don't you tell me about you guys instead? I'm guessing you're from out of town?"

Harper caught that last part and made a choking sound before he reached for his drink.

I ignored him. "I know people in Frisco."

He stopped drying the glass, his gaze stuck on me.

My heart sank. That wasn't a good sign.

I pushed my drink away, knowing it was time to stop. "You know anyone from Frisco?"

"Anyone worth knowing moved away from that town years ago, after their school burned down." He put down the glass slowly. "Who do you know in Frisco?"

A bitter taste came to my mouth. "It's not someone's grandma, if that's what you're thinking."

"Leave town."

My gaze shot to his.

His eyes were serious. "If you're saying you know a Red Demon, you need to go. *Now*. I'm not speaking based on rumors. I know. Personally. We've had run-ins with them, and they are bad news. Go. Wherever you came from, go back. Leave the Red Demons alone. I cannot stress that enough."

Well. This visit just took a turn.

I knew he was speaking the truth, and what he was saying was right. He meant it. He meant well, but he didn't know. I had a sister to find, though I didn't know why. But I did.

My phone lit up.

Unknown: Where are you?

No need to guess who that was.

Me: A place called Manny's.

Unknown: I'm coming for you.

Well. The bad news was coming for me.

I HIT call on my phone.

"Daugh-ter. How's it hanging? You still in California? You know where else you could road trip? To see your old man, that's where. And by old man, I'm talking your pops. Myself. Yours truly. Oh, and the Old Gents got back together. We're thinking of doing a reunion tour."

I had no clue how to respond to that.

Some days my dad could make me speechless. Tonight was one of those nights.

16

KALI

My phone lit up again twenty minutes later.

Shane: I'm outside. Can't come in. You gotta come to me.

I frowned, but okay then. My tab was already paid, so I slipped off the stool.

Aly and Harper didn't notice, both engrossed in their own conversations. Aly was flirting with Brandon, and well, Harper was too. Kinda. I got the vibe that Brandon was straight, but he was cool. He rolled with the little winks Harper sent his way.

I went back out through the door I'd entered.

Just a few feet away was Shane. He had his motorcycle pulled all the way up, and he was locked in a stare-off with the bouncer. Two other Red Demons were beside him, but they were sitting back, waiting. Watching.

I could feel the tension as soon as I stepped outside. I maneuvered around the bouncer, who turned and fixed me with a disapproving look.

"You don't have to go with them."

I opened my mouth, not knowing what to say.

Shane beat me to it. "She's mine."

My mouth closed with a snap. I faintly registered the other Red Demons sharing a look as Shane turned his eyes my way.

He sat up and held out a helmet. "Plans changed. We gotta go."

I frowned. "About my sister?"

He didn't answer, just held out the helmet.

The bouncer reached out, touching my arm.

"Don't," Shane clipped.

I blinked and froze.

He hadn't moved a muscle, but the other two had. Guns now pointed at the bouncer, and neither guy looked scared to use them.

The bouncer went rigid, but said under his breath, "This won't slide."

"You have hands on mine."

I flushed. He said it before, but what the fuck?

I mean, I knew. I'd watched the shows and a fair number of documentaries about the biker lifestyle after Gloves told me Shane was in, but hearing him say that? WTF?

I pulled my arm away.

The bouncer wasn't looking at me. He wasn't even looking at the guns. He was staring right at Shane. *Ghost.* He was looking at Ghost.

I felt the frost when he said, "She wasn't acting like she was yours inside."

I stilled, hearing his implication.

I shot him a look, but again, he was only focused on Shane.

I turned, locking eyes with Shane too. "I don't know what's all going on here, but that's a lie."

Shane was locked down, his jaw clenched. "Take the helmet, Kali."

I frowned. "My friends are insi—"

"We'll get 'em home," the bouncer interrupted. "Don't need more of you lost to those guys."

If he'd been someone I gave a damn about, that would've hurt. He wasn't, so he was starting to piss me off.

I moved to Shane's side and took the helmet, pulling it on. Shane indicated the seat behind him.

I looked back at the bouncer. "You're a dick." Then I swung a leg up and climbed on.

My irritation blocked out the fact that I was getting on a motorcycle, and not just any motorcycle. Shane's bike was the real deal, and then there was the fact that I was behind Shane.

Shane King.

Shane *King*.

Images of us flashed in my head, from the motel room, as he'd pinned me against the wall. As he'd moved in. As he'd lifted me up and begun grinding into me.

My throat was dry.

He walked the bike back before taking off, and I pressed forward into him, my arms locked tight.

He was solid, pure muscle. He'd called me *all woman* before. He was all man.

Foley was a boy.

I never thought that before. He'd been my height, my weight, and a pretty boy. White. Not that the way someone looks makes them a boy versus a man, but there was something about Shane. Something Foley didn't have.

I'd thought Foley was cute when we first met. He'd been charming, but there'd been a feel of authenticity to him—that's what I fell for, not his charm. Not his quick wit or quick grin. I fell for the side to him that had been real, but now, riding behind Shane and having been in his arms just once, I knew Foley had been nothing but a boy.

Shane never had time for the athletes in school. Even at their age, there'd been an otherworldly feel to Shane. He knew things, had seen things, been through things. He was still going through things, and it had made him who he was. I'd felt it even then. And Connor wasn't popular, but Shane hadn't cared.

Shane could've been the popular asshole. He'd chosen not to be. He chose to be my brother's friend.

That, right there, started it all.

Sitting behind him now, I wasn't thinking about Aly or Harper. I wasn't being the responsible adult I should've been. I just wanted to rub against him the entire ride to wherever we were going. I suppressed a shiver, pressing my cheek against Shane's shoulder.

I felt him look back. I didn't move.

It was dark, and the wind whipped against us. I could smell the grease and oil from the bikes.

All of it was heady, freeing in a way. I hadn't felt free in a long time, maybe ever.

But I did right now, and I couldn't comprehend that. Why now?

I should've been worried about Aly and Harper. But instead I was with Shane, going wherever he was taking me.

This wasn't me. I'd grown up cautious—you had to be in this world. I'd grown up smart. I worked hard all of my life. Now here, on the back of a bike, I was someone else.

I scooted even closer to Shane, my front and the sides of my legs molded against him like glue. If he'd stopped and stood, it felt like my body would've lifted with him.

A shiver went through me.

Shane must've felt it, as he glanced back again.

I didn't move, just took a breath in and burrowed my head into his back.

He reached down, took my hands and moved them up to his chest. I flattened my palms there, my fingers spread out. I moved one hand to his stomach, and he squeezed my leg, leaving his hand to rest there. He kept it there for most of the drive, leaving me when he needed to touch the handles.

I wasn't watching where we were going, but I knew we were leaving civilization and headed elsewhere.

I should've been scared, and a part of me was.

But if Shane decided to ride all night, taking me away somewhere, a part of me would want that too.

———

It seemed both too long and not long enough when Shane started slowing down.

For the last part of the drive, there'd been no one else on the road. I didn't know California well, but I was learning that this state had everything—rivers, the ocean, mountains, forest, desert, valleys, plains. If I saw a kangaroo hopping by, I would react, but I wouldn't be that surprised.

I looked up when we turned onto a gravel road, and there were three guys there, guns in hand. We slowed, and when they saw Shane, they waved us through. From there, the driveway went another mile. It was dark, but I could see multitudes of light up ahead. When we neared, it was some sort of ranch. There were bikes everywhere.

A large, three-story house sat in the center, with some campers set up on one side. Behind it was a barn, and beyond that, there were more barns and sheds.

On the other side was a long, extended barn with fences set up around it. I heard horses neighing, and some guys came out to the house's front porch as we drew near. They waved us past and around to the side of one of the barns. More guys opened the large doors, and we drove inside.

I didn't know what I'd been expecting, but this wasn't it.

Shane drove all the way through, parking right in front of the back doors. The two guys parked behind him, and I heard the roar of more engines. More guys were coming inside to park.

A few came over to greet Shane before he was called to the side to talk to another group of guys.

This left me on the bike, and yeah—I had no clue what to do.

I waited, climbing off the bike and stretching.

It was then that my sanity came back to me. I'd left my two best friends—two friends who were family to me, who had taken this entire road trip here to get my sister. I'd gotten a text and left them high and dry behind me.

Shit, shit, shit.

I fished out my phone, seeing the first of a whole chain of texts.

Aly: um, hello.

Aly: Brandon -- his name is BRANDON -- said you took off with some bikers. Guessing that was Shane?

Aly: We're heading back to the hotel. Brandon is taking us.

Aly: Officially waiting for him to finish closing up. I like him. He's hot. But I'm with Scott. Am I being stupid? He's a baby. Brandon is not a baby.

Aly: Harper asked and HE'S OUR AGE! I'm officially not a cougar. Gah. Girl. Where are you? Okay. Putting on a responsible friend hat here, are you safe? I get it. It's Shane. You know Shane. We know Shane, but still. Brandon is not happy you went with those guys. He doesn't know we know Shane. Wait. He's giving me a look. He's flirting with me, hon. Flirting. Sigh. I don't feel old tonight. Is that wrong? I should feel ancient, but he's making me not feel extinct.

Aly: Okay. The universe has spoken. Royce just sent me a picture of Scott at a bar and his hand is up the back of Melly's shirt. Message received, Universe.

Aly: I love you. Be safe. Check in when you can. We realize you getting Claudia back is going to be an ordeal. We're cool with that. We can play tourists, but just check in. I'd feel a lot better if I knew where you were right now.

Harper: Where are you?

Harper: The guys are pissed, said the bikers were dangerous. They said you went with one of them and they'd help us get back wherever we need to go. I'm sober, but honey, I'm pretending to be drunk. The bartender is into Aly. I'm going with it. Don't blow my cover.

Okay. The ball of tension eased in my chest a bit. They weren't too pissed.

I kept scrolling, reading through them.

Harper: The Brandon guy looked ready to spill about the Red Demons, but then he clammed up.

Harper: He's driving us to the hotel.

Harper: He's into Aly. I know I already said that. I might not be pretending to be drunk.

Harper: I asked a friend to do recon on Scott and score! Little fireman was caught red-handed. Aly is into this guy. I got a good feeling about him.

Harper: Full disclosure, I'm in the hotel room. Alone. Aly went with Mr. Hottie Brandon, so on to you, Kali. Where are you? Are you safe? We know you're with Shane, but the guy is scary. Totally aware you bringing Claudia back will be a whole adventure. Keep us updated. Or me.

Harper: Why is Justin texting me saying you reached out to him?

Oh!

Me: I'm with Shane. I'm going with it because I have no clue where Claudia is, but she's with another biker. I'll keep you updated. Don't be mad about Justin. I love you. He loves you. Aly needs to hump The Brandon.

"Hey."

I put my phone away, stuffing it into my pocket.

Shane had come back. He bent down, pulled a bag out of a compartment, and handed it to me.

I took it. "What's this?" This was my bag. "You got my bag?"

His hand came to my elbow. "Made a stop first. Come on." He took my hand, leading me out of the barn.

There were bikers everywhere, and a lot of them were watching me.

"What's going on, Shane?"

He shook his head. "Hold on. I'll explain in a bit."

A big guy came out on the main house's front porch and gave Shane a nod. "We got a room for you in the back, unless you want to be with your guys."

Shane indicated the other barn. "We can bunk with them. I don't want to put anyone out."

"It's no bother, not for the national VP." The guy looked me over. "But we can put you with your guys. I'd do the same."

Another guy came out and stood next to him. "Rash will show you to your place." He said to Rash, "Maybe mention to Shelly about VP's guest?"

Rash nodded. He looked mid-forties, with some skin that had seen a lot of sun. There was a leathery texture to it. He looked a bit thin, but he had a small stomach on him, and as he stepped down from the porch, he walked with long, loping strides. He had dark hair, slicked back into a ponytail. "This your old lady?" he asked Shane.

I tensed, knowing what that meant and remembering how Shane had called me *his* at the bar.

"She's mine," Shane said.

I gave him a look, but he only grinned back.

All of this was new to me.

Seeing him again. The pull of him. The feel of him.

My motel room.

God. How he'd talked to Foley for me.

I wasn't in a position to put up a fight about whether I was his or not. And I didn't know how I felt about it anyway, if I were being honest.

Rash led us to the other barn, where I recognized a few of

Shane's guys, including Corvette from the grocery store, who stopped and stared at me. Hard.

Shane noticed, growling, "Eyes away."

Corvette turned immediately.

One of the other guys who had ridden behind us was coming down a set of stairs, and he jerked his chin toward Shane. "Up here, VP."

Rash stepped aside, but he didn't say anything. He just watched us go up the stairs. I looked back once we hit the second floor, and I saw a few of Shane's club members almost herding Rash out of the barn.

What the what?

But we were walking fast, and I turned my attention to the barn itself. It was a renovated horse barn. The middle section had couches at one end and a kitchen at the other, with tables in between. The stalls had been walled in with doors. A few were open, and I saw beds inside. We were on the second level of bedrooms now, and a walkway attached both sides in the middle, creating a loft over a large table below. In a way, this place was cozy and cool. On the other hand, it was scary too because I was only seeing bikers everywhere.

No. Wait.

I saw two women in the kitchen. One was setting up some coffee, and the other was cooking.

The biker—I didn't know his name—led us down to another set of stairs at the far end. These led up to a third floor that expanded over half of the barn. It was a gigantic room, and as we went up and inside, I saw a private porch, set away from the main house. I could only imagine what that view would look like in the morning.

The guy motioned around the place. "Got your own apartment up here, it looks like." His eyes found me, lingering a bit before moving on. "Thought you'd like privacy, and..." He motioned to the patio. "There's stairs going down for an exit, if you need it."

The guy was young—younger than us—but his eyes weren't. They were very, very old.

He had dark hair, cut short, and he was bulked out, but still lean. He would've been pretty if he hadn't seemed so haunted.

Shane nodded toward him. "This is Stripes."

Stripes gave a nod, but he didn't extend his hand for a shake. "I'm Kali."

"Nice to meet you."

Shane looked around the place. "You good here?" he asked me.

"Uh..."

"I got some business to handle."

Right. So the whole explanation would come later?

But he didn't wait for a response. Stripes was already leaving, and Shane went behind him.

He stopped, reaching for the door. "Don't open this for anyone except me, or if I send Stripes for me. Got it?"

I moved toward him, and as he shut the door, I grabbed the handle, holding it in place. I stepped close and lowered my voice. "You wanna explain what the hell I'm doing here? Or you're just taking off until who the fuck knows when?"

His eyes hardened, but he let out a soft sigh. "Some shit went south. You're here because I want you close. Now, I gotta go handle said shit before even more shit happens because of it. Listen, the guys in my charter are fine, but I don't know the other guys. Stay here. Don't tell anyone where you are, because that could make *them* not safe. Got me?"

Was he serious? "No!"

"Good." He pulled the door shut and spoke through it. "Lock it."

I growled, but did as he'd said.

Now what?

I HIT call on my phone.

"Daughter! What are you up to? Getting tickets for the reunion show?"

I gave him the rundown without telling him where I was, and he got quiet after.

Really quiet.

Really really quiet.

"Say what? You're where? You told me you were road tripping to California, not to go and get your sister! Because Ruby told you to do that. How come this is coming out now?!"

Oh, boy. This was going to be a long call.

I opened my mouth to talk and closed it.

He started in again.

17

SHANE

M y dick was still hard from that ride.

Riding my bike got Kali wet. That was good to know, but this was the wrong time for that realization. She was here in the middle of this, and she was pissed. What woman wouldn't be with the way I was handling her? I just didn't have another choice, and none of that could be fixed right now.

When I stepped out of the barn, Roadie was waiting for me, and he fell in step as I started for the main house. "Machete's not far away," he told me. "He texted. Thirty minutes out. What do you want us to do with Claudia?"

"I don't want you to do anything except leave her the fuck alone."

"Right, but you know, what do you want *done* with her?"

We had a possible war brewing here, and Roadie was asking me about his ex, who needed to stay his ex for our club's sake. I growled and turned, stopping him. "You need to get this through your head. Stay away from Claudia. You don't, and I'm sending you to Texas. For the club, you gotta be up front with me. Are you going to have an issue with her moving forward?"

His eyes widened, and his Adam's apple bobbed. But then

resignation came over him. "No, Ghost. I want to stay with you. I'll steer clear of her, I promise."

"You need your dick sucked, you find someone else. Got me?"

He nodded, his eyes shifting over my shoulder.

I had one guess who was there.

Turning, I already knew I was right.

Crow had his head down, but his eyes were trained on us. He must've come out of his house as we approached. "We got other trouble brewing I should know about?" I asked.

"No." Right now we had church. "Let's do this."

My phone rang—*Heckler calling*. I showed Crow the screen.

He raised his chin, and I stepped aside for the call.

"What's the latest?" I asked.

"We don't know who did the shooting," Heckler announced. "We've questioned everyone here."

"How's Prez?"

"He's bad, Ghost. You need to prepare."

Fuck.

"No one's here, like anyone," he added, dropping his voice low. "We've reached out to all our allies. We've reached out to enemies, and they're all saying the same. If they knew, they'd talk. And that's just the ones who we can find. We're kicking in doors. We're uprooting everyone. This was all timed perfectly—had to be or we'd know by now who got Max."

"Was he alone? How'd it go down? Let's go over this again."

Last time my mind had been elsewhere. Estrada took precedent. Then I thought about Kali.

"No one was with him," Heckler said. "None of our guys. He went for a meet alone, and then we got a call from the hospital. I told you this."

"You don't know who the meet was with?"

"He didn't tell anyone, and there's nothing on his phone."

"Who was he with before? He must've gotten a call?"

"He was with Wraith, but Chris just said Max's phone went

off, and he stepped away for the call. Then nothing. They went to eat, and Chris and my niece went home. Max was supposed to be with our guys, but he wasn't. He never put the call out for them."

"He lied to Chris?"

"Seems he did, and I believe Chris. Kess was there."

Kess was Wraith's woman, but also Heckler's niece.

"You question the hospital?"

"They're saying he was dropped off outside the doors. We asked for the security footage, but all the cameras were down. We bribed the guards for it and looked ourselves, but it's a shit system. Worthless. A nurse knew who he was. She told the front desk to call us."

"Who's the nurse?'

"She knows the world. Her cousin's in one of the prisons here. He's connected."

"Can you ask her to ask her cousin? All the gangs are together down there. He'd know something."

"I'll ask, but she's skittish. Doesn't want anything to do with us."

"We gotta know."

"We already know. Too many coincidences."

He was probably right, but I had to be sure. "I can't declare war now on the cartel if the shooter had nothing to do with the cartel."

"We voted. It was going to happen anyway."

Yeah, but when it was planned for. Not like this. We'd approached Gloves because he was the only one who could put it into action the way we wanted. "That planning was done for a reason," I reminded Heckler. "We got brothers inside to protect."

"You got a plan for handling him?"

I glanced back. Crow was waiting on the porch, a few of his guys with him.

"We're heading into church now."

"Got it," Heckler confirmed. "Call me when you know. The

guys were on the road all night. They'll be pulling in around early afternoon."

"Sounds good. I'll let them know to prepare."

We hung up, and as I walked toward him, Crow turned and led the way into his house, down to his basement, and through to a cellar type of room large enough to fit twenty members. The rest stood in the back. I took one of the seats at the end. Crow took the head seat as the rest trailed in. Every ranking member had a specific seat—VP, sergeant at arms, secretary, treasurer, road captain.

This was Frisco's charter, their home, their church. So their VP would call church to start.

Crow did just that once the doors were shut. The room grew quiet, and he nodded, leaning forward. There was a gavel in front of him.

"Okay. Everyone here?" he asked.

A round of *yeahs* sounded, and he nodded again, looked over at me. "This here is a home-away-from-home sort of place. It's off the books. We shouldn't be connected to it. Now, y'all have heard about our surprise guest and what happened to the national prez, so I'll give it over to Ghost. He's in charge during these times."

All eyes came my way.

I nodded. "As most of you probably heard already, Prez was shot yesterday." I filled them in on what I knew about it. "Half our guys are coming. The others stayed back to guard him, but Estrada being here warrants a threat we can't ignore."

"And if it's not him?" the Frisco road captain asked. "If there's a different threat to the Prez?"

"He'll go into hiding. They won't make a move until I'm back. Heckler stayed for that reason. He'll keep him safe."

That seemed to appease the guys, and most looked Crow's way.

He asked the question. "What's the plan then?"

"We need to gather information, as much as possible. I want

to know who Estrada was visiting near here. I want to know where his men are. I want to know everything we can get. Did you know he's got local connections here?"

"Not at all, but it's not that surprising," Crow said. "They move through Tijuana."

I nodded. Yeah. That was the problem.

"We need a plan for tonight," Stripes piped up. "Just in case." He was standing at my side, and he spoke to me, not Crow.

The rest of our guys nodded their agreement.

"We'll leave guys here," I told him. "The rest will come with us. No drinking. Alcohol should only be served to our guests. And everyone keep your guns ready." I looked at Stripes. "I want half our guys outside, keeping watch."

He nodded.

I focused on Crow. "You're thinking the roast will be at The Bonfire?"

"Yeah. If he doesn't know our other locations, why introduce a new place?"

"He might not even know about that, though. What about where we were before? The parking lot where we met him? It's flat around there, for the most part. We could keep guys behind the building and outside the town."

Crow lifted a shoulder. "Makes sense, but it won't take them much work to find out about The Bonfire. Everyone around here knows that's where we operate from."

I paused to consider that.

Crow was right, keeping Estrada to the areas he knew already or could know easily made sense. "Let's do it at The Bonfire, otherwise we gotta leave more men behind to guard that place. Empty it out except for whoever needs to be there to play a part."

"Ghost."

I looked back, and Roadie leaned forward, his eyebrows pulled together tight. "We really doing this? Pretending?"

"We voted, and we can't throw everything away by making a

move when we don't know for sure. I want him to play his hand, and then we can play ours. I'll pick the guys who'll keep watch." I turned to Crow. "Your charter have any ex-military?"

A few of their guys raised their hands.

Crow motioned to them. "Two Marines and a Ranger, like yourself."

I gave each a study, and all three looked steadily back with knowing eyes. They knew why I was asking for them. "How's our stock?"

"We're loaded," Crow said. "Guns. Rifles. We keep ourselves stocked no matter what."

"You up on sharing some of that with my guys? We were traveling, so we're not as strapped."

"Of course."

Then we moved to specifics. The codes. The signals. The plan if things went bad, the plan if things went fine. We mapped every option I could think of. An hour into the meeting, we could hear a set of boots coming down the stairs, and someone pounded on the door before it opened. A prospect leaned inside, finding me. "Machete's here. Wants to know what to do with the girl."

Right. Claudia.

"Put her in a shed. I want to talk to her before anything else."

"Got it." He disappeared.

"Care to fill us in on that situation?" Crow asked.

Everyone knew our decision to break from working with the cartel. But not everyone knew the specifics, and they couldn't. I pushed up from the table. "It's delicate, but has to do with our exit strategy. She and my woman are connected to someone on the inside who's helping us. I don't want them to know anything, or even *hear* anything." I looked around the room, waiting for each guy to give me a nod in response.

"My guys know how to shut their mouths," Crow confirmed.

"Good. I should handle that situation next."

"All right." Crow leaned forward, grabbed the gavel, and

banged it down. "Church is adjourned. Everyone knows their role."

Stripes moved in close, lowering his voice. "You want me in there?"

I shook my head, as Crow approached. Stripes stepped back.

Crow looked between us as the rest of the guys filed out. Besides preparing, most needed shut-eye before tonight. "I've asked my old lady to put together the food, but I don't like the idea of having the women there."

"Think the sweet butts could serve in their place?"

Crow grinned. "I can ask, but they're not exactly actresses."

I nodded with a smile. That was true. "Just ask a couple of the smarter ones. Keep the old ladies back here."

"And speaking of your woman, you want me to ask some of the old ladies to take her under their wing?" he added. "I mentioned it to Shelly, Rash's sister."

Right. "She's in the room so far. I'm hoping she'll stay there, but she'll need food." I hesitated, but he needed to know. "About Machete's woman... well, just expect trouble from her."

He barked out a laugh before realizing I meant what I'd said. He sobered, his smile fading. "Right. Okay. We got some smart old ladies here. I'll maybe share that tidbit too."

I nodded. Any warning would be good.

Machete came in and headed over as Crow stepped away. "I'll leave you to it then."

"Thank you."

Machete took his place, shifting to watch him leave since the rest of the room had emptied by now. "That looked productive."

I grunted. I liked Machete. "How is she?"

"Pissed. Knows she got handed off to me, but she went along. Now's she even more pissed because she's been taken to a shed, on your orders. What's going on?"

"I don't have time to waste. I need to know if she knows anything."

He raised his eyebrows.

"Kali's here," I added. "They'll cross paths."

His eyebrows shot up. "How'd that happen?"

"Estrada." I gave him a look.

He mirrored it. "Right. What do you want me to do?"

"For now, look the other way because I gotta handle your woman."

"She's *my* woman."

That was the problem. It was club protocol to leave each other's women alone, the old ladies or the girlfriends.

He sighed. "I gotta be there. You know that."

I gave a nod. "Then let's both go and handle this."

He groaned. "I'd rather go in for a colonoscopy than do what we're about to do."

Same, brother. Same.

18

KALI

I was drunk.

No one judge me.

I was surrounded by bikers, I had no clue where we were, and I couldn't officially freak out to my best friends/family because if I did, they could be in danger. I believed Shane when he said that. And now I couldn't sleep. Who the fuck could sleep after that warning?

So, yeah. Drunk.

I found the next best thing when I found the red wine, and now I was giggling to myself because holy *fuck* was my life messed up.

Like, seriously fucked up, and what was worse? I knew that if Shane came in and wanted some, I wouldn't deny him. My God. My hormones were what had gotten me here.

He'd texted me to come, and I had.

I was such an idiot.

I thought what Foley had done to me was the worst thing ever.

Nope.

It wasn't what Shane had done to me, it was what he *could* do to me.

If Foley had texted me after one make-out session to *come*, leaving Aly and Harper behind in a bar, in a state we didn't know, I would've told him to go fuck himself. And, he probably would've—oh. Oh no.

The giggles engulfed me.

Because that's totally what he would've done—or found someone else to fuck him. Not that I could have blamed him... He would've been doing what I'd told him...

But the whole point is that Foley never had power like this over me.

Never. *Ever.*

So, wow.

I'm here, drunk, because of a simple fucking text. But what Foley did to me?

I had some things to tell Foley.

Shane said I couldn't call people I cared about. One, that rule would never apply to my dad, but I was drunk.

So I called Foley.

HE DIDN'T ANSWER, which was a wise decision on his part. I texted instead.

The texts were long and negative.

I didn't want to rehash them. The energy came from a dark place, but I felt better when I finished.

Pretty sure I called him a worm, and actually googled how many different species of worms there were, and then I called him a name in as many of the species I could. At a hundred I had to stop. I did text my dad telling him there's a million different species of worms.

He texted back asking why I was telling him this.
I was too drunk to respond so I went to bed.
I slept great.

19

SHANE

The shed was a rundown building with some straw on the floor, but mostly dirt. Claudia stood at the far end, feet apart, arms folded over her chest, and a glare directed at Machete and me. A few of our guys were outside, the ones we trusted to keep away the ones we *didn't* trust. Likely she had seen them. The boards that made up the wall weren't evenly spaced. There were cracks and some holes, and you could hear and see quite a bit if you paid attention.

"You want to explain what this is about?" she spat.

That look on her face, in her eyes—I hadn't realized that *all* the girls in Connor's family were seriously smart. Every single one of them.

I glanced at Machete. "Is she your old lady?"

He blinked slowly and turned to gaze at her. Then he sighed and started forward. "I guess so."

I almost laughed. Quite a ringing endorsement. That spoke volumes.

I shifted back, waiting to see how he'd handle this. Evidently, she was his, so he'd take the front seat in this interrogation, and that's what this was about to become.

"Claude," Machete started in a low tone, and he stopped halfway between her and me. "We're in a situation here."

I was surprised to see how she softened when Machete spoke.

She kept her arms folded on her chest. "I'm seeing that, considering we took off, fucked a bunch, and now we're back, but where the hell are we?" She looked through the shed's wall at the guys moving around out front. "Roadie told me we were here to party. I'm not getting the party vibe out there." She raised her chin, raising her voice too. "I'm not stupid, Ghost. I remember you, remember how you used to like my sister back in school. I saw how you reacted to her. You stay away from Kali. She's too good for you."

I agreed, but I stepped forward. She'd brought me into this.

Machete knew that too, stepping back as I now took the lead.

"Your sister is here," I told her.

Surprise flashed in Claudia's eyes before she banked it, but she took a step back, her shoulders tense. "She's here for me?"

"She was, but now she's here for different reasons. We're in a situation. You been following us all the way since Friendly. You been hanging around, could've almost been a hangaround if you were a guy. You ain't a sweet butt. You ain't a girlfriend either. So like I said, we're in a situation."

Her eyes clouded over, but she didn't move. Her voice came out small. "What's the situation?"

I sighed because *damn this*. Claudia was smart, and I was exhausted, and I had two more battles waiting for me. Kali. Estrada. I didn't have time to do this the proper way, but I couldn't do it this way either. I couldn't lay out the cards and hope Claudia would do the right thing. She wouldn't. That's just the woman she was. She kept her cards close to her chest, all the time, no matter who those cards could hurt. She didn't care. Never had.

"I don't trust you, not one goddamn bit," I informed her. "But you're here for your safety, and your sister is here for her safety too. You spent a lot of time around the club before we landed here and got you with Machete, so I don't have one clue what you heard. You know who we are, what we can do, so I'm in a bad way here. I don't want you whispering anything to your sister."

I gave Machete a look. As if he could sense my question, he gave me a nod.

We both turned and focused back on Claudia.

Dammit. I had to do this, so I advanced.

Machete held back.

Claudia was his woman, but this was for the club and for my woman too.

Claudia's arms fell, and she started to the side, trying to get away from me.

"Don't! Don't, Claude. Not him," Machete called.

She stopped, a deer-in-headlights look coming over her at Machete's command, and her eyes tracked back to me. She held firm, her face becoming a blank canvas, but I saw a tremble under her chin.

I kept moving, backing her until she was against the wall. I invaded her space, but didn't touch her. I leaned down, leaned over her, and moved so I was completely blocking her view of her man.

"This is between you and me." I kept my voice low.

"Back off or I'll ruin things between you and my sister," she hissed.

"Yeah. That's part of this too."

She raised her chin, but the tremble was still there.

"Normally I would strap you to a chair," I told her. "I'd hook you up to a lie detector and grill you that way. That'd be the humane way to do it. Or if I was pissed, would maybe take a knife to you. I'd cut away all those little curves and pretty appendages you have, like your eyelashes. Your fingernails. I'd pull a third of your hair out. Little nicks here and there to make you squirm, and if you continued to fight, I'd move to your appendages. We don't have time for that, so instead I'm going to tell you a few things. First, if you turn snitch on us, you're dead. Machete will do it. Second, if you say anything to your sister to turn her against me, you're dead in a slow and agonizing way, and it'll be me who does that. Third, you fuck over your man right now, hook back up with Roadie or some other biker here, I will gut you and leave you in the desert. These are not threats or ultimatums. These are promises. You're on my radar. This ain't high school. This ain't Friendly, Indiana. You fuck up here, it's your life. How you go down, depends on you. You got me?"

She stared back at me, not looking away. Not for a second. There was no flinch. There was nothing, but I'd gotten to her.

"You touch my sister, and I'll destroy you," she said.

"Too late for that." I walked out, past Machete. "She's all yours."

20

KALI

W hen I looked up, the room was less dark. It was six a.m. I was in bed, as I'd decided that was the best option. I didn't know what I would've walked into if I'd left the room, and I didn't want to get on the phone. Drunk phone time was never good.

But score! I'd switched out the pillowcase for an extra silk one in my bag.

Also, I was still drunk.

I reached up, my wrap was still in place. I hadn't changed into my usual sleeping clothes because I didn't know this place. I didn't know what was going to happen. Anxiety swirled in my gut.

Where is Shane?

A toilet flushed, and then I heard footsteps. Big, heavy ones.

Guess I knew what or who had woken me. When had I actually gone to bed? Maybe four?

I heard the bathroom door open, and I looked for the bedroom door.

After a moment it opened, and everything was still dark beyond. They must've had blackout shades. Shane came in.

That's when it hit me, and I bolted upright. "Oh no, you don't."

My body temperature shot up as my eyes traveled over the muscles moving under his very tattooed skin. All those muscles. I'd thought the man was lean. I was wrong. I was remembering sitting behind him on his bike, my body plastered against his, my thighs hugging his, and I gulped. He wasn't lean. He was muscle, just pure muscle.

All man. Holy, *all* man.

I was too old to be feeling this way. I didn't know I still had this in me. I felt hot and bothered like... I didn't know, because this wasn't a schoolgirl kind of feeling. This was much more— much, *much* more. I guess Foley hadn't totally broken me.

"Don't what?" Shane rasped. I heard his exhaustion, but there were other emotions too. Tension? Wariness?

"You can't sleep here."

"Bullshit. I ain't sleeping anywhere else." He moved to the side of the bed.

Hearing his determination, I decided to pick my battles. This wasn't one of them. Grabbing my pillow, I sat up to leave as he got in bed, but he snaked an arm around my waist and pulled me back.

"Nope."

"What?" I tensed.

He pulled me closer to him. "Nope."

"Get off me."

His arm slid lower.

My eyes bugged out. "Fine. You want to sleep in the bed, I'll go out there."

"Nope."

Then he tucked me under him and lowered his head to the crook of my shoulder. It was a very firm snuggle.

I had no idea how to digest this. "Shane."

"I'm tired."

"You're not hearing me." I poked him in the arm.

He snorted into my neck. "You're not feeling me, babe."

Feeling?

"Wha—"

He ground his hips into me from behind.

I felt him now. Instant sauna temperatures in here. *Instant.* I almost groaned, because now I was remembering the bike and how I'd wanted to touch him then. This was starting to feel like the hardest thing I'd ever do because I needed to resist him. He had too much control over me, and it was all happening way too fast.

"Shane!" I sunk my nails into his arm, hoping to peel him off, but he just ignored me. I was pretty sure I broke the skin too. "Hey."

"Didn't know you were into that, but we can play around. I'm okay with that."

Okay with—I shoved his arm off me and sat up. I didn't move to get off the bed. I knew where I'd end up if I did that, but I looked down at him, trying for scolding, yet not totally knowing why. "This—"

He flipped us so I was on my back and he hovered above me. His hand slid around the side of my neck and held me there, in his palm. "Things accelerated with us in your motel room. Usually—" He stopped himself, shaking his head. "There's no *usually* about this. I tried to walk away from you in the grocery store, and I couldn't. Things changed, and I'm thinking we've got a pattern here. There ain't no normal for you and me, and *babe*, there is a you and me."

I opened my mouth to argue, but I closed it as he lowered his hips up and into me. I felt what was between us, and I fought to keep from squirming, wanting to push back against him. *Damn.* That felt good. So good.

Every nerve receptor I had was turned *on*. I had no idea how to handle any of this, but in the meantime, Shane had gone quiet, one of his eyebrows raised.

He grinned. "You might not think you're moving, but, babe, you are." He pushed up into me again, and I let out a loud groan, my eyes closing.

Holy. *Damn!*

"Yeah." His word came out as a whisper, and I felt him lower his head, his nose grazing the side of my cheek. "I want you something fierce, but I need sleep, and I'm aware you need some type of explanation. For now, for the next few hours, can we ignore what we both want to do to each other and sleep?"

I opened my eyes. Sleep with him? I didn't know if I could. "I think I might still be drunk."

He snorted a laugh, moving to lie beside me again, still holding me close. "Figured. I saw the wine bottle on the counter —saw it was empty too."

Something about that statement made me embarrassed, but his arm came over me, and he rested a hand on my hip. He tugged me against him once more, one of his legs sliding between mine, and he moved it up, pressing right there, right where I could ride him to my climax.

"I don't know how to handle this," I told him. "It's too fast. I'm cautious and slow."

"I'm aware of that too." He moved in and kissed my cheek, sliding down to my throat, and I was fast unable to think any more.

His hand slid to my stomach, pressing, holding me there.

His leg moved up, grinding into me.

I stifled a moan because it all felt so good.

His mouth tracked back up, tasting me until he got to my mouth. Then he lifted, just the slightest bit. I could breathe his air as he said, "How about right now, this morning, you're not cautious and slow?" He kissed me softly as his hand slid down, into my underwear, and he ran a finger between my folds. "How's that feel?"

I couldn't answer because as he circled me, his thumb rubbing over my clit, he slid inside. All the way inside, and he went deep.

I let out a groan, my eyes closed. I wrapped my hand around his wrist as he moved his finger in and out of me. I didn't stop him. Oh no. I began guiding him, controlling the rhythm, the speed, and when I wanted him deep, I pushed him deep.

He let me, following my every movement, but I realized he didn't need the guidance.

Opening my eyes, I found him right where he'd been before, his eyes locked on mine. He grinned down at me.

I cursed, and his mouth dipped and covered mine.

Only one other time I'd been kissed like this.

It was like he knew me from inside out, my mouth, my body. He knew exactly how to command my pleasure, and I was helpless except to receive it. He moved two fingers into me, stroking deep and hard, then gentle, rolling into me.

"Jesus," he breathed as I felt his body shudder. Then his mouth was gone from me.

"Wha—"

He shoved the sheets away and yanked off my shorts and underwear. His mouth replaced his thumb.

Oh.

My.

Goooooddd.

I was coming apart, my entire body bending up into that touch.

He ate me, and his tongue swept around me. His fingers pulled out, and his tongue thrust in.

So fast. Way too fast.

I wasn't used to this, but I couldn't do anything. The pleasure was almost attacking me, coming at me all at once, and I held on to his head, keeping him firmly between my legs, where he ate, with pleasure.

Then with a roar, he moved back up, his mouth finding mine, and he thrust three fingers deep, deep into me. I nearly folded up at how hard he shoved, but he just kept going, thrusting, thrusting.

I couldn't hold on—a scream began to build that he swallowed, and his thumb moved on my clit.

I came impossibly hard. The tremors ripped through me, tearing me apart.

Shane groaned and moved my body, turning me to the side and putting his hand on my ass.

"Wha—"

"Not going to do anything there, not yet," he murmured against my mouth. His hand smoothed over my ass, taking a firm hold as he pushed his fingers into me again, one last roll and he held me as my body shook.

He was still firm behind me, and I shifted back, rolling my hips against him. "You—"

He cut me off, his mouth finding mine. The long kiss was almost sweet at the end. He lifted his head. "I need sleep more than anything else right now. You'll stay with me?"

I didn't think I could move at that moment. My bones had melted. I nodded.

He closed his eyes, touched his forehead to my shoulder, and settled in, holding me.

I didn't think I'd be able to sleep, but after a while, hearing his long, deep intakes of breath relaxed me, and...

———————————

Knock! Knock!

Shane cursed, but he was up and out of the bed before the knock sounded again. He opened the door, and I heard a muffled conversation before he shut it again. I sat up when he didn't come back to bed.

The clock said it was almost one in the afternoon, and a roar of engines sounded from outside.

I jumped from the bed, going to the window, and I could see a long line of Harleys coming down the driveway, circling and parking in front of the house.

A toilet flushed. I heard water running, and then the door opened again.

"That's part of my charter coming," Shane said, looking toward the window.

I let go of the window shade, turning to him. "I thought you already had part of your charter here."

"Only some." He bent down, picking up his clothes. Rifling through them, he separated some items and picked up a bag I hadn't seen yesterday. He pulled out some new clothes and dressed, a white shirt under his cut. The same jeans as yesterday. He'd left his boots at the door.

"What's happening today?"

When he looked over, I was taken aback by how much more guarded he seemed today than yesterday. His jaw clenched.

I followed him over to the table and pulled on my sleeping shorts. I had no bra, but we were kinda past that. I leaned against the doorframe as he went through his guns.

Guns. On the table.

How was that a normal thing?

He acted like this was a daily occurrence. Instead of choosing what kind of eggs he wanted for breakfast, he picked what type of gun to take—oh, never mind. He was taking them all.

After checking the ammo, he started putting guns into their holsters all over him. His cut was the last thing he put on. He'd placed it beside his guns on the table.

Another reminder of our differences. My mouth went dry.

I blinked a few times, but the image of Shane in all his biker glory wasn't one I'd ever forget. I bit my bottom lip. I didn't know if I liked this look or not. Or if I *really* liked it.

But the fear was real. The guns were real.

I decided then and there. I did not like this. Not one bit.

"Shane."

He paused, looking up from his phone now.

I met his eyes. "I waited. What is going on?"

He nodded, as if coming to a decision. "I can't tell you everything. I just can't. But we work with some powerful and dangerous men. One of those guys came to town, and tonight, we have to go see him. Everyone is here to keep you safe. That's why I brought you in. I didn't want to risk anyone finding out about you and have you not guarded. I know what I'm saying is scary, but right now, I need you to stay put. Don't tell anyone where you are. Got me?"

I tensed, but I kept remembering how he'd held me this morning. For some reason, that pushed its way to the forefront. I didn't know what to think about that either.

I nodded. "Can I leave this apartment? I need coffee."

He cracked a grin. "Yeah. Tell them you're mine if anyone gives you a problem. There'll be some old ladies here too. I think they were asked to look out for you."

Old ladies. I had a bit of a moment, because that term was no longer just a word from a documentary. It was real, and alive, and in my face. This was the biker world.

He came over, a hand at my hip, and leaned in. His lips met mine in a soft graze. Tingles spread through me at the touch, and I bit my lip when he straightened.

He touched my lip with his finger. "I'll be back. Keep your phone on you. I'll be in touch."

I nodded, and then he was gone.

I slid down to the floor, right where I was, and leaned forward, catching my head in my hands.

What had I gotten myself into?

I STARTED to call my dad, but nope.

I couldn't. Just couldn't.

I didn't want to get his viewpoint on an old lady or not.

21

SHANE

The rest of the guys were situated. Crow wasn't too happy to be outnumbered, but he also knew he couldn't say anything about it. Still, I was catching his eye more and more. Suspicion was building, and there'd be a talk brought to the table pretty soon. I could feel it, like an annoying itch.

I did understand his perspective. This was his charter, his area, and we were firmly moving in.

"Ghost."

I was grinning before I even turned around, because *damn*, I had missed this man.

My brother. My best friend. My partner in so many godforsaken situations. Boise was his biker name, and he was my other half—as much as I had one at this point. We called him Boise because of a simple conversation we'd once had.

Where are you from? Boise.

What's your name? Boise.

You ride a lot? Boise.

So his biker name was Boise. One time he'd said he was Shoshone, but he didn't talk much about his tribal family. I respected that, and once he became a Red Demon, he became my right-hand man. It had felt weird to be here without him, so seeing him coming my way, that long-ass dark hair swinging in the wind, I just shook my head and couldn't hold back the smile.

"It's been too damn long."

He hit me hard, and I wrapped my arms around him. None of that masculine bullshit here; we were hugging tight and pounding each other on the back.

I clasped him on the back of his head. "Missed you."

He hugged me tight one last time. "You too, brother. You too."

He stepped back, and we laughed, holding onto each other's arms a moment before we separated fully.

"I thought you'd stay back with Prez," I told him.

His face twitched, and he almost snorted. "I hear Estrada is here and you think I'm staying to guard an ailing man? You loco."

"Yeah. Maybe." Still, the club came first. Boise took that seriously, so for him to choose my side instead of Max's said a lot.

"I'm told you have a woman?" He raised an eyebrow.

Now I snorted. "That's a battle for a whole other day."

He chuckled, and Crow headed our way. All the other guys were on their bikes or moving toward them.

"You still good with the plan?" Crow asked me.

I inclined my head toward Boise. "I'm going to add the new guys around the perimeter. They know what to do, but we'll keep some here to guard the women and kids."

Crow nodded, giving Boise a once-over.

There'd already been introductions. Crow had been the one to greet the guys as they drove in, but he was seeing a new dynamic here. I got it.

"When we ride in, do I need to know the reason you're here?" Crow asked.

I felt Boise tense. I did too. I'd known this was coming. Just came faster than I thought.

"Your president reached out to Max," I told him. "He's in prison for the long haul, and he wanted us here to help situate you guys for new leadership. Said you were having problems with a few of the guys."

Crow nodded because he knew that. He'd been told that. It's the reason our trip here wasn't a surprise, but it wasn't the only reason, and he must've sensed that by now. His eyes danced between Boise and me.

"That's true," he said. "You guys being here has settled some of those guys, but I'm thinking we might need to have another conversation after tonight."

I'd asked Max for three months. I wanted to smooth my way in, not kick over any rocks that had snakes underneath. But with Estrada's presence and the new guys from our charter coming in, I didn't have much choice.

"I got a call," he added after a moment. "The food's ready. A couple of the sweet butts stayed back to play pretend girlfriends. We're ready to go."

I nodded, and since I was the highest ranking member here, I led them out.

Crow came next, right beside me. We interspersed my guys and his guys so they were riding next to the new guys, but at the end of the day, we were all brothers.

The women came out to watch us go. I glimpsed Kali in the window as we rode down the driveway.

This part was sacred.

It was us, our bikes, and the open road—nothing separating us from nature. The wind. The sun.

We were free.

22

KALI

Watching the entire line of motorcycles leave was another reminder that this was an *entirely* different world, different culture. But I was still me, and I needed food. Or more importantly, I needed coffee.

So here I went.

I dressed, keeping it simple with the same clothes I'd had on yesterday. I put my hair up in a thick braid, and I was guessing I'd need some adaptability moving forward. No matter. I could do that. Been doing that all my life.

The barn was mostly empty. There were a few guys on the main floor. All watched me, but none moved to come toward me. I could see a couple women in the back, by the kitchen.

I guess that'd be where I go for food? Or the main house?

As I approached, the oldest woman glanced back as she washed a pot. "You Kali?"

I nodded. "You Shelly?"

She grinned wide and put the pot down. After drying her hands, she extended one to me. "I'm Rash's sister, not his old lady, in case you heard different."

We shook hands. Hers was a firm grip.

She was skinny, but I could see she was wiry with muscle. She had a gaunt face—not pretty, but not homely. Striking. High cheekbones. A bird-like chin and tiny lips. Straight, dark-blond hair, hers in a loose braid. Several strands had fallen free, but she just brushed them back, tucking them behind her ear. I took in her clothes too, now feeling somewhat overdressed. The other woman was dressed the same way.

Both had black biker tank tops that dipped low, showing a lot of cleavage, and skin-tight jeans with sturdy, functional boots—and not the hooker kind.

I'd guess she was in her forties. Maybe. She looked aged, and that wasn't meant in a disrespectful way. She had old eyes.

"I was told to look out for you," she said. "You guys got in late last night. This your first time venturing out and about?"

I almost laughed. "Is it that obvious?"

"Mom." The younger version of her held out another pot, a towel thrown over her shoulder. "That's the last of them."

"Okay." Shelly took the pot and motioned with her head to her daughter. "This one's mine, Katie." She gave me a nod. "Katie, this one's with the national VP. Show some respect."

Katie's eyes widened, and she shot upright, nervously. Smoothing her hands down her jeans, she came over, giving me a quick dip of her head. "Hi. Sorry. I didn't know. There's a lot of—"

"There's a lot of women around here, especially around times like this." Shelly took over, speaking for her daughter. She gave her a smile and nodded to send her along. "I got it from here. Where are you off to now?"

"Uh..." Katie looked between us before turning to her mom. "There's a house party at Jared's tonight. Don't suppose I could go?"

"You know the deal. We stay put until we know everything's done and handled."

Katie glanced my way again. "Okay. I'm going to my room. You need help with supper?"

"Nah. We've got more than enough help around here. If you think of leaving, I'm going to send your cousin after you."

Katie's eyebrows pinched together. "Mom!"

"Just saying." Shelly shrugged. "You know the deal."

Katie snorted before taking off.

"You drink coffee? Tea?"

"Coffee, please."

She nodded to the pot, and I saw there was a whole set up, like this was a hotel. "Help yourself. We try to keep it stocked for anyone staying, and the guys love their coffee around here."

"This is your place?" I asked as I went over and began filling a mug.

"Yeah." She grabbed a few items and waited as I added some cream to my coffee. Then she indicated that we should go the same direction her daughter had.

We walked out of the barn and turned for the main house.

"This is my project," she added. "Crow acts like it's his, but it ain't. It's mine."

"Are you and Crow...?"

"No! God, no." She laughed. "Rash is my brother, like I said, and he and Crow grew up together. Crow's my cousin. My husband used to be Red, but he died ten years ago. I got some inheritance and used that to buy this place, renovate it. It's my business. Katie and I keep an apartment in a town not far from here. It's where she goes to school, and we rent this place out. It does well too. Lots of companies use it for events, whatnot. Then Crow gave me a call yesterday and said the club needs it. So here we go."

"It's beautiful."

"Thanks." She sent me a warm smile, before a wondering look replaced it. "I gotta say, it's a really big deal that Ghost and his club are here. Did you travel with them?"

"Uh." *Oh, man.* She was asking questions, and I didn't know how Shane wanted them to be answered. "No. I know Sha—

Ghost from where I grew up. My sister followed the club out here and well..." It sounded ridiculous, now that I was saying it to a total stranger. "I came to get my sister."

"Is she young?" Shelly lowered her voice, pausing halfway to the house. "If she's eighteen, they're not going to like you sticking your nose in their business. Eighteen and up is fair game to these guys. Since you're with Ghost, maybe rules are different, but—"

"No." I started laughing because at this point, how could I not? "I'm sorry." Still laughing. This whole situation was messed up. I waved a hand, feeling some tears building.

Shelly looked at me like I'd lost my head, but that made it all the funnier.

She was warning me about the guys wanting my sister here. It was *so* the other way around.

"It's not like that. At all. At. All. My sister is–" *Wheeze.* Now I was laughing at myself laughing.

Shelly cracked, starting to laugh with me.

My delirium wasn't just about Claudia. It was about me. Foley. The divorce. Me working at a grocery store. The road trip. Everything—and being told if my sister was eighteen, I should leave it alone.

Finally, after I calmed down and could get some air, I shook my head. "You clearly haven't met my sister yet."

Shelly's eyebrows pitched high in her forehead, and she laughed harder. "Oh. It's like that?"

I nodded, wiping a few tears away. "Sorry. Just—*so* not the situation, and yeah."

"You're such a bitch."

I gasped, whirling around.

Claudia stood not far from the main house's porch. She walked my way, her arms crossed over her chest, and she looked annoyed. She also looked dressed the same way Shelly and her daughter were.

Was that the uniform for women in this world? Claudia had chosen shorts that barely covered her ass.

I looked down. I wasn't too far off. I had the jeans, but I wore a white, v-neck shirt. It was simple, but stylish. Or I'd thought so. Now I was tempted to tie it in a knot behind me, just so I didn't feel too old.

"Good Lord." Claudia rolled her eyes. She turned to Shelly. "Look at her. She's worried she's not going to fit in because her clothes aren't skin tight, and totally not realizing how fucking more gorgeous she is than the rest of us."

Shelly's eyes widened as she looked between the two of us. "Guessing you're the sister?"

I narrowed my eyes. "What are you doing here?" This was sober Claudia. Not fun drunk Claudia.

I ignored the way my question confused Shelly, considering our whole laughing fit, and the fact that Claudia and I looked nothing alike.

"Didn't you come to get me?" she asked. "Where else would I be?"

"Shane said you were gone—like, away."

"Right." Claudia's eyes narrowed, turning speculative. "Let's talk about you and Mr. VP." She came forward, linking our elbows and nudged me away from Shelly. "Excuse us for a minute," she called back over her shoulder. "We sisters need to have a little heart to heart right about now."

Shelly tracked us as we went back to the barn we'd just left, and when we got inside, the two bikers sitting there took one look at Claudia and left.

She grunted as they went, closing the door behind them. "Nice to see I've got a reputation around these parts."

I unlinked our elbows and moved aside. "Don't get pissy that they got smart."

She huffed, rolling her eyes. "More like your man told everyone I was off-limits."

I wasn't going to argue with that. That sounded like something Shane would do. But he had not told me she was here. "Shane talked to you?"

She was looking in the rooms, making sure the ones with closed doors were empty inside. When she got to the kitchen, she turned back, doing the same on the other side of the hall. "Talk to me about what? Why don't you tell me what Ghost would've talked to me about?" There was a bite to her voice.

"About me being here? That Mom asked me to come bring you back?"

She huffed. "Mom does not want me to come back. I guarantee that."

"She was in tears—"

Claudia laughed, coming to stand in front of me and crossing her arms over her chest again. "She was not. Mom hustled you. We both saw how Ghost reacted to you at the bar that night, and trust me, we already knew. Ghost sent someone to ask questions about you all over town—like that would happen and neither of us would hear about it? You're supposed to be the smart one. Mom didn't send you after me. She sent you after Ghost. I was just the excuse."

I opened my mouth.

Claudia fixed me with a look. "I can't figure out why you came. Because of Ghost or because you didn't want to stay in Friendly any longer? My guess? The latter, but now I'm hearing how you came here on the back of Ghost's motorcycle and whose bed you were in last night, so maybe I'm the foolish one. You and Ghost, huh? He's not a rebound type of guy. Not for you, not from Foley."

Aw, snap.

Right there, with that last statement, I realized a few things.

One, Shane had pushed away some of the pain I'd been ignoring from Foley.

Two, my sister didn't care one iota about why I was here.

And three, Claudia was still a bitch.

My walls had been lowered. Shane had done that, but they slammed back up now, and my sister saw the change come over me. She took a step back, her eyes speculative. Or maybe they were calculating.

"What crawled up your ass and got you twisted?" I asked. "You brought Foley up last time I saw you too, and you actually seemed to regret it. This time you brought him up on purpose. To hurt me?"

"Oh." She laughed, mocking me, and started to walk in a circle.

I moved with her. I couldn't help myself.

"You're lying to yourself, Kali, if you think you actually came for me."

"Who cares? I would've found you and tried to talk you into going back to Mom. She did ask me to come and get you."

She shook her head. "You're just running, like you always have. Tell me something, sister. Why the fuck did you stay with Foley? You knew before you married him that he was a cheater, and you stayed with him."

"Like I was supposed to believe everything you told me?" I laughed right back at her, mirroring her mocking tone perfectly. "All you've done is take my stuff. My things. My cars. My friends." We hadn't gotten to that yet. "My boyfriends. My jobs—"

"You're lying on that one. I only took one of your—"

"Two. You took two of my jobs."

She frowned. "Which ones? I remember the school concession stand job, but—"

"Mrs. Bierreto's ice cream shop."

She stopped frowning. "Oh. Yeah. I told her you were lazy and had an eating disorder and would binge on all the ice cream."

I ground to a halt, my mouth on the floor. "You told her that?"

She laughed. "She offered me the job instead, right on the

spot. She had no clue I was telling her about myself. *I* binged on all the ice cream."

"You're confessing now that you have an eating disorder?"

"God, no. That's a lie. I just really like dick, cigarettes, and booze. Right?" She shot me a dark look, starting our circling again. "Isn't that all you think about me? You don't think I actually care about you."

"Because you don't."

"As if. I *only* care about you."

"You only *hurt* me."

"Not true. I just see the shitty situations you put yourself into and try to circumvent you, by putting myself there first. And look, it worked in so many ways. You didn't work at the ice cream place. You would've hated working there."

"I would've loved working there. I would've been working with my best friend. Aly worked there."

"Oh. Right." She frowned. "Aly and Harper. Those two never liked me."

I cackled. "That cemented them as my two best friends. Because they hated you."

Claudia rolled her eyes. "What are you doing here, Kali? For real. You're not here for me, but if you are, I'm here, and I'm not leaving. So what now, my golden and saint-like sister?"

I stopped in my tracks, because she was right.

She did not sound like she wanted to leave. I could hear the finality in her tone, and I knew my sister. There was no talking her into anything. If Aly and Harper were here, I'd ask their input, but I could guarantee it would've been along the lines of getting her unconscious and kidnapping her, then hoping she wouldn't wake until we were back in Indiana.

Maybe it was a good thing they weren't here.

"Why are you so set on staying?" I asked. "For that Roadie guy?"

Claudia seemed to wither in front of me, and that was something I'd never seen.

Well, one time, when she'd come home from a date with a popular senior. She'd never talked about what happened with him, and I never saw her with him again.

"Claude?" My voice dropped low. I didn't know how to handle her like this.

She shook her head, as if to clear it. "I'm not staying for him. He's like all the others. I'm staying for Machete."

"Machete?" I didn't want to know why he had that name.

"He's a good one. You'd approve of him."

I frowned. "You're his old lady?"

"Maybe. I think so." She shrugged. "I hope so. It means something here." She eyed me. "I hear you're Shane's old lady?"

Now my claws were out. "I'm not, but that's none of your business."

She laughed. "You keep doing what you do best, my sister. You keep lying to yourself." She went to the door. "Thanks for this chat. I've gotten what I needed out of it." She stopped and studied me for a moment. "Do yourself a favor this time? Shane's a Red. They've got girls who let them do trains on them. And they all join in—or most of them. If you couldn't handle Foley, you *really* can't handle Shane. Ghost. He's the biggest head honcho here, and they like their power structure. The fact you're still here means he's snuck in and started to dig deep in you. Don't let him in anymore, not even an inch. Foley made you like this, but Ghost will finish the job. You can't handle this life. Get out while you can. They ain't here. This is your best shot at running, but I'm not going. I've got the one guy that's not a piece of shit. Give Mom and Connor my best. I ain't ever going back."

Then my sister, the lovely peach she was, left, and I stood there, going over her words.

"*Get out while you can. They ain't here. This is your best shot at running...*"

I rolled my eyes.

I knew my sister.

If Claudia was telling me to go, I sure as hell *wasn't* going to.

ME: **Updating! I'm still with Shane. Found Claudia. She's not going anywhere.**

Aly: **Good Lord, she'll never change. On the upside, Harper and I have had a divine Saturday. We golfed this morning. (And sucked.) Had a delicious brunch at the country club here. This afternoon was spent at the spa and tonight, Harper has no clue but Justin is flying in. I am planning on spending the evening at Manny's. Bring on some more Brandon and that regular guy. I didn't catch his name last night, but I did meet Roy. He seems like a great kid... if he's a kid. Who knows at this point.**

Aly: **Are you seriously okay, though? Please tell us if you aren't.**

Me: **I am. Promise. Right now I'm pissed at Claudia, so all is normal.**

Aly: **Call us if you need backup. Harper will probably bring a pitchfork intended for me (cause I'm the one getting Justin here), but he might take his aggression out on your sister. You know how we both feel about her. Good old Claudia.**

Me: **Yeah. Good old Claudia. Start stretching to evade and dodge the pitchfork. Harper is fast.**

Harper: **You both suck! THIS IS A GROUP CHAT, DID YOU BOTH FORGET?**

Harper: **Stay safe, K. Share your location with us plz. Aly, start stretching. Start. Stretching.**

ME: Dad. I owe you a phone call. Here's my initial apology before the real groveling happens. Give me a few days. I'm on Claudia duty right now.

Dad: I have news too! We have five hundred subscribers on the Old Gents' YouTube channel.

Dad: Also, I will be waiting.

Me: Oh, boy.

Dad: Was that intended to be a text message to me?

Me: No! Sorry. Again. Or ahead of time. Sorry, sorry, sorry. Love you, Dad!

Dad: I sure do love you back. Tick tock on that phone call, Daughter. Tick tock.

23

SHANE

Normally when we'd roll into Frisco for a roast like tonight's, the gate at The Bonfire would be drawn back, and we could drive our bikes right inside. This time, we drove forward and then reversed, walking our bikes back so all of us were facing the street. We were ready for a fast retreat or a fast chase, and no one was sure which would happen.

I knew one thing, though. I wasn't going to die tonight, and I wasn't going to retreat. Whatever went down, I'd be ending it.

If it came to me snapping Estrada's neck, I'd do it. I knew how cartels worked. They thrived on hitting your family, and no fucking way was anyone touching Kali.

I didn't like Marco Estrada. Never had. I didn't know who did, but Maxwell had put us in business with him, and our club grew because of it. No more. The cartel was too dangerous, too deadly for us, and it was time to cut ties.

Tonight we'd see how it all ended.

I wasn't a great actor, but I knew my role. I'd keep it together until the right time.

Once I'd parked, I called Heckler before getting off my bike.

The rest of the guys went inside, and the prospects came back out a moment later to watch over the bikes.

"I called around, like you asked," Heckler said when he answered. "No one up there has heard about the cartel moving on us. And down here, we're still not getting anything. I'm sorry I can't be more helpful."

I sat back, thinking. "So we're going in blind."

"I'm sorry."

A different thought came to me. "Could he be listening in on this?"

"Our calls?"

"Yeah."

Heckler was quiet a moment. "If he's into that, we're fucked."

We had tech guys, computer guys, who could maybe do what I'd suggested. We'd just never considered putting those measures in place.

"We messed up," I told him.

"Yeah. We did. I was focused on Max."

"I was focused on other things." No way was I mentioning Kali now.

"You want me to call them?" Heckler offered.

"Yeah. We're going to need them moving forward."

Heckler laughed and then sighed. "Maybe that was the point of shooting Max? Distracting us?"

"Maybe." My phone was ringing again. "I gotta take this call. It's Boise."

"Keep us updated."

"Will do." I ended that call and switched over. "Yeah?"

"They're coming. Three vehicles. I'll text if anyone sets up outside the town."

"Thanks." We hung up, and I sent a text to all the others.

Me: Incoming.

A couple minutes later they rolled in exactly the way Boise had said they would: three SUVs.

A little while after that, everyone had settled in. Marco had five men who'd set up in the front of The Bonfire with assault rifles at the ready. Three more stood just inside the gate, and the rest of his men—the ten he'd told us to account for—were sitting, eating and drinking as if nothing was out of the ordinary.

At my table sat Marco, Crow, and Crow's sergeant at arms. One of the sweet butts was all over Crow, running her hand up and down his arm. He mostly ignored her, but when Marco's gaze lingered on her, he pulled her into his lap.

Marco didn't bat an eye, just went back to eating.

His men were drinking, and judging from the way they were throwing them back, they could handle their booze.

Our guys had non-alcoholic beer, because some of them *couldn't* handle their booze.

I was so fucking stiff inside that I could've been the Oscar statue for all those awards. But on the outside, I was pretty sure no one could tell a thing. I wanted to kill this man. I knew that much.

"Ghost."

It was always so odd when Marco used my biker name. He said it as if it were my given name, and we were the best of friends. He smiled. "How is your president? Have you been able to identify who shot him?"

This fucking asshole. To bring him up...

I didn't blink. My smile never twitched. I responded casually, sitting back in my seat. "It's still touch and go, and no. We haven't found who did it yet."

Marco nodded, dabbing the corners of his mouth with his napkin. He switched to Crow. "And you, this is your club, correct?" He put his napkin away, and a smooth smile took its place. "You'll have to forgive me. I'm not very knowledgeable on the biker culture."

Crow shot me a look, leaning forward slowly. He spanked the girl's ass and motioned for her to head back inside. She did, pouting as she went. Crow watched her go, watched her ass sway from side to side before turning to the cartel leader. "Our charter president isn't here. He's in Potomahmen actually."

"That's the prison here?"

"It is, yes."

Marco glanced my way. "And you're here to help them through this time?"

He was wading into Red Demon business, not his, and judging by the spark in his eyes, he knew it.

I gave him a blank stare. "We've covered this before. That's our business, not yours. And I say that with no disrespect intended."

Marco grinned, apparently not offended. "I like you, Ghost."

He shouldn't. But I grinned back. "I'm relieved."

Crow almost choked on his beer before putting it back down. "My apologies."

The music cranked up, and a couple of Estrada's men decided to start dancing. A few of our guys joined, along with the sweet butts.

Marco took everything in for a moment before looking around our table again.

None of us were relaxed. We might've looked it, but we weren't. Crow and his SIA were smiling, but I could tell it was so forced that it was painful to see. Marco's eyes narrowed, and I knew he didn't miss anything, but then he turned and focused on me. Only me.

His eyes changed, growing more serious. "Could I speak with you alone for a moment?"

He asked me, but his question was directed toward the other two.

Both stood, nodding with the same tight smiles on their faces. Crow went inside, and his SIA joined the dancing in the yard.

"I need to repeat myself. I like you, Ghost. Can I call you by your given name?"

No. "Sure. It's Shane."

"Shane."

Fuck no. Fuck no. Fuck no. The last person who called me that was Kali.

He seemed so honored that he knew my real name now.

"Your bike club has done so much for me. You have helped me tremendously. My organization. I've been able to grow my business because of you, and I have enemies. I have many enemies." His face grew rigid, almost like stone. "But no matter. I still keep growing, and I'm aware that your club is a part of that. I feel it was God's hand that had me so near when I heard about your president's attack. And I've always respected you. You, you know how to kill. You know how to make the hard choice, to end a life or not. I can see it in you. I have it in me. I don't wish to speak ill of the sick, but your president, he hesitates at times. I've seen it. I wanted to relay that if anything does happen to your president, and if you should step up to take your place as the national president, you have my support. I'm unaware if that's needed in a situation like that, but I wanted to let you know."

Marco Estrada once hung a family of eighteen from a bridge, all of their heads decapitated—a man, his wife, and their sixteen children. The youngest was eight months old.

This man did that. The one who sat next to me, saying he respected me.

And the reason they'd all been hung and decapitated? Because one of their daughters handed a phone to Marco's sister. That was it. A phone was passed, and the entire family was murdered.

He was speaking nice and acting nice, but this man was evil.

I smiled at him and held up my beer. "That means a lot, Señor Estrada."

His smile warmed, and I could see him relax.

He had no worries. None. If he was behind Max's hit, he wasn't worried about it.

"I am looking forward to many more meals with you. This one has been the most fun so far. I thank you, Señor Shane."

I wanted to pull my gun out, press the barrel against his forehead, and pull the trigger. I smiled instead. "And you as well, Señor."

They partied the rest of the night, until his men could barely stand. I handed out orders. A few of our men needed to start acting wasted, or the cartel would know.

Marco and his men didn't leave, not until the early morning. The sun had started to peek over the horizon when they decided it was time to go.

Marco had a great time. He'd professed it to me many times throughout the night.

And once they'd finally gone, Crow looked at me, with all of our men around us. "Jesus *fucking* Christ," he said.

I texted Heckler.

Me: If it's him, he's the most smug asshole that exists.

Heckler: We got a lead. Following it up tomorrow.

24

KALI

A bunch of bikes had returned thirty minutes ago, early in the morning, with their riders all smiles. No Shane, but the guys rolled up, parked, and a few grabbed the women up in hugs. There were whoops, wolf whistles, and cheers, but I still sensed an underlying tension.

They'd started a bonfire, and now they were partying.

Guys were drinking, and some women hung over them. In some ways, it just looked like a typical family party. Music started, and I could smell weed.

I sat in a chair outside the barn, a few yards from the front door. Some of the guys headed in, giving me looks as they went, but no one approached or said anything to me. These were Shane's guys. I'd come to know that. His charter was staying here.

A minute later, an older guy walked toward the house—maybe a few years older than me. Bald, dark skin, and he was all muscle. Kinda looked like a square box. He gave me a look before heading over.

He wasn't handsome, but he was striking in a rough way.

"Ghost and Boise went to run an errand. He'll be back later."

His eyes dropped to my hands. "Guys will be partying tonight. You want a drink?"

I nodded. "I can grab it, though."

He gave a small shake of his head, already turning around. "I'll get your drinks. Just give me a nod, and I'll know to refill you. Be back."

The sound of dirt scraping had me looking behind me, and my sister was there. She watched the guy leaving, her arms hugging her stomach. It was chilly so she had a flannel on, hanging low and almost covering her shorts. Her hair was free, blown back by a breeze, and her eyes were troubled. Or no... Somber.

I'd only seen that look on her a few times in my life, namely when Connor was convicted. Not when he was arrested, and not any of the days we went to court. Just the day of the sentencing— and one other day.

"He's my man."

She wasn't looking at me, but I knew she was talking to me. I gave the guy a different appraisal.

There was an edge of danger to him, but that made sense. He was a biker, a Red Demon. All these guys wore it in the way they moved, how familiar they were with their weapons, their bikes, but mostly it was in their eyes. They would be violent, without a second thought, if the moment called for it. I knew there were others who *wanted* to be violent. But so far, none of those guys had come near me.

"I thought you were with that other guy?"

She turned, looking at me. After watching me for a beat, she started forward, holding a beer bottle by its neck. She sunk down in the chair next to me, bringing the beer up for a drink.

"He slept with a sweet butt." She glanced at me. "That's what they call the girls who sleep with anyone."

I nodded, already knowing.

She turned to watch the bonfire and the main house again.

"Machete came in when I was getting ready to do something stupid to Roadie and told me I was supposed to leave with him."

That's how most couples get together. "What were you going to do?"

"Something that probably would've gotten me killed."

Candor from my sister. Also something I rarely received. I was pro Machete. He was a good influence on her.

He came back toward us now, holding a few beers in his hands.

She sighed. It was soft, but it was there.

I felt like a frozen animal at this point. Who was this person next to me and what had she done with my sister?

"I like him," she breathed. "I like him a lot."

That was sweet.

She turned to look my way, a hard glint in her eyes. "Don't fuck with mine. I won't fuck with yours."

Never mind. I relaxed. *There* was my sister.

Machete was still coming our way.

I took the time to enjoy this moment. I smiled at my sister, leaned in, and said, "This feeling? Concerned? Knowing you deserve what you've sown in life, this fear from you—I'm loving it. I believe in karma, sister. Do you?"

Her eyes blazed hate. But the sound of footsteps over gravel got closer, then stopped. Machete stood watching us both. "Babe."

Claudia was all smiles then, rising and moving into his arms. "Hi, baby." She tipped her head back for his kiss, and they made out for a moment before she stepped back, her hand still on his chest. "How was your thing? You guys do what you needed to do?"

He studied her. His face didn't move, but his scrutiny was making my sister uncomfortable.

She stepped fully away, straightening one of her sleeves and pulling the shirt tighter around herself. "You want to sit with us? This is my sister, Kali."

Machete nodded to me, holding out one of the beers, but his eyes remained on my sister. "Pleased to meet you."

I took the beer. "Thank you, and you as well."

My sister folded back down into her chair.

That's when he switched his gaze to me. He lifted the beers still in his hand. "Gonna put these in the fridge. Be back." He was respectful to me, but as soon as he said those words, his gaze went right back to my sister.

She ignored his gaze. As he went inside, I saw her cheeks had flushed, and I started chuckling.

"Shut up."

I laughed.

"Shut up!" she hissed, smacking my arm.

I laughed harder.

"You're such a bitch."

"Karma," I said quietly. "Kar-ma. It's a thing. Trust and believe, sister. *Trust* and believe."

"I hate you." She slumped down in her chair.

We heard male voices, and Machete returned with another guy. He was younger. I recognized him as being with Shane a lot. He gave us a nod before he took the empty seat on my other side.

"Up, woman." Machete stopped before Claudia.

She stood.

He sat down, hooking an arm around her waist and pulling her to sit on his lap.

I was glued to this scene. The main house could've exploded, and I wouldn't have stopped watching.

My sister was enamored with him.

They shared a look, holding a moment, before she ducked her head. Her mouth curved up in a faint smile, and her cheeks pinked again. She moved in, settling against his chest, and I swear, she looked so comfortable she could've fallen asleep.

"I'm Stripes," came a voice behind me.

I had to force myself to look away. The guy on my other side was holding up his beer. We'd met before, but it didn't hurt for another introduction.

I gave him a small smile, clinking his beer with mine. "Kali."

He nodded and sat back.

Stripes seemed content to drink and watch the party. Machete was the same. Claudia was *quiet*, seemingly *content* to rest in Machete's lap.

I was speechless.

There was nothing else to say.

25

SHANE

We rode in late, but the guys were all still up and raging. We could see the bonfire from five miles out, and when we drove in, they all made room. I saw Stripes heading our way, but Crow came first. His sergeant at arms was with him, and another guy.

"How'd it go?" Crow asked.

I skimmed over the group, seeing Machete coming up behind Stripes.

Boise stepped up next to me, and I felt the rest of the guys who'd gone with us gather behind me.

I nodded to them, indicating they could take off. They dispersed, but Boise stayed.

Crow gave him a hard look, but Boise didn't react. He never did.

"We kept pace with them. Followed them past Lancaster," I reported.

Crow nodded. "You think they're crossing tonight?"

I shook my head. "Don't know, but they took off after the roast."

"Who's with them?"

"Couple of mine."

Crow's eyes sharpened. "They good? They'll be safe?"

I nodded. "They're good. Special forces. They won't get caught."

Crow's shoulders relaxed a bit. "Good. Uh, I'd like to have a conversation with you later, at some point."

That meant: alone, no one else around, and come find me for it.

"Sounds good."

He was nodding again, and seemed a lot looser. The tension had left him. He waved a hand around. "Everyone's partying. We can talk tomorrow at some point. You and your guys should let loose. Looks like we dodged the cartel for now."

That meant the plan was the same. We'd pull out, but in the coordinated way we'd decided.

Boise was on his phone. "Heckler's calling you," he said as he put it away.

My phone lit up, and I gave Crow a nod. "I need to take this."

"Relax for the night, guys. See you in the morning."

I answered, but didn't move away. Something about Crow's easy acceptance didn't sit right with me. I spoke into the phone, "I'm here. One second."

"Got it."

I nodded toward Crow before facing Stripes. "You're good at blending. Watch him all night."

Stripes didn't blink or react. He nodded once and moved in the direction Crow had just gone.

I glanced back once, seeing Crow on the house's front porch. There was a girl in his arms, so he wasn't talking business yet. Stripes stooped, grabbed a drink, and pulled out a packet of smokes.

"You're giving him a lot of assignments," Boise noted.

Heckler was still on the phone, but I turned to him. "He's been following everyone. He was resourceful in prison, I heard."

"In and out of prison."

Yeah.

"He's still considered a nomad, isn't he?"

I nodded. "Yeah. Max sent him with me on this trip for a reason."

"He seems to be working out."

"We'll see. He might want to go to Florida."

"You want me to feel him out?"

That meant Boise would hang out with him, get to know him, ask him the personal questions a national VP might not get the real answers to.

I nodded, giving Boise the go-ahead.

He took off, but headed toward the barn, glancing at Stripes a few times before merging with the crowd around the bonfire.

Machete was up next. "Sisters are together, outside the barn."

He took off, going right back in the same direction as Boise.

So Claudia had found Kali. I finally spoke into the phone, "How's Max?"

"He's going to pull through, and we found who did it."

I frowned. That got my attention real quick. He hadn't led with that when I answered. "Who?"

"A dad down here. Max was fucking his daughter. Seventeen."

Jesus!

Heckler wasn't done. "She turned seventeen a month ago."

"What are you planning?" My tone was gritty because damn, this was not a good place to be in right now.

"We grabbed the dad. He says he's got proof Max fucked her when she was sixteen, a day before her birthday. He could be a problem, but he says he won't do anything more if we let him live." He paused. "Most of the guys are with you, so I'm thinking it's your call. Max is in a medically induced coma. What do you want us to do?"

Max was the national president. There was no question here.

"Get the proof, then kill him."

26

KALI

I nursed one beer forever.

This was a full-fledged party, so no way would I be able to sleep.

Also, this was a full-fledged party, so no way was I going to get drunk. I didn't care that Shane had said no one would mess with me if I told them I was with him.

Also, a full-fledged party *and* my sister was here, so another reason to say *hell no* to getting drunk.

So I nursed that beer like I was going to win a competition. With a cash reward.

But I was horny, because in the past few hours, I'd witnessed a lot of people getting some action—in the shadows and right out in the light. Hell, Machete had even gone inside and gotten a blanket for him and Claudia. Sure enough, a little while later there was movement under the blanket, and my sister couldn't stop a few groans from slipping out.

Some motorcycles rode in about the time I felt ready to combust, and both guys stood up, which I was a little relieved about.

"Your man is back," Claudia said.

With that, my horniness level went from a decent, steady five to a nine. A nine point five.

I might've been waiting for him. Maybe. I didn't know if I wanted to admit that to myself. But as I watched the guys go over to meet with him... Even seeing him from a distance, I could feel him inside of me. Yeah. I'd been waiting for him.

God.

I wanted him. Now.

My need throbbed a deep, steady beat inside of me, between my legs, and I squirmed on the seat. This guy. What had he done to me? I couldn't handle this.

My body was an inferno.

I remembered all the times—the motel, here, when he ate me out like I was Thanksgiving.

Machete came back, but he only held his hand out. Claudia took it, sending me a furtive look before he pulled her to her feet and led her inside.

Stripes hadn't come back, but that didn't matter. Shane was heading right for me. I knew the instant he saw me. My body went from inferno to active volcano. The rest of the party fled. It was him and me, and the way he was looking at me? It seemed like he was remembering Thanksgiving too.

"You're back." My voice came out raspy, and his eyes sharpened.

"You were out here alone?" he asked after observing me a moment.

"Machete, my sister, and Stripes were with me."

He blinked slowly. "You talked with them the whole time?"

I was back to squirming because why were we talking? I shook my head. "Another guy came over and talked to Stripes, but that's it. I didn't care. This..." I waved at the party. "...is..." I didn't know what to say. "It's a lot to take in."

His eyes sharpened again. "You okay?"

I nodded, my neck stiff, and I moved again, needing to adjust myself on the chair. I was restless. Wanting him. Needing him. Not knowing what to do about it.

He gave me a full once-over, and I licked my lips. I hadn't meant to do it. It just happened, but then his gaze went from studying to dark and smoldering.

He held his hand out.

I took it. A tingle shot up my arm, and as he laced our fingers, that tingle morphed into a sizzle.

He led the way to the barn.

I looked back once and saw Shelly standing not far from where we'd been, watching us. She gave me a small smile before turning back to the house.

Once we were back inside the room where we'd been sleeping, the closed door muted all the sounds. They didn't go away, but they became nice background music, along with the buzzing in my body.

Shane stared at me, not moving to remove his cut, his guns. "You drunk?"

I felt like it. "No." My pulse pounded even stronger, filling my entire body. I pushed out my tits, not thinking about it until his gaze fell to them. He didn't look away, not for a long time.

I couldn't breathe. I tipped my head up, falling back against the door. I was almost panting. How embarrassing was that?

"What's going on with you?"

Fuck it. "Two couples fucking," I announced.

His eyes widened, snapping to my face.

"Three blow jobs."

His gaze smoldered again, darkening. He took a step toward me.

My voice dropped low. "Eight guys did a train on a girl out there."

He moved even closer. Almost touching me. I could feel the heat of his body.

"She seemed to enjoy it," I added.

I held his gaze, my head tipped all the way back now.

"My sister and her new man were doing things too. Right next to me." I took a deep breath. "I'm not drunk, Shane. I want to fuck."

His eyes? Instant black.

He reached for me, but I moved first. My hand went to his chest, and I dropped to my knees. My mouth watered. I'd never wanted to do this. Ever. Not once in my life.

I did for my husband, but rarely. On holidays. Birthdays. It was for him.

But this time, I reached for Shane's pants—unbuckling them, sliding down the zipper.

I reached in and found his cock. This time it was for me.

I'll process all of that later, I told myself as I sucked him into my mouth.

Then I was moving over him.

In. Out.

I deep-throated him.

Licked him.

Tasted him.

Circled his tip.

I stroked him as I slurped like he was a lollipop.

He watched me the whole time, enraptured. He seemed to be holding his breath.

Then I took all of him in again, all the way down my throat. As far as I could take him. I moaned, my sounds stifled around him. Then I braced myself, sinking down on my knees, and I grabbed his hips.

He reached down, taking my hair, and I tried to nod, telling him what I wanted.

He eased in, slow.

I moved farther down, finding a good sitting position, and I tried opening my throat even more.

He eased out. Slowly again.

Yes. I wanted him to do this.

Back in, but he was going too slow.

I'd been sucking him. I wanted him to take over.

I moved my head back, and there was a popping sound as his dick came out of my mouth. I looked up at him.

"Fuck my mouth."

His eyes flared with a dark and primal pleasure there. When I saw he was down for this, I positioned myself again, grabbing his base. I vacuumed him in, and as he wrapped my hair around one of his hands, I reached for his hips and braced.

Then he began moving, fucking my face.

I let him have it.

I was starting to think I would always let him have it. But no, I didn't want to process that either. Not until later.

Much later.

HE TRIED to pull out to finish.

I didn't let him.

I sucked him in, holding him, and then he twitched, filling me up. I looked up as I swallowed. His eyes were still black. He panted.

Then he growled and snatched me up, his hands under my arms. He carried me across the room, as if I were a doll. He tossed me onto the bed and I fell there, stunned a moment. He stripped my pants off, ripped my underwear away, yanked off my shirt, and pushed up my bra. When I was free for his viewing pleasure, he paused to admire me for a moment.

"Goddammit," he growled. "You're so fucking beautiful."

He knelt on the bed, bending over me.

His hand went to my pussy, two of his fingers dipping in. His thumb moved over my clit just before he pulled out and smoothed his hand up my body. Pussy to stomach, between my breasts, all the way up to my throat where his hand circled me and his fingers went into my mouth.

I sucked them in, tasting myself, and closed my eyes as he bent down.

His mouth found my tits, and he circled one with his tongue, his teeth grazing over my nipple.

I gasped, sensations searing through me.

Never. Not ever had another man made me feel these things, do these things, made me hunger for more, demand more. Forget what the guy wanted. This was what I wanted.

Not once.

Shane pulled his fingers away, caressing my breast as his mouth moved to where they'd been. His tongue slid inside, and the kiss consumed me. In that moment, I felt ashamed because I knew I'd never loved my husband.

I couldn't have.

Then I stopped thinking.

I only felt Shane.

27

SHANE

Her phone woke us up.

It was a few hours later, and I grabbed it, handing it over as she began to stir next to me.

I'd had my mouth in her, my fingers in all of her holes last night, but not my dick. Not yet.

She'd blown me twice, and holy fuck, what she could do with that mouth.

I'd fucked her tits.

Not my dick, though.

I was holding back. I didn't know why.

In a barn surrounded by my brothers? That wouldn't normally bother me. It was our way in this life.

But fuck me, I was holding back because *she* was holding back.

She wanted me. That was obvious, but there was a wall inside her. I felt it, and it pissed me off.

Made me rage, but I was patient. When I made love to her, I wanted her. All of her. No walls. Nothing. I wanted to bend her over, twist her into so many indecent positions, but not until I had all of her.

She groaned, answering the phone. "Hey."

I chuckled. Her voice was barely a rasp.

She shot me a glare, which made me laugh harder, and I leaned over her, my mouth dropping down on hers.

"He—" My mouth swallowed whatever she'd been going to say.

I could hear whoever was on the other end bitching, but I didn't care.

I took my time.

My tongue slid inside her mouth, smoothing around her, caressing, enjoying.

She was mine, all mine. I'd have every inch of her too.

She was moaning by the time I was done. My dick was rock hard, and I began to crawl over her, grinding up and into her when the person on the phone got smart.

"Wha—OMG! Are you having sex right now?!"

I lifted my mouth, enjoying the dazed look on her face as she blinked.

I took her phone. I could tell now it was her friend Harper. I remembered him from high school. "Keep it nice and respectful, yeah?" I suggested.

I didn't wait for him to respond. I knew Kali adored him. I pushed up, giving her the phone back, and waited.

She gave me a look, as I was still looming over her.

She put the phone to her ear. "Hey, Harper." But she was focused on me, mouthing to me, "What?"

I grinned. Goddamn. I wanted her.

I couldn't fucking wait until that happened, but I didn't respond, just pushed up and off the bed.

"Don't be mad at Aly," she said, sitting up as I went into the bathroom, shutting the door.

I hit the shower.

When I came out, she was still on the phone, but in the kitchen now.

She'd put the phone on speaker and was looking around for the coffee. She rifled through one of the cupboards, reaching up on her tiptoes.

I went over, my hand to her hip, and moved her aside.

I had no clue why the coffee was kept on the absolute top shelf, but I grabbed it and handed it to her.

She stepped back, her friend still talking in the background, but she didn't take the coffee. She tracked a drop of water as it slid down my chest to my stomach, and she reached for it, her eyes in that haze I recognized from a few hours ago. She touched my stomach and leaned forward. She caught the water drop in her mouth, then moved her mouth up my stomach to my chest.

I loved it. I needed this.

I caught her around her waist, pulling her tight, and then I hoisted her up on the counter.

She squeaked, her legs rounding my waist.

"What?" That was Harper. "Kali? Your man come back?"

I grinned, leaning back to look down at her.

She couldn't blush, but I knew she was embarrassed. Her forehead rested on my chest, her hands holding onto my jeans. They weren't zipped up, and my cock was straining, trying to get to her.

I leaned in, and her legs opened for me.

I slid a hand down to her ass and pulled her to the edge of the counter.

"Kali!"

I moved my mouth to her ear, kissing her there before murmuring, "Better answer him, babe."

She huffed a deep, but quiet sound. But she raised her voice a second later. "No, no. I mean, yes. He's here."

I moved my hand over her ass, my thumb trailing between her cheeks, and she shuddered into me.

"OMG. I'm on speaker, aren't I? I am. Has he been there the whole time?" Harper's voice grew shrill.

I nipped her shoulder before lifting my head, grinning. "Hi, Harper."

He inhaled loudly, then responded very calmly. "Hello, Shane. You remember me?"

I trailed my thumb up between Kali's ass cheeks and felt her body shudder all over again, into me. I was *really* enjoying the way her body was tuned in to me, to every touch from me. I dropped my head back to her shoulder, nipping her again, letting my teeth scrape over her neck.

She shivered.

"I do. I remember the three of you. You were quite a trio back then."

"We still are, except I'm angry at the other one. Has Kali told you what Aly did? What I *so* do not co-sign, and I'm angry at you too, Kali. You encouraged her. You reached out to him first."

I had no fucking clue what he was talking about, and I didn't care. I tuned him out.

Kali's head tipped back, and she spoke to him, but her voice was low, strained. She kept herself in control as my thumb moved farther down under her. I shifted, lifting her up, and she gasped.

"What? What's happening?"

I found her hole, circling it, and she leaned all the way into me. I held her up, rimming her.

I felt her mouth open against my throat, and a strangled sound came next.

"Oh good gawd. I'm calling my mother to complain to her. No one cares. Everyone wants me to marry Justin, and if you want him that much, you marry him."

I paused. *What?*

Kali grasped my shoulders, her nails curving into my skin—not breaking it but close.

She turned, her teeth grazing the side of my neck.

I turned, my eyes finding hers, and I could see the lust. It was that haze again. My girl was gone, and her nails were sinking in.

She wanted this. Realizing that, I reached over, pressed end on the phone call, and lifted her right back up in my arms.

My babe was going to get some play.

28

KALI

I'd been drugged.

That was the only explanation for my behavior, because seriously, I was acting like a junkie. Or the way I assumed a junkie might be obsessed over her next hit. *Drugged*. Yes. All rational thought had left me, and what was worse? *We still hadn't had sex!*

My skin crawled.

What was wrong with me?

Was there something wrong with me?

29

SHANE

Boise found me as soon as I left the apartment. He looked back toward the room I'd come out of. "Going to need to meet this one."

I grunted. Word had spread fast that I'd claimed an old lady.

"I take it she knows she's an old lady?"

I paused, glancing back at the door. Did she? She wanted my dick. I knew that much, but she didn't want me as much as I wanted her. I knew that too. Knowing she was my old lady? That was a whole other battle still ahead of me.

I didn't answer, just slapped him on the shoulder. "Let's handle Crow. Any word from the guys?"

"They called for orders. Estrada is moving east."

"East?" So he wasn't crossing south. "I want to know who all of his connections are in the States."

"He didn't have any when we got into business with him, so this is new and under the radar."

I nodded. Exactly. That's why I didn't like it.

"Heckler texted," Boise continued. "He's waiting for a call too. He wants the guys back with him if we aren't doing battle here."

That made sense, but *damn*. They'd driven a full night to get here, pretended to party, then did party, and now they'd be going back tomorrow.

I nodded, starting down to the main floor. "I want them to rest today. They can head out tonight or in the morning."

"I've made the rounds. Half the guys want to stay with you."

"We might need to head down there."

Boise shrugged. "Your guys want to be with you. Don't matter where you go."

That was true. And I still had a job to do here. "Right."

When we got to the main floor, the guys stood up. They'd been waiting for me, and I led the way outside. They fell in line. Stripes was outside the barn, and he got in line too.

A few of Crow's guys were on the house's front porch, and they stood, seeing us coming.

We'd cover all bases now at church.

"Your VP up?" I asked one of them.

He gave a nod, his face expressionless. "Ready for church."

That was good. Straight to business.

I felt antsy. I wanted to get on the move, do some battle, wrangle Kali so she accepted that she was mine, but all in due time. I needed to be smart, on all fronts. I was about to step up when my phone rang. Seeing it was Heckler, I showed Boise the screen. He gave a nod. He'd handle things for me until I was done with the call.

I answered, stepping right back off and going around for some privacy. "How's he doing?" That was my greeting.

"They're going to wake him up tomorrow. Doc said the swelling is going down, so he's stable. That's the good news."

"And the dad?"

"We got him, bu..." Heckler hesitated.

Heckler wasn't a hesitater. I frowned. "What happened?"

"My niece knows the girl." *The girl Max had been fucking.* "She found out your orders and went apeshit."

Women weren't supposed to know club business, but it

happened. Some always had an opinion and inserted it. We listened to the good ones. Kess was a good one.

I waited for him to continue. He didn't. "And?"

"She's of the opinion that Max might love this girl, and therefore would object if we killed the dad."

"He shot our national president."

"I know."

No one could shoot a Red Demon and walk from it. He shot the *national president* and Heckler's niece was arguing for just that?

"Wraith is wondering if we want to wait, see what Max says, or at the very least do a church call. Just to cover our bases."

"You have the dad?"

"We got him."

"No way he can get free?"

"None. We got Tango on him."

Tango was a sadistic fuck. My orders might've showed more mercy.

"Okay. Let's wait. See what Prez says, if he's able to think right."

Heckler got quiet, because this was an issue. I hadn't let myself ponder what it might mean that Max had been down, and in a coma for so long. But it was in the realm of possibilities that we still might've lost our president.

"Will do," he finally said.

"Heckler."

"Yeah?"

"If anything looks like it's going south before Prez wakes up, the dad has to be put down."

"I know," he grunted.

"I'm told you want the guys back with you?"

"Will feel better having them here."

I got that. "I'm told half of them want to stay with me."

"Are you still moving forward with Max's plan?"

"Think so. Crow's wanting a conversation later today. I'll feel him out. I put Stripes on him last night. His acceptance that Estrada left so quickly didn't feel right to me."

"What are you thinking?"

"I don't know. Something just feels off. I don't like it."

"Got it." He coughed, which meant he was changing the subject. "Heard you got a woman now," he added, his tone lighter.

"Oh, fuck off." I hung up on his laugh.

Heading down and into church, I moved past bikers lining the hallway and stairs. They followed me in, and the room got quiet. Crow was at the front of the table. I took the seat at the end. My guys lined up behind me. Boise had a seat beside me, with Machete on my other side.

Once everyone was inside, the room seemed significantly smaller than the first time we were in here. The door closed, and Crow took the gavel, hitting it down and calling church to order.

"First things first." He nodded at me. "How's the president?"

I filled them in on everything—finding out who'd really shot Maxwell, my initial order, Kess' objection, and the latest call with Heckler.

Crow nodded. "The guy's gotta pay. He's the reason we had our scare here, the reason all your extra guys rode a full night and more to get here."

"Agreed, but let's wait and see how Max is tomorrow. He might have an opinion on how the father pays too."

There was rumbling in the room. Most sounded like they agreed.

"What's the latest on Estrada?"

I gave that update too, glancing to Boise.

"He's going east?" Crow asked.

Boise said, "The last contact I had, they were going through New Mexico."

"They might be heading to Texas. He's got guys working down there."

"I got a cousin out east," one of Crow's guys spoke up. "There's a rumor there about a relationship between the Russians and Estrada."

Crow's head whipped around. "Why the fuck haven't you mentioned that before?"

His guy's face was blank, and he shrugged. "Never thought it was pertinent. We don't operate there."

Crow cursed before sitting back. "We took a vote not long ago. A lot of fucking planning has gone into how that's going to be coordinated. You know about a collab he's got with the Russians, and you don't think it's pertinent?"

The guy blinked slowly.

Seemed to me like the guy was just dumb.

His head lowered. "Sorry, Boss. I didn't think. You know me." He knocked on his head. "Two marbles in here. That's about it."

Crow cursed again.

Rondell snorted. "You might want to lay off the weed, X. I'm thinking you need those last two marbles."

A few guys laughed.

X was laughing too.

Crow looked at me. "Sorry, Ghost. I apologize on behalf of my idiot cousin through marriage."

X grunted.

Crow leaned forward again. "Since it looks like we're in the clear from Estrada... I know you came here initially to help out, but since the national prez is in a bad way, what are you thinking to do?"

The guys all got quiet, waiting for me.

I looked around. My men were waiting for me to decide.

If Max was good, was in the clear tomorrow, he'd want me to stay and finish my assignment.

If he wasn't in the clear, I still needed to do what I came here to do, but I didn't know Crow's true loyalty. And dammit because that shouldn't be a question.

"Half my guys are going to head back tomorrow. I'd like them to rest, and then return to Max. The other half, who want to remain, will stay with me. We'll stick around for a bit, if that's still okay with your charter?"

Their president had asked us here, but I was feeling weird about Crow. That needed to be figured out. And it still made me uneasy how close Estrada had been without anyone knowing until he suddenly appeared.

There were a lot of stones still to be turned over before I could leave.

Crow gave nothing away. His face was a wall as he nodded, looking around. Most of the guys were nodding as well, and he reached for the gavel again. "You're welcome to stay as long as you'd like, but because I don't want my sister to take my balls, everyone's gotta head out of *here* tomorrow. She runs this place, and she's got a wedding party coming in after us."

The guys hooted in laughter as Crow banged the gavel down.

Church was done.

I WAS outside and headed back to the barn, Boise next to me, when Crow called my name.

I turned back, and he motioned to the side. "Wondering if we could have that talk?"

Right. I nodded to Boise, dropping my voice. "Connect with Stripes. I want to know if he heard anything last night. Tell the ones leaving tomorrow to rest today."

He gave a nod, heading off.

I followed Crow to the side of the house and down to where his sister kept her horses. They were penned up in a pretty looking white corral.

"It's real nice that your sister let us hole up here," I told him. "We owe her anything for this?"

He shook his head. "Not for the club. Her old man was a Red too. She knows how it is."

I gave him a sharp look. "Club's not hurting. We can pay. Seems the right thing to do."

He watched me a moment before he nodded. "If you'd like then. She'd sure appreciate it."

We walked a bit farther, going around the corral and toward another smaller barn. Behind it was a walking trail, heading out into the horse pasture.

"What did you want to talk about, Crow?"

He grimaced, his mouth tight before he let out a long breath. "Our president took the fall for a lot of guys in this charter. I know he called you in to help us sort it out. That's the real reason you're here, because we got some guys in here that I don't trust."

He had my full attention because was he talking about himself? Or others?

"But the reason I want to have this conversation in private is because I'm worried. Makes me nervous how close Estrada was, how quick he got to us. When we pull everything off, what about the afterwards?"

"What are you talking about?"

"Estrada's powerful. And if he's hooked up with the Russians, where does that leave us? We're the Red Demons, but I'm worried about when we do pull away from the cartel."

"You talking about safety?"

"I'm talking we might want to team up with another power entity. I wanted to broach the subject, get your opinion."

"Some might say we're getting out of bed with one devil, so why would we want to team up with another?"

"Because who I'm thinking about isn't like Estrada. They don't hang an entire family for passing a fucking phone. They're in the same area we are. Would make sense to team up with them, if they're open to it. But I'm thinking you're national VP, so it'd be up to you to make the approach."

"Why don't we cut the bullshit and you name who I think you're naming."

He eyed me, a trickle of sweat showing on his skin. But after a moment he nodded, coming to a decision. "I'm talking about the Canadians. They're here, mostly in the Midwest, but they'd be open to expanding west. They don't have Texas, and we do."

I gave him another sharp look. "You know that when we pull out, Texas is where we're going to get hit first."

He nodded. "I'm aware. But here too, I think. That's why I'm asking for this. The Canadians do their business in a way that's still a mystery to most. They got men, but they hit in coordinated attacks. Their leader is smart, calculating, but he doesn't kill ceaselessly. That gets me. I got family here. I don't want them killed, and having Estrada on our front door, I want some measures put in place."

Well, fuck me. The Canadians were who Max wanted me to approach. But I didn't trust Crow enough to reveal that, not yet.

"Let's handle the guys you don't trust first."

He gave me another measuring look. Then his eyes closed, and he nodded. "It's the smart move."

We needed to do the ugly business first, because we were talking about Red Demon traitors—one of the worst crimes there was. We'd need to handle those guys first, strip them of their patches and decide who to bury and who to burn.

I could see Crow's reluctance, but it had to be done.

He didn't want to name them. I didn't want to hear the names, but club first. Always.

So I asked the question, "Who don't you trust in your charter, Crow?"

30

KALI

My phone buzzed beside me.

Harper: Justin's here.

Oh boy. I already knew this. Harper knew I knew, so this wasn't that kind of a texting conversation.

This was a something-else text.

I sighed, settling in. I was waiting for Shane to do what he needed to do. Then, well, we'd be doing what we needed to do after that. Until then... My phone buzzed again.

Harper: AND HE'S IGNORING ME! Ignoring me, Kali. Ignoring me.

Harper: He came here for me. Now, he's ignoring me. WTF? Honestly what the effer loving feck?!

Harper: What's worse is that he and Aly are besties. He took my bestie. She's mine. Not his. AND her new man, because holy hannah banana, she and that Brandon are hot and heavy. How long have you been gone? Three nights? She's been with him every night. We're permanent fixtures at Manny's. I'm starting a book club with a crazy lady named Rebecca and another older guy named Gus. Sigh. He's legit nuts, but I like him. I don't think he can read. I'm pretty sure he thinks book

club is code for something else, and I do not want to ask him
what he thinks it's code for.

Me: If Justin is ignoring you, it's because you did or said
something to upset him.

Harper: Whose best friend are you?

Me: Yours. So is Aly. I reached out to him too.

Harper: I hate everyone. Even my mother didn't care.

Harper calling.

I hit accept, and he kept on as if there'd been no break after
his text.

"I called and informed her what was going down, and do you
know what she did?"

I tensed, waiting for the bomb to drop.

"She asked to talk to him!" His voice went up. "Not to chew
him out, or I don't know—warn him not to hurt her baby. Nope.
She wanted to see how he was doing since the breakup. I can't
believe it. My own mother. And then when he gave the phone
back, she warned *me* not to hurt *him!*"

Yep. My guess was confirmed. "Harper."

He sniffled. "What?"

"Did Justin give you an ultimatum? Marry him or break up
with him?"

He was quiet for a moment. "No."

"Do you miss him?"

"Yes..."

"You're scared of getting married. I think that's reasonable,
considering your parents' crazy life, but I'm pretty sure Justin will
understand. Have you talked since that night?"

"No. He proposed, and I left."

Holy—I bolted upright in bed. "What?"

"He got down on one knee, brought the ring out, and I left.
My own house. I left my own house."

"Was he there when you came back?"

"No."

I frowned, something in the way he said that... "How long were you gone?"

"Three days."

"Oh my God, Harper! Of course he was gone when you came back. That's—that's humiliating."

"My best friend." His voice was shrill again. "Mine. Not his—"

I heaved another breath, and he heard this one, quieting.

"I'm being irrational, aren't I?"

"A bit."

I waited, knowing Harper. We'd gone through this since high school. We might age, we might wise up, we could grow internal and external scars, but some things never changed—our hearts. Harper was petrified, and only he could do what he needed to do.

"When are you coming back, Kali? I could do with a Kali cuddle."

"I'm not sure. I'm waiting to find out myself."

"I miss you. It's fun being out here with Aly, but we did come to be with you, you know."

"I know." I lay back down, settling into the pillow once again. "I don't think my sister is coming back with us."

"Are *you* coming back with us?"

I couldn't answer that either. "What are you going to do about Justin?" I asked instead.

"Agh! Do not think I don't know what you're pulling. What's going on with you and Mr. Hottie Biker Badass Shane King?"

"I don't know either." That was the truth. We hadn't had sex yet. "So Aly and that Brandon guy, huh?"

Harper growled. "I totally know you're deflecting again, but I'm going to let this one slide. I could do with some gossip distraction myself. And yes! She's had three one-night stands with him. Keeps saying each night is the last night, until the next evening when we're at Manny's and she's waiting for him to close up. That guy is a workhorse. And I met the sister. I have a crush on her. It's official. I'm going to start my own Instagram page and fill it with pictures of her and her man, who is delicious looking. The both of them? Sex on wheels. *Hot* sex on wheels."

"Aly likes the sister?"

He made a noncommittal sound. "You know Aly. She's all bubbly and nice, but internally she's lying to herself about what she's doing with Brandon."

I frowned. That sounded more serious than I thought. I sat up again slowly. "Wait. What?"

"She's in love."

"It's been three nights."

"Yeah, and you know Aly. We know Aly. She's in love."

"What?!"

"She blushes when he says her name. She gets butterflies before she calls him—or texts him even. She's got the look. Our girl's done fell in love, Kalista."

I shot to my feet, now standing on the bed. "*What?!*"

Panic seized my chest.

Rising.

Squeezing.

The pressure filled my chest, rising to my throat.

The bedroom door opened, and Shane appeared, his face thunderous. "*What?!*"

I dropped the phone, not thinking. "My best friend fell in love for the second time in her life, and I WASN'T THERE TO WATCH IT!" I launched myself at him, knowing he'd catch me. My legs went around his waist, and I peered down at him, glaring. "You kept me here while my best friend fell in love! How dare you!"

Shane caught me easily and shook his head, probably at how insane I was being.

I didn't care. I kept glaring, seething. "My best friend, Shane!"

The thunderous look was gone, and he took a step, dropping me on the bed. My ass hit the phone. I heard Harper squawking under me, but I was so beyond caring.

I felt myself hyperventilating. I had missed this time. I hadn't checked the guy out. I shoved back up to my feet, shaking my hands in the air. "The last time she fell in love, Three-Inch Dick dumped her for a size-two girl. Aly's a size ten. That's it. A ten. He specifically told her he was leaving her for someone who looked like a trophy on his arm. Aly loves *hard*. She's not loved anyone since. Now I find out she's in love with someone, and I wasn't there to check him out—cyberstalk him, interrogate his family members, his friends, look for him on dating sites, see what fetishes he might have. I wasn't able to do any of that because I was here because of you and *oomph*—"

He'd moved in, wrapped his arms around my waist, and put me over his shoulder.

"Shane!"

He bent, then handed something to me. "Your phone, babe."

"Babe?!" I could hear Harper again. "He calls you babe?!"

Oh Jesus. I took the phone, putting it to my ear in a very uncomfortable way. "Hey."

"Hey? Hey yourself!" Harper was all chirpy now. "He calls you *babe*?!"

I cringed, some of my anger melting, because yeah, he called me babe. "Um, I think I need to call you back."

"You do that! You definitely do that. Take your time. Babe. Oh my gawd. *Babe*. I have to call Aly right now." He hung up on me this time.

We weren't too far from the bed, so I tossed the phone as Shane moved out through the apartment and into the bathroom. He placed me on the counter, stepping away to turn the shower on.

Say what?

We'd not had sex where his dick was inside my vagina, but he wanted to shower together?

I was putting my foot down. Consider it down. My foot. Now.

Then he turned to me, and his eyes got all hooded. Gulp.

There went my will, literally melting out of me. He reached back to take his shirt off, and I gulped again because holy goodness, his chest was something else. He dropped the shirt coming toward me, and his hands went to his jeans.

I swallowed, forcing my gaze upward and away from those very magical fingers. "What?" I winced. My voice was seriously high-pitched. I lowered it, coughing. "What are you doing?"

"You were on your phone with the guy friend?" His eyes still smoldered.

I looked away.

He came closer, his hands on my knees, sliding up my legs.

"Yes." My voice broke. I would've been embarrassed if I wasn't so focused on the way his hands were sliding up my legs, right to where I wanted his dick to tunnel inside of me, but it still hadn't. "What about him?"

"Getting my bearings here." He tipped my chin up to meet his gaze and moved in even closer. I could feel his jeans rubbing against mine. "And your other best friend, the girl, has fallen in love with someone?"

"Mmm-hmmm." No way was I telling him it was a guy adamantly against his motorcycle club. Forget my sister. She'd made her bed, and to be honest, I wasn't sure if she wasn't better off here than at home. I liked Machete. Red Demon or not, I had a good feeling about him. But forget her. My new goal was getting back to Fallen Crest and checking in on this guy Aly was falling in love with.

"And you weren't there?" Shane asked.

I nodded, starting to feel dumb. Slightly.

"Harper said she's in love, and he's only said that once," I tried to explain.

"About her ex?"

I frowned. "How do you know about her ex?"

Shane moved in closer, now standing between my legs. His eyes softened. "Your brother and I talked more than you think."

"Connor mentioned Aly's ex?"

"Gloves kept abreast of everything in your life. He shared most of it, or I thought he did. He didn't share that you were back in town. Did he know?"

I nodded. "Yeah. He knew."

Shane made a noncommittal sound. "Looks like he kept that to himself then, but it is what it is. To handle the present issue, I'm taking it you want to get to your friends?"

His fingers kneaded my legs, his thumbs rubbing along the inside of them, but he wasn't moving farther up.

Why hadn't we had sex?

I wanted it. I'd told him in a very direct way, and nothing. He'd done everything else. But no dick insertion.

What did that mean?

I could feel him, even now. His hardness. It was right in front of me. He studied me, and I studied his dick.

"Why haven't we had sex?"

The instant the words were out, I regretted them.

His hands lifted, and he stepped back.

Instant cold washed over me, like a bucket of water splashed in my face.

That was dumb.

I shouldn't have asked... Wait. No. That's a legit question.

I tipped my head up and shoved aside all my stupid insecurities. I wasn't twenty anymore. "We've done everything else. I told you last night I wanted to fuck, but so far..." I reached for his waistband, drawing him to me. "This guy hasn't been inside of me yet."

His eyes went black, suddenly serious.

Widening my legs, I moved him until he fit right there. A flick of a few buttons, and he could've surged inside.

I waited.

I would wait him out.

Dark lust shone from his eyes.

I ached for him. I'd never, ever felt this before.

"I asked you a question, Shane. I want an answer."

So direct. So assertive. Who was this new Kali? I mean, I was usually assertive, but not about sex, not when I felt like the vulnerable one.

He made a growling sound as his hand came up, gripping the back of my neck. He took hold of my hair and slowly moved fully against me.

I closed my eyes, just briefly, at the touch, the connection.

He felt so good there. Then again, that's where all this had started—grinding against a motel wall.

"You want to know why my dick hasn't been inside of your pussy?"

I panted as he moved against me, rubbing.

"Yeah." I stared right up at him. "I do."

I wasn't scared of him. Not anymore. I let him see that. In this area, I'd never be scared again. No man was going to take that power from me.

He bent down, his eyes glittering, his hand holding tight to my hair, keeping me frozen in place. But I wanted it. I liked it.

As he got even closer, his mouth almost to mine, I shifted and wrapped my legs around his waist, yanking him even closer.

His mouth dropped to mine from the motion, and while he wasn't expecting it, I was. I nipped at his lips, but his mouth widened and took over, suddenly very commanding. His hands cupped my face, tilting me back for him, so he could plunder my mouth.

His tongue claimed me. Taking over.

Then he picked me up all over again and turned, walking us into the shower. Water rained down over us as he pressed me into the wall.

He massaged my ass, both cheeks, as he kept kissing me.

The kisses. I could die from just the kisses.

He removed my clothes, dropping things one by one on the

shower floor until we were both naked, writhing against each other.

He grinded into me, rotating, moving, repeating.

I was back to panting, but he wasn't letting go of my mouth, not once, not even as his hand swept between my legs. Then his cock was there, paused at my entrance.

I groaned, my head falling back.

Finally, he lifted his mouth only enough to growl, "My dick's not been in you because I've been waiting. I want all of you. Not just your body or your mind. I want *all* of you."

And as he said those words, he thrust inside. He went deep, his hand holding the back of my neck. "I know I don't have all of you—not yet. But you want this? You're getting it."

He slid out, and then thrust in again. He went hard, almost aggressive, punishing.

I grasped his shoulders. I wanted this.

Yesss.

I gasped, as he moved again, I felt like I was being branded from the inside out.

I was his.

He had commanded it.

His thrusts were hard, rough. They weren't smooth, but this wasn't smooth between us.

It was raw. Desperate.

And so fucking needed.

My hips moved with him, and he kept my head anchored in his hand, but the rest of my body slammed into the wall. Over and over again.

He continued to kiss me, his tongue now in rhythm with his dick.

My fingers sank into his skin, holding on. We were frenzied. Both of us together.

Pleasure soared through me, rising, building...

He kept moving inside of me. In and out.

I dropped one of my hands to his hip, the other to the shower wall, and I began riding him, pushing up and out on my own. We moved into and against each other. Now that I was holding myself in place, his hand moved to my clit and began rubbing there slowly, almost tenderly—in total opposition to the way he moved inside of me.

He looked into my eyes, and I knew he could see inside of me, but I could see inside of him.

He needed this as much as I had, maybe more. No. Definitely more. Need flared bright in his gaze, and my emotions pressed up and threatened to burst out of my chest.

I was coming, but God, no. I didn't want to. Not yet. I wanted to wait, to savor this.

He saw me fighting it back and shook his head before he grabbed both of my hips. He held me there, pausing before he slid out, almost all the way, but then he repositioned me. He held me higher up, moving in and I couldn't do anything except wrap my arms around his neck, my legs closing around his back, my ankles hooking over each other.

I tucked my head as we bear hugged, and he began pounding up and into me, almost pistoning.

It sent me over the edge, and I shattered in his arms, my whole body seizing on my climax.

He kept moving, losing some of his intensity as he waited for me to come down, for my body to calm after the waves had crashed through me. Once I did, he pulled out and turned me in midair before pressing me against the shower wall. His hands found mine, his fingers lacing with mine as his cock slid back up inside of me.

He fucked me from behind, up and up and up until I starting to feel the tingling all over again, and I fell back into him. My head rested against his shoulder. He still thrust up into me, and he moved our joined hands between my legs, touching me there with my own fingers. We worked me to the edge together, and he paused until I cried out all over again. Then I felt him surge up, one last time, grinding and rotating until he came inside of me.

I was replete, boneless.

He eased out of me, pressing a soft kiss to my shoulder, and his hand moved up to circle my breast. I thought he'd say something, but he didn't. He only held me. We were both shaking a little. After a few moments, he carried me out of the shower, grabbing some towels on the way.

Back in the bedroom, he tossed one down before settling me on it.

I eased back, shaken by what had just happened.

It'd been violent at moments, almost a domination sort of sex, but I was shaken because it had felt right for me. With him. Only him, though.

He stood, staring at me.

I stared right back.

There were no words. No feelings. He'd wrung every single one of them out of me.

But I knew I could sign up for a lifetime of sex like that.

That scared me.

31

SHANE

I was just dressed when there was a knock at the door. It was Boise, and I went and closed the bedroom door. Kali and I had not talked after whatever the fuck that had been, and she was getting dressed too.

I went back, opening the main door.

Boise stepped inside, his gaze going to the bedroom door, but he didn't comment. He moved to the kitchen table where I had my weapons out. I began putting them back on, one after another. My cut was last.

"Crow?" he asked.

I shook my head. I couldn't talk about that with Kali able to hear.

It wasn't that I didn't trust her. She was a steel trap, the strongest there was. But this was club business. I didn't want her in the position of hearing anything. It was also against policy.

He nodded. "You still looking to head to Frisco tomorrow?"

The door opened and Kali came out, but she paused, seeing Boise. She wore shorts and a tank top, and her hair was loose. She pulled her fingers through the ends. Avoiding my gaze, she gave Boise a small smile and slipped into the bathroom. I heard the shower turn back on a second later.

"Do I ask what that was about?" Boise glanced at the closed bathroom door.

I grunted. "I don't even know what that was about." I nodded in her direction. "Ask around. She wants to get to Fallen Crest."

"Fallen Crest? What are we doing there?"

"Nothing, but she's got friends there, and she wants to meet up with them."

Boise, not one to indicate emotion, was this time showing his surprise. His eyebrows went up. "We're not supposed to be in Fallen Crest."

He was referring to a past agreement we'd come to with people who were just that—in the past. He was wrong about part of it. "It's Roussou we're not supposed to go through. Fallen Crest was never a part of that agreement."

"Still. There's cops there. Rich folk."

I nodded, giving the bathroom door a hard look. "She wants to go, and I'm not letting her go in alone. Not yet."

He glanced back too. "So what? You're the national VP. No way you're going in alone."

This meant some concessions. "No cuts? A small group of us?"

He gave me a long, hard look. Then swore. "Stripes is out."

I nodded. He had history with both towns. "Grab Corvette. Roadie."

"Me."

We shared a grin. "No other person at my side."

"Okay then. What do you want me to tell the others?"

"The truth. I got to give some attention to my woman, and she wants to go to Fallen Crest. We'll take her, go from there, and meet the rest when they're rested?"

His eyes narrowed. "No one's going to want to be here without you."

Yeah. I got that.

The shower cut off inside.

I had to make a decision.

I reached for my cut. "Tell them to suit up. We'll head to The Bonfire and stay there. It's not that far from Fallen Crest. That's something."

Boise gave a nod, then took off.

I finished getting my stuff together—not that I ever had much with me. A bag. That's about it. Kali was still in the bathroom, so I went and put her stuff together too. Her phone was out. I left that alone, leaving her bag next to it. I took mine with me, heading out.

Stripes appeared once I had closed the door, which wasn't surprising. The guy was everywhere. That's why I'd put him on Crow.

He glanced around. "Boise said we're heading out?"

"If you want. I'm going to Fallen Crest. The rest can head to The Bonfire."

He nodded, his hands going into his pockets. He did this when he had something he wanted to say. "You got something to say?"

His head lifted, but went right back down. "I got history there."

"I'm aware."

"Boise said you're taking Core and Road."

"I'm aware of that too."

We cut across the front driveway, going to my bike. Crow was waiting for me on the front porch of the main house. He had a whole bunch of his men with him, and his eyes were tracking us. I recognized the look on his face too. He had something to say as well.

"I'm thinking there might be a line of people waiting to converse with me," I told Stripes. "Say your piece. What's up?"

He took a breath, then expelled it. "I want to go with you."

"No."

"Ghost."

"No." I stopped, facing him. "We're going in without our cuts. It's not something I feel comfortable with, but I also don't feel comfortable about some other things. You're not coming. Cops will spot you, recognize you, and you know they'll want payback. Or some of them will."

He cursed, turning away.

"What else do you have to say before I go over there and Frisco's VP finds something to talk to me about?"

Stripes shot me a grin, his hands still in his pockets. "I got nothing then. Wanted to put my pitch in to go with you. I know Fallen Crest, know where all the dirty assholes are."

"I'm aware of your history, but my woman's friends are putting roots down in a place called Manny's."

His head jerked back, his whole body stilling.

Yeah. That was the reaction I knew he'd have. He had serious history with a few people who were close to that place's owners.

He cursed. "I didn't think it would get that close."

"It's that close."

He drew in a breath. "Yeah. Okay. Maybe I'll stick it out here a bit, do more of what you asked me to do before heading back."

"Ask a brother to go with you. One of ours."

He nodded, already starting to walk away. "Will do." His eyes went past my shoulder, and he gave me a small heads up. I didn't need the warning. I heard the gravel and knew who was coming my way.

As I turned around, Crow was alone. His men were still on the front porch, all watching their VP approach me.

He gave me a chin-lift. "Heard a rumor you're heading out."

I grunted. "Boise's fast."

He laughed. "What are your plans concerning what I talked to you about?"

Right. All the brothers he didn't trust, and he'd given me good reason not to trust them as well. I gave him a hard look. "What you said was serious. It's not against the rules to have side jobs, side hustles. You know that, but Estrada's moving southeast, right toward where our national prez is currently still laid up. Trust and believe that I'm going to take what you're proposing into strong consideration, but I need to handle a couple things before making that move. You hear me?"

What we weren't saying had to do with digging six feet down for a few guys, guys we called brothers, and finally doing what I came here to do. But before all that, I needed to tend to Kali.

Crow gave a small nod, easing up. "I hear you." He scanned the front yard, seeing some of the other guys packing up their bikes, and some that weren't. "Plans for your men?"

I relayed the plans I'd hashed out with Boise and Stripes just now.

As I spoke, Machete crossed the yard, coming from the barn. Claudia came behind him, her hands stuck in her back pockets. As he angled toward me, she shifted to the house, moving past the guys on the porch. She almost had a bounce to her step, but she wasn't looking my way.

I doubted Kali's sister would look my way ever again, not unless her life was on the line. Just my guess.

"I'll keep in touch with you?" Crow asked.

I nodded his way as he went toward the house, and Machete came over.

He glanced in Crow's direction. "That one's got a different look to him."

I frowned. "What do you mean?"

Machete watched as Crow conversed with some of his men before they moved off the porch, going for one of the other barns.

He shook his head. "Just got a feeling. The guy's off."

I had that feeling too. "Got nothing to go on with that, though."

"No, but we got computer people. They can be steered to look a certain way." He gave me a look.

Yeah. Maybe he was right. I'd have to make that call as soon as I could.

"You came over for a reason. What's up?" I asked him.

"Just seeing how the sister is?" He glanced at the house. "Claude's a little worried, thinks Kali's out of her depth, considering her recent divorce."

Fuck's sake. I gave him a long look, a very hard look too. "It's cool you and the missus are clicking, but you know her. This is her wading in, and you know I won't be receptive."

He grinned, a dry chuckle coming out of him. "I said as much, but she wouldn't stop yapping until I told her I'd say something. For what it's worth, I think part of her wants to mess with your relationship and the other part of her *is* concerned. The ex did a trip on the sister."

I stifled a sigh because I knew all this too. "Tell your woman that if she wades into mine, I'm wading into hers."

His eyes narrowed. "That a threat?"

"No, but she'll sure as shit take it as one. The way she thinks, she won't be able to get that out of her mind. Might give me and Kali some peace for a few days, at least."

He grinned, but Machete had ceased to exist for me.

Kali was coming my way, her bag in hand. She trudged across the gravel, her shoulders bent forward and one of her hands in her front pocket. *Goddamn.* Her long legs showed through jeans that were ripped and torn. I wasn't one for trends, but I thanked all fashionable people out there for these good-ass views of those long legs of hers.

She had a tank top on, a black bra showing underneath it, and my dick was hard all over again.

This woman.

She looked up, and her eyes warmed at finding me watching her.

Fuck. One look from her like that, and I'd kill anyone she asked.

She slowed, just out of my reach, and drew upright, shifting back on her feet. "Saw my bag. Saw your stuff was gone. Made an educated guess."

I reached forward, taking her bag from her and making damn sure my hand grazed her fingers and arm in the process. Her eyes got all dark at the touch, and she swayed toward me. I was pretty sure she didn't know she was doing that either. Then she sucked in a breath and jerked back.

She rolled her eyes. "I turn into a mindless, sex-starved woman with you." She laughed at herself, her mouth curving up.

That made me want to swoop in and kiss that smile until it was mine. I refrained. "Me and a few of the guys are going to take you to Fallen Crest."

Her eyes snapped to mine, widening. "Really?"

"You gotta know, the club has some history in these parts, but I've no mind to let you walk in there by yourself. I'm coming with you, and we won't be wearing our cuts. I'm hoping that'll make things a little smoother." I gave her a small nod. "Doing that for you."

Us taking off our cuts, or hiding our cuts, meant something. Our cuts were our most sacred possessions.

Her mouth formed a small O.

She got it. "Thank you."

I leaned in, touching my mouth to hers. A sweet, lingering kiss. She tasted like fresh lemonade on a hot day, making me want to curl my toes up and pretend I was a kid again with no worries, not knowing the shadows in the world. She was like that to me.

I lifted my mouth, just a bit, and said, "Give your friends a call, see where they are? We'll hook up with them tonight."

She nodded, her mouth moving against mine with the

motion. Then she lifted up on her toes, grabbed the back of my neck, and pressed her mouth, hot and hard, to mine.

Well then. Looked like I'd just made an impression.

I wanted to make more of them.

32

KALI

We started out riding with most of Shane's club, but then we turned south for Fallen Crest as they continued somewhere else.

I didn't ask where. I didn't want to know, but riding behind Shane, feeling nothing between us and the wind and nature, I knew the exhilaration they felt. I understood why people dedicated part of their lives to being just on their bike.

It was addicting, thrilling, and dangerous.

We rode in, keeping to the outskirts of Fallen Crest and pulling in behind an auto repair shop. An older guy—lean, weathered skin, bald—came out and waved us through to the back. Shane led the way, and we entered a backyard with a small house. There were also patches of dirt and gravel, sandwiched between abandoned vehicles, a few bikes, and grass that didn't look like it'd been cut in a decade. A propane tank sat on the far side of the house, which looked more like three motel rooms put together with a cement sidewalk in front of the doors.

Shane drove right up to the house and parked.

The older guy came over, his hand in the air. Shane met it, and they pulled each other in for a backslapping hug.

"Ghost. It's good to see you." The guy's gaze skimmed over me, but didn't linger. He turned to the others as they parked next to us. "Good to see you, Corvette. Roadie." There was a twinkle in his eye. "I'll make note to warn Tracey, though maybe I should warn you. My girl's visiting from West Virginia, and she's got a man now. Hands off."

Roadie came around the back end of his bike, frowning at the older guy.

I'd finally put two and two together and realized who Roadie was minutes before we took off from the barn. Roadie and Corvette were the bikers fighting in the grocery store that first day. He gave me a sheepish look while Corvette's eyes turned hard.

Corvette approached from the other side, pulling off his road gloves. "Nah. No warning needed. This one's fucked up so much with the ladies, he's on dick lockdown."

The older guy's head tilted. "That right?"

Shane grunted, grabbing my bag and his. "That's almost too bad to hear about Tracey. She would've eaten him up and spit him out. Maybe he would've learned a lesson."

The guy's smile was blinding, and took me back a little. He laughed. "Maybe, but my girl's in love. He's a big fella too."

"He's here with her?" Corvette asked.

He shook his head. "She came to help with her aunt for a bit. We made the decision to put Helen in a care unit."

All the guys sombered.

"We're sorry to hear that, Granddad," Shane said. "Helen's a good woman. Spitfire."

Granddad blinked a bit, before he coughed and turned away. "Yeah. You know how it is. Those diseases take the brain and all, but she's still a spitfire. Got a call just this morning that she'd locked two nurse assistants in her room while she beat an escape."

Corvette grinned.

Roadie chuckled.

"Tracey went in to help them out," Granddad continued. "Found Helen on the road, trying to hitchhike. I gotta get there myself. Helen's throwing a fit, and she's still able-bodied, so who knows what kind of damage she might do in the meantime." He gave another cough and nodded to the house behind us. "Rooms are yours as long as you need 'em. When I get things cleared up, I'll give Maxwell a call. Miss the old fella."

Shane nodded. "Thanks, Granddad."

Corvette and Roadie stayed silent, letting Shane speak for them.

Granddad held up a hand, heading inside.

I didn't know the history or who this guy was, but it was obvious all three men were concerned. No one spoke, not at first, but then Corvette smacked the back of Roadie's head.

"Ow!" He twisted around, rubbing at the back of his head and scowling. "What was that for?"

Corvette shook his head, eyes still where Granddad had gone. "You're just an idiot. You need reminding every now and then with a smack. Thinking I'm going to take that on as my job." He bent, grabbed his bag, and headed to the back house. "I'll be in my room, thinking of more ways to add to my new role with the club."

Roadie continued rubbing the back of his head, glaring at Corvette. "What a douche."

"Heard that!" Corvette pumped his fist in the air before going through the door to the room on the right, the screen slamming behind him.

"You were supposed to!" Roadie shouted. "What's the plan, Boss?"

Shane touched my hip. "Go to your room, shower, and change. We won't be wearing cuts tonight."

Roadie frowned, but headed to the left door.

Shane had our bags and took my helmet, stowing it away before we went into the middle room.

It *was* like a motel, except our room opened to a hallway, and I could hear the guys moving around in their rooms from there. Shane came up behind me, touching my back and shutting the door. "Can't see it from the outside, but there's a back section that extends. Living room, kitchen, and behind that there's a whole bonfire eating area outside."

He went to the front, shutting that door too, and clicked on a fan.

I almost melted because the fan was super loud, which I liked —reminded me of riding and also, privacy.

Shane put the bags on the bed.

He glanced over his shoulder. "You okay?"

I closed my eyes, suddenly exhausted. "Yeah."

He put the bags aside and reached for me, drawing me to his lap.

I climbed on, curling up, and he angled his head back to see me better. "What's in your head?" His frown deepened. "You okay to see your friends?"

I nodded. I'd texted Harper and Aly before leaving, and pulling out my phone, I saw they'd responded.

Aly: YOU'RE COMING BACK?! SCORE. HELL YEAH. TOUCHDOWN.

Harper: It's GOOOOOAAAAL, not touchdown. Kali, don't mind Aly, otherwise formerly known as our Best Friend. She watched a hockey game with her new man and also Justin and now they're trying to teach her the terms.

Aly: Formerly known? Wtf? Don't be butthurt because you're choosing not to acknowledge the man of your life, who TRAVELED ALL THE WAY TO CALIFORNIA FOR YOU! That's on you. He's here. Justin is amazing and you're just jealous because we're enjoying him. Yolo, Harp. YO-LO

Oh boy.

Me: We're here. Where are you guys?

I wasn't expecting an immediate response so I tossed my phone on the bed, but it started ringing.

Aly calling.

I showed Shane the screen and started to climb off his lap. He held me in place.

Oh, okay. I hit accept and settled back, yawning. "Hehhhlo?"

"What kind of greeting was that? You must be tired, huh?"

Warmth rushed through me. It was good to hear her voice. I smiled. "Hi, Aly."

"Hey yourself." I heard her own smile through the phone. "Girl, have we missed you. I know Harp's been on the phone with you, and you're getting reports on what we're doing, but how are you? How's your sister? What's going on with you and Shane? The husband of Manny's owner is a bounty hunter. I don't think it would take much to get him to do some pro bono work and find you." She paused. "Kidding."

She wasn't.

We both laughed, but Shane tensed at the mention of the husband.

I frowned. "Um, well..."

Shane looked back at me, and whatever he'd been thinking, he'd moved on. The tension left him, and he gave me a soft smile, his eyes warming.

I reached up, touching the side of his face before another yawn left me. I wasn't able to stifle this one.

"Oh, man. I can hear how tired you are," Aly said. "Why don't you take a nap? Let me know where you are and we can swing by? Maybe we should do a meal in? Netflix and chill, that sort of thing?"

Shane shook his head, just slightly.

"Um..." I searched his eyes and made a decision. "Can I call you back in a second? I want to get on the same page with Shane real quick."

"Okeley-dokely."

We hung up. "I know they can't come here." Shane looked ready to talk, but I kept going. "I'm also guessing you don't want them to know about this place."

He settled down to hear me out.

"But I know not wearing your cuts is a big deal, so what about if I went there and hung in their room for the night? They're at the hotel at the country club, totally safe. You guys can go have a beer or something?"

His eyes had a soft, but knowing slant to them. "First." He reached up, taking the phone from me and putting it on the bedside table. "That's considerate of you, thinking about us and knowing what it means for us to go without our cuts. I really do appreciate it, but it's unnecessary. Second..." He kept a hold of me and stood.

I gasped, but Shane had me firmly in his arms.

He turned and lowered me to the bed, stretching out next to me. He propped his head on his hand to look down at me. "No place is safe from the people we were initially hiding from. No country club, nowhere, and we're not operating as if they're a risk anymore. They've moved on. They're in a whole other state by now. But you and I are new. I'm possessive. Not in a bad way, but I caught feelings and I don't want to lose you so soon. Because of that, you're going to have to indulge me. There's no place you can go that I won't worry about you. You got me?"

I cocked my head, raising an eyebrow. "How many times have you done this before? Catching feelings for a woman where you're possessive of her?"

That wasn't jealousy stirring inside of me. Nope.

I was fully lying to myself.

His eyes smoldered, and a faint grin showed. "None before you."

None.

Before you.

Oh... *oh man!*

Warmth sizzled inside of me.

He watched me, waiting until I let out a small gasp of air.

"You serious?"

He nodded. "You're the only one, Kalista."

"You're telling me you have feelings for me?"

He smirked. "I think that's a given, based on what I just said and how I've been acting. You know that."

I swallowed, feeling a lump there. My voice dropped low. "I wasn't aware that this wasn't a usual occurrence for you."

I felt like a schoolgirl here.

"I've laid claim to you," Shane said. "In our world, that means a lot. But I meant what I said this morning." His eyes looked through me, slipping right through any walls I had. "Your heart— I'm aware you hold it precious. But babe, it means something to me what we did this morning. What we've been doing the last few days."

Oh.

Wow.

That wall he referred to? It wasn't as thick as it used to be, but I didn't know if I dared share that. Not yet. It'd be giving too much away.

"What are you thinking?" he asked.

He was still studying me, seeming to know my insides better than I did.

I squirmed in bed, stretching and letting out another yawn. "I'm thinking I like you." My voice dropped to a whisper. "Maybe a whole lot."

He gave me a searing stare. "Same, Kali. Same."

My phone rang, and he glanced at it. "It's your friend again, but what I was starting to say is that no matter where you go tonight, we go too. You want to grab a pizza and movie in their hotel room? Fine with us, but we'll be close by. Parking lot. I might stick Roadie to hang out in the end of your hallway, but hotel or grabbing a beer at Manny's, either works for us. You do what you want. These are your friends, your time to catch up. Sounds like a lot of drama needs to be shared, and I get that."

The phone kept ringing.

We ignored it.

"The owner's husband. Is that history I need to know about?"

He shook his head. "Nope. In the past. We picked guys who wouldn't be recognized, if that's your worry. He don't know me. I don't know him. That's just club business, and with our club, that's going to happen in a whole lot of places. It has nothing to do with you, or even me, really."

That didn't quite make sense, but I was getting how the club was its own entity.

The phone stopped ringing.

A beat later, it started again.

Shane waited for me.

I gave him a nod, and he reached over giving me the phone.

I hit accept. "Hey, I'll meet you at Manny's. I want to meet this man of yours in a more official capacity."

I HIT call on my phone.

"Daughter! It's been forever. Felt like a year. You alive? Married? Pregnant? You better not be any of those, by the way. Not without your pop's blessing. So. Tell the haps. What's going on out in Cal-i-for-nia?"

"Aly's got a man."

"Aly's got a whattie?"

"A man."

"His name isn't JustinBanana, is it?"

"His name is Brandon."

"Whooee. A Brandon. I don't think I've ever met a Brandon. Stevie's here. Hold on.... STEVIE!"

From his end, "WHAT?!"

"YOU EVER MET A BRANDON IN YOUR LIFE?"

"WHO?"

"BRAN-DON. BRANDON. LIKE LONDON, BUT WITH A BRA INSTEAD. LIKE THE FEMALES WEAR."

Silence. Then, "Nah. I've never met a Brandon. Met a Caden one time. It was the most hipster name I'd ever met in my life. I thought he was going to challenge me to a smoke-off, on the account that I like my cigarettes and he was smoking one too, but not what I was smoking. You get my drift?" He dissolved into laughter. "Oh, and he was a white boy too. I kinda wished I'd hung out with him more. He seemed real cool."

My dad coughed into the phone. "Nope. He never met a Brandon either."

33

KALI

We were leaving the room when another Harley pulled into the lot, coming to park on the end by Corvette's bike. It was the guy who'd come to our room back at the barn, and as he got off his bike and came over to greet Shane, I noticed that they were close.

I hadn't paid much attention back at the apartment. I went into the bathroom to try to do some damage control on my hair. But now was different. *So* different.

First off, this guy was gorgeous. Beautiful long, dark hair that hung free, past his shoulders. High forehead and cheekbones that were kinda set low, but rounded out his face. His jawline was strong, prominent, and those eyes were dark, intense. He was tall, maybe an inch shorter than Shane, and wiry.

He went straight to Shane and the two hugged. Not a manly hug, just a full-on hug.

The guy was smiling when he stepped back, and that transformed his face, making him a little blinding to look at.

Corvette was good-looking in a rough and gruff manner. Roadie had a pretty boy feel to him, mixed with a flirty and sly vibe, but this guy was almost on Shane's level. *Almost.*

He stepped back, taking me in, and his eyes warmed. "Your woman is checking me out, Ghost."

Shane snorted and stepped over, sweeping an arm around my waist. He pulled me to his side. "Kali, this is Boise."

"Hi." I felt shy. *Gah.* This was not me. Then again, this whole experience wasn't me either.

He stepped toward me, his hand out. He watched me intently as we shook hands. "Kali. It's a pleasure to meet you." He gave Shane a nod. "This one here hasn't said a word about you, makes me even more intrigued."

Yeah. My tongue was tied. *No* clue what was going on with me.

"Guys are good?" Shane asked over my head.

Boise straightened, his face growing serious. "All settled in. We've got the night."

"Good." Shane's hand spread out over the small of my back as he stepped away. "Time to go then." He nodded at Boise. "Cut off for the night."

Boise went into our room, and a moment later came back out cut-less and wearing a black long sleeve Henley shirt. It hugged his frame.

Oh boy. I was rolling with the definitions of bad boy hotness. If Aly hadn't beaued up with this new guy, she would've gone crazy. Same for Harper. They knew Shane from high school, but as far as I knew, they hadn't seen him since, or any of these guys.

Butterflies fluttered in my stomach, nerves, as I got behind Shane, wrapped my arms around him, and hugged him the whole ride to Manny's. The fluttering only intensified as we parked at the end of the lot and walked toward the building. It was busy. There was a different bouncer at the side door this time, and he didn't give the guys a second look.

He was the only one, though.

The rest of the people, those standing in the parking lot and hanging out on the outside decks, were all about watching our group. The guys. Most were fixated on Shane, but the rest of the guys got their fair share of looks.

I understood. I had tuned into them myself. It was in the way they walked, the way they held themselves. Their jeans were well-worn. All the guys had on long sleeves—maybe to hide their tattoos? It was all classic. Nothing these guys wore were trendy. They were the real deal.

I knew they were carrying, but I didn't know where. I didn't want to know where. But it was clear these guys weren't to be messed with. They were dangerous, like camouflaged wolves coming in from a recent hunt.

I sent a text.

Me: Here. Are you guys?

Aly: Yes! We're in the back bar section. Is Shane with you?

The bouncer stepped aside, letting us in, and I paused, tilting my head up to Shane.

He bent down.

"They're in the back bar section."

He nodded, his hand still on my back.

Boise had been leading the way, but he paused, looking back.

Shane gestured the direction we needed to go, and Boise continued forward.

Manny's was packed inside too, but not as bad as the other day. Today, at least there was space to breathe. I looked over the bar and spotted the guy from the last time I was here. I guessed that was Brandon. He was taking care of a customer, but as if feeling my eyes, he looked up and spotted me.

Recognition flared, and his head jerked up, but then his eyes narrowed as he took in Shane behind me. His mouth pressed into a firm line, but he didn't do anything, just watched us move down the hallway past the bathrooms. Right before we moved out of his eyesight, he reached to pour a beer.

If anyone was going to raise an alarm, it would be him, so we'd have to see what happened.

I took a deep breath.

Aly and Harper.

I was walking into some drama, and they were going to see Shane.

I wasn't ready.

But we'd entered the back section, and it was happening anyway.

It was go time.

"KALISTA CALLIOPE MICHAELS!" I heard a beat later.

That was Harper, and he rushed toward me as Aly let loose with a full squeal.

My besties were coming.

I braced myself, and their bodies hit mine a second later.

"Oh my God." Aly was behind me, her voice muffled into my neck. I could feel her boobs pressing into me. "I have missed you!"

Harper's head was buried into my shoulder. His arms held me, just underneath Aly's. "Not more than me."

When they let me go, I could only stare at them.

It'd only been what? Three days? But I'd missed them right back.

Aly brushed her hand over her eye. Harper just smiled, brightly and widely, still holding my shoulders. Then, as if remembering, he straightened and jerked his head to the side. His eyes got big and he sucked in his breath. "Is that—who are they?!"

Shane and the guys had gone to a table in the corner, not far from where Aly and Harper had come from. Shane was watching, and when I looked over, he gave me a nod. He was giving me space.

I nodded back, letting him know I was good.

Harper and Aly both had big eyes when I turned back to them.

"Holy shit, woman." Harper grabbed my arm, leading me to

their table. It was a high-top in the corner.

There were other people in the back section with us, but they were on the other side of the room. In the middle was a plethora of pool tables, an air hockey table, and other games. The bar was in the corner with a door to the outside next to it. People were coming in and out, and you could catch a glimpse of a couple picnic tables outside.

Again, I was impressed. This place had it going on.

Both Harper and Aly had drinks already, and an appetizer sat in the middle of the table.

"So that's him?" Harper looked over at Shane, studying him like Shane was about to come over and rob us.

Shane noted the attention, giving me another look.

I shook my head. I needed to catch up with my friends before he came over.

"He's not who I remember from high school," Harper said.

I couldn't tell if that was good or bad.

Aly had been watching me, not Shane, with a knowing look on her face.

"What?" I asked.

She shook her head slowly, a grin appearing. "You look good, that's all. Like, real good."

Harper's attention turned to me. He nodded, but sounded miffed. "You both are getting some. What am I doing here?"

Aly's smile fell. "Self-pity, much? Your man flew to California for you. Not me. Not Kali. You."

"He shouldn't have come! I left him—"

"You've been miserable since he left."

"I have not. We were doing *SNL* dance routines just the other week."

"Yeah," she shot back. "We do those when you *need to be distracted from your misery.*"

Her voice rose, and we were now getting attention from more than just Shane's table. Corvette and Roadie seemed to be enjoying the show. Roadie was grinning. Corvette gave me a smile and lifted his beer in a salute.

"Okay. Enough," I told my friends.

They stopped bickering and flushed, giving me a guilty look.

"Sorry. It's been a few days, you know?" Aly's words were to me; her dark look was to Harper.

He raised his chin, pointedly ignoring her. Then he turned to me and softened. "It's really good to see you. All the drama here —we were worried about you. What happened?"

"I..." I flinched. "I can't tell you guys except to say there was a guy in the area. Shane was worried about me, and I had to stay where they were for a few days." I held my hands out, seeing their instant concern. "It's all good. The bad guy left, and it ended up helping in a way because I saw Claudia."

"Oh." Harper's mouth turned down.

Aly's face went blank.

"She's definitely not coming back with us, so there's that." I remembered that was the main reason I'd come out here. "Ruby just will have to go without her favorite daughter for a while."

I'd also come out here to escape Foley. Or the memories of Foley. Or... I wasn't really sure anymore. I just remembered feeling a mountain of pain sitting on my chest, and over the last few days, that mountain had gone.

I felt lighter. Freer.

Thinking of Foley didn't send me into a blind rage of suffocating pain.

Weird, right?

Or maybe not.

I looked over at Shane.

Yeah. Maybe not weird at all.

The waitress came to their table with another round of beer for them. She lingered, giving Shane a smile. I noticed, but he didn't because he was watching me.

He responded to something she'd said, but he didn't take his eyes off me.

My body warmed, but I wasn't surprised. It was the Shane effect. I'd named it.

"Holy fuck."

I tuned back in. Aly and Harper's gazes were stuck on me. "What?"

"Nuh-uh." Harper shook a finger in the air. "You can't play that card. We saw that whole exchange. You... You got it bad for him."

I rolled my eyes and looked at Aly. She was biting her bottom lip. "What?"

"You love him."

I felt like a frozen fish came out of nowhere and hit me in the face. "What?"

"You do." She nodded. "You fell in love with him. What are you doing?" She leaned across the table, her arms crossed tightly over her chest, but that head—she was giving me an owl impersonation right now. "Hon, you were shattered when we came out here. I thought *distraction*. Sexual fling. Hot and intense, but short. Emphasis on the short. You've not even talked to us about Foley, and you've moved on to a new guy? And *that* kind of guy? Do you even know anything about him?"

Oh. Whoa.

I leaned all the way back in my chair, because this was not my friend.

"I don't know, Aly. I mean, I knew him in high school. He's remained good friends with my brother. I've spent the last few days in his world, and I mean, *fully* in his world. But you're right. I'm thinking you might know more about my man than I do." I held a hand out. "By all means, educate me on the person I've been with the last few days."

Her face went blank, making it even harder to read.

"Guys..." Harper attempted to cut in.

I don't think Aly knew he'd spoken. She raised her eyebrows. "Fine. I do have things to educate you on. Do you know your boyfriend and his club have murdered people? They work with the cartel? They helped make an entire family disappear, just like that." She snapped her fingers, looking so cold. "Just like that, Kali." She inched forward. "You're my friend. I love you, and I am worried. The stories I've heard—"

"Stories."

She stopped, frowning slightly.

"You've heard. Stories that you have heard." I did not need a guess where these stories had come from. "Your new man, who I don't know anything about either, must've been filling you in with all these stories."

I had nothing to say on that matter. It was beyond my control. Her new man, whether she loved him or not, had an opinion, and he had shared it.

"What's funny is that I never thought I'd get this, not from you," I told her. "Maybe Harper in a drunken night when he's feeling dramatic."

"Hey."

I ignored him. "But you? Aly? You don't judge. You never have. You're the one who's *been* judged. I thought..." I shook my head. "Never mind what I thought, but it's definitely not what this turned out to be."

I pushed back to slide off my chair.

"Hey! Whoa." Harper had his hands in the air, between us. "Time out, okay? Kali, you do not move from that stool. You hear me? And Aly, lay off the judgment. Kali's right, but not about the drunken dramatic thing. Don't get too big of a head over there."

I had to smile at that, a knot loosening inside of me. Just a little, and not enough. No matter what else was said, damage had been done. Aly had slammed the door before I'd even gotten a foot inside.

We both quieted.

"Okay, now what the fuck?" Harper said. "Honestly? What the ever living fuck? I've not heard about any of these things Aly just said, so she's not been talking behind your back or anything. And you know she's just concerned, *really* concerned based on the absolutely horrible delivery, but you know what I mean." His tone softened. "She loves you, and you came in knowing about her situation. You were prepared. None of us were prepared for your situation. It's a lot for anyone to digest, much less family."

A younger me might've asked them to be happy for me. But that wasn't me now, not anymore. We were beyond that stage in our lives.

I shook my head, because there was another elephant in the room. "Where is Justin?"

Harper's mouth dropped.

Aly started laughing.

That eased a bit more of my knot. But again, not enough.

"I can't even," Harper sputtered, flinging his hands in the air. "Fine. You two battle it out." He picked up his drink and slid off his stool. "Unlike Aly, I'm going to actually go over and get to know your man, because I want to know who his buddies are. See ya, bitches. Harper's out."

Aly seemed stricken.

I didn't care why. A pounding had started behind my forehead, and it was building fast. "You're the steady one," I murmured. "The kind one. Warm. Humble. Loving. I don't know who this new Aly is, and I'm not saying she's wrong, but man, she was quick to speak in a way the Aly I know wouldn't have. I do know that much."

I was done. I'd said enough. But I ached. She'd punched a little hole in my chest.

"Brandon knows the club," she said after a moment.

"The club. Not Shane." Because there was a distinction.

"True," she agreed. "He doesn't know Shane, but in these clubs, it doesn't matter. You know one, you know all."

Bullshit. I was already shaking my head.

"Yes, Kali." She raised her tone, but not in a bad way. An assertive way. "His brother-in-law has had run-ins with Shane's club. He told me about them, and he's terrified of them. Terrified. He's worried about you. He's worried about me—"

She wasn't looking at me now. She was staring off into the distance, her concern clouding everything again. "He said if you stay with Shane, he doesn't know where he and I will stand."

"That's a lot of power you're giving him."

Her eyes found mine, and I saw a tear forming in there. She blinked it away. "It's not like that. We're older. We know. We don't have time to waste anymore, not if we know what we want." Her eyes glistened, and she lifted a shoulder, looking helpless. "I've loved you all my life, but you can't give me babies."

Damn. Harper was right. She was there, *all* the way there.

"Harper said you were there, but I was kinda hoping he was exaggerating." I gave her a sad smile. "I wanted to be here when you fell in love. I wanted to talk to you before your first date, get the 411 after—or the next morning."

She laughed softly.

"I wanted to help with the guessing game of *what is he thinking*, reassure you that he was into you as you freaked out that he might not be, even though it's so obvious he is. And the cyber-stalking. I was prepared to go overboard too. We're talking PI stalking, that sort of thing."

She fought back tears, blinking rapidly.

"I missed it."

She closed her eyes, a serene sadness coming over her. "I thought Shane was your rebound guy—a badass after dealing with a serious asshole. I'm so scared of losing you. I spoke too quickly. I judged, but I'm not wrong about his club. They're dangerous."

I nodded, feeling her sadness tunnel inside of me. "I know, Aly. You didn't tell me anything I don't know."

Her eyes widened a fraction. "But, what?"

"Shane and I talk. Not about that stuff, but about the things I need to know. That stuff."

Harper was over there, laughing, sitting at the end of the table. He was flirting with Roadie, who was lapping up the attention. Corvette rolled his eyes, laughing and shaking his head. Boise was doing nothing. He was staring, and Shane? He was watching me.

From the look in his eyes, it seemed he knew what was happening over here.

"Brandon has a whole family here," Aly said, pulling my attention back to her. "I mean, not blood. He's got his sister and her family, but from the way he talks, there's a group of friends. His sister is tight with them, and he's on the outskirts. He's always welcome, but he's got freedom to do his own thing. I can't tell if he likes that or not, or if he's hurt about being on the edge. His sister has kids, and Brandon adores them. Their older brother is in Florida. Married. Got some sales job or something. Their dad is there too. His older brother kinda takes care of the dad—like, he checks in on him. Their mom is gone. He's not talked about her that much, but it's like he doesn't think about her, so it's not a big deal, whatever happened."

She was sharing. Okay. We were at that part now.

I kind of had whiplash, but I wanted her to keep sharing. I nodded, trying to smile.

"He knows about my grandma. He knows about my ex. He knows about all the guys I've dated and wasted my time with. He knows about you, about Harper. He loves Justin."

Oh, man. That was a point for him.

"He likes Harper. He said you seemed cool that night you were here. He told me you guys talked a little." She stopped, her eyes changing, getting hard again.

I prepared myself.

"The run-in with Shane's club was serious and real. It's very, very serious. I—"

"Stop." There was no heat to my tone, just tiredness. I waved a hand in the air. "Just please. Stop. I don't want to hear all the things I know and I'm scared about too." I didn't know what else to say. I couldn't tell her things I was scared to admit to myself.

"I don't know what to do now."

I nodded. "Do you even want to meet him?"

"I already know him."

That was a no then. She'd made up her mind.

Alright.

I needed a break. Sliding off my stool, I said, "I'm going to the bathroom."

Aly reached for her drink.

I moved toward the door, indicating to Shane where I was going.

He lifted his chin in response, but didn't move to follow.

I took my time in the bathroom before washing and heading back out. When I did, Shane was there. It was déjà vu from the hotel. He put his hand on my stomach and ushered me back into the bathroom, grabbing a *Closed for Cleaning* poster and sticking it to the outside of the door.

Back inside, I stepped away, not liking how he was looking at me. "Don't."

"What'd she say to you?"

"Can't you guess?" Going to the mirror, I washed my hands. Again. I needed to do something. My stomach rolled, and Shane could see inside of me. It was uncomfortable. "She's with the bartender, whose sister owns the place."

"I know that already, but what'd she say to you?"

I jerked up a shoulder. "Nothing you haven't said yourself or that I didn't already pick up, but the gist was that if I stay with you, I lose her." I stopped fiddling with my hair, meeting his gaze in the mirror.

His eyes were dark. He wasn't letting me read him.

"You've known her all your life."

I nodded, my throat swelling up.

There was no leeway here. It was what it was. It was harsh, but it was smack dab in front of my face. No way around it. How could I make a choice like that? So soon?

He took the pain away.

She didn't know that.

"Okay then." He turned to leave.

"Hey!" I was across the room, my hand on his arm. "What are you doing?"

"I'm letting you have some space. She's family to you, and she gave you that. Seems like you'd need some time to sort your thoughts."

Good grief. I wanted to shake him and kiss him at the same time. "You followed me in here. Why don't you stay and hold me?"

His eyes never changed. They were still so dark, but he put his arms around me and pulled me to him. We weren't teenagers. I wasn't going to get worked up about it. Aly could be handled. It might take time, some delicate maneuvering, but as Shane held me and I savored it, I knew I wasn't going to lose Aly.

I also knew I wasn't going to give Shane up. Before tonight, I hadn't known I'd made that decision.

I knew now.

"Kali," he murmured.

"Hmm?" I tipped my head up.

He was looking down, so intently. "It gets to a time where you gotta make a decision between me and your girl, let me in on it."

"Sure, but it's not going to come to that. We're too old for that."

"Just let me in on it, no matter the decision."

I could tell this was important to him and I frowned slightly. "Okay. Yeah."

"I have a thing about masks. I don't want you to ever feel like you have to wear one with me. I could tell you wore one in high school. Broke my heart even back then. I don't want you to do that, not with me, not where we are. You get me?"

I nodded, my mouth dry again. I got him.

No masks.

34

KALI

We were leaving the bathroom.

Shane took the sign down, putting it back in the closet right next to the bathroom. And as we turned, his hand to my back, we stopped right away. Brandon was coming through from the back section, holding Aly's hand right behind him. "Oh."

He stopped.

I stopped.

I felt Shane's hand press harder on my back and he moved up right behind me.

Aly looked around Brandon, her eyes going big. "Hey, um–" She began to try to move around Brandon, but he held her back. His gaze was steadily on Shane.

"Why don't we let the friends have the night?" Shane spoke first, his tone sounding casual, but I could feel the tension inside of him. "You and me can maybe come to an understanding? Outside?"

Aly's mouth dropped. "What? No–"

"Sure." Brandon cut her off, turning and looking down at Aly. "We got this. Okay?"

She closed her mouth with a snap, her eyes finding mine and I saw the plea there.

A part of me hurt even more because I knew what she was afraid of. She'd gone through so much hell already, had her heart shattered and now she found a guy she could see herself having babies with. She didn't want someone to come in and take that away. I was pulled in two separate ways because she thought the person who'd take that away was a guy who'd taken away my pain.

I moved ahead, linking my elbow through Aly's. "Come on." I gently bumped my hip to hers. "Let's go and grill Harper about Justin." She was so stiff, but went with me. I glanced back, taking in both Brandon and Shane's gazes. Shane's was locked right on me, his expression unreadable. Brandon was watching Shane, and his was very readable. He looked like he wanted to murder him.

We headed to the table where Harper was. At our presence and at Shane's absence, his guys each took a sip of their beer before sliding right off their stools and heading where we'd just come from.

Aly saw them go. "Wha—no!"

I stopped her, getting in front of her. "They won't do anything. They'll just go and have his back if Brandon swings on him."

She squeaked, her eyes bulging. "That's what I'm worried about."

"Will Brandon swing for no reason? He didn't strike me as that type of guy."

"What? No. He'd never do that, but if he's provoked, he's got friends here."

"Exactly. Brandon's not alone. He's surrounded by people who will have his back. Let Shane have a few too. We're on Brandon's territory, remember."

Aly frowned, taking a step back and reassessing me. "I have to say I'm not a big fan right now. Where's my friend gone? Feel like I'm just seeing a biker bi–"

"Okay." Harper was between us, wedging his way in there. "Stop. Both of you on either side of that table. Now." He pointed at our previously emptied one. He reached back, grabbed his drink and rounded up the rest of the guys' beers. He brought all of them over to the table and pointed to a stool on one side, then the other. "Sit. Now."

I went to the one facing the back door.

Aly went across from me, her stool facing the door to the other end of Manny's.

Harper hesitated a second before taking the stool next to Aly.

Justin moved in and took the empty one by me.

"Hey." It took a second for his presence to register. I melted. "Hi! Oh my God, Justin." I reached over, giving him a big hug.

He hugged me back, cupping the back of my head. "Hey there. How are *you* doing?" He said it only for me to hear and we kept hugging, holding each other, because Justin was that kind of guy. He wanted to know, real quick before we got to business, how I truly was doing. That's how he spoke, how he handled himself. He truly cared about people. He was loving. Gentle. Patient. And Harper was terrified of losing him, so of course he pushed him away. I was suddenly so angry at my best friend.

I hugged Justin a little bit longer, harder. "I am mending."

Justin leaned back, looking at me, his hands still around me lightly. "Well, that sounds healing." He smiled, raising an eyebrow in an inquisitive way.

I smiled back, answering the unspoken question. "And you?"

Some of his smile faded and his hands fell away. "You'll see that part." He raised his voice, turning to include the table. "Because we're going to hash out things between me and Harper tonight too."

"What? There's nothing to hash out." Harper sat upright, doing the best impersonation of a rod being stuck down his back.

"Yes, there is because I'm tired. I'm going back and I'm moving on."

"What?"

I reached over, touching Justin's knee for comfort. He was so tense and at my touch, a breath wooshed out of him. He gave me a sad smile before responding to Harper again. "It's time, babe. If you really don't want me, I'm going to go. I have a lot of love and I know there'll be a guy out there who'll appreciate me. I've been waiting for Kali to come back, help here, and if you still say you don't want me, a guy can only take so much you know? I gotta go then. I can't keep harassing you."

"But," Harper heaved a deep sigh. "You're not harassing me, Justin. You never could do that. I'm the harasser."

"I know, but you've not been harassing me. You've been avoiding me."

"I didn't last night."

Aly and I shared a look. Last night?!

"One night doesn't mean you've changed your mind. If anything, it just opens the wounds again. Gives me hope."

Harper looked away, his mouth pressed up and looking like he was having a hard time swallowing. "Man. I-" He took us all in before closing his eyes, hanging his head. "Put me on the spot here."

"We can go outside? Talk privately, but I want the girls to know that I'm done waiting." He covered my hand with his on his knee, patting it gently. "It was good to see you. I can see that you're almost glowing."

I felt like crying. "Justin, don't go."

He tilted his head to the side, that sad smile moving so he had sad eyes. "I can't take much more. Harper's made his decision loud and clear. I have to listen at some point."

I knew, but I wanted to argue. Harper was wrong. Knew him all my life to know he was wrong, and he knew he was wrong too. I glanced at him, saw he was fighting with himself.

We all got off our stools for the hugs.

Justin hugged me. Hugged Aly.

Harper looked defeated so he got a hug and I knew he'd need more of those by the end of the night so no matter what happened he'd be getting all the hugs from us. Aly and Harper hugged, so I got one last hug from Justin.

He squeezed me hard, saying into my ear, "Don't let him become like his mom."

I hugged him back just as hard. "I won't. I swear."

He pulled back, taking me in before giving a final and firm nod. His eyes were set, determined. As he led the way outside, there was a resolved look to both of them. Their shoulders were hunched forward and down.

"Why do I feel like we're breaking up with Justin?" Aly moved next to me.

I sighed because damn. That was the case. But no. No way. I knew Justin would do what he'd have to do. He'd move on, which meant he'd move away but Justin was amazing so he'd get snatched up so quick. He'd find a great guy, and all of those guys' friends would fall in love with Justin. There'd be some visits every now and then, maybe a couple emails, texts, but those would dwindle because Justin would become loyal to his new guy. At some point, he would have to cut ties with Aly and me.

I shook my head. That wasn't going to happen. "We need to stop Harper from destroying Harper."

Aly asked, "We need to protect him from himself?"

I looked sideways at her, seeing she was giving me the same look right back.

She added, "You thinking what I think you're thinking?"

"Chances are high."

A whole different resolution came over her. She lowered her head. Her eyes got serious. Her mouth went firm. "Let's do this, whatever this is that we have to do."

I finished, "We're doing it."

"Got it."

She started forward, but I touched her arm. "Hold up." We had four drinks still left untouched on the table. I took mine and drank it, handing Aly the rest of hers.

When ours were done, we eyed Justin and Harper's.

"Normally I'm not about drinking what someone else started, but ..."

I reached for Justin's, giving Aly Harper's. Both of theirs were basically untouched.

I said, "Booze is booze. It's a cardinal rule in our group not to let good booze go to waste."

"Exactly."

After I drank Justin's, Aly was back to eyeing me. She informed me, "Justin had them do two long islands together so..."

"What?!" Oh–no. Oh boy. No, no, no. That meant I just had like eight shots all mixed together. I forgot he could seriously drink. He had a tolerance level that I'd never witnessed before.

She started laughing. "You are going to be so drunk and soon."

"Shit." I covered my face. I had no idea how to handle this, what to do.

Aly started laughing, and I heard the snort at the end.

I groaned. Once the snort-Aly-laugh started, we'd both be rolling because that laugh of hers was infectious. Really infectious. She'd soon be sounding like a chuckling donkey. And soon enough, the haha got longer, louder and I was smiling, chuckling alongside her because the *he-ahhhaaa-eee-haaa* was emanating out of her body.

Goddamn.

"He-ahhhaaa-eee-haaa!"

I was laughing, and that made Aly get worse, louder. It was now "HA-AHHHHAAA-EEE-HAAA," and the people around us were joining in.

"Oh my God!" Aly gasped between laughs, holding her stomach. "I can't breathe HA-AHHHHAAA-EEEE-HAA!"

"I've never heard someone laugh like that," a woman said, shaking her head as she went to her table, but she was smiling and as Aly kept doing her thing, her whole table was joining in. She hit my hand, half bent over as she was still laughing and motioned for the door. "WE have to go–that way–" Another laugh came from her.

It was a whole out-of-body experience when these happened. "Ha-ahhhhaaaa–eeee-haaa–HA-AHHHHAAAA–EEE–HAA!"

I was laughing too, but mine was more contained. I moved ahead of her, grabbing her hand. Our fingers laced as I dragged her behind me, and out the door where I assumed Justin and Harper would've gone. We got out, but the guys weren't here. I'd taken her out the back door. People were at tables in the front and on the north side of the bar. They had a whole setup up there for everyone. I walked to the south side. A house was set back a little bit, with gravel traveling up the side of Manny's and connecting to the parking lot. Spotting Corvette, I didn't think Justin and Harper would've gone by them. I was on a mission before the booze really hit me and wading into whatever was going on between Shane and Aly's new man wasn't it.

"There." Aly had settled down, her laughs more normal by now.

I looked where she was pointing. There was a driveway on the other side of that house, that was attached to a whole different road. I frowned, but saw two guys over there. They looked in an embrace.

"Wait. Maybe they made up?"

Aly's hand squeezed mine. "Or doing way more than that?"

That didn't seem like them, though. Justin looked heartbroken in the bar earlier. Those guys were hugging or something more. I doubted Justin and Harper would be at the hugging goodbye stage so soon.

I shared a look with her. "You think we should go make sure it's in a good way or leave 'em alone?"

"Are you kidding me?" She gave me a dark look while still chuckling. "It's Harper. We have to do this for him."

I gave a nod right back to her. "You're right. It's Harper."

We didn't need to hold hands going over there, but I didn't pull away and neither did she. Either the alcohol was kicking in or I was feeling some sentimentality about Aly. I was scared about what would happen after this mission was done? A part of me was trying to reassure myself that nothing would happen to Aly and me. Our friendship was solid. Had always been strong. But...

Yeah.

I didn't want to think about it anymore.

We eased up, seeing the two guys move around the side of a shed.

Aly started forward, but I pulled her back. Frowning.

"What is it?"

I shook my head. "I'm not sure, Harper is shorter than Justin. Those two guys were equal height."

"Oh, yeah. I noticed that too, but thought Justin was leaning down or something."

This was dumb. There were five bikers just on the other side of Manny's. Nothing was going to happen with Shane so close by.

I led the way, saying, "Harper? You and Justin out–"

I took two steps, rounded the shed, and woosh! It went dark. Something was shoved over my head. "Hey–" A hand covered my mouth and before I could register what was happening and sink my teeth into that hand, it was replaced. I got half of a scream out before something was shoved into my mouth, and then I felt tape going around my entire head.

I began fighting, harder once my brain caught up to me.

I could see a little through whatever had been shoved over my head, but it was so dark.

Two guys were there, and just as I tried running, two arms wrapped around me and I was lifted off my feet. I was struggling, kicking and wiggling around.

"Jesus. Shit!"

"Shut up!"

"Get their phones."

Hands were pushing into my pocket, searching. They pulled back out, and I heard a *smashing* sound soon after.

I didn't recognize either voice, but they were males and I was being carried quickly into a vehicle. I registered what it was just as I was thrown inside. They had covered up the back lights and a second later, I felt a body land next to me. Aly's groan identified her and I tried to reach out, grabbing her hand. I couldn't find her hand, but her head was pressed into my chest. I rolled around, scooting around just in time to see two other guys had jumped out from the back of a van. One guy disappeared. The other reached for the door.

I was trying to roll my way out, but he saw me coming and laughed. He shook his head before slamming the door shut.

That's when I realized they had tied my hands together too, and behind me.

Funny. I hadn't even noticed that part.

35

KALI

They kidnapped us. I couldn't believe I was freaking being kidnapped!

We were in the dark and I couldn't see much inside. A seat or something was blocking from where we were and where *they* were, but I felt around and found Aly's hands. I was thinking either adrenaline was going hard in my body, or the booze were kicking in because I wasn't scared. No shock either. It was just, okay. This is the situation. Now, let's get out of this situation.

So I was trying to do that, by pulling on Aly to roll with me to the door.

There was no one else out here. I didn't know of a vehicle that would keep a door locked from the outside in, except cop cars but no way was this that. There were three guys in the front, and this was a big van. They had the windows rolled down in the front, which was either ingenious on their part so we couldn't identify their voices, overhear them, or it was stupid.

I was hoping it was the stupid part because that meant they couldn't hear us either. Or hear us rolling around.

Every time I tried to make a sound, I ended up eating fabric, from whatever they'd stuffed in my mouth. I couldn't see, but I was assuming they'd done the same to Aly.

Hence, why I was trying to tug her for the door.

She wasn't budging. So, ugh. I moved over to the other side of her, put my shoulder into her side, and began pushing her for the door. She moaned, struggling around. I groaned, deep in my throat until suddenly, she went where I was pushing her. Now this was the hard part. My hands were tied so when she got to the door, I sat up and leaned in so she could see me. It was so dark, but I knew this road. We'd traveled it with the bikes so I knew a light post was coming up. I waited until one flashed over the van and as it did, I motioned to the door with my head.

Aly's eyes got big, but the light was gone and we waited until another post passed over us.

I nodded. She nodded, and I began to sit up, turning around and reaching for the door with my hands.

This would be hella uncomfortable, but no way was I waiting around here for wherever they'd take us. That was Staying Alive 101. Don't go with your kidnappers. Aly must've sensed my nerves, because she moved in, leaned her head to my shoulder and let it rest there.

That felt nice, but okay. Oh man.

I was so nervous. Another post went over us, Aly gave me a nod, and I jerked mine up and down but waited until it was dark again before opening the door.

It did–hell yes! But I was falling and oomph. I landed hard on my wrist. I was pretty sure it was broken or strained, and then I heard Aly fall just a little after I hit the pavement. I groaned, hoping against hope that they wouldn't know that door had opened. It'd been dark when they had the door open when they put us inside so I didn't think it would kick the light on again. I looked, but I didn't see their lights on at all. They weren't braking.

They kept going.

But then I needed to get to my feet, and I felt liquid going down my arms. Pain lit up the entire right side of my body, but I couldn't focus on that. I got up, struggling, my head was pounding but I made my way over to where Aly was struggling to sit up.

I turned around, grabbed her arm and tried to help her up.

It took a little bit. Some struggling. She almost fell twice, but once she got up, and was steady, I looked around.

I didn't know this town or where we were. I just remembered driving on the road, but we were surrounded by trees.

Aly made a moaning sound, but was tugging on me to follow her.

One side went south. The other side was north, and up a hill. Manny's was behind us and on the south side of the road. That's where Aly was tugging me, but I stopped her. Those guys would come back and they'd guess where we would go. I shook my head, and pulled her the other way. We'd go up, north and hope to find someone who had a phone and would be willing to help us. I didn't think those guys would think to go up the hill for us.

I had no idea if it was best friend telepathy or not, but she went with me, and as soon as she did, I felt a burst of energy go through me. I tore out of there. There was no way in hell I'd be here when those guys came back, and they would. That was a given.

We tore up through the woods, climbing up until we were a safe enough distance from the road.

Aly pulled on my shirt, stopping me, and then went to her knees. I felt her teeth trying to cut through whatever they'd used to tie my hands together. It might've been tape because when she started pulling on it, it was peeling off my skin. I gritted my teeth until she made enough headway before I could move my wrists around, pulling the rest off myself. As soon as I did, I turned her around and was pulling at her wrists.

She moved around, some moans leaving her bound mouth.

Finally! I tore it free and then I was pulling off the tape around my whole entire head. Assholes.

I swallowed a cry as I pulled it free, feeling my hair getting caught up with it too. But then I spat out whatever was in my mouth, sweeping everything up and stuffing it into my pockets because you bet your ass I wanted police to grab some evidence off of them against these dicks.

"They're going to be coming back. We have to keep moving."

God. It hurt my ribs to talk. My voice felt funny too. It sounded funny.

I felt funny.

I couldn't feel my feet.

Or my one shoulder.

I couldn't think about that. None of it.

"Who were those guys?"

"I have no clue, but we have to go." I grabbed for her shirt and began moving forward. "Come on."

Aly let me take the lead. Her and Harper weren't the tough sorts like I was. I was rough and tumble, needed to be growing up with my sister, but we spent a good amount of time out in the woods and around the lake. I figured we had another while before Aly's shock would really set in. Mine too, but I'd bear through mine. Been through worse shit than this, or, well... no. I'd never been kidnapped so no. This was the worst I'd been through, but spending time in Chicago where my dad worked and being biracial, yeah. There'd been some scary times there too. Nothing in Friendly. Thought the whole place was scared of getting on the bad side of Ruby and Claudia, which had me feeling a certain way about my mother and sister now that I was thinking on it.

What was I doing? I didn't have time to suss this out, but that was me thinking. Keeping my brain busy so I didn't have to focus on those guys coming back and finding us.

I kept moving forward. My plan had been to go up north, get

on a hill over that road and then follow it down back to Manny's. Or wait until we heard Harley engines roaring through the street and sprint as fast as I could down there to bisect Shane. So I wanted to be away from the road enough that if those guys came back, we could hide easily, but not too far where I'd miss the road if I heard Shane.

Did that make sense?

It made sense in my head.

...I think the shock was starting to set in.

We kept going. Branches tore at us.

I probably had a nest in my hair, but I kept going. Had to. Needed to.

Then I got to a stage where my head was fuzzy, and I stopped running.

I was getting confused. What was going on again?

I looked around.

I wasn't alone, but I couldn't see anyone.

Aly! Aly had been with me, but she wasn't anymore.

I started to take a step back, but I came down on a log and my ankle went one way. My body went the other way.

Crack!

Oh, no. That didn't sound good.

But I was down, and I lay there a minute. If I could've seen anything, I knew I would've witnessed birds flying around my head.

Crash.

Snap.

"Kali!"

I sat up, my head all woozy. That was Aly. She sounded so scared.

She saw me, just as we both saw headlights peaking over a hill.

A hill? I thought we'd gone up to the top of the hill?

I must've got that wrong.

I think I must've gotten a lot wrong.

Where was Shane?

"Kali!" Aly fell to her knees beside me. I heard her sniffling and she was touching my leg. "Oh no. What'd you do?"

I reached forward, grabbing her hand, and I fell back. I couldn't hold myself anymore. Maybe those headlights wouldn't see us? We weren't on the road. They should skip over us, easy-peasy.

"I fell down."

She settled next to me, a heavy dense thud so I knew she landed hard on her ass. I doubted she felt it. She was probably in shock like me, and she leaned into me. "I'm pretty sure we'd only been running for a few minutes, but it feels like hours."

I grunted. It did.

The shock was wearing off, and I was starting to feel the pain.

I hissed, knowing not to move my foot, but damn. I wanted to move. Had to move, but also couldn't move at the same time. What a situation we'd found ourselves in. I was hoping it was a strain and not a sprain.

"I'm sorry."

"About what?" She turned my way.

I shook my head. "I don't know, but I'm figuring this was because of me. Chances are high, considering Shane. You know."

"Oh." She settled even more into my side and arm. Her head rested to my shoulder. "Silver lining?"

I cracked a grin, which also hurt, but I had to play along. This was another thing we did.

I suggested, "Silver lining, I bet Justin never left."

She barked out a laugh before choking on it, a moaning sound coming out of her throat at the same time. "Jesus. Every-thing hurts."

I moved my shoulder a little, lightly jostling her. "Silver lining? Your turn."

"Right. Um, what Brandon worried would happen did

happen so it already happened. Statistics wise, chances are low of it happening again."

I knew where she was going with that. "See. You can use that logic against him when he'll argue about you and me being friends." But my turn. "Silver lining... you can see what kind of guy Brandon is when they find us."

"That's true." She was moving her foot around. I didn't know why. She whimpered on a hiss of pain. "I really do like him."

"I gathered. You said I couldn't give you babies."

She snorted. "I mean, you could. 'Cause of science, you could give me babies, but you know what I meant."

"That means you *really* like him."

"I do. I didn't expect it. Never expect it anymore, honestly. Not anymore. I gave up. I thought Scott was my best shot at a family, but knowing how his family was, I had no hope. I was relieved when Harper showed me that image of him kissing that girl back home."

"Slut."

She laughed. "I know you're meaning him, not her."

"Of course."

"Thanks, Kali."

I'd forgotten all about the headlights, but remembering, I lifted my head and I couldn't see any light anymore. They must've gone on. I didn't even know where the road was because where those lights were didn't make sense to me. I thought the road was to our side, but now that I was analyzing that, I didn't see any light posts either.

"I'm pretty sure I got us lost."

"Let's make it through the night, and when the sun comes up, we can get our bearings."

That was a good plan. "I can't sleep. I'm pretty sure I might be concussed."

"Then you can't sleep."

"Okay."

A minute later, Aly was sleeping.

I struggled, but she had settled even more into me, lying by me. She was warm. I moved in, trying to get as close as I could because it was still cold out.

I'd stay awake.

I could do it.

I'd have to do it.

Think of Shane.

Think of Harper. Justin.

Connor.

Claudia.

My mom.

My dad–oh man. They smashed my phone.

I was really screwed.

But...

36

KALI

A wet nose and a pounding headache greeted me when I woke.

Arms swept under me, lifting me, and I was being carried/ran across a field. I looked up. "Wha–" It was Shane. He hugged me tighter. "Hold on, babe. We're going to get you to a hospital."

Oh.

That sounded good.

Also, Shane!

I closed my eyes, resting my head against his chest and a feeling came over me. I'd be fine. I'd be safe. Everything would be okay. I'd never got that feeling from a guy. Ever. Even Harper. It was my job to reassure him, but with Shane–I was noting that here.

Then I remembered Aly.

"Aly!"

"Corvette's got her. We need to get you to the hospital."

Oh, good. That was all good.

"Babe." We were still running.

"Hmm?"

"You shouldn't fall asleep. You look like your head got hit."

Right. Yes. I was concussed, very very sure to where I knew I was. My head was still hurting. And things were still woozy.

Still. Logic was kicking in. It'd be better if I stayed awake.

"Why don't you tell me what happened to you? We've been looking all night for you."

Yes. He would've had no idea.

Panic seized me. "Those guys!" They couldn't come back. They couldn't get Shane. Wait. I was okay. Shane had a gun.

"In here." That was another voice and Shane was slowing down.

"I got her. Make room." Shane's voice was now rough as he passed me to someone else.

I looked up. It was the new guy from yesterday. Idaho? No. That wasn't right. Why couldn't I remember?

"Okay." That was Shane.

And I was being passed right back to Shane, who was in a truck. He held me in his arms, going all the way to the inside and a second later, Corvette slid into the seat next to us, Aly tucked in his arms. He was cradling her like a baby, and I knew Aly. Her huge size of ten (I'm being very sarcastic here) did a number on her self-esteem, but he was cradling her like a baby and our eyes met since he had her the other way on his chest. We both were noting the same thing, and she started laughing a little.

Corvette froze, his head jerking down to take her in.

I started laughing, which made Shane hug me a little tighter. "Ow. My ribs."

He loosened his hold immediately.

I looked up. "No. It's from laughing." I looked back to Aly. "How are you feeling?"

"I'm not really sure."

The Idaho guy got behind the wheel, and another guy jumped in the passenger side. Both slammed their doors shut, as Shane opened his window a little. "Thank you for the use of your dogs."

I heard a muffled voice, but then we were off and we were going fast too.

Shane put his window back up, saying, "Hit the heat, Roadie."

The heat's fan blasted a second later.

"Should we call her man?" I couldn't tell who that came from. Shane's heat was pulling me back down, and we were in a moving vehicle. Sleeping in a moving vehicle was my favorite.

"Not yet."

I heard Aly say something.

Shane responded, but ...

"THEY WERE OUTSIDE ALL NIGHT?"

I woke again, hearing that question as I was being put on a bed, then wheeled down a hallway.

Shane answered, coming with us, "Yes. We found them this morning."

"What time?"

"A little after five."

"And they were outside, why?"

I was a bit more coherent this time, and I waited for what Shane would respond with. He didn't.

"Sir, do I need to call the police?"

"No fucking cops," he growled.

We were moving into a room, and as we did, I lifted my head, taking in the scene around me. At Shane's growl, Roadie and Boise moved next to Shane, all three giving the doctor a meaningful look.

"I see." The doctor's response was tight. His eyes narrowed. "I need the room. You three will need to step out. We have a lobby where you can wait. I'll have one of the nurses show you."

"We're not going anywhere. We'll be right out here." Shane stepped back, his anger simmering under the surface and he took one step out into the hallway. His gaze went to mine just as a nurse came in and whisked the curtain closed. She came to the bed and started setting up an IV right away. The doctor was looking me over as the nurse mentioned, "Red Demons, huh?"

I looked up, giving her a different look because she didn't sound scared. "You know them?"

"I think the better question is do you know them? They friends of yours?"

She was worried about me. I nodded, slightly just as the doctor said, "Don't move your head. Not yet."

I said to her, "They're friends. He's my man."

Because he was.

Shane.

My man.

I liked telling her that, and I liked that it was true. I wasn't scared to claim him. I also wasn't scared that he was my man. Felt right.

Yeah. I'm pretty sure I was concussed. Only thing that made sense right now.

"What's your name, sweetie?"

"Kali. I'm a nurse. Hoping my ankle is a strain and fairly sure I have a little concussion going on."

"All right, Kali. I'm Rena, and this is Dr. Vioeri. You just give us some of your time and we'll make sure everything is okay with you. Okay?"

"Yeah. Okay."

"Good."

After that, the doctor moved in and I was checked out.

———

THE FINAL DIAGNOSIS was a slight concussion, my ankle was already better so the strain was super slight, and some seriously nasty scrapes over half of my body. I'd *really* not liked when they cleaned those up, but when they wrapped everything and gave me antibiotics, I was more inclined to like the staff from the Fallen Crest hospital. The doctor told me I needed rest, keep away from too much stimulus with my concussion, and I'd need to have my bandages cleaned once per day. The stitches would dissolve themselves, for where I needed to get stitches.

He headed out, but Rena stayed back and I noted the look he gave her, also the looks the other nurses all gave each other as they walked out. I was readying myself for a good talking-to from Miss Rena since I saw the wedding ring on her finger. The last nurse pulled the curtain shut and I could now hear the ER door slide shut. I'd not been with it earlier to notice it. It was nice and quiet. Smooth.

"This is about them?" I started it off.

One of her eyebrows raised from surprise before it settled back, and she gave me a knowing look. "You know anything about New Kings Bounties?"

I started to shake my head, and remembered I shouldn't. "No."

She gave a small nod, letting out a tiny breath. "My husband works with them. He's a bounty hunter. Reason I'm sharing that tidbit with you is because there's history between them and your man's motorcycle club. I've listened to them talk about the Red Demons in the past. Don't remember hearing a Shane so I'm not saying it's with your particular man, but I do know that they are supposed to keep clear of this town and another not far from here."

"You're telling me this, why?"

A look flashed in her eyes, and she dipped her chin down before stepping further back. "Just be careful. That's all." She was going to leave.

I asked, "My friend? Aly. We came in together."

"Oh, yes. She's already been discharged. Her scrapes were less minor than yours." She reached for the curtain, but paused and looked back. "I shouldn't do this, but I am. What the hell." She came back, took her pen out, scribbled on a piece of paper and handed it over. "That's my number. If you're staying in the area and need a job? We've got a serious shortage. If you need anything and I mean, anything, you call me. Text me. I don't care. Just know that there are people here who can help if you need it."

I took it, putting it in my pocket.

She was giving me another reassessing look before a wall came down over her face. "Though, I'm thinking maybe I got it all wrong and you can handle yourself just fine? I hope I'm getting that right."

"I'm good. Thank you."

One last nod before she left. Then it was just me and my thoughts.

So, Shane's club had history here. Right. I didn't know what to take from that, but it was what it was.

I wanted to check on Aly, find Shane, and then get those assholes who came after us. Those were my priorities now.

The doors slid open and I felt Shane before I heard him. "Kali?!"

"I'm here."

The curtain was flung open, and Shane was at my side in two steps. He started to hug me, but paused and stepped back. "I don't want to hurt you." He was looking me all over again, and this time, now that I was a whole lot more clear-headed, I was seeing the strain it was taking him to keep himself under control.

He was almost shaking.

I reached out, touched his arm, and his hand came over mine instantly. I could feel his tension. He felt like cement under my touch, but he drew in a sharp breath at my touch. "Jesus, babe." He came in, his voice hoarse. "Do you know how many years I lost when I realized you were missing?" Still shaking, but his eyes closed, and he stepped in, resting his forehead to mine.

"Oh, baby." I touched his waist.

He let out a rueful sigh, half grinning. "Do you know how much I didn't know I needed to hear you call me that until you just did?"

I grinned, feeling an assuredness that it would all be okay.

It had to.

Had to.

"How's Aly?"

"I should be asking you. They closed ranks as soon as they got her in there. Her man got here and they took off."

"Oh." I didn't know how to process that. Happy she had someone that cared that much about her? But also, pissed because Aly was my family and he just met her. "What about Harper? Justin?"

A whole different vibe came into the room, and my stomach dropped.

It sunk low, a ball of dread nestled right next to it and I saw a transformation come over Shane.

This was biker Shane looking back at me. Ghost.

A shiver went down my spine, because I could understand why everyone was so scared of him, of them, if this was what they got to see.

I swallowed around a lump in my throat. "What is it?"

He blinked, once, before saying, "They're gone."

"What?" I shook my head. "What does that mean? What do you mean they're gone?" My voice was rising with each question.

"When I realized you were gone, and when her man realized your friend was gone, we all went apeshit. The whole bar locked up, and I mean, we locked everyone inside. Lights were on. Music was off. We went through every person in that bar, checking phones. Everything. If we'd been cops, none of that would've been a legal search, but good thing we aren't. I gotta warn you now, though. We pissed off a whole lot of people doing what we did, but Aly's man was right with us. We couldn't find you guys, and we couldn't find your friends. We started a search right after, and Stripes called in a favor. Got us in touch with a local guy who uses search dogs. That's how we found you when we did, but it took a while."

The air was pulled out of me. I... I couldn't comprehend this. "Justin and Harper? They're gone too?"

Wait.

I gasped, grabbing Shane's arm. "You didn't–no, no. Their bodies?" God. Pain seized my insides. I couldn't finish that thought.

"No. They were taken like you guys, or that's what we were thinking until you both showed up. Two sets of wheels left the back house's driveway that's attached to the other road. Security cameras picked up two vans leaving. One went south, yours. And one went north. We're assuming that was theirs."

The room became stifling. The air was thick, pressing down on me.

Justin and Harper. They were kidnapped.

"Babe." Shane stepped in again, his voice gentle. He cupped the side of my face, tracing a thumb over my cheek in a tender touch. "We need to know who these guys were. What do you remember about them?"

Justin. Harper.

They couldn't have them.

I grasped his wrist, holding it tight. "You have to get them back."

His eyes widened, just a bit at my ferocity, then they softened again. "We will."

"No. I mean it, Shane. We have to go now."

His eyes narrowed, and his head leaned back an inch. He was reassessing me, not that different from how Rena had moments earlier. "We will, but we handle this in-house. You gotta know that about us, this life. We don't deal with cops. We take care of everything ourselves."

He'd get no argument from me there.

He was still watching me, studying. "You okay with that?"

I stood up, looking around for my clothes. Seeing a bag he'd brought in with him, that he put on the counter behind him, I pointed to it. "Those for me?"

"They are. Roadie went and bought you some. Figured you wouldn't want to wear the others."

I suppressed a shudder because he was right, but reached for them. "Give 'em to me."

He passed them over, still eyeing me from my sudden change of attitude. "You okay, Kali?"

I took the bag and began to change clothes. "I'll tell you everything I remember, but I don't know much." I told him what I did as I finished dressing. Once I put on my old shoes, I was ready to go.

"You're supposed to take it easy."

But the way he said that, he knew me. I gave Shane a look. "You expecting that of me?"

He flashed a smile. "I'm a bit worried about your head, but no. You're forgetting I remember you from high school. I know just how much you love those friends of yours, and I've heard how fond you are of the boyfriend. I'd expect nothing else."

Good.

Some of my own tension left me at hearing that. He wouldn't fight me. He wouldn't try to contain me. He wouldn't tell me to stay home and be a good woman.

We left the room, and I put my head down to help with keeping out the extra stimulus. "They took our phones. Smashed them."

Shane was right next to me. "We found 'em. I got a replacement for you. Waiting until you were ready for it."

He handed over the phone just as we got to the hallway leading from the nurse's desk to what looked like the waiting room. I saw Shane's guys standing down there, waiting for us, but looked back over my shoulder.

Nurse Rena was standing, handing over a file to another nurse, but she was watching us right back.

Her eyes caught and held mine. She took me in, her gaze sliding to Shane, who had gone ahead, but was waiting for me now. He wasn't touching me. He wasn't coddling me, and Nurse Rena was noting all of that.

Her warning, Aly's warnings all flared through me but when I gave them much thought I kept coming back to the key terms that they were based off of history. In the past. That was back then, and not now and I had to make a decision if I would care or not.

I chose not to, right then and there. I'd heard the warnings. I wouldn't forget, but I wasn't going to let them affect me any more than that. That was a history that didn't pertain to me, so I was going to let it go.

That decision made, a whole renewed sense of desperation filled me up.

Justin and Harper. We needed to find them now.

I turned and *I* was the one who said to Shane, "Let's go."

37

SHANE

E verything stopped when we found Kali missing.
My world stopped.

But she was here. She was banged up a little bit, but *she was here.* Whoever did this to her, I was going to enjoy killing. I was also thinking I'd have to get in line because Kali might insist on doing it first.

She felt my gaze and looked my way. I was letting her see how I was feeling her, and unlike the past times when she'd shy away from me because I got it, a guy like me feeling how I felt and feeling how I felt it, it could be a lot. Made her uncomfortable at times with the bullshit her ex did to her, but not today. Not this time.

She was gazing right back at me, holding my look steadily and I saw the same fierceness she shifted into at the hospital. My woman was ready to declare war on whoever took her friends. Made me fall even more for her. She was fucking breathtaking.

"Oh whoa." Boise was slowing down for our turn into Grand-dad's place.

He came to the road, his arm waving in the air. A big ring of smoke was going up in the air from behind, where our bikes would be.

"What the fuck," Roadie growled.

Corvette glanced at me, but as soon as Boise pulled into the driveway and paused, both he and Roadie were out the truck.

Granddad was sweating, with blood dripping from his head. He was messed up and he started shaking his head, coughing. I asked, "What happened?"

Roadie and Corvette were sprinting back to check on our bikes. When we switched them out for the truck Granddad let us borrow, we'd grabbed our cuts so those were safe.

"Estrada."

"What?" From Boise.

Granddad was still shaking his head, but he was having a hard time standing. "I'm sorry. It was his men. They tore in here, looking for you guys. Took Tracey. Smashed our phones."

Holy.

Fuck.

The world went still when Kali went missing, but it stopped once again because holy fuck.

Roadie was running back and he came to an abrupt halt. "The bikes are fine. They left those, but they tore through the rooms. All our shits everywhere."

"What's smoking?"

"Ah." Granddad grimaced. "That's my fault, not theirs. They were in a tear looking for you guys and I was so mad, I grabbed my fire torch. Strung it up to my water blaster, but I used air instead. Turned off the water. Tried torching them. Got one, so they might be heading to a nearby hospital. They grabbed Tracey on the way out, but I think they took her as a hostage to get me to stop torching them. Thinking they were going to do something to your bikes, but when I turned that fire on them, they took off real quick."

"They took Tracey?"

My phone started blowing up. Heckler.

Word got to him, I was sure.

I answered it, but continued speaking to Granddad, "They smashed your phone too?"

"Oh yeah. They did that first. Came in, guns drawn, speaking Spanish. Not that I wouldn't know they were Estrada's. They had the Estrada tattoo on their neck, but Tracey knew one of them. I have no idea how she knew them, but she did. She started hollering about her man and his team coming after them. That's when I turned the torch on. I mean, it all kinda happened at the same time, but it was Estrada's guys."

"Shit." Roadie went still.

So did Boise.

So did I because this was huge if this was true.

I was out of the truck, my phone to my ear in another second. "You hear that?"

"Yeah, but holy shit. What's going on? You told me your woman was missing last night, but Boise sent me a text saying she was all good and that you'd catch me up. That's why I was calling."

Goddamn.

GodDAMN!

This was huge, fucking huge. Monumental.

"How's Prez?"

"He is not up for this shit."

"Goddamn, Heckler! We're at war if this is true."

"It's true and you know it. Since when does Granddad lie?"

"Never." I wanted to hurl this phone, but other thoughts were racing through my mind.

This meant war.

This meant we were behind already. That meant who knew how many bodies were on the ground already.

That also meant all our planning was up in smoke, the planning we took very careful consideration with Connor. But...well fuck, because that would still have to happen, but probably way sooner than we'd anticipated. Than I had anticipated because I wanted time to tell Kali, needed that time.

I was so desperate for it now because I'd lose her.

There was no if about it. It was when I'd lose her.

Fucking Estrada. He came. He knew. He figured it out somehow.

"Ghost, it's on you. That's another reason I was calling. Prez suffered a mini stroke last night. He's back in ICU. They caught it early, but he's unconscious. This true, and you have to act as if it is, then that means the entire club is at war against the cartel. You need to tell us your orders."

My mind was still racing. Hadn't stopped, not since hearing that news and I couldn't process Prez either. Heckler was now my number two in place. I was now acting national president for the entire Red Demons motorcycle club.

First things first. I spoke, motioning for the guys to come over. "I need to know where Estrada is. His guys hit us last night, tried to take my woman. *Did* take Granddad's niece and I'm thinking they also got two of my woman's friends."

Heckler cursed from his end.

Boise was on his phone. "I'm calling the team who has eyes on Estrada."

Corvette had his phone out and I said to him, "Call Crow. Tell him we're out of time. I need the list of those guys now, and then we need a group to be dispatched to round them up."

Corvette nodded, putting his phone out and walking away a little distance.

I said to Roadie, "Call our computer guys. Tell them the make and model of the van who took Justin and Harper, and let them know we need to find the guys who also took Tracey, Granddad's niece."

He gave a quick nod before stepping away, his phone to his ear already.

Granddad was taking it all in before hobbling over to me. He wiped his face off with the back of his shirt, squinting around. One hand went to his hip and he let loose a long sigh. "Can't say I fully know what's going on, but can see that it's a big deal those guys coming for you–"

"They might've been looking for me."

Kali had gotten out of the truck and was standing not far, hugging herself.

"Kali." I started for her.

She shook her head, stepping back. "No. Don't do that. Don't coddle me–"

"Boss! Hey, Boss! Ghost." Corvette came running back over, his eyes panicked. "Just hung up with Crow and got a call from Machete. He was jumped. Him and his woman were on the highway and he said a van pulled up. They shot at him, and took his woman."

GODDAMN!

"He okay?"

Corvette nodded quickly, his eyes skimming over Kali, who wasn't reacting. "Boss. Shot one of the guys, but he said there was a guy in the van that looked burned. Machete was hit, but they don't think it's serious. Bullet went right through him. They're taking him to the hospital now."

"Okay. Tell Stripes. I want six of our guys with him at the hospital. Once he's cleared, he's going to be hightailing it after Claudia. We need to figure out the situation before he gets there."

Corvette nodded, relaying my orders to Crow.

Kali spoke up. "It's the guys who took me and Aly. We got away, but they can't go back without hostages. So they're rounding up who they can. I mean, I don't know, but it's a hunch. Makes sense. How many times are people kidnapped? Can't be a coincidence."

Tracey. Now Claudia. Two females for two females.

I shared a hard look with Boise, who was coming back. "You hear all that?"

"Most of it. Team still has eyes on Estrada. He is sitting tight in Texas, in the Valley."

I nodded, but dammit I did not like that. "He's protected more down there than anywhere else."

"What's your call, Acting President?"

At the term, Roadie, who'd come over, and Corvette looked at me a little different. They grew more serious, more alert, less panicked. I looked at Kali and she was watching me back, still steady, the same look she had at the hospital and in the truck. She was waiting.

She wanted vengeance.

First things first, though. "We need to alert all the clubs between here and Texas. Estrada's guys got those hostages for a reason, to take back to Estrada. I want them stopped. Hostages rounded up, safely, and I want all of his men still alive. Send the word out."

Boise, Corvette, and Roadie all got to work, sending out the texts.

"Boss," Roadie was texting as he spoke up. "Computer guys hacked into the transportation system. They're checking street cams, but picked up a speeding van ten miles from Frisco. Makes sense if those are the guys who hit Machete."

Relief flooded me, but something else too. Something darker. Something harder. Something that I didn't want to admit was inside of me. "I want the exact coordinates. We're going to converge on that van and we're going to do it the same damn style we've done in the past. Organized and smart." Which meant, we just found our first battle.

I turned for Kali, and it's like she knew. She started backing up, shaking her head. "Don't cut me out. Not now. They have my family. And my sister."

I shared a look with Granddad, sending him an unspoken question.

He got it, raising his hand, and he gave me a nod.

"Kali."

"No, Shane!"

"Kali." I lowered my head, drawing closer to her. "You got a concussion. I don't care if it's a slight one or not, it's still a concussion. I made myself a promise when I discovered you missing. I told myself that I'd never put you in harm's way again, not intentional or unintentional. Now, some of that I can't hold to, but I gotta try for my own heart. You hearing me?"

"No," she cried out, a single tear slipping and falling down her cheek. "I can handle it. I'm a nurse. I know my own head."

My girl. She never once brushed the tear aside. Didn't think she even knew it was there.

"They have Harper. Justin." There were deep sobs in her voice, but she was holding them back. "Claudia will probably rip them apart, but Harper. Not Harper."

"I know." I moved in, my hands closing around her arms. I just needed to touch her, but I made a point not to make her feel like I was closing her in. I was learning or it was cementing she had an issue with that. "But I gotta go do what you've been getting all those warnings about me, with what we do. I need you safe, and baby, how your head is, you would not be safe with me."

She let out a growl. "Goddammit, Shane."

"I know." I motioned to Granddad. "He's going to stay with you while we go." To him, I said, "I'd be worried about the both of you here. We got guys in Frisco. I'd feel better if the both of you were there."

Granddad tightened his mouth, taking in his place, the big ring of smoke rising up from his place. "Yeah. There ain't much more I can do right now. Fire and police will probably be heading here, and to tell you the truth, I've got no interest in being here when they are. I feel a certain way about police."

It was decided. "Granddad, pack a bag. You got five minutes. I'll have you drive the truck, you and Kali."

He took off limping back to his place, wiping his face again with his shirt.

Roadie yelled, "Got 'em! We know where they are."

Thank Christ.

I shared a look with Boise before saying, "We need guys on them now, watching, following."

"I'll do it."

I gave him a nod and he took off, going for his bike.

Kali motioned for the truck. "I'm going to wait here."

I went over, pressing a kiss to her forehead. "Means a lot, you being okay with going with Granddad."

She glared up at me. "Don't get comfortable. It's cause I got a damn concussion."

I grinned, needing a taste of my woman. She was like heaven, just like always.

"I'd expect nothing less."

We rolled out five minutes later.

38

KALI

I tried calling Aly later that day.

Shane took off as soon as we got to this place. It was The Bonfire bar in Frisco, where I'd first been scared just to stop at. Needed to take that back because here I was, getting comfortable like this was going to be a temporary home. I shuddered at that thought, hoping it wouldn't happen. I'd go crazy, but who knew how long Shane would be gone.

We were put in a back bedroom. Shane said to let anyone know who might ask that I was his old lady. I gave him a look, but I knew what that meant and knew it'd keep anyone off my back.

As soon as we got here, I lay down, but now I was restless.

Shane was out there.

Aly was... I had no clue. She wouldn't take my call.

Justin. Harper. God. I held off on another shudder because they had to be okay. Had to be. If they weren't... I couldn't finish that thought.

And Claudia. I mean, I was more scared for the kidnappers in her case.

"Hey."

I'd wandered outside to the street, and went down a little to sit on a bench. This place was a ghost town, or just about, and they had four prospects guarding the front door. I thought going thirty yards away would be okay. Shelly thought the same. She was coming my way. Dressed in long sleeves, she had the ends pulled down over her hands and stepped up from where the front of The Bonfire switched to the front of this store. It was a small diner, but it was closed. They had better upkeep. The benches in front of The Bonfire were nonexistent. It looked like what an old watering shed might look like in an old western movie, with low bearing shafts on top and posts out front as if in the old days they'd tie their horses to them. All that was missing was the actual watering tubs for the horses. There was none of that here. The place behind me was all windows. No awnings overlooking. No posts. Nothing. Just a couple benches and now I had company as Shelly sat down beside me.

She added, "See you got pulled in for the second round, huh?" She glanced to my phone. "You making a call? They usually try to keep that down to a minimum."

"It's to my friend. I think she's on lockdown like me so I thought she might be okay. Besides," I motioned to the bar thirty yards away. "The bad guys know about this place."

"That's true." She laughed, but the sound was half empty.

I texted Aly instead.

Me: Hey, it's Kali. I got a new phone... and now realizing you probably did too.

I hit send, knowing she wouldn't respond back.

I started to tuck it away when it buzzed back.

Unknown: It's Aly. We got my phone switched over this afternoon. Have you heard from Harper?

I took a breath before typing back.

Me: You should call me.

Aly: I can't. Brandon is extra sensitive right now. He's worried, thinking all sorts of bad things. You know.

Oh, boy. I did, and he'd been right to worry.

Me: Are you safe?

Aly: Yeah. Worried about you. Worried that I can't get a hold of Harper. Brandon said they don't know where Harper is or Justin. I assumed they were with you.

Me: You should really call me.

Aly: Now I'm getting scared. Just tell me. I'll handle it.

Me: Where are you? Just tell me you're safe.

Aly: Yeah. We're at Brandon's brother-in-law's house. He's a bounty hunter so his whole team is here, and there's a bunch of others as well. It's a full thing but you're making me scared.

Things changed so fast. Aly had 'her people' and I was here with 'my people.' We were at two different places, being protected by two different groups.

Me: Do they have guns?

Aly: Um, I don't know. There's some HUGE guys here though. I feel safe with them. Stop stalling. Where is Harper?

"Just tell her."

I jumped, screaming.

Shelly sat back, grimacing a tiny bit. "Sorry. I got bored and you weren't hiding the phone. I did try not to read them, but couldn't help myself." She nodded to the phone. "Just tell her. She's asking about your friend, the one that was taken right?"

I stilled. "What do you know about it?"

She shrugged, pulling the ends of her sleeves further over her hands. "Nothing much except that Crow said there was a couple attacks. Estrada tried to take you and your friend. I'm guessing that's the friend? On the phone. He said that they took others instead. I'm also guessing that you're meaning your friend 'Harper.' Am I right?"

"You always this quick with business that's not yours?"

She flashed me a grin. "I'd like to tell you that this doesn't happen or this isn't a common occurrence, and while it's not really that common, this does happen. Your man's a Red Demon. They're not a riding bike club. They're the real deal. You should know whose bed you're getting into because what Crow says, your man is now their president. Or soon-to-be their national president. You're with Ghost and that means your whole world is going to change. The Reds aren't small time. They're going against a cartel for a reason."

A cartel?!

I inhaled my gasp because I couldn't let it out. I wouldn't. No one could know how I was reeling on the inside. "What did you just say?"

"The Estrada Cartel." Shelly sat further back, giving me a set look. "They're a 1% club. You know what that means, right?"

I bristled. "I know."

She settled down beside me. "Good. For a moment, I was getting nervous. Thinking you had no clue whose dick you're blowing. I'd get educated real quick if that was the case."

I gave her a look, but she wasn't noticing it. Then my phone started ringing.

Aly calling.

Oh boy. I heaved a breath, trying to squash the nerves as I answered the call. "Hey."

"Where is Harper? Brandon's all grrr right now. I don't know how to explain everyone's relation here but some chick just showed up and said that they got reports that 'some others' were taken. Those were her words. Did they take Harper?" Her voice went up a notch.

I stood, and started walking. My mind was a mess, literally. My stomach was a mess. Everything was a mess. "Aly."

"Oh God. It's really bad if that's how you're speaking to me. What is it? Is it Harper? Did they take him too? We didn't find him and we were going to look for him. What is going on, Kali?! Tell me."

"I—"

"Kali! Just tell me."

I stopped, my head falling back. My stomach was emptying

out to my feet. All my insides were being dumped. "I don't know who took him, but someone did. I think... I think it was a cartel."

There was absolute silence on her end.

I couldn't bear it, waiting for her.

I knelt down, wherever I was. I had no clue. I didn't care. I squatted as low to the ground as I could go. "I'm so sorry, Aly. This is all my fault. We came out here because of me. I went with Shane, and now, these guys–I think they tried to grab us to hurt Shane's motorcycle club. I'm so sorry."

"You're saying," her voice ground out. "You're saying a cartel took Harper?"

I pressed my eyes closed so tight. I was holding my phone against my face, so hard that I'm surprised I didn't crack it. "Justin too."

"Justin too?!"

"I think they got my sister too. And some other lady."

"OH MY FUCKING GOD, ARE YOU LISTENING TO YOUR-SELF?! FOUR PEOPLE, KALI! Four people! Your boyfriend is the cause of all of this. And you're right, if we'd not gone out here, then NONE OF THIS WOULD'VE HAPPENED!"

"Babe?" I heard from her end.

She sucked in a dramatic breath, but I could hear her crying.

That was me. That was my fault.

All of this was my fault.

"I'm so sorry, Aly. I'm so sorry." I didn't know what else to say, or do. "I'm so sorry. We'll get him back. I promise."

Her tone was chilling. "You cannot promise that. Do not even dare touch that."

Another shiver went through me at her voice.

She hated me. I could hear it. There was pain, but there was loathing.

I'd lost my friend. And I just hoped that I hadn't physically lost Justin and Harper too. Or Claudia. Goddamn Claudia. I'd not been letting myself think of her either. Claudia chose this life.

She knew more than me so her being taken wasn't on me, but it didn't matter.

My heart hurt for her too.

Shane needed to find them. He did. He needed to bring them back. All of them.

Please, God. Please. Just, please.

"I'm going to share with Brandon and his family what's going on, and then I'm going to pray that Harper and Justin are found. Because if they aren't, Kali, then I'm coming for you because this is all your fault. Damn you."

Every word she said was a punch to me. I felt them, blow after blow, and by the time she hung up on me, I was right there with her because damn me. This was all my fault.

"Your friend's a bit unhinged."

I whirled around, seeing Shelly standing behind me, a lit cigarette in her hand. She'd stood facing the street, her arm crossed over her chest, under her other arm that was holding her cigarette. She looked all casual, but she had followed me.

"I don't need you to watch over me."

She took a drag from her cigarette before motioning to my phone, exhaling. "I'm thinking you do if you let that 'friend' get in your head. She's wrong, you know. Nothing is no one's fault. It just happens. I heard enough to gather that you guys came out here for a reason? You force your friends to get in your car?"

"You don't know what you're talking about." I started to head back, but she touched my arm, stopping me.

She gestured down the way with her head. "We're fine down here. Also, some of the girls are going to be arriving. A bunch go to a beauty school not far from here and they will go crazy when they get a load of us being in their place. That's what they think. I'm hoping to wave some of the guys down here and sneak in the diner behind us for some food when it opens for supper. You in? I'm betting you're hungry."

She was right. My stomach growled as if on command. "What do you mean girls?"

"The sweet butts. You know, the girls that sleep with anyone as long as they're hanging out with the club."

"There's actually women who do that?"

"Oh yeah." She took another drag from her cigarette. "All sorts, but don't worry. I've never heard of the infamous Ghost taking a woman."

I was still feeling raw from Aly. "Don't think you know him since he's not from this charter."

Shelly laughed, taking a drag again. "You're right. He's not and I don't, but give me a break. Been around enough guys. I can tell. Your guy, he's a good one. Solid. Loyal. Smart. He's like my old husband, or I'd like to think so don't take that away from me. He's dead after all."

And I was feeling like a heel. "I'm sorry."

"No worries. I'm not normal. Life and death doesn't affect me like it does with others. My husband is gone, on the other side, and I'm here, spending my days out trying to enjoy life as much as I can until I go over and join him. Don't get me on past lives because that's a whole other thing with me." But she took a fourth drag, exhaling, and pointed the cigarette at me. "You know that I have friends who do believe in past lives? They think we're just energy in these bodies, for this life. Like I have some friends who fully believe they were an Apache in another life. One is convinced she was a horse. And I got another friend who is convinced she was some goddess from Africa. You believe in that stuff?"

I... had absolutely no idea what to say to her. "Why are you telling me this?"

She glanced back to the bar, then to me. "Honestly? One, because I think it's cool. And two, I'm stalling because the girls all arrived and are inside. Now I'm going to use your phone and give one of the guys down there a call. The owners are opening this diner up behind us in five minutes. Trust me. We *want* to eat at Mama's Diner, and not at The Bonfire. They mean well, but their food is shit."

She nabbed my phone and did as she said.

And me, I was trying not to think about Harper or Justin because if I did, I was going to fall apart.

I HIT call on my phone.

He didn't answer, but I knew he wouldn't because he didn't know it was me.

I texted instead.

Me: Dad. My phone got smashed. This is my new number.

39

SHANE

W e walked to where Boise was stationed, all of us quiet and dressed in black. We needed to be stealth so the bikes were left on a back road, pulled off so no one would find them. He'd taken point on the nearest hill to where Estrada's guys were holding up, in a house. Who knew if it was theirs or one they broke into, looking for a rest stop? I had no idea, but I intended to find out.

He shifted aside, giving me the night vision goggles. "There's three of them, but they already ditched the burned guy. He was making too much noise so they shot him. See that plastic pile behind the house?" I moved the goggles, seeing it set next to their garage. He added, "That's him."

"Jesus," Corvette said quietly behind us.

"That mean there's two or still three targets?"

"Still three. One in the back that's been checking on the hostages, and two in the front. From watching, it looks like there's some problem with the first two. They're upset about something, one guy keeps pacing. He's come outside a few times to check for a cell signal." Boise was grinning as he held up his device. "Don't know I grabbed this handy dandy cell blocker."

Corvette whistled low under his breath. "I didn't think those get good distance. How far are we out?"

"We're two hundred yards, not that far, but yeah, farther than the normal. I got ambitious last winter, decided to try my hand at inventing shit."

Boise was being modest. He was a genius when it came to tech and weapons.

I settled more firmly on my stomach, my elbows helping keep the goggles steady for me as I scanned the rest of the house. Heat signatures showed me where each person was, including the hostages. Both were on the floor. One looked restless, or antsy. The other was holding still. I had a guess the one being antsy was Claudia.

"What do we know about Granddad's niece?"

I passed the goggles off to Corvette as I replied to Boise, "There a reason you're asking?"

He gave a shrug, turning to watch the house with his own set of binoculars. "Just a feeling. Something's wrong. I can't hear anything, but they're treating her differently than Machete's woman."

"We know how Machete is doing?"

Corvette answered, "I've been getting updates. He's getting stitched up. Stripes knows the nurse and asked her to take her time."

Boise grinned. "He's going to hurt for that one. You know Machete is fully aware of what we're all doing."

"Yeah. They confiscated his phone. Same nurse passed it to Stripes or Machete would be blowing up all our phones."

"No, he wouldn't. He'd track our GPS and hunt us while we're hunting Estrada's guys," I commented.

The guys all grinned because they knew I was right.

"What's the plan here, Boss?"

Plan. Fuck. We always needed a plan.

I got serious. The slight moment of jokes was refreshing, but now it was onto the killing business. "You have reason to believe they know this place? Have traps set up for some reason?"

"Nope. I think they are fully and completely alone. I don't think they've even been able to send word to their big boss, which is why that one guy keeps pacing up the place."

"Okay. Then the plan is that we converge on the cabin. Use silencers. Masks. Plan to capture all targets if possible."

"And if that's not an option?" Corvette asked the question, but all the guys were waiting.

I had to be the one to give the go-ahead.

I said, "Then you take them out. I want Roadie and Corvette handling the women."

"I call Granddad's niece," Roadie piped up quick.

Corvette threw him a glare. "Fuck you. You know it doesn't happen that way."

Boise asked me, "How many Reds do we have back there waiting for your order?"

"They're waiting for us to return and then figure out a plan."

All of my guys stopped and stared at me.

They knew me. "That's why we're going to go in now, and I'll call them once everything is taken care of."

Crow said he had men he didn't trust. I sent orders for him to round them up, put them in a location, but the truth of that matter was that I didn't know if there were men I shouldn't trust or Crow himself. And with the attacks, getting back who we could took first priority. So I wasn't going to bring in anyone that I didn't trust to have my back in a situation like we were going to enter.

Knowing that, all of these guys got real serious real fast.

"Suit up."

We went in, silencers added to our guns. We were already in camouflage, but as we converged on the house, Boise and I went to the front. Roadie and Corvette went to the back. I wished we had more of our guys, but there hadn't been time. Half needed to stay back, watch over Kali and whoever else was there. The others were with Machete. And just as we arrived, Roadie told me he got a notice from our computer guys. They found the second vehicle.

It was already in Arizona by now.

We got to the door, and over our comms, we did roll call.

"I have eyes on target one." That was Boise.

I said, "I have eyes on target two."

"I have target three."

"Roadie?" That was me.

"Ready."

"On three." I led the count. "One. Two."

As I said three, the plan was that Roadie would open the door, and toss in a flashbang. Corvette would go in, stun the man back there. At the same time, we'd smash into our door and each stun our guys from the back.

We heard the flashbang go off, and we were moving.

Boise pulled the door open.

I went in first, sweeping to the left.

He moved to the right.

Both our targets were going through the doorway, but they turned at hearing us.

Guns were up–bang!

Bang!

Their bodies fell. After that, we cleared the house just to make sure.

There were no surprises on the first floor, second, or in the basement. We were good so still keeping the lights off, we got to work. Boise and I made sure each guy was knocked out with another tranquilizer, then the guys were carried to the front of the house. I could hear Roadie and Corvette over the comms and in the house as they were talking to the women.

Claudia seemed fine. Pissed, but fine.

The other lady was more of a surprise because none of us really knew Tracey. She grew up in the biker community, but her folks were out east. Something happened and she decided to move to West Virginia, took up with her sister and her sister's husband. Granddad always talked about Tracey as being smart, tough, and someone not to cross. She was also described as having a big personality, but when he was once asked what that meant, he shrugged and said she did hair.

She should've been someone that was snatched up by mistake, and on another operation I would've chalked that up to what it was. But that didn't fly with Boise, who said she was being treated differently. I wanted to know more about that.

Boise went to check the truck, then did a search inside. He showed up, dangling some keys and flashed a smile at me. "Transpo."

Solid plan.

He went, reversed their own truck up to the house and we began putting their bodies on the back of it. At the same time, Roadie and Corvette were bringing the women around from the back of the house.

I checked, not sure what to expect, but stone-cold expressions on both women was not it.

That was until they saw the guys we were loading up.

"Goddamn, you assholes!" Claudia screeched, going after the one Boise and I were currently carrying. She began hitting him on the chest and when that wasn't good enough, she tried kicking at him. He was too high for her, so he got a few hits to the back.

"Grab her," I barked at Roadie, who swept her up. He began backing up, his arms around her waist.

His head was down and he was murmuring something to her. It wasn't working.

She had her hands in fists and her legs were still trying to get free, but she wasn't struggling too hard in getting away from him. Suddenly, after we loaded him up, and he was the last one, a sob erupted from her throat. "Goddamn," she whispered before she hung in Roadie's arms.

He lifted his head, meeting my gaze and I was getting it.

Something very serious had happened before we got here.

Glancing at the other woman, she seemed more put-together. Withdrawn. Quiet, but standing close to Corvette. Her arms were wrapped around herself. Catching my gaze, she didn't jerk her eyes away. She flinched, and her face tightened on some emotion I couldn't place, but she held my gaze.

"Roadie," I said it quiet.

"Hmm?" He was still holding Claudia.

I motioned to her. "Help her get situated in the truck."

He gave me a nod, putting her back on her feet and ushering her gently, with caution, to the truck.

Boise was doing a pass through the house. If there was something there he thought we could use, he'd grab it. I trusted him. He was more thorough than myself. So I moved toward Corvette and Tracey.

She might've been a good-looking woman, heavy makeup even under these circumstances. Her hair was flat, and I could tell it was bothering her because she kept fussing with it. But those eyes were hard and aged. She struck me as in her thirties, but I couldn't quite get a read on the exact number. She had meat on her bones and she carried herself in a way that she was proud of it. She was watching me watch her, and she took a breath, one, right before I settled in front of her.

"You're the leader."

I gave a nod. "Suppose that's what they call me."

Her eyes went to the guys in the truck. "Those are Marco Estrada's men."

"You know that before they swept you up?"

"No. I would've known them without because of their neck tattoos."

Claudia was in the truck by now, and Roadie had half of an arm around her, on the back of the seat. She wasn't curled into him, but she wasn't on the other side of the seat. Her head was buried in her lap and she was shaking from silent sobbing.

I gave a nod in their direction. "You want to fill me in on what they did to my man's woman?"

She looked over, another heavy sigh leaving her. "They didn't touch her in any way, if that's what you're asking. They told her that they killed her sister. They do that to mine, I'd take a knife to their balls. Unconscious or not."

"They told her what?"

She looked back, her eyes flaring a little. "They murdered her sister—"

I was moving before she finished, going to the truck. "Claudia."

I rested a foot on the bottom rung, a hand on the top of the door and I waited for her to look my way.

She didn't. She kept shaking from the middle of the seat.

"She ain't dead, Claudia."

She sniffed once and lifted her head. Her face was wet from the tears, and she sniffled again, using the back of her arm to wipe over her face. "Say what?"

"They took her, but they didn't keep her. The brainiacs that took you were the ones who lost her."

Her mouth parted, and she was absolutely still. "It's not a good idea to fuck with me right now, Ghost."

"Not fucking with you, in any way. Your sister's alive and sitting in Frisco territory right now, far away from these assholes."

"You're saying Kali is alive?"

A firm nod from me. "My woman is alive."

Roadie snorted, now relaxing and slumping a little in the seat. "If she was dead, you think he'd be standing here all calm-like and talking to you? Fuck no. Ghost would be *ghost*, hockey mask and all and he'd be *gone*." He whistled, shaking his head. "These guys would've been toast the second we found 'em, and he'd be off, going for the next round all by himself if he could've. Nah, woman. Your sister is alive."

Claudia's eyes were bulging at me, and she was breathing hard. Her chest was rising. "My man?"

"Probably pissed as fuck at us, but he's alive too. Bullet went through him."

"Why'd he be pissed at you?"

"Because we came to get you without him. I wanted this mission done with one of the guys alive to be questioned. That wouldn't have happened with your man here, whether you were hurt or not."

She blinked, and her whole body shuddered. She slumped back. "Thank GOD! Thank GOD!" But she was yelling and punching the dashboard before she tried to twist around to look at the guys in the back. "I want at 'em, Ghost! They fucking told me they killed my sister. They said that shit to me."

Oh, Christ.

I eased back from the door, but said to Roadie, "Contain her."

"I'll try."

Tracey moved next to me, and she motioned for the open seat. "I'm guessing that's for me?" She scanned the horizon around us. "They were trying to call Estrada to get his orders. I don't know if they got through or not, but speaking on behalf of my hide, I'd like to move on out of these parts? Maybe have a meeting somewhere else? Somewhere that's safe?"

I eyed her, but gave a nod. As she got into the seat, I gave a short whistle to Roadie and signaled him for no cell phones, then I motioned to the two women. He gave me the slightest nod before starting the engine.

After that, Corvette and I hopped up into the back.

Boise was coming back out of the house, and he lingered long enough to throw a match inside.

He took off, and jumped into the back with us. All of us got down, just in case, but it wasn't long before the house was burning bright. It was always a good idea to torch any possible evidence behind us, if anything to slow down Estrada on making his next move. Or I was hoping, thinking he might want to wait for reports of bodies found in that fire.

ROADIE DROVE us to where our bikes were.

We'd called ahead so a few of our guys were waiting when we arrived. One was a prospect and he hopped off the back of a bike, heading over to the truck. Roadie got out, and the guy got in. He'd be the driver.

Stripes was one of the guys who came to meet us, and he came over to me. "Machete is pissed at you."

I grunted. "Where is he?"

"He's at The Bonfire. A few of us slipped away to meet you, but he ain't going to be happy that we did that."

"I know." Keeping guys out of the loop was not in our culture, but neither were handling cartels, bad club politics, and splitting your club up in four fucking different ways. "I'll talk to him, but did you let him know that we got her?"

He nodded. "Yeah, and speaking of, I know of a warehouse we can bunker down in." He jerked his chin up toward the back of the truck, meaning he knew of a discreet place where we could have our interrogation.

"It's safe?"

"It's the middle of nowhere. My uncle tried doing a shop here, but it didn't take. It sat abandoned when he got carted off to prison."

"All right. Send everyone the coordinates."

My phone buzzed then.

Crow: What's the plan? We're twiddling our thumbs up our asses here.

"Stripes."

"Yeah?" He'd started back for his bike.

"Text it to Crow too."

He paused, just briefly before he gave a nod.

Me: Meet us at the coordinates.

Boise came over. "You sure about that? He's got guys we might not be able to trust."

I was watching Tracey and Claudia in the truck and I tracked down to where those guys were still lying unconscious. We had more battles on the way concerning Estrada. I wanted to handle the one with Crow or his men before we did that.

"Yeah. I want to get it all out in the open, once and for all."

Boise went still, hearing what I wasn't saying. He let out a swift curse under his breath. "Gonna be fire, that's for sure."

"Yeah."

I was past caring.

They tried to go after my woman. They shot my brother, and they were planning on doing more, a whole lot more. These were just the warning shots as far as I was concerned.

I was itching to go after them.

40

SHANE

Heckler was calling when we arrived to the place Stripes told us about. The place looked abandoned, like he said, so he had to kick in the door a few times before it finally opened.

"Oh, man. Are you serious?" Roadie was griping, waving his hand in the air before him as he walked inside. "This place is covered in dust and probably rat shit. I got allergies."

"Cry me a river," Stripes sent right back.

My phone was still ringing so I answered, starting to walk right back on the gravel driveway we just came down. "Give me some good news."

He laughed. "I'll do that, no problem. Prez is going to pull through, and we have him locked up tight. He is hidden and no way anyone can find him."

I stopped because what. Did. That. Mean? I was scared to hope. "You shitting me?"

"I would never shit you. We are heading your way, or I should clarify that we are heading to stop that second van. Thinking we can cross paths with them in Albuquerque. You think you can meet us?"

"I'm thinking you're going to get there way sooner than we can."

"You got the other van?"

"We got the other van."

He let out an amused grunt. "That is fan-fucking-tastic."

I looked back. The warehouse was lit up so there was electricity. The guys were starting to bring Estrada's men inside. And as I watched, I saw Tracey start to grab one of the guys and after a second's hesitation, Claudia took the other end of him. Together, they carried the man inside. He dipped low to the ground, but Tracey was a strong woman. She was holding her own. Claudia struggled, but out of sheer spite, she held up the guy's arms and head. It was almost comical to watch.

Corvette moved in and relieved Claudia before she did head damage to the guy.

Once they were inside, I asked in a low tone, "You know anything about this Tracey?"

"That's Granddad's niece? The one they grabbed?"

"The very one."

"Not really, but she's not really in the community anymore. I thought she wifed up with someone? Out in West Virginia? Doing hair, right?"

"Could you ask around, see if you hear anything about her."

"Sure, but what's the reason? What are you looking for?"

"I don't know, just a wonder right now. Boise said Estrada's guys were treating her differently. And she wasn't too tore up when we found her. Makes me wonder. She helped bring in one of the guys just now too."

"Yeah, yeah. Consider it done. I'll call the computer guys, have them do a search."

"Good. That's a good call."

"See you, Boss. Call me when you got things figured out where you are."

"Will do."

I was heading inside when Tracey stepped out, and she did it in a way like she'd decided this was her time to talk to me. There was a purpose to her step, and she stood in the middle of the door. Her head lifted. Her eyes met mine, and she asked, "Thinking we could have a talk before you lay into those guys back there?"

Well, then.

I stepped back and to the side. "After you."

Her head went back down, but everything about her was reading she knew exactly what she was doing. Her shoulders were set. Her gait was strong, stable. She led the way, taking us to the far end of the parking area, and then farther down a walking path, past a few trees.

She noted where the road was, and the driveway, seeing we were hidden if anyone came out looking for us.

I sent a text to Boise.

Me: Be a minute.

Boise: You want me to start questioning? One of them is waking up.

Me: Have at it.

She had settled back on her heel, watching me text.

I gave her a nod. "I'm all yours."

She opened her mouth, but a blood-curdling scream filled the air.

Boise must've decided to start with the hard questions first.

"I've noticed that I've not been offered a phone."

"Yeah. I wanted to talk to you first."

Her head moved up and down, chewing on that. "Right. Well, I'd like a phone. I'm sure you've talked to Granddad, told him I'm good, but I've got a man that'd take it a certain way that I've not notified him as quick as I could've."

"About your man, he someone I should know about? My man was set on you guys for a bit before we pulled up. He watched while he was waiting for us, and he told us that you were getting different treatment from Estrada's men. I'm wondering if you'd be open to sharing with me the reason for that treatment. That being said, I'll share that I've been told they treated you differently. I'm assuming it was better considering how Claudia lit into them and you didn't."

"Right." She was back to chewing on that information, looking like she was literally chewing the inside of her cheek. "So, I'm not a part of this fight, but since they took me, thinking I was one of your women, I'm thinking this changes things a bit. Having said that, you need to know that my man works for someone who works with Estrada. They found out, and freaked. It's why they were trying to call Estrada, or I'm assuming, because I educated them as soon as I learned who they were."

Well. Fuck.

Things made more sense now.

"You're from West Virginia. In my books, that ain't considered east. The people who Estrada has aligned with are known to be in the east." I gave her a once-over. "And Russian. Assuming you're not from where he lives in Mexico or those guys might not have mistaken your identity."

Her lips parted, half in a grin, half in a grimace. "Look, I come from biking stock. Grew up with my dad riding for his club. My loyalty is strong with you, but I'm in a situation where I don't feel fully prepared to share the name of my man or how it is that he's partially in employment with Estrada's ally. Also, saying all that considering the very abrupt turn of events because up until a few days ago, the belief was set that the Red Demons motorcycle club was the reason Estrada was so powerful in the States. It gets out that he doesn't have you anymore, and well, I'm just giving a subtle hint that could affect other relationships he's got but I still don't feel comfortable giving you my man's name. Tip my hand too much and I'm not real sure if I'm in enemy territory or with friends of my family. I can say that I don't mean you any harm and you letting me call my man would go a long way with some people."

Now my lips parted because she was asking for a show of faith without giving me much.

Goddamn it all again because I already knew what I was going to do, and seriously hoping this wouldn't kick me in the ass later on. I gave a nod. "Okay. I'll dispatch a guy to take you back and give you a phone. We'll get you where you need to go."

"I appreciate it. A ride to the nearest town and hotel, and a phone for a call will be all I need. I'll be good after that."

"Nearest town? Not to see your uncle?"

"I was planning on checking in with him via the phone, but guess I could ask you. He's okay?"

"He's okay. He's in Frisco at one of our places."

"Good. Keep him safe, but the nearest town and a call to my man is all I need."

We were heading back as we heard the engines first, then the headlights started showing. A line of motorcycles was coming around the corner.

Crow and the rest of his charter had arrived.

But the first to me was Machete. He parked, almost catapulted himself off his bike, and he was marching right to me.

"Now, Machete–"

Punch!

A right hook landed on my face. I went with the punch, but threw my hands up because Machete was my brother and I understood his anger. "I'm sorry–"

"Goddamn you, Ghost." He threw another punch, hissing as he did.

I dodged that one, and evaded yet another as he tried to get me with an upper cut.

"Stop!" I stood my ground, because I was the boss now. Whether he was weighing that into his anger or not. Vice Prez and I might've thrown down a few punches back his way, just to have some fun. I couldn't, not this time, not with what we still had to get to. "I had to make sure they were alive to question. That's why."

"Goddamn you, Ghost!" He stopped swinging, but he was still riled up. He had wild eyes and he was looking around. "Where is she?"

"Machete!" came from inside.

"Claude!" he yelled right back, moving toward her, but slower and grimacing. He was pressing a hand up to his bandaged shoulder.

Stupid fucker. Throwing punches when he just took a bullet there?

Stupid fucker that was my brother, that's who he was. I loved the guy. I'd do worse, I knew that much.

"She's fine. She was more worked up. They told her they killed Kali."

He threw me one last look, and not a happy one, before Claudia cleared the doorway. She sprinted for him, tears rolling down her face. She launched herself, her legs wrapping around his waist. He caught her, bullet hole be damned, and he carried her off to the woods.

They'd need a minute.

Tracey had been watching, and she cast me a grin. "Some days I really really miss this life. Feels damn good to be back, even if it was for a minute."

I gave her a half grin back, still hoping I wasn't going to regret letting her walk. "Even being taken hostage?"

She grunted. "Hell. That was the fun part."

41

KALI

Knock, knock!

    I was on the bed, lying there waiting for something. Anything. I'd not undressed and I wasn't even under the covers, but hearing the knock, I bolted upright.

"Yeah?" I scrambled for the door, opening it.

A woman was there, wearing a tight tank top and the skimpiest of skimpy jeans. I gave her a brief glimpse because she was one of the 'sweet butts' that Shelly pointed out to me. There was a hierarchy even among the women in this world and according to Shelly, I was at the top since Ghost had been saying I was his old lady. The term sounded offensive, but it meant something to them. I was trying to get that, I was, but right now I was only focused on getting Harper and Justin back. After that, I needed to see where everything would lay between myself and Aly, and also Shane and myself.

"What?"

She stepped back, her head moving down and up as she gave me a once-over. She sniffed at the end, literally sniffed. "Guys say that you need to get packing. You're going on a trip real soon."

"What?"

But she turned and was heading back.

I stepped out into the hallway, but I didn't say anything more.

A trip?

I had nothing to pack up, but I went to the bathroom. Washed up. Got as ready as I could and then I grabbed my bag before leaving the room. Those women were in the bar, some sitting on a few of the guys' laps. Others were bellied up to the counter.

I scanned the room, looking for anyone I recognized. There was no one and seeing a few of the guys going through a door to a back section, I followed to see who was all out there.

Seeing Shelly in the corner, having a smoke, I headed over there. "He–"

She snatched my wrist and pulled me around the corner, and I didn't even know there was a corner here.

I was looking around because where were we? This looked like a private section. We weren't in the back anymore, but we weren't on the other side of the wall either, where the street was.

"Listen."

"What is this place?"

She waved her cigarette in the air, dismissing me. "It's for private hookups. You know, if one of the guys wants to get his dick sucked in private or something else."

Oh.

Ew. I was looking around at it differently now, though, again, I knew that was part of their lifestyle. They wanted to live life to the fullest and doing a threesome where others could be seen was something they did without blinking an eye. Had Shane ever done that? And because the question was now burning in my head, I asked, "There was a woman who came and told me to get my bag."

"Yeah. About that–"

"Do you think Shane ever hooked up with her?"

"What?"

"Her and Shane. That's their purpose, right? To hook up with the guys?"

"Uh. Yeah. I mean, it's not so clear-cut. They get protection from the club, but not the respect. But they know that signing up. It's their choice to be a sweet butt."

"What kind of woman would do that? Or a girl would do that? Sign up, service the guys, get looked down on by others and for what?"

"Protection. A sense of belonging. The guys really like them."

"I don't understand that."

"That's because you're not made that way. They are. You aren't. Some don't know better. Some like it, but listen." She ground out her cigarette and touched my arm, stepping close again. She lowered her voice. "A little after we came back from dinner, a bunch of Shane's club came in. Then, a bit ago, they took off again. They didn't ask if you were here and Crow and a bunch of guys went with them, but I overheard something that I don't think I should've."

"What?" Also, why was that dread coming back to me? "Does it have something to do with my friends?"

"What?"

"Uh." I shook my head. "Never mind. What'd you overhear?"

"I don't know how much of club business you know, but I know a little. There was recently a vote put where they're not working with a cartel anymore. Some of the guys aren't on board and I overheard a conversation that some are going to go ahead and ambush the rest. I'm not sure what that means, but I heard where they're going."

"What?" Oh God. My heart slammed against my chest. "Where?"

"They're heading for Texas. A town there. Amarillo." She pulled me even closer. "I think we should go."

I backed up. "Wait. What?"

"Yeah. I tried calling Crow, but I know something when

they're on these missions, they use cell phone blockers. And I'm a little edgy about keeping mine with me. They got computer people who could track ours, but I can't sit here and wait to see what happens. Not if we can get to them. Stop them or the very least, warn them."

Yes.

Everything she was saying I was down for.

God. Not just Harper and Justin now, but Shane.

I pulled my phone out. "I could call Shane right now."

She shook her head. "I wouldn't. I mean, who knows who could listen in, right? And if we let him know, that's great, but the wrong person might hear too."

"What are you saying then?"

"I think we should go. The guys are off somewhere else, but if they're heading to Texas, we should too. If anything we can get there and then call, and find where they are. By then, they can't stop us." She was studying me intently. "What do you think?"

They already tried to hurt me, hurt Aly. They had Harper and Justin.

This was a fucking no-brainer for me.

"I'm in."

She closed her eyes, her relief evident. "Good." She looked down, seeing my bag. "Oh good, you have that. Where's your phone?"

I pulled it out.

She motioned to it. "Turn it off, and let's just go. The guys are still here. I know the route they use. My car is around the block. We could do this, get there ahead of them."

"Then let's do it."

I turned my phone off, and we snuck out.

42

SHANE

C *alling Kali.*
        "The person for this account has not yet set up her voice–"

I hung up because what the fuck?

"What's wrong?" Boise came over.

I sent off a text before putting the phone back in my pocket.

Me: Where are you? Call me.

"Can't get a hold of Kali. She's back at The Bonfire, right? You been in contact with the guys back there?"

"No. Our guys are here."

"Kali is there."

He grimaced. "Uh, if she was keeping her head down, I don't think they would've known she was there. I didn't tell them. Did you?"

Shit. "No. Everything was hitting the hay here."

"None of the guys would've told them. We pulled the rest of our club here, they rode in with Crow and the others."

This wasn't sitting right with me. "I need to talk to Crow. We might need to send some guys back for her, some of ours."

"Sounds good. You want me to send him out?"

I was outside, and it was nearing five in the morning. The night had been about interrogating Estrada's men, who told us nothing. It wasn't that I didn't believe them. I did. We let Machete loose on them. He'd been feeling a certain way since they took his woman. But it was that they didn't know anything. They were told to grab two Red Demon women. Kali had been specifically mentioned, but when she went missing, they had to improvise. It happened exactly as Kali guessed it had.

"And the two guys?"

The guy was crying and bleeding, but he wasn't holding back. It only took two hits before he broke. His friends had been the same. "I don't know. We were told two women. The other van might've been told to get people friendly to the Red Demons. They were easy pickings. Right there and talking. We saw the one at your table in the bar so we knew he was an ally of your club. That's all I can say. Honest. You don't get it. We have to go back with someone or it's our head and our family's hanging. You can't mess up with our boss."

"Yeah. He's a great guy. We're aware."

I nodded to Boise now, and added, "Send Stripes too."

He went inside. After we were done with the interrogations, we were getting ready to go to New Mexico and meet with Heckler. Or at least that was our plan. I'd not given Crow the exact details, instead announcing to everyone to get ready to ride.

He was coming now, and Stripes showed up a second later. He paused, seeing Crow with me. "You want me to come back?"

I motioned for him to come over.

He did, and I asked Crow, "I left my woman at your headquarters. Now I can't get a hold of her. What guys do you have back there?"

"Some prospects. We cleared out the hangarounds until this was all cleaned up with Estrada, but I left a few of my most trusted guys there. Shelly's there too. I asked her to watch over your woman, and the last she told me they were eating at the diner with my guys. She sent me a text saying they were buckling down until she heard more from us. That was it. You want me to call her?"

"I do." I glanced at Stripes, who was taking in the exchange with narrowed eyes.

An unspoken question formed from him to me, and I gave him one slow nod.

He nodded back, already starting to pull his keys out, but we waited while Crow was putting a call through to Shelly.

He ended the call, frowning at the phone. "Called three times. Keeps going to voice message." He hit another number, putting the phone to his ear, and telling us, "I'll call my guy. Have them find Shelly or your woman."

His guy answered.

"Yeah. Hey. Shelly around?"

We waited as his guy went to go and find her.

A second later, his voice came over the phone, "She's not here, Boss. Neither's her car."

"What about Ghost's old lady?"

I gave Stripes a nod, telling him, "Keep your phone close."

He took off, lifting a hand to let me know he heard me. He went to his bike and a second later, he was tearing off.

The same time, the guy said, "Yeah. She ain't here either. She was in the back room, but she's gone and her bag's gone too. You want us to keep looking for her?"

Goddammit. I was going to rip heads.

I growled, grabbing the phone from Crow. "You *tear that fucking place apart*. If you can't find her, get your bikes and haul ass to where they might've gone. That's my woman."

"Yes, sir!"

I wanted to shove Crow's phone down his throat, but he didn't fuck up. I had. Kali was my woman. I should've designated one of my guys to watch over *only* her. Goddammit! What had I been thinking?

"What do you want to do?"

I wanted to find Kali, but my woman or my brothers? I had to pick right now.

I wanted to rip everyone's head off, including my own.

Crow's phone started ringing.

I snatched it up, answering it, "Did you find her?"

"No, but Carol said that Shelly had her tell Kali to grab her bag and get ready to leave."

"When was this?"

"Thirty minutes ago. Another one of our guys said he saw both of them dip outside, but he didn't think anything of it because they'd been hanging out in front of the diner earlier anyway. Thought they just wanted some air."

"What about the prospects? They would've been watching the bikes."

"Prospect we had out there said he saw both of 'em go around the corner. A second later, he saw headlights leaving a block north. We're thinking that was Shelly's car since it's missing too. They were heading east."

Crow was waiting for my orders.

"A prospect just let them go? When we're *under attack by the cartel*?"

"He's real sorry, Ghost. Me too. All of us. Carol is crying. There's no reason not to do what Shelly says, always done it before. Shelly's the Lady Boss in this charter."

"You find out *exactly*, word for word, what Shelly told Carol to say. I want to know every fucking thing she said or saw or did from the time she walked in that fucking bar until right now. You get me?"

"I get you. On it."

This time there was no restraint.

I took Crow's phone and whipped it as hard and as far as I could, and I was two seconds from whipping Crow himself right after it.

"Now, Ghost." He began backing up, his hands going in the air. "Think, brother. We're both Reds here–" He choked off the last part on the account that he *couldn't fucking breathe*, on the account that my hand was around his throat and on the account that I was squeezing it harder with each second that passed.

"Hey!" Feet scrambled over gravel and I felt hands at my hand, trying to pull me off.

I wasn't moving.

This fucker. His charter had been nothing but bad news from the beginning.

"Shane." Boise wrapped an arm around my chest.

I felt others, all trying to pull me off.

Someone wedged his way between us and he pushed as Boise was pulling. Someone dipped down, and lifted me up. A few guys. I was carried back and only then did I stop squeezing.

I shoved off them, pushing Boise away and whoever else. "Get off me!"

I was going for Crow again.

He was being carried into the warehouse, and his club guys were getting between him and me. The same was going for my guys until Boise was in my face, and talking sense. "He is their president right now. VP or not, he's theirs. They're going to throw down for him, whether he's in the wrong or not. You know that. I got no clue what transpired in the last five minutes, but I saw Stripes tear out of here so I'm assuming it has something to do with why he's gone. You want to fill me in? Let someone who's thinking a little clearer than you are at the moment know what's going on?"

"That woman, Shelly, whoever the fuck she is to him she took my woman somewhere and Kali's got her phone off. She'd only turn her phone off if she was taken or she was told to turn it off, and no reason she'd be told to turn that phone off unless it was a fucking lie!" I began pacing, fury raging through me, but dammit.

Damn! Boise was right. The guys were looking at me a certain way.

Fuck this shit.

I started forward.

"Ghost–" Boise tried to get in front of me.

"I ain't going to touch him, but I *am* going to deal with some shit right here and now." I signaled to one of Crow's guys. "You tell him what make and model Shelly drives and you," I said to Boise. "Get the computer guys on it. She's got Kali with her and I have no idea where they're going. I want her car found now. Tell Stripes what's going on. He lit out after her."

He gave a firm nod, stepping back with Crow's guy.

After that, it was time to clear the air. I was prepared for some digging to happen tonight.

Six feet down.

"Let's have church."

Everyone filed into the main warehouse after me. Crow's guys stood to one side while mine went to the other. Roadie and Corvette lined the doors. Boise took my right side. I saw Claudia lurking in the background, but since this wasn't actual church for us, I let her stay. Machete moved from her side, stepping in line with our other guys.

He raised his chin up, asking me, his eyes steady, "What are you doing, Boss?"

I motioned to Crow's guys. "Your president called us here, for your charter. We were told there were members of your charter that we couldn't trust. I was supposed to move in, take over, and suss out the guys who bled Red Demon and those who don't. Now I've got the beginning of a war against the cartel happening under my watch, right here, and they tried taking my woman. Who knows. Maybe they got to Shelly and might get her in the end, but what I do know is that the fuck I want to be here when I should be on the road, riding to save my woman and her friends, and then after that, moving forward against the Estrada Cartel. Want to know what I'm doing instead? I'm here dealing with your charter's politics. Who doesn't bleed Red here? Let's deal with this shit now. I got no time for politics."

They were all quiet.

My guys looked resigned.

Crow stood in the back, and a lot of his guys kept sending him looks.

"Jesus, Crow. Your guys are giving you the call to step up for them. You are their current acting president. What do you have to say?"

He took a breath, also looking resigned, and stepped forward from the crowd. "You're kinda blowing up my spot."

"I don't have time to deal with it. Estrada came to your charter, not where Prez was. Yours. I want to know why and I want to know why my woman and her people were targeted. Start talking or we're doing shit the hard way."

His eyes narrowed. "You want to run that by me? What 'hard way'?"

I shook my head. "I don't have time for this, but I'm sure as shit not going to ride into another fight and worry about who's got my back. We cut your group out and magically, we were able to get two of their hostages back. Doubt that's a fucking coincidence."

One of the other guys spoke up, "Our president called you in?"

"Yeah. I mean it, guys. Start talking or we're cutting all of you and starting new. I do not give one shit what that might mean moving forward. Every second we're not on the road, is a second my other brothers are going into a fight without us at their backs. START. FUCKING. TALKING!"

"It's Crow."

"Rash!"

"I'm sorry, but it is." Rash stepped forward, looking tired. "You're my cousin, but it's you. Some of the guys know, some don't. You set up Prez. He went to prison covering your ass, he just didn't know it was you. But I do."

"Rash, I swear to God–" Crow launched himself at him, but he was caught by some of his own men.

Rash didn't jump back. He didn't react. He just seemed tired, that same resigned look coming from him too. He jerked his chin toward Crow. "It's him. He was selling to minors, which is against club policy. He roped in about five others in the club. When it fell apart, they planted evidence on Prez, who was getting suspicious. I got proof of it all."

"You're goddamn fucking lying!"

Rash barely blinked, just shaking his head. "I heard you. You called Marco Estrada. I heard you the first time, and after that, I made sure to hear all the other times. You told him about the vote. He showed up when he did because you also told him the national VP was coming our way. He came in, sussed everything out, and left. You told him who Ghost's woman was, and that she had friends that they were going to Fallen Crest to meet. You gave him the location. You gave him the time. You told him everything, but when they fucked up, you also fucked up. You gave them too much, and a man like that, Marco Estrada, he's a snake. He's always going to turn on you. Mark my words."

"You're the snake." Crow was glowering, but one by one his men were starting to distance themselves from him.

"I got it all on tape. Like I said, it was luck when I caught the first call. I was pissing outside and you hadn't closed the window. Dumb luck on my part, but the rest, yeah. I made sure to put something on your phone. Got all your calls recorded. Some of that shit no one needs to hear."

That was enough. That was all I needed to hear. I stepped forward. "You got the proof here?"

He nodded, closing his eyes a moment, his shoulders slumping. He reached into his pocket, brought his phone out, and after a second of fiddling on the screen, Crow's voice sounded out. "Yeah. They did a vote. The whole club is leaving. They're deserting you. All of them. But those of us loyal, Señor Estrada, we weren't given the proper chance to voice our feelings on the matter. I guarantee you that there's more than just me who don't want to stop working for you. I promise you that."

Marco's voice was next, eerily calm. "You like the money, but I need more proof than your word before I make a move."

"YOU FUCKING PIECE OF SHI—"

Crow was quieted. My guys moved in, replacing theirs and Corvette punched him, knocking him unconscious.

Rash was waiting, watching me.

I jerked my chin toward him. "I need to hear more."

He went back to the phone, and a second later, Crow's voice came out again, "Just got word. Maxwell is sending the national VP our way. I think our charter Prez snitched on us, that's why, but he's coming here. The fucker terrifies me, but if you want to move on them, here's your shot. He's going to be as alone as you can get him."

Rash stopped it, but I shook my head. "More."

For the first time, uncertainty lit up his gaze, but after hesitating, he played another one.

"Yeah, yeah." Crow's voice again. "No, listen. I got him. Told him some of our guys can't be trusted. I'm working him, and I think he's buying it. Even mentioned maybe teaming up with some folk up north. He seemed open to it."

"I need to know his weaknesses. Where do we hit him?" Marco's voice, still calm.

"He's got a woman. He brought her here, and he seems real into her. They're heading to Fallen Crest tonight, and he's alone or more alone than normal. Only a few guys are with him. There's territory issues there, but yeah. You want to take out his knees, take his woman. He'll go crazy to get her back, and," Crow's voice rose, his excitement was audible. "She's got friends in Fallen Crest too. That's why they're going there, to meet with her friends."

Rash stopped it, but held his phone up. "You want more?"

A stillness came over me. It didn't calm me, but it made me go slow. With purpose.

I was closing in on a kill. Didn't matter who it was that I was going to kill, but it'd be someone and I walked forward, and held a hand out. "I'd like that phone."

Rash looked from me to the phone, did it twice, before handing it over. "You get in this way." He showed myself and Boise, who'd walked with me toward him, how to get into his phone. Boise nodded, taking the phone for me. I knew within the hour, he'd go through whatever evidence was on that phone.

But we had another matter.

I asked Rash, "I want the names of the men Crow was working with."

"Done." He listed them off, and those guys began running, cursing.

It was short work, but their own caught the men, and handed each one over to my club. They were hauled off and we'd handle them after this. After that, there was one more item.

"Where is your sister taking my woman?"

Rash hesitated this time before saying, "I got no clue. She's going rogue."

43

KALI

Something was wrong.

Felt it thirty minutes into driving, and knew it in my gut hours later. The problem, though, was that I didn't know who or what was actually dangerous. If I turned my phone on, who could tap into my GPS? We stopped at a gas station and I wanted to call Shane, but Shelly came around the corner at that moment. Could I call Shane? Would that alert someone that I didn't want being alerted? I had no idea, and I tried again in the bathroom, but she came into the next stall.

When I left, she was right behind me.

It happened at the next gas station.

I was starting to think she was scared to leave me alone, which added to my gut feeling that something was seriously wrong here.

I wished I had Aly to bounce ideas off, or Harper? Or even Justin, though Justin was always way more calm than the rest of us.

We were entering Arizona when I broached the topic, "Where in Amarillo are we going?"

"Huh?" There was an edge to her tone.

My stomach dropped.

How to explain when the unspoken very much moves into the realm where it's very obvious and you need to act on it? Because we were there. Or I was there. We needed to 'head off' the Red Demons so it wouldn't make sense to stop at a hotel, but I was getting this feeling more and more that I needed to stall.

I needed more time.

I was so out of my depth here. Dealing with Claudia, handling Foley, approaching my mom with caution, those were familiar terrain for me. This, whatever this was, I had no clue, but I wanted a gun and why would I want a gun? Though, anyone knowingly going to stop a bunch of Red Demons against the Cartel... guess that made sense.

I felt like I was going crazy, but in my gut, I didn't think I was nuts at all.

Shelly was flat out lying to me, and I was starting to feel like I was the kidnapped hostage.

"Where are we going? Can we go over the plan?"

She dropped her cigarette, ground it out, and got into the car.

I didn't. My door was open, but holy God. Could I run now? Was that what I should do? I had no idea.

"What are you doing?" she barked.

I jumped, but frowned. "Okay. Lay off the attitude with me."

"Come on! If we want to get there in time to figure out where the Reds are coming from, we gotta go now. They don't stop and chill. When they ride, they go hard. They party after their job is done. We gotta go."

I was still hesitating.

"Now, Kali!"

I jumped again, but got in, shut my door, and immediately I was cursing myself. Why did I do that?

Oh, screw it. "I have to go back."

"What?"

"I forgot to get water. We're going to need more water. Turn back for the gas station."

"Are you shitting me?"

"No. Water. Come on."

She kept going, her face hard, but letting out a dramatic sigh and a curse, she swung the car around. As soon as we got to the station, I jumped out and went to the water aisle. Knowing her, if something actually was wrong, she'd be watching me. As I moved, I pulled my phone out of my pocket and turned it on.

A guy was lingering in front of the water, so I got right behind him. Perfect. He had no idea I was there. I had time.

None of this could be obvious.

He picked out one. No, two. No, he put them both back. Then he saw me. "Oh, sorry! I can't decide. You go ahead."

"It's okay."

He was still moving aside.

And I was panicking. "Uh, are you getting the water for yourself?"

"My girlfriend, but she always has to have a certain brand. I can never remember what the bottle looks like. You go ahead."

"No. I'm good. You remember the lettering of the brand?"

Suspicion started to creep into his gaze, but he only moved away a step.

My phone started buzzing and ringing.

His eyes went down, saw I was holding the phone and staring at him as I was unlocking my phone, and then moving to silence it. No buzzes. No alerts. Nothing could get through.

"Uh–"

"You remember seeing pink from her bottle?"

"Huh?" He was still distracted, watching me working my phone.

"The bottle. Sometimes when the water is drunk, there's a

flamingo on the inside of the bottle. Guys remember the pink, but don't remember the flamingo."

His eyes lit up. "You're right! It's that water." He frowned. "What brand is that, do you know? Also–" His head went down and he was going to ask about my phone, or worse, he was going to make it obvious I was doing something.

I stepped forward, grabbing the bottle his girlfriend probably liked and I grabbed two for myself.

Anything else?

I handed it off and moved past him, my finger moving over the texts and trying to remember Shane's number. I had no idea. Dammit. But, man. I bet he'd been calling, texting me. I put the phone in my pocket, remembering there was a mirror above that could see down all the aisles.

In my pocket, I moved to the texts and hoping against hope that the last text sent my way was his. Not my dad's because oh my God, I had no idea what would happen if he got involved. He'd call the National Guard on us, but first he'd probably call Ruby and see if she knew what was going on.

Please, please, please.

I grabbed some snacks, going the long way to the counter.

There was a line of people so I waited, finishing my text and hoping it wasn't too jumbled. I hit send as soon as the last person moved and put my items on the counter. She rang me up. I had to make a show of pulling my wallet out, paying for the items.

As I did, I hit call on my phone, still hoping it would go to Shane.

Shelly made me promise not to use a card, use cash. And I could feel her eyes on me. She was watching, so I counted out the cash and handed it over. The front desk worker gave me change back, and I put everything back in my pocket. Grabbing the water and bag of chips, I headed back outside.

"Hey, Shelly."

She glared at me, but that turned to a frown when she saw the chips. Snatching it, she opened it and put it between us. "I'm starving. Ready?"

Not on your life. I smiled. "Yep."

I had to do something. I needed to stall.

44

SHANE

We were an hour on the road when we met up with Stripes. He was waiting on the side of the road, so we pulled over. All of us. He stood up, heading over to me, but looked at the rest. "Some of the guys stayed back?"

"They had some guys to handle."

He gave a slow nod, his eyes flicking to Boise. Neither of us got off our bikes. This was a quick meet and we were heading off again.

"I was in contact with our computer guys, and they found 'em. They think she's sticking to back roads, staying away from any street cameras, which is smart. That's good for us. They've got a head start, but we can go interstate, get past them, and move to intercept. Their last spotting was in Arizona."

I cursed under my breath because we were so behind. "Let's get going."

Stripes dipped his head down, and went back to his bike.

After that, we rode.

We rode fast.

My phone started vibrating not long after, and I grabbed it up, but then immediately pulled over. I hadn't saved her new number, but that was Kali. I knew it.

As soon as my bike was parked, I turned off the engine and hopped off, running ahead so I could hear better. "Kali?"

I couldn't hear.

The other guys' bikes were taking too long to shut off, so I sprinted farther but I pressed that phone as close to my ear as I could get, plugging my other ear. After a few more seconds, all the engines cut out behind me, and I was able to figure out what I was hearing from her end.

"...a game? I Spy?"

That was Kali, her voice sounded coming from a distance. I could hear movement on her end, static. They were driving. She'd turned her phone on, though. That was good, so good.

Hearing gravel from behind, I lifted my head. The guys had come over, all quiet so I hit it on speaker and held it out. As soon as I did, Stripes was on his phone. He'd be calling the computer guys, trying to locate her phone. We would need to ride, but while she was on the phone, we had a line open. The computer guys would move on somehow keeping her on the line, but also letting us ride. Until then, we were waiting and listening.

And I felt like pissing myself because Kali was alive and she was thinking. She was planning.

That was my woman. I was damn proud of her.

Shelly was saying something, but I couldn't make out her words.

Kali, "What town did we just leave? Was that Kingman?"

More from Shelly. Her words were jumbled, but her tone was sharp. Tired. She was going to lose it on Kali if she kept pushing.

Stripes came back. "They got her phone, and they got Shelly's car. There's an iPad in the back that they were able to trace so if we lose Kali's line, don't matter. We still got her."

"We need to ride, but I can't hang up."

"Yeah. They're working on that too." He held up a finger, moving back and listening to his phone again.

"...should've grabbed coffee. Can we stop in the next town?" Shelly snapped back at her.

"I know. I want to get there ahead of them too, but I need some caffeine. I'm going to wipe out before we stop them. Did you want me to help drive?"

'Ahead of them?' 'Stop them?' And she's offering to drive, so Shelly got inventive with how she got Kali to leave with her. And Kali being Kali, started getting other thoughts and turned her phone on. Whatever the lie was, it must've been believable to get her to turn her phone off in the beginning.

But Shelly never took the phone. That would've really alarmed Kali, which meant Shelly was operating in a cooperative phase, meaning she was coercing Kali to be cooperative. I didn't want to find out what Shelly would do if Kali stopped being cooperative.

"We gotta go."

Stripes was coming back. "Give that to me." He took my phone and began working on it. At the same time, he was speaking into his own phone, "Got it. Now what?" Then he went to work.

Boise motioned for me to step aside.

We did. Machete and Roadie came with us.

"We're not going to get there in time, so if they just left Kingman, that means Shelly is doing back roads, but she's still trying to keep to as straight a shot as possible. We have the Flagstaff charter. We can loop them in, ask them to intercept until we get there."

I was already nodding because I was thinking the same thing. "Let's do it. Make the call. Roanoke's a good guy. He'll try to help if he can. His whole charter is good."

Boise was on it, stepping toward his bike with his phone out.

Roadie and Machete moved in, but I was looking at Machete's bike.

I asked him, "How's she doing?"

Both turned to where I was watching where Claudia was sitting.

She remained on the back of his bike, and she was just watching us right back. No look. No defiance. No attitude. She didn't look like she was sulking, sad, or had any pep to her. After she reunited with Machete, I hadn't given her much thought, but when he said he wanted to bring her, I hadn't cared. I only replied, "Just as long as she doesn't slow us down."

"She loves her sister too. I think if we slowed down for her, she'd take a gun to all of us."

Then that had been just fine with me.

Machete answered now, rubbing a hand over his jaw, "They didn't touch her, but they took her. Said they killed her sister. That made a mark on her, even if it's in the head. It'll always be there."

Our life, what we do for a living, how we do it—sometimes there would be collateral damage. That happened to his woman. My own was in a fight of her own right now, and after all of this, the whole reason both got pulled in hadn't happened. But it would, and when it did, that'd be another mark on both of them. They just didn't know it.

I glanced to Machete and saw his eyes were on me. They were haunted, and I had a thought, wondering if he was thinking the same thing as me.

He was when he said, "We gotta do it a different way."

My gut clenched. "There isn't. He told us himself."

"There has to be. Both of them–"

"I know, but..." I couldn't finish, because first, I needed to get Kali back. If I didn't... I couldn't finish that thought either.

We just had to get her back. Period. There was no other way out of this.

"Okay." Stripes came back, bringing my phone with him. He handed it over and showed me his screen. "So, the guys have her call linked in and this is for you." He handed over an ear piece. "Put that in your ear, and you can black out your phone. I put the call to a collective line so if you lose the connection, we'll still have it from their end." He waved his phone so I was guessing he meant the computer team. "They're tracking her and they're able to guess the route she'll go, you know, since it's not such a straight shot if she's taking back roads."

Boise came back, putting his phone away. "Looped in Roanoke. He's on board and he's putting the call out to his guys." He said to Stripes, "Since you're the Tech Contact right now, can you tell the computer guys to loop in Roanoke on their end. They'll probably be able to intercept before we even get to Arizona."

I didn't like it. I didn't like that another charter would get to Kali first. On that meet, so many things could go wrong. If she didn't trust them? If Shelly had a gun? But it was better than anything right now.

"Oh." Stripes' tone got all our attention, and he was listening to his phone. His gaze went to mine and he didn't look away, not one time until he lowered the phone. Things were already serious, but I had a fucking feeling things were going to get a whole lot more serious with whatever he was just told. "They hacked Shelly's phone. They know why she's doing what she's doing, and they know where she's taking Kali."

I turned to him slowly and squarely. "You gonna fill me in, or are we playing I Don't Have the Patience to Read Your Fucking Mind?"

He didn't blink before he said, "They took her daughter. Estrada didn't send two teams up. He sent three. Shelly's supposed to deliver Kali to a location or they're going to kill Katie."

I was right.

Things just got way worse.

"Let's go."

At this rate, there was nothing more I could do so I did what I could do.

Stay alive, Kali.

45

KALI

Two hours later, and I was out of things to say except for, "I gotta pee in Flagstaff."

There. Not obvious at all.

Shelly let out an exasperated sound, her eyes bulging as she glared at me. "Are you serious?"

I shifted in my seat. "It was the coffee. And I'm a pee-er when I'm nervous." Totally lying. I was not a pee-er when I was nervous. "You're all tense and I don't know what we're driving into."

Another exasperated half growl before she turned on the signal and slowed down to turn onto another road. I had no idea what her exact route was because she kept changing and taking other roads, and then other roads, and other roads until I was pretty sure one time we did a full circle and started all over again. The only thing I could get was that she was trying to stay off the main roads and trying to be unpredictable? Either way, I was glad when a sign popped up saying Flagstaff was nineteen miles ahead. I was also relieved when I saw other cars on the road with us.

I was not expecting to see all the trees.

We'd definitely been north of this area when I was road tripping with Aly and Harper before.

Harper.

Fear and panic seized me for a moment.

I hoped he was okay. I hoped he was alive? I hoped he was being fed chocolate covered strawberries and being fanned by hot shirtless guys. He joked that it was his fantasy. I doubted that was happening, but I needed to focus on that and not the other thing that I was thinking might be happening, him being hurt or starved or I didn't know. I just needed to get away from Shelly, see if my call ever went through to Shane because I'd been terrified to check and then get my friends back. Safe. I wanted *everyone* safe.

When we got to the station, she pulled to fill up with gas. I guess she was being extra cautious, but I went inside and this time, she wasn't following me. I pulled my phone out and saw the line was still connected. Holy—thank God for helping! "Shane?!"

I only heard motorcycles' engines.

"Shane!"

There was a click, then silence. I panicked, thinking I'd lost the line, but a different, calm voice said, "Is this Kali?"

"Yes." I frowned and looked at the screen. It showed I was connected to Shane's phone. "Who is this?"

"My name is Seth. I work with the Red Demons. We're their IT department. You're at a gas station on the north end of Flagstaff?"

"Yeah! How'd you know that?" I needed to quiet down, but my heart was picking up. If they knew where we were, then things were starting to look way up for me.

"That's not important. What is is that you need to tell me the exact whereabouts of Shelly. Where is she right now?"

I looked, and stepped out of the hallway, moving to a window where I could see the car.

The car was gone.

"Wha–" I started to go outside, seeing if she pulled to the side. "She's gone."

He got quiet on his end.

"Hello? You still there?"

"What do you mean she's gone?"

"I mean," I stepped more fully outside, looking to the right and left, "she's gone. I can't see her car anywhere and she wouldn't go inside with the car not being here." I was so happy that I was almost shouting. I was free. "She totally left without me."

"Kali," the voice came back, insistent. "You need to listen to me. Shelly would not have left you behind."

"Well, she said that she overheard–"

"No. What she told you was a lie. She has to take you to Marco Estrada. If she doesn't, they will kill her daughter."

"What?!" I whipped around, feeling a presence at my back.

It was an elderly man. He jumped back, startled from me.

"Sorry. So sorry." I moved out of the way, but I was processing what he'd just said.

"They took Katie?"

"Yes. Since you are currently away from her, remain among groups of people. Is she armed?"

My mouth went dry. "Yeah. She has a gun."

"Okay. I'm coordinating with a local Red Demons charter. They're coming to help. They're closer than Ghost and his men. Now–"

I felt the press against my back before I felt the presence of another person.

Every cell in my body was telling me that was a gun at my back, and as I went still, I heard the safety being taken off.

"I'll take this. Thank you." Shelly was behind me, and she lifted my phone out of my hands, pressing it to her ear. She listened a second, saying, "Move around the corner. Walk casual."

Oh, shit. This wasn't good, but I moved forward, going slow.

She tossed my phone to the ground and a second later, I heard a crunching sound. As we kept going, she said, "When did you figure it out?"

"Figure what out?"

She laughed, the gun still pressed so tight to my back. "You know what I'm talking about. That I was lying to you. I didn't overhear shit, but when'd you figure it out?"

We were around the corner. Her car wasn't back here, but she urged me to keep going.

"Thirty minutes into leaving."

She whistled under her breath. "Keep going. I moved to the back."

I did, but my heart was racing with each step because what would happen when I got back there? Would she let me stay conscious? My heart was up in my throat. I felt sweat dripping down my back.

"It's nothing personal. I want you to know that, but I have to do this. Marco's men came back and they took my daughter. That Jared kid had another party, and of course, we weren't under lockdown. They nabbed up Katie when I gave in and let her go. Thought I owed her one night after having everyone move in, take over the place. She helped clean the whole place up too. Did a good job. She's a good *kid*," her voice got thick, choked up. When she spoke again, it was hard again. "They took her, and they said to bring you for her so nothing personal. You know I have to do what I have to do. That's my baby–"

We were around the corner, in the back of the gas station. There was one other car parked back here, but no one else was around. A chair was set up behind their back door. A can next to it, and I was betting there was a load of cigarette butts inside of it. "Let's go."

She went around, the gun still pointed my way. She opened her door, bent and pulled the trunk.

I took a step back. "Come on, Shell–"

She ignored me, going to the trunk and she pulled out some rope. She tossed it at me. "Pick it up. Wrap it around your wrists."

"This isn't neces–"

"Do it or I'll have you finish the ride in the back of this trunk. I'm betting you don't want that."

I didn't.

I picked up the rope and began looping it around my wrists. This was foul in so many ways.

"Tighter."

I looped it around, making a knot as best as I could.

Think, Kali. Think.

I didn't know anything about knots, but what a time to wish that I had a full career in yachting. A trick knot would've come in handy.

"Okay. Enough."

I tried pulling it down over my hand, a little leeway.

She was going to tighten it.

Anything? What could I do?

I tried twisting my other hand around, getting a finger under the other side of my wrist.

Sheathing her gun in her pocket, she came over and grabbed my wrists. She jerked me around, moving my arm. Seeing the finger, she slapped it out of there. Her gun was pointing down, but the safety wasn't on.

Oh, God.

Oh, dear.

Could I?

She was tightening the rope–I had to.

She was still holding my wrists up so I lunged, going hard and fast, hoping to get her surprised.

I did.

"Wha—"

BANG!

OH MY GOD!

I jumped back, my whole body feeling like I'd been shot.

My ears were ringing.

My vision was blurring.

What had I just done?

I blinked a few times, waiting for my eyes to come back to focus and when they did... Oh. My. Jesus, Jesus, Jesus.

I was fully praying to Him.

The blood was everywhere. On my hands. On my chest. My stomach. My legs.

But, no, no, no.

I couldn't have—it wasn't my blood.

I choked back a cry, stumbling backwards.

Shelly was on the ground, her leg a wrangled mess.

Oh, I was just hoping she still had a leg. I didn't want to look anymore, but she was staring down, then at me, and she was losing color fast. "You—you shot me?"

Um. I started nodding. I had.

"Whoa. I'm sure hoping you're Ghosts' woman and not the one who's shot, because, honey, you better start brainstorming your cover story because there's no way you're getting out of this one."

A guy with dark hair, a face that could be on billboards, and wearing a Red Demons cut stood just around the corner. More guys came filtering in behind him, seeing us, and some whistled under their breaths.

Another guy stepped around, cursed, and pulled his phone out. "We need Doc. Now. Gunshot wound." He scanned me. "Uh. I don't know. There might be two."

I shot her.

I couldn't believe I shot her.

She was—Katie. This was for Katie.

OH—I shot Shelly and now they'd kill Katie.

The first guy strolled forward, cursing with a little more insistence. "Oh yeah. She's about to lose it."

I heard from the phone guy, "You might need a tranq. One looks ready to lose her shit."

Yes. I started nodding, crying, and laughing all at once. I was *so losing my shit,* because I *might've just killed two people.*

I crumbled, falling to my knees and bent over. The blood was on the ground too.

It was caked to my hands. My arms.

The blood was on me. It was *all on me.*

"Yep. Totally losing her shit. Someone call Ghost."

46

SHANE

S he was the first person I saw.

I was trying to tell myself I could breathe easier, but there was no light breathing after this. But still. She was here. She was curled up in a ball, in a corner, with a blanket pulled around her. Her chin was propped up on her other arm and she was watching them as they were trying not to watch her back, to make her feel less uneasy.

The second I cleared the door, she saw me too and she took off running for me.

She launched herself in the air and I caught her. Her legs went around my hips. Her arms were hugging me fiercely, and her mouth was on mine. She was hungry, but I grunted, because holy–I was just as hungry right back. My dick was rock hard, sticking up into her ass.

I heard laughing from behind me, but flipped them off as I lifted my head a second. "Room?"

Roanoke had been approaching, but he was fighting back a grin and gestured to the hallway. "Down there. Third door on the left. It's all yours for the night if you need it."

I carried her right into it, but as soon as we cleared the door, Kali was off me. She jumped down, and shoved me back. Hard.

Once wasn't enough, she did it again.

And again.

I barely moved, but I saw the tears and she just kept shoving at me until her hands weren't leaving my chest and her head was down and her shoulders were shaking.

"Babe," I whispered, my insides searing from the emotion pouring out of her now.

"You left me!" Her head tipped back, big fat tears streaming down her face, leaving trails but she backed up. Shaking her head. "You left me, and they took my friends. My sister. They could've taken you. They could've–you left me."

"Kali." Jesus, she was broken inside.

I did that. Me. Not her asshole ex.

I broke her.

Never again, I vowed.

Moving in, gently, cautiously, I reached for her and when she didn't hit at me, or shove away, I pulled her into my arms. I needed to do this the right way. Everything had to be the right way from now on. "Kali, I am so sorry."

She started to shake her head.

"I am," my own voice broke. Damn. Damn! I had so much shit to make up for. "I thought you were safe, and I wanted to get your family back as soon as possible. I wanted to keep my guys alive. I wanted to–there's so much shit I wanted to do and I messed it up, and it gave them an opening to get you. And they did. They got you." On my watch. *My* watch.

Never. Fucking. Again. "I'm sorry."

"They didn't get me. They almost got me."

I suppressed a shudder.

I got the call. Roanoke told me how they found her, but she had to pull that trigger. She was in a situation where she needed to reach for a gun to pull the trigger.

I let my head fall to her shoulder.

She tensed at first, but relaxed. A hand came up, catching the back of my head and she held me back.

"They almost got you."

She moved in closer, hugging me.

God. I needed her. I needed this touch. I needed everything about her.

"I love you."

She was *it* for me. It was her or no one.

She had tensed, but I didn't care. I said it again, "I love you."

She leaned back, and I lifted my head up.

"No masks, Shane. Your rule." She was searching me. "Are you sure?"

I nodded. "I love you more than my club."

A fierce emotion pushed forward in her eyes, shining bright at me. Tears filled them, and she tried blinking them away, clearing her vision but she couldn't. More and more were flooding her until she reached up, grasping my face. "I love you too, Shane."

I was lifting her, not even thinking.

I just needed to feel her, hold her. I'd never go a day not needing this.

She hugged me back, just as hard, harder even. Pressing her face into my neck, she broke out against my skin, "I love you so much it scares me."

I moved my head back until she lifted hers, looking at me and I moved in.

I needed to taste her.

Her mouth opened under mine, and God, she tasted like my ecstasy. Pure heaven. My paradise.

I groaned, wanting more, but she had family that still needed to be rescued. I started to pull away, but she stopped me.

Her hand went to my chest. "No."

I looked at her again, wanting to make sure I heard her right.

She began to lift herself up so I bent down, and caught her. Lifting her instead.

Her legs wrapped around my waist and they tightened. Her eyes darkened. She bit her lip, but I felt her heart picking up and her breathing deepened. She needed me too. This was for her.

I waited, feeling like she needed to dominate me this time. I didn't know why I felt it. Could never explain it, but I waited and she reached between our bodies, unzipping me, slipping in, finding my cock. She began working me up, her hand holding me, moving down, sliding up and down. Her thumb moved over my tip, and I let out a breath, because *fuck* that felt good.

I was already aching for her, felt my balls were ready to burst when she lifted her hips up, going to her own jeans.

I shifted her to one hand, and helped, undoing her pants and then my fingers slid in. So tight. So beautiful. As I moved my fingers up and began a rhythm, she reached back for my dick, returning the favor.

We kept going.

Faster.

A little harder until she let out a small whimper.

That was enough for me.

I lifted her up, kicked her pants off, and I stepped on them, shoving them down the rest of the way. Then I held her up in the air, two hands under arms, and when I moved her back down, she found my dick. She aligned up, and I let her slide down over me.

We both moaned from the contact.

I was inside her and it was perfection. Utter and complete perfection.

We both began to move at the same time. I wanted to go fast, rough. I wanted to burn the feel of me into her soul, but this moment, today was different. It had to be perfection too, so I moved inside of her slow. Delicious.

She gasped, her eyes watching me the whole time, moving with me.

This was both of us together making a moment.

She gave in to me. It hit me on the fourth stroke. What I'd been waiting for from the beginning, it happened, and it happened after all the shit. She was mine, really truly mine.

I'd move mountains for her if I needed.

Anything.

She was mine, but I think she was finally accepting the other truth.

I'd *always* been hers.

47

KALI

"Y ou should start smoking."

I almost dropped the newest phone Shane gave me. The building inside was filled to the brim with way too many men. There were women, I assumed this new charter's sweet butts, but it was a lot of people.

"What?" I'd not been expecting to hear my sister when I stepped outside for a breather. "What are you doing here?"

"Your boyfriend rescued me." She flicked the end of her cigarette before putting it back between her lips. "Now I'm of the mindset that I don't want to let Machete out of my eyesight again." Her body twitched in a shudder, and she crossed her stomach with the free arm. "Or you know what I mean considering he's not actually in eyesight this very second. And I said that because this world is stressful. Smoking helps. You should start smoking."

My sister was sitting on the top of a picnic table, trying to give off attitude because that was her, but she was affected. And she was scared.

I grinned, stepping up and sitting next to her, facing the back of this building, wherever we were. I thought Flagstaff, but at this point, I would've believed we were in an alien spaceship. I ignored the smoking comment. "My boyfriend?"

"What?" A tentative grin teased at her lips before she rolled her eyes. "You're going to start calling him your old man now? Because, newsflash, little sister, you are officially his old lady."

"Little? I'm the older sister."

She snorted. "I'm the older sister coming into this world. You can come to me for advice. I'm here for you. You don't need to feel self-conscious with me." She patted my knee.

I reciprocated by shoving her off the picnic table.

"Hey!"

The door opened and a few of the club's women came out. They slowed, taking in my sister on the ground. When they started to laugh, she scrambled up and pointed her still-lit cigarette at them. "Don't even think about starting. She and I have been through hell and we got no problem pulling you down with us."

They took her in, took in the promise in her eyes, and turned to me.

I was glaring right back at them, knowing they could see my own promise too.

One wrinkled her nose. "Ew. Old women." She shoved her friends ahead. "Let's go before they breathe their talcum powder on us."

Her one friend's mouth dropped before she let out a startled gasp. "You did not just say that."

The bitch shrugged, going around her. "What are they going to do?"

She took a step forward, and stopped because in that moment, Claudia crossed the distance and took hold of her swinging hair. She answered, still holding her cigarette, "Let me show you." And she took one step back, put her hip behind the girl, and flipped her right over. As she fell to the ground, her two friends gasped, but took me in.

I stood, every cell in me ready to launch myself at both of them. I had meat on me, good strong meat and if I twisted my body a certain way, I could just bowl right over them.

"Oh my God! Are you serious right now?"

I stood taller and narrowed my eyes. "Yes."

Claudia let out a snort laugh. "So wise and forbidding, Kal."

I flicked her off, still glaring at the other two. "Choose, little girls. Run or fight. That's the only two options I'm giving you."

"You don't have any say here. Who are you anyways?"

Claudia bent over, laughing. "You're so fucked, but I should thank you for being you. Idiot–" The door opened right at the end of her word and she cut off, seeing Machete step outside. He took her in, his eyes going from the girl who Claudia was still holding down because she'd stepped on her hair, the other two, and then me.

He shook his head. "Oh, boy."

The door was pushed wider behind him.

Roadie, Corvette, and another of Shane's guys pushed out, taking in all of us.

Roadie's grin went wide. "Whoa. Did we just interrupt a chick fight?" He touched Machete's shoulders, pretending to pull him back inside. "Please, ladies. Keep on as if we were never here."

"Get off my hair!" the one whined, trying to sit up.

Claudia gazed down at her, literally looking down her nose at the girl and took a slow drag of her cigarette. She was plucked up by Machete, and he carried her back to the picnic table. "No more fighting, babe."

She pretended to pout, but I could tell she was really loving how Machete was still holding her. He climbed up, settling behind her and she leaned back against his chest.

Roadie was helping the one girl back up to her feet, who took in the sight of my sister in Machete's lap.

Claudia smirked, raising an eyebrow. "You were saying, bitch?"

Roadie started laughing, one of his hands lingering on the woman's waist.

Claudia pointed it out with her cigarette. "Be careful with him. He's always going to be someone's sloppy seconds."

"Hey!" Roadie's hand dropped from the girl's waist, but he didn't look insulted. Instead, he gave the girl a slow smile. "We might stop by on our drive back to California? I'll look for you."

She was cutting her losses, shaking her head and going off with her friends, but she looked back, looking him up and down before returning a small grin.

Roadie started laughing. "All right. Look at that! Still got it."

Claudia snorted, running a hand down Machete's arm.

She said something back, and I recognized her tone. She was laughing something off in a cocky way, but I startled. Not at how she sounded, but from the contrast of her arm against Machete's arm. She was always usually a dark tan, but her skin was so white.

I realized how pale she was.

She'd not been this pale a few days ago at the barn.

And gaunt.

I was now looking her over, but without the usual filter I normally had with Claudia. She was tough. A smart-ass. Usually loud. Sometimes endearing like at Ruby's and most times mean like at the barn, but now I was just seeing my sister as she was. Fragile.

She'd lost weight in those days too.

Emotion rose up, choking my throat and I struggled to keep it from moving to my eyes, forming tears, but damn. I loved my sister. Couldn't stand her most days, but I loved her. Always would.

I didn't care how she'd react. I cut off whatever she'd been saying to whoever and scooted over.

I wrapped my arms around her, and hugged her.

She stiffened, and I felt her one hand still in the air, no doubt holding that cigarette, but catching movement from the corner of my eye, I saw how Machete took the cigarette out of her hand and held it out to Corvette.

Claudia melted into me, wrapping her arms around me right back.

It was so cliché, but I hugged my sister, and she hugged me, and we just needed this.

Yes. So cliché.

I didn't give a damn.

I HIT call on my phone.

My dad answered with, "WHAT THE HELL IS GOING ON? WHERE HAVE YOU BEEN? I HAD TO CALL RUBY I WAS SO WORRIED. YOU BETTER ANSWER ME, KALISTA CALLIOPE MICHAELS! The doc said I have high blood pressure and you put my levels up. Worried my doc." He took a breath, quieting, calm, but still stern. "I've not even been able to practice with the Old Gents, I've been so worked up. You better start talking, and you better start talking right now!"

I started talking.

48

SHANE

The decision was that we'd stay in Flagstaff for the night, let the guys rest. Let Kali rest.

Then my phone rang. *Heckler calling.*

Kali was sleeping soundly next to me, so I stood and went to the bathroom. It was from the team that we'd put on him, to watch him. I shut the door, turned on the shower and leaned back against the counter. I accepted the call, saying, "Too long without contact. I was getting nervous."

His chuckle was dry. "I know, but we needed to go silent for a bit here. Where are you?"

"Flagstaff, Arizona."

"Are you shitting me?"

"Not one bit. I got a woman and I don't want to scare her off this early."

Another short laugh from him before he went serious. "You should sit down."

I readied myself instead. "Tell me."

"We got 'em."

I shoved off from the counter. "What do you mean?"

"Communication got to us that Marco Estrada sent three

teams to California. He knew he was being watched by the club so he's been acting as a decoy. That was until he got a phone call and he was told that one of his two teams never showed up. He was also informed that their line of contact with who had your woman also went cold. His team and that line of contact are all considered dead. So you know what he did?"

"Bunkered down in The Valley?"

"You'd think. Nope. He is on the move. I just got word and I'm letting you know. We have eyes on the other two teams. We also have ears on them too. They're too scared to move. We've been driving hard around their neighborhood so they're convinced the entire Red Demon club is converging on them."

This was music to me. Pure absolute music.

"So Marco is going to them?"

"Yes, indeed. He's coming up with five trucks of men."

Man.

This was it, the whole fucking culmination for everything we'd gone through. Heckler was calling me because it was my call now what to do. "Prez?"

"He's still in lockdown, but he's not conscious. This is on you."

Yeah. I was getting that.

Standing here, in the bathroom of another club's headquarters, a woman in my bed, the irony was not lost that I'd been the one to make the push to leave the cartel. The price was too much. Things I've done, scars on my soul, my own haunts following me, but here I was. Alone. By a toilet and I had to make the call for the next move in this war.

"We do this, we have to move forward with Connor."

"I know."

I wanted to curse, a whole fucking litany. I wanted to let loose, kill someone like Marco, but to do that, to really do that and make sure it didn't come back to further haunt us, I didn't know if I could handle that collateral. "I can't do it, Heckler. That's my woman's brother."

"I know I'm supposed to tell you that you need to follow through and what we've all started, but I'm not going to do that. I can't. Situation reversed, I don't know what I'd do either. It's your call. I know things have changed. Everyone is aware, but I guess my duty is to remind you that this is for the entire club. There. Done. Now it's on your back. You're going to be the one shouldering this."

For the club.

My woman or my club.

I was having to choose, and not too long ago I was vowing that I'd never hurt her again. I was sharing that I loved her more than my club, but I was thinking about all the brothers we had. Every single one of them.

"It's lonely at the top." That was from Heckler. He added, "I do not wish to be in your place."

"Yeah." Goddamn. "Yeah."

"What's your orders so far?"

I moved over and opened the door, seeing Kali still sleeping. She was at peace, and I was about to rip her from it.

I said into the phone, "Keep track of Estrada. If we can isolate him, I'd like to do that first."

"We?"

"You heard correct. We're coming. I want to see this through to the end."

"Will do, Boss. See you when you get here."

I texted Boise.

Me: Wake the guys. Get ready. We're moving now to Albuquerque. Estrada is on the move.

I also texted Roanoke.

Me: We're leaving shortly if you or anyone from your club would like to join?

Boise texted back first.

Boise: On it. What's your decision about Gloves?

Me: Give me a bit.

Boise: I do not envy you right now. Good luck.

The second guy to tell me that in less than two minutes. Yeah. I was getting it. No one would or should do what I was about to do, but I was still going to do it because it needed to be done.

Roanoke: We're all with you.

49

KALI

"Kali."

I didn't want to wake up, and I started to roll over when who was saying my name got through to me, and then everything came back in a flash. I sat up, instant alarm pumping through me. "What is it? What happened?" My heart was racing.

Shane was sitting by me, and at my reaction, his eyes widened a little. He let out a breath. "We need to talk."

No.

No.

I shook my head because noooo.

The alarm moved aside, and impending doom sank deep inside of me.

I closed my eyes, one second. "Why do I feel like I need to start crying right now? Just to get some of the tears out of me?"

There was no good look on his face. Nothing that was telling me to feel otherwise. No reassurance. Just resignation, like he was about to tell me someone in my family was dead. "Shane, you're terrifying me. Tell me this feeling is wrong."

"I can't." His eyes matched his tone, sad, but ready. He nodded to the bathroom. "You need in there? Maybe get dressed? You're not going to want to go back to bed when this is done. If you're going to trust me on anything, it should be that."

Enough said.

I shut down. Everything.

The gates came around my heart. The lock was turned. I went numb because that impending doom was a monster that took root in me. It was growing with each word he said, each look he refused to give me, each tone he used.

When I was finished, I came back to the room. Dressed. Washed up. Fucking ready for whatever was coming my way.

I stood just in the room, and crossed my arms over my chest.

"You want to sit?"

I ignored that. "You're a dick."

He sighed, and ran a hand over his face. "I know."

Nothing I said or did was going to shield me from whatever he was going to tell me. I knew that, and my heart was already splintering. "Just tell me, Shane. Get it over with."

He nodded, his head hanging down for a moment before he went and sat in the chair in the corner of the room. He leaned forward, elbows on his legs, his hands clasped together and his head was down again. "I gotta break the code in order to tell you what I have to tell you. I need to tell you club business. We're not supposed to, but sometimes we enter into gray areas and I think we're in one. Or, hell. Maybe I'm just saying that to deal with my own guilt. I don't know, but you already know we're battling with a cartel. What you don't know is why or how it all started." He lifted his head now, and his eyes were so haunted I felt them pierce through me. A shiver went down my spine. "We got in with them from the beginning. It was supposed to be one trip. We'd carry something for him, and by him, I mean Marco Estrada. One time trip, lots of money. It worked. Money was great. The guys were happy, but Estrada wasn't. He wanted another trip, and another, and another until we find out that he's using us as his pitbulls. He's got a hold in the States because of us. We helped cement it. Then..." He stopped, and his Adam's apple moved up and down. Once. When he continued, his voice was thick. "I don't mind doing shit to bad people. Never grew up worrying about that. No skin off my nose. Had no family growing up. All I did overseas, couldn't do what I did there if that was the case, but bad people. People who steal, kill, lie without a second thought. Got no problem taking them out. It's another thing when it's someone innocent."

My heart felt like it was being crushed.

"The request came through, but it wasn't a request. It was fucking blackmail. We had to kill someone, and who Estrada said to kill wasn't who it turned out to be. They were innocents. Not even in this life, but it didn't matter. Estrada is a snake. His whole cartel is set up in a way where it's not just him at the top. He's got other guys who can step in if something happens to him. They can make a call and end families. Lines of families. We know this because we're the ones who set them up because they ain't hiding down in Mexico. Oh, no. Marco was smart. He thought his 'second-in-commands,' that's what he calls them, wouldn't be safe down where he was, and he didn't want to worry about them being free. Being able to walk around, infiltrate, take over before he was ready for them. I need to be real clear about these guys. They know the names, the codes, the bank accounts. If for any reason, someone takes Marco. He's kidnapped, taken, whatever, these guys can be let loose and they will do what he's already ordered them to do. He stashed them away and they're making millions from him, but that money isn't going to just them. It's going to their families, extra insurance for keeping them where they are. Their own families want them there so even if they did get free, they got no one to turn to. Family is everything to them, and he was smart in who he picked."

"Where are they being held at?"

"East Bend Penitentiary."

"What?" That didn't make sense.

None of it–what?

I frowned. "That's where Connor is."

He was just watching me. One blink. One nod. "I know."

"No."

Nope. I wasn't believing him. That made no sense. "Why–they're up here? That makes no sense."

"They're in Indiana. At a prison. At a prison where all of the guards are being paid by Marco. All of them. There was a new hire and he turned down the payout. His family was decapitated the next morning. He has every single guard in there on his payroll."

"No, but..." Connor.

Not Connor.

My chest was caving in. An invisible pressure was pushing down on me. My knees were threatening to buckle.

Please. Not Connor.

"The favor?" Everything in me was hurting because the pieces were coming together now. "The favor he's doing for you, he hasn't done it yet. Has he?"

Shane shook his head, so slowly.

I was being torn open, slowly by one piece of skin being pulled apart at a time. It hurt to breathe. Felt like I was inhaling blood. I could taste it.

"They were big favors. Sending bikers to Ruby's, that'll set her for life. My sister, you were going to buy her a hair salon."

"The club was, not me personally. You didn't ask for anything."

I was remembering and that wasn't right. "I asked for you to leave."

"We did. It's why we left, for you."

But Claudia. Fucking Claudia. She followed, and I went after her. "My friends went with me because they thought I was running from Foley. I pulled them into all of this based on a lie. I wasn't running from Foley." I couldn't take much more, but I had to face the truth. "Ruby asked me to go after my sister and I went because I was following you. I pulled Harper and Aly into this life because I wanted to fuck you."

He let out a soft curse. "Kali–"

I shook my head. "No! You're not done. We're not done. No masks, Shane! Your words. You're going to finish telling me everything. You're going to tell me the favor my brother is doing for your club and you're going to tell me why this all had to happen how it happened. I want answers. I want..." I couldn't get air. My chest was imploding.

"Are you okay?"

I nodded, my neck was so stiff. "Just finish it, Shane. Tell me fucking everything."

"Okay. I will."

"No *more* masks."

He agreed. "This is all the cards."

He told me about their club's meeting. That he brought it to every charter they had, that he was the one who was pushing to leave the Estrada Cartel. And I got that. I did. My heart was still hurting, but I understood. Marco's hold was strangling them. I didn't understand that part, but I didn't need to. No one would want to work with a cartel. No one who had family and loved ones and children, and some of these men did. I also knew I only saw the tip of the iceberg, but I got it.

"What is Connor supposed to do?"

"Marco couldn't put them in separate prisons. It'd be too much for him to control to keep them safe, but one prison was enough. And it's set up where all four of those men are never together except for one time. And the expiration is running out. It's an animal training course. The men signed up for it. They themselves did. It's short-term. It's only given to the best inmates. One instructor. One guard. And those four men."

I was really getting it now. All of it.

"Connor loved animals."

"Yeah."

I knew what he was going to tell me, but he had to say the words. I had to hear them out loud. If I didn't, I'd never believe them. I'd have hope it wouldn't happen or that it didn't happen.

I grated out, "Say it, Shane. Just fucking say it."

"Connor's going to kill all of them. Every one. We got a weapon smuggled in for him. He's going to take out the guard, and then he'll take out the rest. They won't be able to get to him to unarm him, and they won't be able to run. The room is locked down. The guard will go first so he couldn't call for help. It'll be like shooting fish in a barrel."

"It's suicide. *This* is the favor. He's going to kill Marco's four 'second-in-commands' so you can kill Marco and know that his cartel won't be taken over. Right? *That's* the plan?"

"*His* cartel will fall. Another will take its place, but it won't be the same one. It'll be chaos in Mexico for a while until another gets in power. That means we're free. We're not under his hold anymore. You don't understand how sick Marco Estrada is."

They were going to kill my brother to save their lives. That was the bottom line.

He was right about one thing. I did not want to go back to bed. I would never want to go back to bed, not with him, not ever again.

I would never be the same.

"You killed my brother."

He didn't answer, but that was fine. I heard it all, knew enough.

"How could you do that? How could you go to him and ask him to do this for you? Find another person, another way!"

He didn't answer. He just sat there, looking down until he said, "I didn't."

"Bullshit! *Bullshit!*"

"Kali." His voice was soft, but lined with regret. "I never went to your brother with this proposal."

"What?" Again, he wasn't making sense. None of this made sense. All this death. All of it was pointless. Except, God. It wasn't. It wasn't at all, and I hated that the most.

"*He* came to *me* with this."

"No."

"He knew what was going on. You know in prison. You hear the worst of the worst in there, and he was hearing how Estrada was controlling us. He did this. He set it up, all of it up. He knew what was something in common those four men had. He knew. They all liked dogs. He asked for the animal training to come into their prison. He researched it and he rallied the inmates to want it too. Kali, *he was the instructor.* He was the *only* inmate that was allowed to be in the same room as all four of them. The only one. Ever. *He* did this, and he asked us to finish it, and then he asked us to take care of his family. That's what we're doing. We were trying to do this for him!"

I snapped, unleashing, "IT MAKES NO SENSE! Why would he suddenly *decide* to create this whole program?! And what inmate is allowed to instruct a class on their own?!"

"He was!" Shane roared back. "He was because he's fucking perfect. Because he doesn't deserve to be in that place, but he's in there and you know how he is. He's a good person."

Tears were rolling down my face, but I wasn't feeling them. "He's getting out. He went in for burglary–"

"He burglarized a judge's house. He killed the judge's kid. He's never getting out. That was just one charge they brought against him."

"No." I was adamant. Just, "No."

"Yes."

"NO! It was an accident. He didn't mean to hurt that kid. He thought he was taking a toy gun with him."

"They don't care. They didn't then, and they won't now."

"But–" Why did the world have to feel so heavy all the time? "Why? Connor's not a mastermind manipulator. He's dumb in

some ways. Why'd he decide to do all this? That takes thought
and planning and reason. He had no reason to..." I trailed off
because it was in his face.

Guilt.

"What'd you do?" I asked.

"He did it for me. Because of me."

"Why Shane? Why specifically because of you?"

"Because he heard about someone that died, and he knew
who really killed the person. She was an innocent. She didn't
even know about this life, but your brother's cell is next to one of
Marco's second-in-command. He's privy to information that most
don't know, and he knew that *I* was the one to kill the person. I
found out afterwards that she was an innocent, but yeah. It's me,
Kali. He did this for me. He knew I would never have killed the
woman if... He did this all for you, for me, for your family, for the
rest of my club. He had time and he planned it all, knowing that
it'll cost his life, but he doesn't care. *Trust* me. I have tried to talk
him out of this so many times. He's doing it. And he said that it's
on me to make it mean something. So that's what I'm trying to do,
and Marco Estrada is as vulnerable as he's ever going to be today.
We have a chance right now to do this. RIGHT. NOW. There's no
going back." He stood and picked up his cut, pulling it on. "The
club is ready. We're riding out so you have a choice. You can stay,
I'll make sure someone stays back with you and gets you to wherever you want to go. Or you can come with. The choice is yours."

He left after that.

50

SHANE

She came out a minute later, an attitude cold enough to give a guy pneumonia and eyes that were lit with hate.

I didn't care because she was here. She was coming with us. She stopped, perused over everyone and I shook my head when she finally looked at me. She wasn't riding behind anyone except me. Her eyes went flat, her lips thinned, but she came and swung up behind me.

She snuggled in, dressed for the cold in a jacket, but I could still feel her breasts pushing up against my back. I liked that. I liked feeling all of her against me.

I led the way, and an army of Harleys pulled out behind us.

We were weaving down the roads and in a way, it was a nice ride. Peaceful. Not a lot of others out and about because of the hour, and when we rolled close to Albuquerque, I turned into a gas station. We stopped already once, but we'd all need to fill up again.

As they did, a prospect handled mine, and as Kali stalked inside, I sent off a text.

Me: In NM at a stop. Where should we go?
Heckler: Coordinates.

Heckler: Park the bikes in the shed. There's someone there to help, but you'll need to head on foot to where we are.

Me: Sounds good. See you soon.

There was no chitchat, not with what we were heading into so I was surprised when I felt someone coming up behind me.

I turned, and turned right back. It was Claudia.

She chuckled, her hands pushed deep into her jacket's pockets. "Don't think I didn't register the little snub, but no worries. Not the reason I'm here. Noticed my sister's attitude when she came out. So." She moved her foot around on the pavement in front of her. "She usually reserves that pure hatred for me or our mother. You're neither. What'd you do to piss her off?"

"You can ask her." I leaned forward on the bike.

"Claude," Machete tried to call her back.

The door's bell pinged on Kali's exit, and she slowed, seeing us talking, but just narrowed her eyes and kept coming for us. I sat up, and she touched my back as she got behind me. "You should piss, Claudia. I saw the coffee you took with you after the last stop."

Claudia snorted, but sashayed inside.

Corvette laughed. "You've got a woman, Machete. I don't know what else to say about that, but she's definitely a woman."

Machete laughed. "She's fire. That's what she is."

Kali snorted behind me. "That's one adjective to use for my sister."

I glanced over my shoulder. "We're talking?"

"No." But she slid her arms around my waist, and leaned forward, resting against my back.

When everyone was done and ready to go, Kali never moved a muscle as I took off again. I knew better than to think she was going to get over what I told her about Connor. Not my girl. She was plotting, and when we pulled up to the place Heckler gave us coordinates to, she got off my bike and I saw her watching her sister.

One of the prospects ran into the house, and a moment later, he came back with another guy. We were being waved to pull in and park our bikes so they were hidden. I went to find Kali, but Roanoke found me.

"What's the plan now?"

"Heckler and the rest of our charter are back that way, watching where Estrada's men are. We don't need everyone for this job so I was thinking you and the rest could stay here, keep an eye out for anything."

"Sounds good." He shifted to the side, seeing Kali had come back out to the front porch. She sat, and watched us right back. "She's in a better mindset than when I first met her."

"Yeah. She's got a new purpose."

Roanoke frowned. "Don't know if you want to know, but the other lady is going to be fine. Got word from my guys at the hospital that she's stitched up and given a severe warning to keep her mouth shut, but she's worried about her daughter."

"I know. We'll get her kid back, then decide how to use her moving forward."

"I figured as much."

There was an extra edge to his tone, so I asked, "You got an opinion on that matter?"

"They took her kid. She was trying to do what she needed to save her kid. Everyone here can relate to doing extreme shit for our loved ones."

"I know, but considering her cousin was the one selling us out to Estrada, I think we need to tread lightly here."

"I was told it was her brother who turned him in too."

He brought up another good point, and I understood what he was saying without saying it. "I hear you, Roan. We've not done any unnecessary killing so far. We even handed over Estrada's guys."

He snorted. "Estrada's guys won't say shit. And you know they'll get killed in the county lockup within a day."

"But it won't be at our hands, and they're given a chance this way. The vote to leave the cartel was also a vote to try to turn our club around, to a better path. We're trying to do that too."

He gave me a look, but sighed and nodded. "Okay. We need to remember that Shelly's husband was a Red. That shows some respect there."

"I know."

My response seemed to appease him, because he reached out and clasped my shoulder with his hand. "I've respected Raith, but if for some reason he doesn't pull through, you'll make a good national prez. I'd ride into battle with you any day."

I gave him a grin. "You're going to make me all choked up, Roan."

He barked out a laugh. "That's what I'm known for, making grown bikers cry." Spotting Kali watching us, he nodded at her again, his tone growing more serious. "Assuming you'd like us to watch her while you take off?"

"I would indeed."

"Consider it done."

I got the text from Heckler then.

Heckler: Heard you arrived. Follow these directions to our spot. Come in fast because we're getting movement outside their house.

"We gotta go."

I gave Kali one last look, but she was still hating me and I couldn't blame her. I was hating myself, had been for a long time, but I loved her. I'd never not love her, but well, I'd have to handle whatever she cooked up to save Connor. She had to be her, and I had to be me.

We ran in hard, and drawing up to where Heckler said they were hidden, I pulled out my flashlight and sent a quick reflector their way.

They flashed us back so that was a signal we could approach, knowing it was safe.

As we drew up, Heckler and the guys were all on the ground, all in black. He sidled out of his hiding spot, moving farther down the hill and then standing to find me. "Hey."

It was good to see him. The rest of the guys too.

"Damn, man." Heckler was taking me in too, shaking his head. "Been way too fucking long." He pulled me in for a hug, which shocked me. Heckler was the unpredictable sort. Rough around the edges. Never could get a read on what he liked or what he didn't. He could bring home a stray cat one day, and the next day pistol whip a teenager who dared to touch his bike, all the while holding the stray cat. I loved the guy, and even in all black clothing and a black hat, the dude's weird almost albino-coloring couldn't be squashed. He and his niece. Both didn't look from this world. Almost white hair. Crystal fucking clear eyes. Someone could tell me they actually were not human and I'd entertain the idea, but Wraith, Max's nephew, had the same striking clear eyes and since there was no shared blood between them, that they must be human.

The rest of the guys did their hellos, but I wanted to get to business. "Are you tracking Estrada?"

"Yeah. We've got nine hours to handle this before moving in on him."

"Okay. Let's figure out a plan and get this done."

Ten minutes later, we had our plan.

That's when Heckler asked me, "You got the mask?"

I didn't like wearing a mask when I loved, but when I killed, that was a whole other matter.

I gave a slow nod. "I got the mask."

51

KALI

Claudia came to find me as soon as the guys took off.
I didn't feel like talking, and she read that so she didn't push. Which I was grateful for because today was not the day to push my buttons. So, we sat on the back porch.

"You two want to watch something?"

It was the biker that first came around the corner after I shot Shelly.

"Depends on what you think we'd like to watch." Claudia's narrowed eyes on his junk was an indicator where her mind was. And she didn't seem happy about it, which almost made me start laughing because my sister had changed.

He barely reacted, instead giving us both a set of binoculars. "Those are long distance, but take a look. Swing it down and to your six o'clock. Might spot some guys you recognize."

I took them, and aimed where he said, and I saw them right away.

My breath was caught in my chest, for a moment.

Two houses. A main one with the lights lit up like it was Christmas, and a shed in the back. There were men walking around in the main house, and one was currently coming out to smoke, but it was his assault rifle that really got my attention.

Zooming out a bit, I saw the guys moving in.

My breath was taken away once again, because I'd never seen anything like it. Not in person. In movies, yes. Television, but not in real life. I was seeing it now, though and I didn't know if I should be impressed, worried, excited, or pissed. I had no clue. My reactions had shut off since I found out about Connor, and I didn't know if I should tell Claudia or not. Everything was shut down for me.

But they were moving in, all from different angles. All converging on the main house as two figures approached the shed. They moved up, hugging the side of the building until they got to the door. I couldn't tell exactly what was going on, but they had paused before the door swung open.

The guy on the front porch heard and began to move to the side to see what was going on, and he was reaching for his rifle when suddenly a figure stood up from the ground. A gun was raised. The front porch guy stumbled back, his hand raising to his neck. He swung around, and tried scrambling to bring his rifle up. The black figure stepped forward, that gun still being held steady. The front porch guy went unconscious.

I wasn't seeing any flares and I wasn't hearing any shots so I was guessing they were using suppressors.

"Look," Claudia gasped.

I went back to the shed and sagged in relief. "That's Katie. They got her out."

Or it looked like her, but her head was down. It was a female, and soon after, two guys came out. Justin and Harper. Thank goodness. Two guys moved to help run them back, and they were covering them, but once they disappeared, they began moving in on the main house.

It was a slow and steady approach until they were lined up right next to it, bent down under some windows.

And, acting as one unit, the windows were smashed by one guy. Another guy on the other side threw something inside.

The air looked like it exploded and right after that happened, the front door was kicked in. A line of guys surged in, guns up, and gas masks on.

I couldn't see what was happening on the back end, but was assuming it was the same thing.

These guys moved like military. They were professional and organized, and a whole new chill went down my spine thinking Shane wasn't just one of them. He was their leader.

It happened so quick. It wasn't long before they were hauling men outside. Five in all. Zip Ties were put on them, and they were laid on their stomach. Other guys were going through the house, and this was just as organized. Phones were collected, thrown to a pile. Weapons went in another pile. Files. They brought out laptops. All sorts of items, and other guys were bagging everything up. Others were going through the weapons while four guys stood around the men on the floor, their guns pointed right at them.

Then, like rising out of fucking mist or something, I saw Shane walking in from a hill.

He wasn't dressed like the others. He was all in black, but no gas mask. God no. A whole different chill went through me at what I saw. He was wearing an old hockey mask, white. There were marks on it, one going right down from above the eye to the cheek below. I knew it was Shane because I knew his body.

Another shiver wracked my body.

When he approached, the guys looked up and even I could tell everything got quiet. The guys lay still. Even the men going through everything, bagging everything up, seemed to go a little slower, more cautious.

Shane—no, this was Ghost.

Ghost went to the group and stood there.

Abruptly, one of his men grabbed one of Estrada's and jerked him to a sitting position.

Ghost stood over him, saying something.

The guy wouldn't look up.

Sha–Ghost stepped forward and pressed the end of his gun to the man's forehead. He said something again.

The guy started shaking his head, and his lips were moving fast, frantic.

Shane/Ghost suddenly jerked the gun to the side and shot. There was no suppressor on that one. The bang traveled to our ears seconds later, but at the same time, the Red Demon who'd pulled him to a sitting position, slammed the butt of his gun on the guy's head. He fell down, unconscious.

The others hadn't witnessed what happened, and they began moving around.

The bikers surrounding them moved in and Estrada's men stilled again.

They repeated the process, all the same until they got to the last remaining guy.

He was lifted up, but he was shaking too hard. When they tried sitting him down, his legs weren't working. He kept flopping down, so they were forced to hold him up. He was almost eye level with Shane, who raised his gun, pressed the barrel against his forehead and like the others, he kept shaking his head. He was weeping. His torment was hard to watch, but I hardened myself. He was part of the group that took a daughter, took Harper and Justin.

Fuck him.

"Hey."

I almost screamed. I'd forgotten Roanoke was there. He patted my shoulder, and ignored my shriek, though he was sporting a grin. "Incoming. Think these are your people."

I whipped my binoculars off and looked. A four-wheeler was speeding our way. I didn't recognize the guy driving, but I did recognize Katie. I saw a glimpse of two guys in the back, but it was enough for me. I jumped off the porch. My feet hit the dirt and I was running.

Katie was in the front, and seeing me, recognizing me right back, she flew off the four-wheeler and right into my arms.

I snatched her up, my hand cupping the back of her head. Her mom might've not been my favorite person, but I understood why she did what she did. Didn't agree with it. Thought there would've been a better way about it, but I did understand the fear.

I was passing her off, turning and prepared to grab both Justin and Harper for a hug when I stopped.

My arms were already up. I was going for them–that wasn't Justin, or Harper.

Two strangers stared back at me.

The guy who'd driven them to me took off his front mask, and I recognized Corvette. He stepped toward me, his hair messed, sweat streaks over his face. "Yep. That was our reaction too, and just to be very clear here, these are not your friends?"

I shook my head. "No."

Also, what the fuck?!

I HIT call on my phone.

My dad answered, but he heard me crying. "Kali? What's wrong?"

I told him what I could.

My heart was breaking and I needed my Dad.

52

SHANE

"Dumbasses over there." Stripes approached. He indicated two of Estrada's men, who were currently still tied up and sitting on the front lawn where we were. "Did not think to make sure they were the two individuals they'd previously identified from our table in Manny's. Those two guys, who were identified as Harper and Justin, Kali's friends, went out the same door, but we're pretty sure they did not go out the back way and instead probably turned to leave from the front."

"Which means they would've walked right past us when we were having our 'To Do' with Brandon Jax."

"Pretty sure. We're coordinating with Monroe now, Jax's brother-in-law, the one who does not like us. They picked up the trail where the real Harper and Justin are. Just got off the phone with..." He hesitated a moment. "With Monroe's sister, she's also a bounty hunter, and she said they found two airline tickets booked for Vegas."

"Are you shitting me?"

He started chuckling. "Nope. They were booked the following morning, so when Kali and Aly were at the hospital, their friends were boarding a plane for Sin City. Bren—er, Monroe's sister, said they're looking for a hotel they might've been using."

"There's been no attempt for them to contact Kali or Aly?"

"No, and Bren, Monroe's sis–"

"I know who Bren is. You don't have to keep explaining."

"Right." His shoulders relaxed a little. "Bren said that Aly was taken in to get a new phone, but she was just able to sync it to her old one. She tried calling Harper, but he's got his phone off."

Roadie had come over to listen in, and he began laughing. "So that means either they were also taken by a way smarter Estrada team or those two guys went and got hitched and don't have their phones on because they're still partaking in Sin City and the many pleasurable activities the city has to offer."

Kali was pacing back and forth on the front porch. I'd tried to get her to go inside, away from Estrada's men and where Katie was, but she wouldn't budge. She kept shooting me looks so didn't take a genius to know she wanted an update asap.

"Okay." I asked Heckler, who'd come to join our circle. "What's the update on where Estrada is?"

"They're in Amarillo."

Right. Fuck. That meant we'd need to get word to Connor, so he could do what he wanted to do and then set up the attack for Estrada. "You guys make the call to get these guys picked up?"

Roadie raised his hand. "I did. We're coordinating with local bounty hunters so all of us won't be here when they come to get them."

"Good." I motioned to the two guys who none of us knew that were now sitting on the other end of the porch. "Did they get identified and call whoever they needed to call?"

"We did. They were just two guys hanging out at Manny's that night. Went outside to smoke a joint, and wrong place, wrong time. Bounty hunters are going to take them in too. Police will want to question them."

"They been instructed on what not to say?"

Roadie flashed me a grin. "They were given a story to tell when asked how they came to be rescued. They've been informed that *we* didn't rescue them. The *bounty hunters* coming to pick them actually did. They seemed amenable, especially when we found their families on social media. Good old social media. Always so informative of tagging friends and family in all those pictures where they like to brag, or maybe that's just how I take it. I might be jaded."

Corvette snorted. "I can think of a lot of words to describe you, but sure as shit that jaded ain't one of them."

Heckler said over them, cutting through the bullshit, "When are we leaving? We need time to set everything up for Estrada. We're going to kill this time, right?" He was always the most serious of everyone. Also older since he was in his forties.

Everyone got real quiet, real quick.

"What if we tell someone in law enforcement who Marco's second-in-commands are. Someone who can actually do something about them."

I shook my head. "We've thought of everything. Everything. No one will get to them in time before they'll all be transferred out and somewhere else. He's got everyone in his pocket there. We checked everyone." But... goddamn. There was one chance. One shot, but it was such a long one that I didn't dare put any stock into it.

It was a wish on a star, that sort of shot. But looking at Kali right now as she was trying to hear us, all the way across the lawn, and knowing she couldn't, I knew I had to try. For Connor, for Kali. I had to make the call.

But everything needed to be ready.

"Who's got the current line to Connor?" There was a guy in Connor's prison that had a cell. The number tended to change frequently. We were never told the reason why that happened, but we would get an update on the current number. That person operated on the basis that if we sent a message, it would be only one time, and he would need to give that message to Connor. The phone operator didn't know what the message was about, or even who was on our end. It was a deal set up, and when that message was delivered, we'd pay that person a fuckton of money, but if that person also ratted on Connor, all that money would go away. It never surprised me what people would do for money, and a ton of it too. It's a currency that made the world go round so we used it when we needed to.

"I do." Christopher Raith, Maxwell's nephew and also known as his biker name, Wraith, raised his hand. "Once you tell me to send the message, I will."

"Good." I skimmed the group. Heckler was right. We needed to get set up. "Let's get going."

As they moved to do what they needed to do before once again, going into another battle, I stepped aside and pulled my phone out.

KALI

Shane wasn't talking.

I was going with the flow by now, and knowing they still needed to handle Estrada, I was figuring he was next on their list. Claudia had no clue. I don't know what she was told, or if she'd been filled in by Machete. I was guessing not because she seemed almost chipper.

I didn't have the heart to tell her and I'd been thinking of all the different scenarios to get Connor out of this, but I kept coming back to the part where he was in prison. He was in *prison*. I couldn't get to him. I couldn't get him out. Not in the time I needed, and not ever.

Shane was right. My brother was never getting out.

I *hated* this plan, but it was a Connor plan. Had everything

Connor about it. *Of course* he'd put himself in the line of fire to help someone he considered a brother. *Of course* he'd be adamant to make sure his family was also taken care of, because Shane didn't know this, but I knew that was part of why Connor put all this together.

It was as much to take care of his family as to help Shane. In his mind he was killing two birds with one stone. Shane. Us. And a third might've been that he was choosing to go out how he wanted to go out.

God. I didn't know. How could I?

I just loved my brother. I wanted him back.

But he killed a judge's kid. He confessed to it, knowing he was signing his life away when he did. He still did it because my brother was a good person in his heart. Did stupid stuff, seriously atrociously dumb stuff like getting addicted to drugs and sinking so low to putting himself in that judge's house in the first place. But he pleaded guilty because he killed a kid, and I couldn't help but to wonder if that was the last part. My brother couldn't take the guilt?

My brother would never be free again in his life, but I didn't want this to be the way he went out.

God, no. Please.

"You going to clue me in on whatever the fuck is going on? You're wound up tight. Your man's wound up tight. Machete is not making eye contact with me lately, and now everyone just got real serious and my tits are so perked up from all the tension in the air that I have those tied up assholes eyeballing me."

I started crying.

I couldn't stop it, and I couldn't control it.

The dam burst and my sister jumped back ten feet from me. "Oh, fuck my tits. She's lost her mind."

I heard gravel crunching and then Shane's voice, "Go elsewhere, Claudia."

"I—"

"It's not a request." Then his hand touched my arm, and I didn't have the strength to fight him.

I should hate him, I knew this. And maybe a part of me always would, but for the life of me, I could not think of a way out of this. Not one that wouldn't get a whole ton more people dead.

So because of all of that, because I was gathering up my strength to do what I just now decided to do, I let him hold me. And I let him pull me away from the group.

He folded his arms around me, his head burying into my neck. "I'm sorry. I'm so fucking sorry."

My whole body jerked on a shudder. My baby brother was going to die, and I could do nothing to stop it. What new hell was I stepping into? "He can't go."

Shane stiffened right before he lifted his head. A dull and almost dead look was in his eyes. It washed over me, and a third fucking shiver wracked my body. "He set all this in motion. He did. Not me. Not my club. He told me he was going to do this whether or not my club followed through. I visited him thirty-nine times. Thirty-nine, Kali. He took me off the list so I couldn't do it for the fortieth time. This shit didn't happen overnight. It took an entire year of his life to plan it. You tell me, knowing everything I told you, you tell me what to do. Don't go through with it? You tell me. What should I do?"

"Not fucking yell at her, how about that?"

I tensed because someone had overheard.

And I tensed even more recognizing Claudia's voice, but I was going over what he just said. He gave nothing away. She wouldn't know any details, but the guilt I was feeling at not telling my sister? A black hole opened in my stomach and it was swirling and it was angry and it wanted to eat my soul out of me.

Was this how Shane felt?

I reached back, not intending to, but once I touched him, I couldn't pull my hand away either. "It's fine, Claudia."

"My right buttocks, it's fine. He's yelling at you about our brother. First, what the fuck are you talking about and second, DON'T YELL AT MY SISTER, YOU BIG FUCKING ASS–" she cut off with a gasped cry, but then began yelling again, "Put me down! Marshall. What are you doing? That's my sister..." She trailed off when he put her down, but he shoved a helmet over her head, lifted her onto the back of his bike, and a second later, he was in front of her and they were leaving.

"Yep. She's all woman, that's for sure."

A few of the other guys had migrated over. That was Corvette.

Roadie laughed. "They're going the wrong way."

"No." Shane moved in behind me, his hand coming to my waist. I didn't want to, but I felt more centered at his touch, at feeling him at my back. He added over my head, "He's not. He's taking her home."

I leaned back into him.

His arm curled around my waist, his hand splaying out over my stomach.

"Get on your bikes. It's time to go."

He sounded so tired when he said it, and my heart was aching.

But I moved forward because I had every intention of being there when they took Marco Estrada down.

———

I DIDN'T CALL, but I texted.

Me: Dad, I love you. I'm proud to be your daughter. I'm proud of who you are as a man and a father. You are the best person I know in my life.

Me: I just wanted to tell you that.

Me: I really love you, Dad.

Me: I gotta turn my phone off. I hope you're not breaking a hip with the Old Gents.

Me: If you are, call your doc.

53

KALI

I wasn't privy to their plan, but I stayed back and I watched. When I left his bike and followed behind the large portion of guys, he hadn't argued. He wasn't going to fight me on a lot, I realized. Maybe it was guilt? Maybe it was because I needed to see this through, considering what it was going to take away from me. I didn't know.

I didn't care.

None of the guys said a word either, and I glimpsed a few with pity in their eyes so they all knew.

All of them. It hit me then, *really* hit me.

This had been a plan for a long time. They all knew. They knew when they came to Friendly, Indiana in the first place. Roadie knew when he was fucking my sister. He knew when he cheated on her.

Machete knew when he 'took over' with my sister.

Shane knew when I showed up, following him.

When he kissed me.

When he claimed me.

When he defended me to Foley.

They all knew, and that was a truly shitty feeling.

But was I different because I hadn't told Claudia? Because I already knew that when we got the call that he was knifed in prison, and was dead, that I wasn't going to tell her the real reason behind it? I already knew I wasn't. And in my mind, there was only one thing I could do that would make any of this worth it. One thing that would appease my soul.

So because of that, I kept quiet and I stayed in the background, and I watched.

In a way, it was anticlimactic. The road getting here was the most harrowing, with all the pitfalls and realizations but I guess it was fitting.

Marco Estrada was just a man. He may run a cartel and he may have his men to take over as a backup, but he was still just a man. I didn't know if he loved. If he had a woman, or women? Or a man? If he had children? Or parents? Or siblings? A part of me wanted to think he was soulless. He cared for no one, but himself. It was a guarantee that he was narcissistic. Who could run a cartel and not be a narcissist? The lack of caring? Empathy? Being so ruthless? That person must've been hard inside themselves when they were first born, or were raised in a world where you killed or were killed?

It was all that made sense to me.

The Red Demons had separated into three groups.

A third went down the road by a mile. Another third went ahead. I went where Shane went because in the end, it'd be him with Estrada. Felt that's how it was going to play out, all the way down to my bones. He was with the middle section.

Five trucks were driving down a gravel road. They'd pulled off a main highway and were weaving through the hills to where we were. I was watching with the same binoculars as the caravan of trucks were speeding when suddenly an explosion went off by the road.

It cut off the last two trucks from the rest, but because they were dickheads, they went even faster. They left those two trucks behind, and a barrage of gunshots rang out. I could see as the Red Demons were moving in from the top of the hills, shooting down into those two trucks.

Boom!

Another explosion, and this time the front two trucks had been separated from the middle truck. The explosion caused a whole crater in the road so the middle truck literally couldn't go forward. One of the trucks had been upended by the explosion. Men were starting to crawl out through the windows, but like the last two trucks, they were under fire.

So much death.

It was all senseless. Every one of them. But I wasn't doing anything to stop it, nor did I want to.

What did that say about me?

The middle truck reversed fast.

There was a crater in front, one behind. They had nowhere to go, so they went into the ditch. That didn't last long because we were in the middle of a forest. I wouldn't have believed it myself if I wasn't here, but we were. Desert. Cliffs. And trees everywhere.

The truck crashed, which was a given by now. The driver was panicked, and he looked like he was tossed out.

The guys that I stood with, they raised their guns and they lit into him.

He was dead. I was certain.

I noticed movement in Shane's direction and saw he was pulling on that same white hockey mask as before.

Then I was distracted as I heard more gunfire.

They threw another guy out from the truck. Same result.

I wasn't understanding the logic, but suddenly there was an explosion on the other side of the truck.

Now I got it, or I got the Red Demons' logic.

There was nowhere to go.

They began moving down, converging like they had at the

other house, and I went with them so I guess 'we' were converging.

I wasn't shooting so I didn't know if I should think of myself as one of them. Though, in a few minutes that wouldn't make a difference, I suppose.

One more guy came out, but he didn't shoot so he wasn't shot.

He held up his hands in surrender, and a few of the Red Demons moved in, grabbed him, and dragged him away.

There was yelling.

They were yelling at the truck.

They were yelling at the guy they just pulled away.

I wasn't listening to the words. I didn't care.

I was watching Shane, and he wasn't moving.

I thought back to that old hockey mask he put on.

What did it mean? Did that signify something?

I wasn't too concerned about the chaos that was happening right now. No, no. I was watching and waiting.

There was another explosion. This one felt smaller, and closer. I felt the heat on my face. My hair was whipping around from its impact but I was still only watching Shane. When he moved, I would move.

He was my calm in this storm.

As if feeling my gaze, he turned, sparks of fire going in the air between us. His head tilted to the side, just barely. Then I heard someone call his name. It penetrated this weird vacuum of sound. He started forward, and I felt his footsteps, though he was a few feet away from me, I felt every step he took. The deep thud as he walked, his foot meeting the earth, and I felt that vibration going up through my legs. Up to my chest.

I didn't know what was going on with me, but I was in a daze of sorts. I'm sure. I was only seeing Shane as he went forward. I was only hearing his footsteps. There were yelling and other sounds of gunfire or explosions in the background, but they were barely filtering in.

It was like we were in a bubble. Where we were, nothing could penetrate. As Shane kept going forward, so did I until he got to Marco Estrada's truck. A man was pulled out, and he was being held up, shoved against the back.

It was not Marco Estrada.

I didn't know what Marco Estrada looked like, but I could tell by the eyes that this young man wasn't him. He wasn't a boy, but he wasn't quite a man. He was scared, and his mouth was moving fast. He was saying something, and judging from the plea in his eyes, he was pleading for his life.

I hoped, for the first time since the first explosion, that this young man wouldn't be killed. But it wasn't him, and I knew that they were expecting Marco Estrada to be in the middle truck. Made sense except to Marco Estrada himself. He would've wanted to trick anyone who might set out to attack his convoy. But if he was in the back, he might've been taken out.

If he was in the front, he might've been taken out.

So where was Marco Estrada?

I knew where he would be.

I turned, and this time the vacuum left me.

All the sounds from around me hit me hard.

I heard all the shouting, all the cursing. But no more gunfire. No more shots were being exchanged. I liked that part, and I ran back up the hill, hearing Shane yelling my name too.

I ignored him.

A part of me didn't want him to come for this last part, because as soon as I figured it out, I knew it was true. I felt it in my bones. I was supposed to go, but I didn't know the reason.

I didn't care.

They had brought a truck. One, among all the Harleys. I ran to it, jumping in, and I turned back to where the house was.

I didn't go to where we'd left, where I knew bounty hunters were arriving to pick up Estrada's men. I drove to the first house, the one that had the shed where they kept Katie and the two men I didn't know captive.

It looked so ragged and abandoned now, but as I drove down the driveway, I saw another truck parked on the backside of the house. It was an old truck, a classic that I might've gone crazy for in another life. This time, though, I just knew who that meant had arrived.

A man stepped out from the front door, his gun raised. He was dressed all in black, and he looked military. His gun was pointed at me.

I stopped, my hands going up, but then another man stepped out from behind him.

There.

That was Marco Estrada.

I knew it this time. I could tell from his eyes.

They were old and dead. Like him. It was a weird sensation because I already saw the life leaving his body, though he was fully connected. I still saw it. Parts of him were shedding and flying away. Or maybe I was just seeing his soul wasn't a part of him. On the outside, he looked almost handsome. Cheekbones that curved high. He had big lips. He was tall, maybe six three. A wiry body. He was in a business suit.

He held up a hand and his lips moved. He was almost smiling as he stepped forward. Then I heard what he said. It took a second to get to me, and no, I didn't understand the cause for that. "Wait, Manuel. I'd like to hear what she came to say."

He walked down the stairs and approached, the ends of his mouth curved upwards. He had a hand toward me, and he was waving for me to come to him. "I've come to enjoy these moments, when I get a pocket of time to talk with my enemy's woman. This has happened before. Another woman. Another time and place. Another enemy, but still the same. Though, that time she had a dog with her." A full smile beckoned to me. "Do you have a dog, Miss Kali Michaels?"

So he knew who I was.

That would make this easier.

I didn't care to make this a big to-do. There didn't need to be conversation. There was no point, really. Before a few days ago, I never heard about this man, but as I started to hear yelling again, as my heartbeat began to pick up, I brought out the gun that I snuck.

I watched as they took the weapons out of that house. And I watched as they bagged them up. And I watched where that bag of weapons were put when they brought them to the house. And when Shane was having a 'meeting' with his men, when everyone wasn't paying attention to me, I went and grabbed one of them. And I checked, because my dad once took me to a shooting range because he thought it'd be a good idea if I knew how to defend myself, and I saw there were three bullets still in the chamber.

There was shouting again.

I saw from the corner of my eye as the guy behind Marco, the one who was with him, was shooting behind me.

Marco was focused behind me as well, and he was starting to turn to run, but then I brought my gun out and he stopped.

Slow motion.

That's what this was.

This was all happening in slow motion to me.

Even better because I raised the gun, and I pointed, and as his eyes widened, he realized what I was going to do–I did it.

Connor's death *would* stand for something.

I pulled the trigger.

EPILOGUE
KALI

K atie was okay.

The random men were okay.

I found out where Harper and Justin had been the whole time, and they were more than okay.

But me, I wasn't okay.

That day when I shot Marco Estrada, I got him. I know I did, but we didn't have his body.

Shane had driven in, guns blazing and he drew attention from me. It's the whole reason I was even able to shoot Estrada. Thinking back on it, I realized that I would've been killed the moment I pulled that gun. The guy with Marco Estrada had been that good. He wasn't like the other imbeciles who worked for him.

He ran in, grabbing Marco's body at the same time that Shane ran in and scooped *me* up.

They were like two opponents having a ceasefire for a moment as they each got their partner to safety. Shane had come alone, his other men were back at the other 'battle.' So in a way, I still blamed myself for why Marco got away, if he did indeed get away. I put it that way because it's been a whole year later and no one's heard a word about him or from him.

His cartel didn't fall. After all that planning, there was no chaos in Mexico. But there wasn't an all-out war either. It was like one side went silent, and our side... just continued living.

The Red Demons were free.

And my brother, he went through with what he promised. He killed those four men, and then another surprise happened after. Instead of getting a call informing me about his death in prison, I got a call saying that my brother had *escaped* prison. It was kept very hush-hush. No media covered his disappearance. I never once had law enforcement knocking on my door, asking about him or looking for him. To my knowledge, my brother literally vanished from prison.

I had no idea where he went, and when I asked Shane about it, he would say the same thing.

He made a call to the one person he trusted in law enforcement.

He never thought it would pan out.

And he had no idea where my brother went.

But, no news of my brother's death was very good news to me. I liked to think, like on days like this, as I was standing on our front porch in our house just outside of Frisco, that everything was a happily ever after.

Aly and Brandon got married.

Brandon didn't quite 'hate' the Red Demons anymore, but he didn't necessarily like us. What he did was thaw toward Shane and me specifically. That meant Aly and I got to hang out. I helped plan her wedding. I helped plan her bachelorette party and her baby shower. I also got to know her in-laws more, and while I enjoyed her sister-in-law, I was always uneasy around her too.

But we weren't the only ones here.

Harper and Justin did indeed get married. They decided to

leave Manny's that night, and instead of going out the 'back back' as Harper put it, because it was 'creepy,' they went to the front. They enjoyed the show of machismo going on between Shane and Brandon, but they went and 'had it out,' also as Harper put it, in their hotel room. After a few hours of yelling and crying, the make-up sex had been Hot (also as Harper spelled it,) and after that, he had an epiphany.

"What the fuck was I fighting him for?" he explained to us. "I mean, like duh. I was being so dumb and being so scared of not wanting to get hurt, that all I was doing was hurting myself. I realized that Justin was *actually* going to go, and he would find a great guy and I would've lost him forever." He started tearing up, his voice went hoarse. "I couldn't do that, so you know, Vegas."

They went to Vegas, got married, and turned their phones off to the world.

They didn't turn their phones back on until a rather mammoth-size man showed up at their hotel room and informed them if they didn't call their friends back, he'd shoot them right then and there.

Justin says the guy didn't actually say that threat, but that's what Harper stands by.

As for me and Shane–"Hey, hooker."

I grinned at the same time I rolled my eyes. "Claudia."

She grinned, ruefully, at me. "Hi."

Machete was right behind her, his arms full of equipment. He gave me a grin. "Where do you want this?"

I pointed to the back. "My dad's already here. He's set up."

He paused. "Grill Master?"

"Grill Master."

Claudia frowned.

He said, with a small grin, "Cool. This will be awesome."

A second later, the air filled with beats from Tag Team. The Sugar Hill Gang would be on deck, and there were a ton others right after. I lifted up a thumb, heading down the porch to Claudia. "That music won't be stopping till late tonight. Hope you're okay with it."

She gave me a look. "This is not the first family cookout I've been to." She gave me a hug, wrapping her arms around me.

"We got a DJ."

"What? Really?"

"Yeah. I mean, it's my cousin Trevor, but he DJs as a side-gig. Also, are you ready to eat, because there's going to be a lot of eating. *A lot.* There's going to be dancing all night too. Karaoke. You do know the rule?"

Her smile was wiped clean.

"What? No. What is it?"

"You gotta dance as if no one's watching. That's the whole point. And definitely you have to dance if someone points to you. No matter who it is. My niece? Dance. My cousin–"

"You have like thirty-eight cousins! What do you mean if one of them points to me?"

"Dance." I wasn't done. "And if my great-grandmother points at you, you *really* dance. You hearing me? I only got one left. All the others are gone, so Great Grandma Martha is kinda like a goddess to us. I'm not joking."

Claudia had met my Great Grandma and a few of my cousins from Chicago, but not a ton. A few. And in small doses, but there was a whole event happening tomorrow and a ton of my family flew in to be a part of it. It was enough to make me cry and laugh at the same time.

Love. Laughter. Togetherness. Dancing. And eating. That's what it was all about.

I patted Claudia on the back. "You'll get it. Just wait till Great-Grandma Martha gets here."

"Kali!"

I twisted around, Claudia's arms still around me. My dad had an apron on, a t-shirt under that said *Kali's Dad*, and giant-sized tongs in one hand. He held them up to me. "I don't have enough spices. We *are* the spices. This is a big deal." He barely blinked, waving his tongs. "Hi, Claudia."

"Hi, James."

"Your mother coming tonight?"

She nodded, her whole body stiff in my arms. "She and my dad got a divorce. Did you hear?"

He gave a nod, not showing a thing. "I heard. I hope she's doing okay."

She gave another nod. "Me too. I think she is. It was a long time ago, just making sure you knew."

Again, he barely blinked. He was picking up what she was putting down. "Her bar doing good?"

"Yep. It's doing real good, Mr. Michaels."

"That's good." He flashed me a grin. "She as tight as she always was?"

I dropped my arms from around my sister. "Dad!"

Claudia laughed. "You know Ruby."

"I do. Oh, boy, do I. Kali." He waved his tongs back in the air. "I need the seasonings. This food takes hours to properly season!"

I had no idea what he was so stressed about, but then again, I was not a Grill Master.

I headed for him, pulling my phone out. "Okay. Tell me the seasonings you need."

———

THEY WERE PLAYING Catch Phrase when I walked by, hearing my Uncle Toby saying, "It's a Southern word for *pop*." I was pretty sure he was describing Coca-Cola.

A second later, I heard, "You can't say soda!"

"I didn't."

"You did."

"I said pop."

"You said pop, and then you said soda."

"It's on the card!"

"Those are the words you *can't* say."

"Oh! Well, why isn't *that* in the rules? Should be in the rules."

"It's in the rules. I've told you seven times."

———————

"Hey."

An arm circled my waist later, when I was watching my dad and his dance crew on the dance floor. I was pulled back into the shadows. I knew whose arm that was, and I was already smiling, turning around to meet him. I reached up on my toes, pressing my mouth to his. "Hi."

Shane smiled down at me. "Hi back."

It'd been a year since I pulled that trigger.

Since then, he picked me up. Literally.

He carried me at times when I couldn't walk.

He was there when we went back.

When we met Aly. When Brandon hadn't been such a fan of Shane then.

When I called my father, told him what all happened, he had so severely not been happy. He refused to meet Shane until months later. Shane was with me at every step of the way back, and the way back was a long trip. But we were here, and I was feeling we'd finally arrived once more.

I killed Estrada, or I thought I had, and his club swarmed me. They covered me, but there's been no investigation. Nothing. The most I saw was when I woke one morning and two cops were talking to Shane, Boise, and Machete in the driveway. They left and none of the guys ever said a word to me what that'd been about.

We came back.

We lived.

I got the call about my brother. I told Claudia about the call about our brother, and well, life went on.

It was a weird event.

We went to Texas for a while.

We went back to Indiana. When Aly called and asked if I could help make plans for sending her grandmother to California, I *really* got it. Aly was staying in Cali, and since she was there, and since I was kinda a nomad, that's where Harper said he was going to settle down. Justin had family from California so it worked for them, but we helped get Aly's grandma transferred out there.

And Shane asked me one night in bed, his arms around me, "Where do you want to be?"

I paused, my legs had been wound around his hips. "What?"

"Max is asking me. I still got stuff to handle in Cali, but if you don't want to settle there, then we won't. Where do you want to go?"

I told him instantly, no hesitation. California.

So here we were.

I called Rena when we arrived, knowing we'd be staying and I had a job at Fallen Crest not long after that. I didn't know the specifics, but Shane was taking over the Frisco charter. But changes were happening. On my request, he was making a move to help rebuild the town. They moved their charter's headquarters so it was more out of town, and put money into building whatever needed to be done.

The latest I heard was that the plans were approved to start rebuilding a school. A new development recently started too. The Red Demons had an investment into it, but it was happening. There were talks about setting up a small clinic too. Three other bars had popped up in and near town.

It was all good.

But we'd built our own house, a renovated horse barn. It was always my dream, and Shane had a whole shed for his bikes too on our land. Plus, that shed was added onto it so he was housing half of his new charter too.

I got it. I understood. I liked the guys.

They were family to me too.

Harper didn't quite understand. Neither did Aly, but they were supportive. Once Brandon got to know Shane, and he did that over many nights of rummy and drinking bourbon, but it happened. Brandon's family was another thing. There was no gray meeting or compromise between his family and Shane or the club, but it was what it was. I didn't care as long as I still got to have Aly, and she would've made sure that happened no matter what. After our night together, Aly was a changed woman with me or she'd just remembered who she was. I got it. I really did. There was real reason to be worried about the Red Demons, but I loved Shane. He was a Red.

That meant I was a Red.

Aly had a whole moment, but she said she loved me no matter what.

So in a way, that meant Aly was a Red.

I mean, not really, but we were still going with it.

It just meant I still had both of my best friends in my life, and I was Shane's old lady, so I was happy. And now with my family being here, I was extra super happy.

Life was good. If you had people who loved you and were in your corner, life was damn good.

"You ready for tomorrow?"

I tipped my head back, feeling his arms around me, and I smiled up at him. "You mean when we get married?"

His smile deepened. "Yeah. That's what I mean."

I put my arms around him, raising up on my toes. "Yeah." I moved so my head was right in front of his, a few inches separating us. I dropped my tone. "I am very ready."

"Good." He smiled at me.

I smiled back.

IT WAS THAT NIGHT, after dancing and laughing for hours, when I was lying in his arms that I asked, "You told me you had a thing about masks."

His arms tightened, just barely. "Yeah?"

I rolled so I was facing him more directly. "Why do you wear that hockey mask? I saw you."

We were not conventional.

Our wedding tomorrow would not be conventional.

Because of that, or maybe despite all that, we were sleeping together the night before we got married.

Maybe I was having a moment where I wanted to know all the secrets. It'd been something on my mind because I hadn't been able to get the image of him putting that mask on, wading into battle how he had both times. I wanted to understand the reason.

"It's a symbol."

I rolled to my back, looking at him. "A symbol for what?"

His face grew tight, but then he softened. "I'm their leader. In that moment, in that time, all the danger going on, it's me. Every responsibility rides on my back. When we go into places where the guys wear masks for whatever reason, camouflage, gas masks, etc, *my* mask will stick out. Or that's the hope. It's twofold. It's supposed to symbolize what we're doing. Wreaking havoc. Justice. Fear. But mine should stick out the most. That's the point. If someone is going to draw against us, I want them to point at me first. I'm the leader. I stand for my men, just as much as they stand for me. It's me giving back to them. I protect them while they protect me. It's a yin and yang balance. I'd be nothing without my men, whereas they would still be fine. They could get a new leader and they'd keep moving forward. So in a way it's also my ode to them. I love them and I want to protect them, and it's a way I might help them back as much as they've undoubtedly helped me already."

I moved closer in his arms, touching his face, and cupping his cheek. "You send the message, but you are the message and you are standing for your men. All at the same time."

"Yeah. Something like that."

I got it. It was beautiful, but it wasn't one-dimensional or even two-dimensional. It was a multi-layered answer and in some ways I felt like it could stand for so much more than it did. Then again, maybe it always did and that was the whole purpose.

The bottom line was, "You wear that mask to protect your men."

"Yes."

It was pure Shane, and another reason why I loved him, why I was marrying him tomorrow.

I moved up, touching my mouth to his.

My man.

My husband.

My other half.

IT WAS LATER, after I kissed him, and he kissed me back, and he rolled on top of me.

It was after that when I told him, "You know I asked my mom today why she sent me after Claudia." I lifted my head up, gazing at him. "She had to know Claudia would never leave. Claude does what she wants. It's just how she is."

"I know. It's why we're building a salon for her in Frisco."

I smiled, another advance for the dying town.

"What'd she say when you asked her?"

I lay all the way back, making sure he could see me. "She told me she sent me after you."

"*Kali, honey. You stupid? I took one look at how you were looking at that man and I knew he was the one. I'm not a perfect mama. I know that much, but I do love you and I knew that man was yours. I just gave you the excuse to go get him."* She gave me a wink and moved in, pressing her mouth to my forehead. *"I love you, baby girl."* Then she looked around. *"Now, where's your father because he's single, ain't he? Saw him earlier and he's looking damn good. That dance crew is doing wonders for him."*

"Are you serious?" Shane was fighting back his laughter. His hand slid to my stomach and then moved down, resting between my legs.

"I am." My smile got all secretive because he also knew the other secret I found out today, just from going to see Dr. Vioeri who was now my regular doctor. I had to ask, "Speaking of parents, what do you think?"

I moved in, touching my mouth to his, a kiss for a kiss because I loved him so much.

And I asked, "You think I'm having a boy or a girl?"

If you enjoyed Frisco, please leave a review!
They truly help so much.
www.tijansbooks.com

ACKNOWLEDGMENTS

I never planned on writing an MC before, but when the Red Demons first showed up in The Boy I Grew Up With, they slowly took on their own world. And then Always Crew happened and yeah, I was obsessed. I *had* to write a book for Shane. So thank you to the Red Demons themselves.

A special thank you to the whole team that helped me with Frisco. Jessica, all my proofreaders, Crystal, Serena. You guys are so amazing!

Heather and Crystal, thank you for helping with the audiobook. I truly appreciate it so much.

A special thank you to Renita and Curtis for all your help with Frisco!

A very special thank you to the ladies in my reader group. You guys are so active in there and it truly helps me to keep writing.

I couldn't end this without a huge thank you to my cuddle partner, and the guy who is always checking on me, Bailey! My pup. Love you so much!

ALSO BY TIJAN

Frisco is a standalone, but it is the *latest* story in a universe that I've created. The timeline is set after:

Canary

Kess

Before Kade

If you wanted to read more about the Red Demon's history mentioned, check out:

The Boy I Grew Up With

Crew Princess

Always Crew

Latest books:

My Anti-Hero

Pine River

Hockey With Benefits

A Dirty Business (Mafia, Kings of New York Series)

A Cruel Arrangement (Mafia, Kings of New York Series)

Sports Romance Standalones:

Pine River

Hockey With Benefits

Enemies

Teardrop Shot

Hate To Love You

The Not-Outcast

Rich Prick

Fallen Crest and Crew Universe

Fallen Crest/Roussou Universe

Fallen Crest Series

Crew Series

The Boy I Grew Up With (standalone)

Rich Prick (standalone)

Hockey With Benefits (standalone)

Nate (standalone)

Aveke (standalone)

A Kade Christmas

My Anti-Hero (standalone)

Motorcycle club romance:

Frisco

Series:

Broken and Screwed Series (YA/NA)

Jaded Series (YA/NA suspense)

Davy Harwood Series (paranormal)

Carter Reed Series (mafia)

The Insiders

Mafia Standalones:

Cole

Bennett Mafia

Jonah Bennett

Canary

Paranormal Standalones and Series:

Evil

Micaela's Big Bad

The Tracker

Davy Harwood Series (paranormal)

Young Adult Standalones:

Ryan's Bed

A Whole New Crowd

Brady Remington Landed Me in Jail

College Standalones:

Antistepbrother

Kian

Enemies

Contemporary Romances:

Bad Boy Brody

Home Tears

Fighter

Rockstar Romance Standalone:

Sustain

Christmas novellas:

A Kade Christmas

A Christmas Song (Ryan's Bed holiday novella)

More books to come!

CANARY

1

I should've been fazed that I was about to witness a murder. I wasn't.

Sad to say, but this was my new normal.

I was in a motel room. A large plastic sheet covered the floor, and a guy sat on his knees in the middle of it. My boss stood over him. He took his gun out, pressing it into Knee Guy's mouth.

He leaned forward.

"You're going to tell me who sent you, you motherfucker," he growled.

That was my boss. Raize. He was on a kick today. The "motherfucker" bit was new.

He'd used it to the point that I wondered if he called his mother *motherfucker*, and if so, did she reply with who actually fucked her? Probably not.

I couldn't see Raize having a mother.

Knee Guy was sobbing, making pleading sounds around the gun's muzzle, and a distinct smell filled the room.

"Ah, man." One of Raize's henchmen groaned, shifting on his feet. "He just pissed himself."

Henchman Two gave him a look. "Shut up."

Henchman One was new. I called him Henchman One because he acted like there was a hierarchy, and he was on top. I didn't know his name. I'd learned it was easier not knowing their names. Raize had hired him a week ago, and I was surprised he was griping so much. Raize didn't put up with attitude from his goons. Maybe this one hadn't been around long enough to realize that.

Raize took the gun out of the guy's mouth and turned, pinning Henchman One with a look. "You got a problem?"

Henchman Two glanced my way. Then we both made sure not to make eye contact with Henchman One while he was looking around for allies.

Oh, wow. Look at that floor.

It was a beautiful myriad of...plastic. All different colors in that plastic down there.

Yep.

Plastic.

"Can't hear you, motherfucker." Raize took the safety off his gun.

Yep. I recognized the slight sound of that by now. This was something else that should've fazed me. But all I did was move to the side, farther away from Henchman One.

Knowing my boss, I knew Raize didn't miss. But the blood would be a bitch to wash out. I'd have to shower here, and there was an ick factor involved with showering a door away from two dead bodies.

Henchman Two moved with me.

He'd been with Raize for the last month and was proving to be smart. He'd last longer than Henchman One, that was for sure.

There were two main rules you had to follow if you worked with Raize. One, do whatever he tells you to do. And two, don't bitch about it. This guy was bitching. Our boss did not have patience, hence why this guy had been hired in the first place. He was filling another guy's spot who hadn't followed one of those two rules. I didn't know which. But he was there one day and gone the next. This new guy showed up for lunch, and then we were off to do whatever Raize needed us to do.

"I—I'm sorry, Raize."

Raize glowered at him, and it was ugly.

Not that Raize was ugly. One night when I was drunk, I realized that Raize was good looking—hot even, but he was dead inside. That was obvious, and the fact that he had no problem killing snuffed out any attraction I might've had. I tended *not* to look at Raize, or did it the least amount I could.

Another unofficial rule of mine? Don't make eye contact with Raize. He might think you're issuing him a challenge.

I'd been working for him for six months, almost seven. In this world, that was just about tenure. I was pretty sure I'd been won in a bet. I'd gone to a poker game with my previous boss. He went inside a room. Eight hours later, Raize came out, grabbed my arm, and we left.

I'd looked back, but my boss' guys were just standing and staring. If they'd been going to put up a fight, they would've done so the second Raize touched my arm.

And, well, anticlimactic, but that's how I came to work for Raize.

He'd turned to me in the car after I left with him. "You got a place here?"

I'd eyed him, warily, as I shook my head. "I was staying at Slim's." That was my previous boss from an hour earlier.

He'd grunted. "I got a room. You can use that." But he must've had a new thought come to mind because he'd squinted at me after that. "You want your own place?"

I'd wanted to ask why. I'd come into this world knowing the score. If I worked for someone, I worked wholeheartedly for them. There was no half-in or half-out. We didn't do taxes. Forms of ID were issued from what was 'heard' about you. Everything was cash. There was a normal world, that wasn't this. We were all the way in the 'other' side of society.

You were all in or all out. And all out meant death.

I wasn't ready to die, not yet.

I still had shit to do.

So I'd shrugged. "What's the point?"

He'd grunted, his mouth curving up in a slight grin.

That'd been the only time I saw Raize come close to smiling, and it wasn't even a half-smile. It'd been a hint of a smile, like a glimmer and then poof—it was gone. He'd returned to being scary the next second when he'd pulled a gun out and aimed it at the guy in front of him in the car.

I sat behind the driver. Raize was behind the front passenger.

There was no warning.

He'd put the end of his gun against the headrest and pulled the trigger—I'd missed the silencer on top.

White fuzz and blood went everywhere. The guy's body slumped forward.

Raize had settled back, cleaning his gun. He'd wiped blood from his face and hands.

The car made a turn and pulled over in an alley.

"You want?"

My heart had been in my damn throat, my body on the razor's edge of flight or fight. Everything around me had intensified. Colors were brighter. Voices were louder. Stronger. I was on a stimulus overload, so it had taken a second to realize that as the driver opened his door, Raize offered me a piece of cloth—the same one he'd just used to clean his gun and face. He had folded it back so a clean section faced out.

He held it up. "We're going to stop for food. If your face isn't clean, you can't come."

Of course.

Food.

With blood on me.

That wasn't good.

I'd shaken myself out of the weird state I was in and reached for the cloth.

The driver had walked around, opened the front passenger seat door, and taken the dead body out of the car.

I'd started to wipe my face.

Raize had been watching, seeming almost bemused by me. Then he'd offered up some alcohol.

I'd been confused, but hell, I'd figured it might help at this point.

I took the bottle and dipped my head back, taking a long drink. The burn was good, warming.

Raize had frowned. "You need it to wash your face. The blood is caking. I don't have anything else to offer you."

Oh.

Oh!

I'd snorted and poured some of the whiskey onto the washcloth. I'd never needed alcohol to wash my face before. It wasn't the first time I'd seen someone executed in front of me, but it was the first time Raize had killed a man in front of me, and the first time I'd used alcohol as a cleanser.

New things.

Exciting.

By the time I'd finished, the driver had returned.

He'd leaned over, grabbed some wipes from inside one of the car's compartments, and started cleaning off the dashboard, the seat, everything around him. He'd used one to clean his face as well, and then he'd looked back at us.

"Chicken nuggets?"

Raize had grunted again, settling back, and we'd gone to get chicken nuggets.

I never asked why that guy was killed. No questions. It was a rule, but in working for Raize, I had learned that he didn't kill unless there was a reason. A further 'problem' that might happen.

There'd been no warning that first night when he'd killed the guy in the car. So as Raize stared at Henchman One now, I was ready.

His eyes narrowed, and for a moment, the guy kneeling seemed forgotten.

Raize lifted his gun toward Henchman One. "You got a big mouth on you?"

This guy was fucked. He'd be a 'problem' and Raize knew it in the way he worded that question.

I also knew what else was coming.

My stomach clenched in preparation.

The guy swallowed. I could see the sweat pouring off of him. His hands twitched, and he shifted his feet around, the plastic crackling underneath him. "No. No, sir. No, boss."

"You've been having a lot to say." Raize's gaze was cold, but there was a twitch beside his mouth, and he turned his eyes to me. "You."

Fuck.

But I'd known.

He nodded toward Henchman One. "He gonna be a problem for me?" he asked me.

Shit.

Fuck.

Shit.

Fuck.

This. This was what I did for these men. It was something they'd learned right away. Or almost right away. When they asked me a question, I always knew the answer in my gut, and I hated it.

Hated it. Hated. It.

I hated being the reason there'd be another body to clean up today.

"Girl!"

I jerked at Raize's bark and answered, because if I wanted to remain alive, I had to be truthful. "Yes."

I'd barely gotten the word out before *bang!*

Henchman One's body fell against the door behind him, then slid to the side and down, a dark, red hole smack in the middle of his forehead. His eyes remained wide, as if watching us, but he was gone.

Raize was an ace shot.

I bit back my remorse. Dammit. But I'd told the truth because this guy would've been a problem. When I'd gone against my gut in the past, I was always proven wrong, and my bosses tended to get pissed at me.

I wasn't psychic, but my gut knew the true answer to any question. If it was a yes/no question, I'd know.

Raize sighed, his gaze lingering on the blood that left a trail down the wall behind Henchman One. It'd be a long night of cleaning. With all that done, he turned and stuck his gun back into Knee Guy's mouth again. He cocked it and raised an eyebrow. "You gonna tell me now, motherfucker?"

The guy's mouth moved around the muzzle, his words unclear.

Raize took the gun out, his face locked down, waiting.

The guy coughed and said, "Bronski sent me."

"Why?"

The guy glanced up at me, and I felt a chill pass through me. Nausea rose up, my stomach churning and twisting. I knew Bronski. He'd been my first boss, and the worst boss. He hadn't known about my gut. That shit was discovered by my second boss. It was the reason he'd taken me to work for him.

My time with Bronski had been short, *thankfully*.

"He wants her back."

Raize swung his head my way. "You worked for him?"

I had to tell the truth, and it tasted bitter coming out. "Yeah."

"As?"

"As nothing. I wasn't with him long, a few days."

"What'd you do for him?" He cocked his head.

"Not what I do for you."

He didn't comment on that, but his gaze traveled down and up my body.

Another blast of cold seared my insides.

Then he turned back to the guy and *bang*! A second body collapsed.

Henchman Two went to work. He started rolling up the kneeling guy first since he was smack in the middle of the plastic. That was an easier cleanup job. Henchman One would be last.

Raize stuck his gun back in his pocket as he crossed the room to me. "Bronski ever fuck you?" he asked, his voice gruff.

My stomach twisted again. "Yes."

"You wanted it?"

I looked up at him, wanting to be a smartass because no one wanted to think back on memories like that. "No," I said instead, hating that my voice came out sounding the way it did.

Henchman Two stilled and turned to look at Raize.

A vein throbbed in Raize's neck as he turned away, motioning to the body. "Clean it up. Get this shit done."

Henchman Two went back to work.

Raize focused on me again. "Hey."

I looked up to him. I'd never seen Raize soften, ever, and I knew this was probably the closest I'd ever get. He wasn't soft, but he was less hard than he usually looked.

"I don't want to go to war with Bronski, but we'll make this right. Yeah?"

I had no idea what he was talking about, but I nodded.

Raize wasn't about using girls or forcing them. He didn't need to. He had a slew of women who came and went from his place whenever he wanted them. That wasn't his business.

He motioned to Henchman One's body. "Help clean that fucker up."

As I did, he went outside for a smoke.

Forty minutes later, both bodies were gone, the room was

clean, and we left, leaving no trace of the two murders just committed there.

Then we went for chicken nuggets.

I didn't have any.

For more Canary, go here!